THE ECLIPSE OF THE CENTURY

The people on the steps arose and held out their arms. They were long-haired, men and women alike, wearing robes, jewellery, trailing scarves, and they were not his long-lost dead loved ones. He had never seen any of them before in his life. He reached the foot of the steps and was about to ascend to those welcoming faces, the outstretched arms, when something caught him by the elbow. He half turned, half saw behind him an urgent presence, an impression of long swinging skirts, bright floating hair, mouthing something as it tugged at his sleeve. "No, it is too soon. It is much too soon. You must come away."

He thought, remembered thinking, I was wrong, this is heaven, they let me see it and now I am being dragged to hell. He gazed back imploringly at the yearning welcoming beings as if they might save him. One, a shining golden woman, came down a step or two and said, "Go now, we'll meet again."

He cried despairingly, "Where?" and she answered, "Why here, in Kantoom, under the black sun, at the end of a thousand years."

THE ECLIPSE OF THE CENTURY

Jan Mark

■SCHOLASTIC

Scholastic Children's Books,
Commonwealth House,
1-19 New Oxford Street,
London WC1A 1NU, UK
a division of Scholastic Ltd
London ~ New York ~ Toronto ~ Sydney ~ Auckland
Mexico City ~ New Delhi ~ Hong Kong

First published in the UK by Scholastic Ltd, 1999
This edition, 2000

Text copyright © Jan Mark, 1999

ISBN 0 439 01482 4

Typeset by M Rules
Printed by Cox and Wyman Ltd, Reading, Berks.

2 4 6 8 10 9 7 5 3 1

For Ursula Le Guin

Part One

"Leave the train at the junction and follow the rails," the man in the corner said.

"How far?"

"Thirty kilometres."

Keith wondered if he were translating correctly. "That's almost twenty miles."

The man in the corner shrugged. "Thirty kilometres."

"Qantoum is thirty kilometres from Qantoum Junction?"

"You'll make it by sundown."

Keith looked out of the window. There was no sign of civilization or any human settlement. To the south-west the sun hung high over the plain. To the east, on his left hand, the shadow of the train, slightly elongated, jolted over the uneven terrain of green scrub. Seeing his own shadow in the window of the second car from the rear he waved to it, and it waved right back.

"Are there wild animals in the desert? Wolves?"

"This isn't the desert. The desert begins at Qantoum."

The shadow sloped sharply, dwindled and slithered out of sight beneath the wheels as the train followed a curve in the

track. A sign ambled past the window, QANTOUM JUNC-
TION, and the train, which for the last hour had proceeded
at a walking pace, stopped moving altogether.

"Here. Now. This side," said the man in the corner. Keith
rose, swung his backpack from the seat beside him and
opened the door, stepping down on to a narrow strip of
boardwalk a little below the sill.

"Thanks for your help," he said, as he turned to slam the
door. The man in the corner grunted. He might have been
laughing.

Keith shouldered his backpack and set off along the
boardwalk towards the front of the train which was
immensely long and virtually empty. The only sounds were
of his own hollow footfalls on the warped planks, the whin-
ing of a thin wind in the wires that linked the telephone
poles beside the track, sundry clicks and twangs from the
stationary cars and the exhausted hissing of the distant locomotive. The boardwalk ended in a broken ramp. Keith
dropped to the ground and continued beside the line, the
train looming above him. If this were a junction the line
must fork. When he reached the locomotive he might ask the
footplatemen which way he ought to be walking, but without
warning the smokestack erupted, the cars heaved and con-
certinaed together, clanging fearfully, as the train plunged
into reverse. He stood stupidly watching as the locomotive
drew level and passed him, slowly enough to leave the disagreeable impression that the cab was empty and the train
was driving itself, stopping and starting *en route* from habit,

like a horse with a blind-drunk rider that nevertheless knows its own way home.

He saw that it was not returning the way it had come but dawdling southward, butt-first, the locomotive nudging it along. He dropped his pack, ran after it and vaulted up on to the boardwalk. Now he could see the fork. Opposite the platform stood the switch gear. The train had driven on to the single Qantoum branch line, somebody, presumably one of the footplatemen, had thrown the switch and then reversed on to the southern line to Iskanderabad. Qantoum would lie ahead, then; due east, or near enough.

He jumped down, returned to his pack and heaving it on again stepped on to the gravelly track that lay between the rusted rails. He began to walk. Behind him the receding train clattered through the silence, coughing smoke and steam into the clear air. For a long while he could hear it and, if he turned his head, see it, as they drew apart, the train to the south and he to the east, to Qantoum. He thought, Did I really die for *this*?

One

As Near Death Experiences go it had been irregular, as he discovered when he read up on the subject afterwards. Everyone else who died and rose again was permitted a glimpse of heaven, was greeted by long-dead loved ones, welcomed effusively and then abruptly shown the door when some doctor galvanized the failing heart. He did not believe in an afterlife. When he saw the articulated truck waltzing side-on across the central reservation he had expected to be extinguished. But he was not dead, only sleeping. If he had had a vision it had not been of heaven or of hell, therefore it must have been a dream.

Up to a point his experiences tallied with the accounts in the books. He had risen above the snarled traffic, the converging police cars, fire-engine and ambulance, to look down upon the fuming tangle of mashed steel in which he supposed his mangled body lay leaching life. Drifting upward and backward. He was so enjoying the sensation that he failed to notice when the sky thickened and closed in and he found himself in a softly luminous tunnel from which he had emerged not into an Elysian garden but in a broad city square with a fountain, formal flower-beds, ornamental trees, surrounded by public buildings. Through the trees he saw a great gate and a tower, limpidly blue, but there was no time to look. On the steps of a church sat a group of people. They noticed him, beckoned to him, and without walking, without any effort at all, he approached the steps, moving through a lilac twilight that was not dusk or daybreak but noon, for almost overhead hung a black sun, and he did not think it strange.

The people on the steps arose and held out their arms. They were long-haired, men and women alike, wearing robes, jewellery, trailing scarves, and they were not his long-dead loved ones. He had never seen any of them before in his life. He reached the foot of the steps and was about to ascend to those welcoming faces, the outstretched arms, when something caught him by the elbow. He half turned, half saw behind him an urgent presence, an impression of long swinging skirts, bright floating hair, mouthing something as it tugged at his sleeve. "No, it is too soon. It is much too soon. You must come away."

He thought, remembered thinking, I was wrong, this is heaven, they let me see it and now I am being dragged to hell. He gazed back imploringly at the yearning welcoming beings as if they might save him. One, a shining golden woman, came down a step or two and said, "Go now, we'll meet again."

He cried despairingly, "Where?" and she answered, "Why

here, in Kantoom, under the black sun, at the end of a thousand years."

He was not going to hell, he had not been in heaven; he had been in Kantoom, but his frantic companion was dragging him away, no time for questions, he was alone, he was back in the tunnel, he was lying at the side of the green Mercedes that had picked him up on the slip-road to the M40, and a voice was saying, "He'll do. The other one's gone."

He did wonder, uninterestedly, as he lost consciousness again, if by some celestial mistake he had taken his journey on behalf of the dead driver who was being cut out of the wreckage by a masked man with a thermal lance.

Later, sitting in Leyton Public Library, his still-sutured head propped on his hand, he recognized his tunnel as identical to a thousand other tunnels. It was what lay at the end of it that was different: Kantoom. Had the dream not been quite so vivid he would have forgotten it in the febrile, stuporous days that followed the accident, but the woman's voice remained with him, insistent in his inner ear: "We'll meet again . . . here, in Kantoom, at the end of a thousand years." The end of a thousand years was close enough, nine months away, but where was he meant to be when it happened?

Khartoum? At first, recalling the dream encounter, he had been sure that she had said Khartoum; but not quite sure. Kowloon? Canton? He went to the reference section for an atlas. There were eighteen Cantons alone listed. Kanturk, Kahntah, Khantau, Cantu, Cantuar Saskatchewan.

He hunched over the atlas, running his finger down the tiny names, until he looked up to meet the amused eyes of a schoolboy seated opposite and realized that he was rehearsing the names aloud, searching for the right inflexion; Gantang, Gantheaume, Gantung. . . He replaced the atlas on the shelf and slunk away from the daunting gaze of the schoolboy, his physics books, his folder of prim diagrams. Little tit, he thought; why isn't he out behind the bottle bank with his draw instead of wasting his youth in here? He knew now, as never before, that time was short, time was precious, time could end in the fraction of a second. He might not even complete the step he was taking, the breath he was breathing, the thought he was thinking. In nine months the end of the thousand years would be accomplished, two millennia would touch, the black sun would rise and he could not find the place.

No one he asked recognized the name, or the sound of it. When he stumbled upon his first clue it was by accident that, with hindsight, could surely be no accident. Two weeks later, searching unsuccessfully for sweaters in an Oxfam shop and not liking to leave without buying something, he cruised the bookshelves. In a basket on the floor was a pile of pre-WWII magazines, the size of paperbacks. It was the future he was seeking, not the past, but he leafed through them, smiling at the chaste nudes and empire-building advertisements for sola topis and humidity-proof socks. At the bottom of the basket was a single copy of *The Rover's Monthly*; more nudes, but foreign and therefore less chaste, cartoons and brief articles on voyages, explorations, far-away places. A word caught his eye as he browsed. *Monsters, Mummies and Mermaids by Lt. Col. Sir Oswald Dornage-Strynge*, and halfway down the page; *Qantoum*.

He said it aloud, "Qantoum", and heard the voice of the dream woman. This chance discovery must be more than chance.

The seasoned traveller leaves nothing to the hand of Fate, particularly when traversing the steppes and deserts of Turkestan, but in the early spring of 1913 it was Fate herself that directed my camel eastward to the ancient town of Qantoum, grown from its origins as an oasis on a caravan route to a cosmopolitan curiosity where one may rub shoulders with the wily native (do not rub too hard!), the international criminal, the adventurer, the adventuress, the dregs of Central Asia, the explorer, the archaeologist and the soldier.

These last three met in the person of Prince Andrei Zherdin who entered Qantoum in 1874 and never left it thereafter. Prince Zherdin famously travelled with his own caravan of household servants and a camel train that transported his collection of antiquities, acquired between military campaigns and on them. Deciding in his climacteric that it was time to settle down, and learning that the principal Russian museums declined to accept his collection, he remained in Qantoum and commenced to build his own museum to house his treasures, which he described as a 'Kunstkammer' or Cabinet of Curiosities, in humble imitation of his illustrious countryman Tzar Peter the Great.

The Prince was an eclectic collector of monsters, mummies and mermaids. When an ingratiating native appeared at my elbow. . .

The next page was missing. All that remained of the article was part of the concluding paragraph . . . *on the edge of the desert. Once one might take the train from Moscow or Tashkent but the Bolshies have put the kybosh on these simple pleasures, drawing boundaries that have placed the ancient Tajik centres of Bukhara and Samarkand in Uzbekistan, and Qantoum, briefly capital of the Qantoumi Autonomous Republic, inside the borders of Iskanderistan. As I write a Soviet garrison occupies the barracks at Qantoum. Only armoured trains run from this strangest and most remote of outposts, and the curious collection of Prince Zherdin may even now be sinking beneath the encroaching sands of Iskanderistan.*

What had become of the museum in that "strangest and most remote of outposts"? What had become of the loot, for, reading between the lines, loot was clearly what it must have been. Why had no one ever gone to find out? Why had no one ever heard of Qantoum? He looked at the date on the front cover of *The Rover's Monthly*: September 1939. By the time that issue hit the news-stands the world had had other things on its mind.

Back at the atlas in the library he turned at once to the index; Qantoum, Iskanderiskaya ASSR. Autonomous Soviet Socialist Republic. There was no Soviet Union now, the atlas was out of date, but there on the map, hanging like a bead on the tenuous thread of the railway line from Tashkent, dangling between steppe and desert, was Qantoum.

Michelin, Fodor, Blue Guides, Odyssey Guides, Rough Guides, Hitchhiker's Guides, Lonely Planet; one thing became eminently clear: no one ever went to the Independent Republic of Iskanderistan for fun.

The library could not help and if Qantoum were ever to appear on the Internet he would have to be the one who put it there. His only hope was to go second-hand again, serious research in specialist shops, and he headed for the streets around the British Museum, tossing the name of Zherdin at bemused booksellers in the hope that the old bastard had written a book. Everybody wrote a book eventually, didn't they? He might have one to write himself.

Lady Charlotte Crow rode to his rescue, eccentric youngest daughter of a more eccentric earl who, pressed into marriage with a rising politician, sensibly eloped on her wedding night with a passing officer of Hussars, abandoned him in Paris and, dressed as a man, vanished into Central Asia, emerging after seven years to write the inevitable book; *In the Footsteps of Genghiz Khan*. He might have guessed that Genghiz Khan would have passed through Qantoum at some point. Wasn't he the one who left heaps of skulls behind him; *Genghiz woz ere*? No, that was Tamburlaine.

Lady Charlotte dropped by in 1873, narrowly missing Prince Andrei who was approaching from the opposite direction. Territorial disputes had been more or less continuous in the region for centuries, Lady Charlotte recorded, the Khanates of Khiva and Kokand having laid claim to the Khanate of Qantoum, until the troops of the Tzar conquered all three. Keith began to suspect that Qantoum, prized on account of its water supply, had been hard to find because it rarely remained under one regime long enough to appear on a map. Originally an oasis on a trade route, stopover for caravans, brigands and Genghiz Khan, it had grown into a village, then a town, doubling its population almost overnight when a particularly protracted border dispute trapped a tribe of nomads, the Sturyat, who after six years gave up any hope of moving on and stayed put. *They have, as they say,* wrote Lady Charlotte, *set up the bones of their ancestors and laid down the stones wherein they keep their souls.*

The nomadic hordes, he thought; hard-riding free spirits who played polo with each other's heads. He turned the page, eagerly. At last he was going to learn something. *They are a degenerate people with little culture, no written language, a most debased form of pantheism and an utter want of interest in the arts of war.*

No interest in war – clearly a bunch of no-hopers. He pictured the Sturyat, placidly detached on their oasis, while all hell broke out around them and the disputed border surged back and forth like a tidal wave; ultimately settling, as it turned out, 100 kilometres to the east.

Next morning I left for Khorassan.

And good riddance, you old cow, Keith thought. They set up the bones of their ancestors and laid down the stones wherein they kept their souls and you call that a debased form of pantheism?

He thought, I have to find these people, and then his first really constructive idea for weeks struck him. There was absolutely no reason why he should not find them. True, it was barely two months since the accident and he was still officially under doctor's orders, but family and friends had tactfully acquiesced in his wish to be left alone. He could be gone and return before anyone thought to come after him. He had his unspent loan for the rest of the year; he could afford a return flight to Tashkent and a ticket to Qantoum. He would not be returning to university yet. The accident had left him in a state of permanent *déjà vu*, perpetually on the verge of knowing what would happen next because everything seemed to have happened before. The only true future lay in those few words from his dream; "We'll meet again . . . here in Qantoum, under the black sun at the end of a thousand years." If this were destiny he must be in Qantoum on 31 December 1999 to meet it.

But he could not wait so long to find out if this were even possible; he must go now. Iskanderistan did not run to a London Embassy, but the Russians advised him to contact a tour operator.

He did not want a tour.

"Then travel to Tashkent with a visa for Uzbekistan. You will be allowed a stay of three days without an additional visa in any other Central Asian Republic."

"And is it possible to visit Qantoum?"

He might as well have suggested Chernobyl. "It should be possible . . . there are trains. . ."

The vagueness ought to have alerted him, but at least Qantoum was still there, or part of it at any rate. He learned that the region had suffered an earthquake in 1994.

Telling no one of his plans he made his arrangements, and only at the last minute did he sit down and e-mail interested parties. *Keith has gone to Qantoum to find the black sun at the end of a thousand years.* Then he walked to the station, took the train to Paddington and changed on to the link line for Heathrow.

Large dark birds swam in thermals overhead. The going over the bleached sleepers and the weedy pebbles between them was not smooth but made for easier walking than the shifting gritty soil on either side. Now he heard nothing save his own footfalls and occasional small scurryings in the scrub. The song of the telephone wires had fallen silent some way behind. The poles still marched beside the track but the wires, he noticed with unease, had been pruned at intervals. He had been walking for more than two hours and still nothing broke the eastern horizon. The foothills of the mountains to the south appeared no closer.

It was near to the end of the third hour when he finally discerned something that might be his goal. Incalculably distant, a dim bubble seemed to hang in the air a little above the earth's edge. His shadow pointed towards it. He accelerated, and as he advanced silhouettes began to shoulder out of the ground and assume firm shapes. The bubble was a water tank on a skeletal tower. He saw roofs, walls, windows. His eyes were so focused upon the distance that he did not see the boardwalk until he was almost beside it. As dilapidated as the one he had stepped on to at the junction, this one also carried a chipped enamel sign: QANTOUM INDUSTRIAL.

The track forked again, the main line curving away to the left. To the right a spur ran through the scrub to lose itself among low concrete sheds with broken roofs, pylons bearing loose swags of cable, cranes, gantries, winches, lifting gear. But if this were industry nothing was working; no one was working. There was no one in sight, there was no sound. He thought, this was not in my dream.

He followed the left-hand curve towards the buckled legs of the water tower. The lettering on the tank at the top read QANTOUM. He drew alongside a station platform, no boardwalk this but a paved terrace; another sign – QANTOUM BARRACKS – but the doors in the station buildings were padlocked, there was no way in or out. Qantoum advertised its presence everywhere he looked. Where was it?

The track hugged an iron fence in a tight curve and as he rounded it he saw another station in the distance. Fifteen minutes' walking brought him to the platform, long, broad, canopied and deserted, with buffers beyond it, and its name was QANTOUM CENTRAL. He had arrived. This was the end of the line.

He climbed on to the platform and stared up into the canopy, all dusty glass and cast-iron lace-work. The glass was shattered into fangs and from the vaulting hung signs on rusty chains. Peeling paint disclosed several layers of lettering, Cyrillic alphabet over Latin characters, Latin over Arabic; *Lavatories, Tea Room, Tickets*. A slight breeze set the signs swinging gently on their chains as he walked beneath them. They were all lavishly punctuated with bullet holes. He heard the silence. He thought of massacres.

As at the Barracks station all the doors were padlocked, windows shuttered, the paint blistered and faded. Ragged notices were pasted to walls where here and there a line had escaped the bleaching sun. *No spitting . . . Cockroaches are not to be introduced into eating houses . . . All loose dogs to be shot on sight.*

Flies carry disease. Kill a fly for the common good. He moved on to the door of the booking hall. *Do not accept lifts in unauthorized vehicles . . . Do not encourage wolves . . . Anyone impersonating a widow will be liable to judicial proceedings.* The door was locked like all the others, but farther along the platform a gate stood ajar in a row of spiked railings. When he reached it he found a final notice mounted beside it. *All aliens to report to Control Point E.*

He stopped at this one, large enough and clean enough to be eye-catching. A map was attached to it showing the station area, and an arrow, pointing to the station itself in the lower left-hand corner was labelled *You are here.* A second arrow helpfully indicated the proximity of Control Point E. He opened the gate, looked up and finally saw Qantoum.

The notices had led him to expect taxis, touts, possibly a bus, but the plaza in front of the station was as empty as the platform, surfaced with cracked asphalt and sprouting lamp-posts round the edge. A burned-out Lada was marooned in the centre. To his right the station's overhanging façade loured down at him and beyond the farther edge of the forecourt lay the town, low, massive; sprawling blocks of concrete and purplish brick, all livid in the late afternoon sunlight and all in some degree damaged. The arrow directed him to a broad street, Oktyabrskaya, that led out of the forecourt, and he set off across the asphalt towards it. A notice on a lamp-post reminded him, *The throwing of rocks in public places is forbidden.*

Control Point E was a small concrete cube on a street corner, a single-storey cabin, grey and unadorned among the rampant brickwork and stucco that surrounded it. Five steps led up to a recessed door beside which a little metal frame was affixed to the wall. A name-plate inserted in a slot at the side read, *Officer of the Day A/C Tcherk.* A Lada without wheels or windscreen was parked outside.

There was no knocker or bell on the door, no entryphone beside it. Keith pushed at the bar handle and entered a small square lobby with another door to the right. After the stillness of the street his ears were instantly receptive to the sounds of human activity behind the door; a throat cleared, a drawer pulled open. The upper half of the door was a reinforced panel of dirty glass. Something moved on the far side like a shark in an aquarium. Mindful of the bullet-scarred station and his thoughts of massacre, Keith slipped one arm out of the backpack straps, leaving it to hang from his shoulder, and peered sidelong through the glass, ready to drop the pack and run for his life. A man in an officer's cap and faded uniform tunic was bending over a filing cabinet. Keith knocked on the door.

"Come in." Russian.

He opened the door. The man at the filing cabinet turned and straightened up, kicking the drawer shut with his boot heel, and a tremulous rattle betrayed the presence of his pistol lying on top of the cabinet between a tin mug and a pile of loose change. He was about Keith's height, although of a marginally more martial bearing, clean-shaven but with his hair brushing his collar and flopping in an unsoldierly swatch across his forehead. It was brown, with many flecks of grey in it, but he looked fairly young and very, very surprised.

"Acting Captain Tcherk?"

"No," the officer said, and sat down suddenly, indicating a chair for Keith on the far side of his desk. "Lieutenant Kijé." He paused, as if expecting some reaction, and getting none went on, "What can I do for you?"

"I've come to report."

"What?"

"What?"

"What do you want to report?"

"Me. I'm an alien. The notice. . ."

"Oh. I see." The lieutenant continued to look astonished. "It really doesn't matter any more."

"What doesn't?"

"Reporting. The regulations. We are demilitarized, didn't you know? Didn't you *notice*?"

"I'd rather do things properly." He wanted a record of his arrival in this place, some proof that he actually was here and not hallucinating on the railway track back at the junction.

"Well, all right," the lieutenant said, doubtfully. He opened a drawer and scrabbled randomly in it until he found a pad of forms, picked up a pen and assumed a businesslike expression. "Name?"

"Chapman. Keith Chapman."

"Age?"

"Twenty."

"Nationality?"

"British."

The lieutenant immediately switched to English which he spoke with a slight American accent. "Occupation?"

"Student. Here's my passport."

"They've changed the cover."

This must be the first EC passport in Qantoum. "Could you stamp it?"

"There's no need."

"I'd rather you did."

"If I can find the . . . the. . ." He leafed through the passport and copied a line or two on to the form. Looking at it upside down Keith noticed a circular space at the bottom for an official stamp. The lieutenant drew a face in it. "There are some *things* here, questions. Do you want to answer them?"

"Certainly." He felt ridiculously bureaucratic, insisting on form-filling, passport-stamping, when the man in charge clearly could not care less, but he had to have proof. It occurred to him that Kijé's vagueness might be the result of speaking a language he had not used for some time, although it was clear, by the eagerness with which he had switched, that it was markedly better than Keith's phrase-book Russian.

"Uh – what is your purpose in visiting Qantoum?"

He could not bring himself to tell the truth to this stranger. "Tourist."

"Really? Are you planning to stay or are you just passing through?" A thought struck him. "How did you get here?"

"I walked from the junction."

"Oh." He seemed to find this reasonable, a twenty-mile stroll. "How long did you think of staying?"

"As long as you'll give me a permit for – if you'll give me a permit?"

"Of course I'll give you a permit. How could I keep you out?" Keith's eye wandered tactlessly to the pistol. "You really don't need—"

"Yes, yes. Go on."

Kijé turned the form over and began to drone: "Are you or have you ever been a member of a prohibited organization? Is it your intention to in any way damage, hinder or subvert the democratically elected administration of this region? Don't bother to answer. Do you have any convictions for theft, embezzlement, fraud, affray, assault, homicide in any degree, arson, rape, drug offences or conspiracy to contaminate a public water supply?"

"No. You can check."

"I can't, you know. Have you ever kept a disorderly house? Have any members of your family – oh, life's too – too *short*. See that list of communicable diseases on the wall? Had them? Got them?"

"I've got vaccination certificates."

"Let me have them. I'll just clip them to – oh, no, keep them, why not? Now, if you'll just sign it?" He handed Keith a map and his passport with a carbon copy of the form folded into it.

"Don't you even keep that?"

"Oh God, what for?"

"I might break the law."

"Go ahead, break it, do. Which law did you have in mind?"

"Well, if that's it, then?"

"It is."

"Perhaps you can tell me where I can get a bed for the night. Food? Drink?"

"You'd better go to the museum."

Zherdin's museum? "Aren't there hotels, rooming houses? Shops?"

"There's a market and – look, the best advice I can give you is to take a walk around and see for yourself. Leave your luggage here, it'll be quite safe. If I'm not here when you get back I'll be at the museum."

"Where's that?"

He pointed haphazardly over his shoulder. "It's on the map."

"Won't it be closed?"

"The museum doesn't close," the lieutenant said.

Keith stood up. As he turned to leave he said, "What time do *you* close?"

Kijé almost smiled. "I wasn't actually open."

"Then what—"

"I live here."

"You aren't on guard duty?"

"What's to guard? I was just watering the mushrooms when you came in."

"Mushrooms in a filing cabinet?"

"They like the dark," said Lt. Kijé.

Without his backpack Keith walked away from Control Point
E into the soft evening sunshine. The sky was cloudless but
the light seemed filtered through a dusty lens. He looked at
his watch and saw that barely twenty minutes had elapsed
since he left the station, in which time the shadows had
lengthened, although the scene at the crossroads was
unchanged. Windows were still shuttered, doors closed and,
now that he came to look at them, either boarded up or
chained.

The map was old, printed in Cyrillic characters much
scored-out and scribbled on in a variety of languages. He
located the crossroads: *chorsu*. If he turned left past Control
Point E along the side of the *gimnaziya* he would fetch up in
the railway sidings. To the right the road led to an area
labelled *Consular District*. Along Oktyabrskaya, the curving
road from the station, lay the town centre, according to the
map which showed many buildings, although to the north-
east the place was sheared off in a dead-straight line: *Border*. A
few millimetres to its right was a parallel line, *1917 Border* and
a wavering trail of dots beyond that: *Disputed Territories 1868*.

The declining sun was behind him. In the deserted street
his footsteps rang hollow, the roadway curved before him,
silent. He crossed side turnings, the mouths of alleys, and
looking down them saw nothing, no one. The doors did not
open, no faces appeared at windows. The only traces of

humanity were the abandoned Ladas, rusting where they stood. The only movements were of his steadily advancing shadow and the occasional lazy passage of a cruising bird. No birds alighted in the street, there were no basking cats, no dogs; all shot on sight, as threatened? *Had* there been a massacre as he at first suspected? Conducted by whom? By Lt. Kijé, drifting around Qantoum in a fog of dozy good humour, shooting people in the back of the head as he ambled past? Had he in fact imagined the scruffy lieutenant and the meeting in Control Point E? Had he imagined the walk from the junction, the journey in the train, the flight from Frankfurt? Was he here at all or was he still dying in the wreckage of the green Mercedes on the M40?

But he was not imagining the map, or the permit folded into his passport on which an angular black tangle of pen marks like a squashed crane fly, represented the signature, and the existence, of Lt. Kijé. All right, *he* was here, Kijé was here, but where were the voices of children at play, the revving of vehicles, the clamour of workmen; where was the chatter of daily life? Where was everyone else?

The street completed its curve and straightened into a wide boulevard. The buildings stood farther apart, here, some in overgrown grounds that had reverted to stubbly thickets. For all their grandeur they were as firmly shuttered as the ones in the side streets, and where those others had borne signs of damage, these looked seared, scorched, destroyed above the first floor. The boulevard ended in a square, *Registan* on the map, where budding trees stood around four sides of a central garden. In the middle was an ornamental fountain surrounded by empty flower-beds. It was dry, but he stopped and stared at it. He had seen it before. He had stood in this very place and looked at that fountain when an ostrich plume of white water had jetted from the spout and cast cooling spray on the surrounding pavement, and the trees, in full leaf, had murmured in the lilac light of a black sun. He saw, as he had seen then, that on one side of the square wide shallow steps rose up in front of a church where a group of people in flowing robes had held out their arms to him in welcome, where a golden-haired woman had come down to meet him before he had been dragged away.

"We'll meet again."

"Where?"

"Why here, in Qantoum, under the black sun, at the end of a thousand years."

His exhausted legs gave way and he sat down heavily on the rim of the fountain. The steps were empty, the square deserted, but this was the place he had dreamed of without ever having seen it. Whatever his expectations had been since the moment when he had looked into *The Rover's Monthly*, they had not included the possibility that his dream might come true. He had expected revelations, the fulfilment of inarticulate yearnings, adding Qantoum to the mystical litany of far-away places: Khiva, Bukhara, Samarkand, the song of the Silk Road. He had not expected to come again into his dream.

*

A bulbous green dome ripened like a boil above the gable. According to the map this was the cathedral of St Vasili. Its doors and windows were boarded up. Next to it, similarly sealed, was the Gorki Theatre and on the nearer corner an hotel, the Sogdiana Serai, Intourist. On the east side of the square stood the remains of an Ensemble, mosque, madrasseh, a truncated minaret clad in the remains of blue-glazed tiles and all derelict; to the south, still whole but apparently abandoned, another hotel, the Iskander, and a concrete blockhouse, the cinema. The Iskander stood at the top of Market Street which was almost as wide as Oktyabrskaya and sloped downhill. He struck out cater-corner across the Registan towards it. Along the centre of the street ran a row of stalls under dingy awnings, where small birds pecked and scuffled among the trestles, looking for scraps . . . scraps of food . . . evidence of humans. He saw a single discarded cabbage leaf and was almost moved to tears by the possibilities.

Crossing Market Street he turned a corner, then another. The buildings here were smaller, lower. Suddenly they ended, the metalled road crumbling into shingle and coarse vegetation. For a moment he thought he had walked in a circle and was approaching the railway line again, but the sun was still at his back although hidden by the bulk of the town. It was close to setting now and shadows stretched infinitely into the mauve haze that obscured the horizon. The mountains, which he was noticing for the first time since he glimpsed them from the railway, reared golden and remote to his right.

He was not looking out over the western plain but eastward, into the desert. For fifty or so metres the ground was occupied by abandoned building lots, forlorn rectangles of brick barely waist high. Away to the right stood a high wall with observation towers at either end; he could just make out the words *Old Citadel* on the map. Here and there stakes were driven into the earth, some linked with slack tendrils of wire, the redundant border, all the borders except the current one more than sixty miles to the east.

If he could find a way up on to the citadel wall he might look out and down, over the town, over the desert, to the mountains, blazing now in the last moments of sunshine, but while he wondered, squinting at the map, the sun went down at last. The angle of its setting was steeper than he was used to; there would be no leisurely English twilight here, and he had not yet got his bearings. Worse, he had taken no note of his route since leaving Market Street. He had better return there before darkness fell, but he had left it too long; at once the mountains were extinguished and the rufous light drained from the sky. The air grew noticeably cooler.

A flicker of movement caught his eye. He was standing by iron gates in the railings that surrounded a little cemetery and the gates, for a wonder, were open. He went in. Small stones stood among the shrubs and long dry grass. Beyond them, farther in, he could make out shadowy mausolea, a twisted ancient mulberry tree, beneath which a very old woman in a long duster coat was scattering crusts and crumbs from a paper bag. She was humming quietly to herself, swallowing the high notes, and swaying as she broadcast the crumbs. When she saw Keith she stopped humming and rippled her fingers in his direction.

"You should have gone home long ago," she said. "One is entitled to one's privacy."

"I've only just arrived," Keith said.

"Oh no." Even when speaking her voice fluttered from note to note. "No no. I shall say nothing on this occasion, but if it happens again. . ." Clearly she had no idea who he was, or rather, she thought he was someone else. "There must be no one here when they come for their supper." Bending from the hips she strewed more crumbs in a semicircle. "La la, there, my darlings, my pretties. We shall go away now and you shall have your supper in peace." She up-ended the bag, folded it neatly and stowed it away about her person. Then, ignoring Keith entirely, she turned towards the gates, wearing and tacking on the uneven pavement. As she reached them the shadows absorbed her while he watched.

Keith followed her out of the little burial ground and looked down the lane. For all those street-lamps posted about the town he could not see a single light. He took a few steps along the lane, but the dusk was closing around him like a fist. Above him the stars ignited one by one; the planets burned with steady fire. He searched for a constellation he might recognize and as he stood his head was pierced by a high sweet note at first felt rather than heard, a needle in the ear; then a second lower, softer tone made harmony with it. The air was breathing music, louder, fainter, higher, ebbing and surging: one voice, two, three, a choir. Out in the eastern darkness beyond the squalid border zone the grains of sand lifted their voices; the desert was singing.

He thought he was retracing his steps but in the lampless darkness that thickened by the minute, he misjudged a turning and instead of regaining the unmistakable breadth of the market found himself in a lane which, dwindling to an alley, led him blindly into a series of right-angled corners at the foot of featureless walls that closed in behind him to shut out the song of the sand.

The sound was undoubtedly caused by the silicon contracting in the first chill of evening, but the prosaic fact could not blunt the astonishment of that moment when the twin needles of C and B flat first drew their threads of melody through his head.

The first chill of evening was becoming solid cold. He imagined his breath steaming above him, although he could not see it. He could no longer see anything, he discovered, and wondered for how long he had been walking with one arm extended, feeling his way from corner to corner. He ought to put on the sweater that he had discarded at the junction, but his sweater, all his sweaters and his torch, were in the backpack at Control Point E in the care of the creepily affable Lt. Kijé; or not. If he ever found his way back to Control Point E would the lieutenant still be there? If only he had returned before darkness fell, but it had fallen so suddenly, and he had never expected to find Qantoum so utterly benighted, so deserted, so silent.

Still, he had not been expecting Las Vegas. Everything, which was not much, that he had discovered in advance about Qantoum, suggested that the place was not quite what it had been; successively oasis, trading post, village, town, frontier garrison, transit camp and fuel dump. Even a museum would seem like a roaring nightspot in this godforsaken wilderness – though it might have a tourist information centre of some kind. That must be what Kijé had meant. His first port of call, after escaping Kijé's limp clutches, ought to have been the consular district, except that his meagre researches had revealed that there were no consuls left in Qantoum.

From the moment he had found the atlas in the library, and seen the glorious company it kept, the mantra had recited itself in his head; Khiva, Bukhara, Samarkand; the minarets, the domes, the great-gated madrassehs, Jummi mosques that could contain the entire male population of a city for Friday prayers, the courtyards, canals and chaikhanas; the carpets, the textiles, the silks, the azure faience tiles. Qantoum was not of that company.

Without warning, the corner he was turning, instead of drawing him farther into the maze, led into an open space, and the close-burning stars cast enough light to reveal that he was at the lower end of the market-place, opposite the lane by which he had left it. Market Street evidently narrowed to a point where he had crossed it without noticing, and he had come round in a jagged half-circle to the far side. On the left he made out the mass of the Sogdiana Serai Hotel across the Registan, St Vasili's dome and the slightly lower façade of the

Gorki Theatre, wearing its beat-up tiara of obelisks and balustrades.

He approached the Registan, conscious now only of cold fatigue, passed the Hotel Iskander and the cinema and made his limping, shivering way back down Oktyabrskaya to Control Point E. The little building was in darkness and the door was locked. Lt. Kijé had obviously gone to the museum. It was too dark to read the map, and he could go no farther. Wrapping his coat around him he sank down at the top of the five steps, huddled against the door and was asleep in seconds.

At some time during the night he awoke briefly and heard music; not the pure sopranos of the desert sand but the whooping notes of a fiddle, the friendly wheeze of an accordion, and lay listening to it until he fell asleep again, wondering if he were delirious, and dreamed that he was on board an airliner in a nosedive above the polar ice-cap. Over the intercom the pilot remarked chattily, "We are about to crash. Please do not block the exits." The man in the next seat turned and said, "Well, it's better than being in Qantoum, anyway," as the plane hit the ground and burst into flames. Keith said wasn't it just? and died happy, but when he woke up he was still alive and he was still in Qantoum.

TWO

It was light, the bleached light of just before sunrise which, even as he watched began to take on a faint warmth, a pinkness, as of blood returning to frozen fingers. He unfolded, in an agony of stiffness, and descended the five steps to the pavement as the sun came up over the borders.

Taking out the map he remembered the phantom music. He found the market-place, the border zone, the site of his encounter with the crumb-throwing crone, and discovered where he had gone astray last night. Bypassing his intended turning in the twilight he had proceeded to lose himself in what the map described as the Old Town. Sensibly, the map did not attempt to reproduce the myriad alleys and the whole area had been left blank, but he had been right about Market Street. It was a dead end except for a narrow lane in one corner which he must have crossed in his wanderings. Not two minutes' walk from Market Street, he estimated, was the Museum of Anthropology, occupying a whole block of, not surprisingly, Museum Street. It was scarcely ten minutes from where he stood now and he thought of the direction from which the music had seemed to emanate. "The museum does not close," Kijé had said. An all-night museum? Here, anything was possible.

From the direction of the Registan footsteps were approaching and he looked up to see someone rounding the shallow curve of Oktyabrskaya, a couple of hundred metres away. He thought at first that it was Lt. Kijé but as the figure drew closer he saw that although similarly dressed this man was a little taller, a little thinner, thatched with fair hair in place of Kijé's mousy mop-head. As he came close Keith withdrew to the top of the steps so that he was looking down from a vantage point when the stranger turned in at the doorway.

He looked up at Keith, grinned and said, "You didn't find the museum, then."

"Acting Captain Tcherk?"

"Lieutenant Fitzgibbon." He tapped the name-plate. "Rusted in. Tcherk was before my time. He's probably been dead for a long while. Where did you spend the night? We were expecting you."

"Expecting me?" *We'll meet again.* . . . This character had not been in his dream. "You know about me? I got lost in the dark – I slept here on the steps."

Lt. Fitzgibbon took out a key. "Kijé told us you'd arrived. I'm sorry you couldn't get in. We have to keep it locked at night or the bear comes poking about."

"The bear?"

"Szusko's bear. It's a good thing you didn't run into her."

"Szusko?"

"The bear. Do come in."

Keith followed him inside. "Do you live here too?" He intended to sound ironic but Fitzgibbon nodded. "What about the barracks?"

"What about the barracks?" Fitzgibbon said discouragingly. "You must be frozen. Take a nice brisk walk to the market and you'll be able to buy food. Hot tea."

"I came back for my luggage. I left a backpack here yesterday. The other guy said he'd look after it."

"He took it to the museum. It'll be quite safe, you can collect it any time. Where are you going to stay? *Are* you going to stay?"

"I hope so. For a while. Your fellow officer told me there were hotels—"

"There are."

"I've seen them. I'm not fussy but I was really thinking of somewhere I could get into. You know, a door that opens. . . ?"

"I'd go to the museum. Ernie Fahrenheit will fix you up."

"*Who?*"

"Ernestine. The Sturyat call her the widow Fahrenheit."

So the Sturyat were still here, were they? "She isn't a demented old biddy who feeds the birds at sunset in the cemetery?"

"Wolves," Fitzgibbon said.

"Wolves?"

"She puts out crumbs for the wolves."

"I thought that was forbidden."

"Cockroach races are also forbidden. Maisie doesn't care."

"The old lady is Maisie?"

"She *is* a lady; Lady Hooke. She really ought to have gone home to her pension but she's come to love the place. It gets to you."

"It's got to me already," Keith said. "I had a dream—"

"I'm not joking," Fitzgibbon said. "I don't mean Qantoum, it's the desert – kind of hypnotizes people after a while – fatally, sometimes. But Maisie's a rare case. It's usually the chaps who succumb, as far as I can tell. Normal as you like one minute, the next, they hear the sand singing at sunset, fling off all their clothes and rush out into the desert. Never seen again. Rough on their wives, of course. Known as sand widows."

"And this Ern – Mrs Fahrenheit, she's a sand widow?"

"In a manner of speaking."

"When can I see her?"

"At any time, I suppose. But don't worry, there's always someone around at the museum."

"I'm a stranger here," Keith said. "I'm lost. I have been separated from my luggage. I haven't eaten in twenty-four hours."

Fitzgibbon opened the bottom drawer of the filing cabinet. "Have a mushroom – no, seriously, go down to the market. You'll be able to get food there. I'll give you a map."

"I have a map."

"Money?'

"Yes. I changed some before I started out. What happens if I need more? I was going to ask if there was a *bureau de change* here but that's probably a silly question."

"It is. But if you run out of cash you'll be able to barter."

"Barter what?"

"You've probably got some spare socks."

The street and the Registan were as deserted as they had been yesterday, but the market-place was a comparative hive of activity. Six of the twenty-three stalls were operational and clusters of people stood about them. Others were walking up and down, like extras on a film set rhubarbing in the background before crashing into the big production number.

The stallholders were not specialists; whatever they had to sell they sold it. The first display was of heaps of root vegetables and cabbages, with worn felt boots and leather shoes arranged among them. The fruit stall offered cartridges and skeins of wool, the fruit resembling shrunken heads, threaded on string. The third stall sold samosas and bread, broad flat loaves with seeds scattered like mouse droppings over the crusts, and a couple of glazed yellow bricks. Beside it a man stood by a wagon with a samovar, selling tea and a thin sepia liquid out of a barrel. He had also a basket containing a species of dried frog, which people nibbled at as they talked.

Beyond this was a display of leather goods, belts and pouches, none of them new, and second-hand clothes, then a kind of a gibbet from which hung lumps of gluey meat. Towards the end of the line was a board spread with enough spare parts to build a whole Lada and beside it a table over which were scattered unidentifiable metal implements that looked as if they had been in the ground for some years. Among these lay a stiff leathery thing about the size of a cricket pad, thin almost to the point of transparency and curled at the edges, the colour of old wallpaper paste.

No one took the slightest notice of him, but it was a kind of studied neglect, almost courteous, as if he looked to them very strange but they knew that it was rude to stare. Both stallholders and shoppers seemed to be locals, the Sturyat nomads so despised by Lady Charlotte. To them, he supposed, he was just another foreigner stomping uninvited upon their turf, the latest of thousands, but no one showed him any hostility, they were simply indifferent to his presence. Just as birds that took wing at the sight of a distant human would feed confidently at the feet of elephants, so in their scheme of things he did not matter. Keith Chapman, Prince Zherdin, Lady Charlotte, Genghiz Khan; others came and went. The Sturyat stayed.

He returned to the bread stall and took out a coin which seemed a more productive approach than wondering what to say and in which language to say it. The stallholder was immediately alert, beaming; the smile was almost all that was visible for in spite of the increasing warmth everyone was wearing a hat, pulled down over the eyes, jerkins, sweaters, scarves, overcoats, shawls. It made them all conical and asexual. He had taken the bread seller to be a man, but the voice was a woman's.

He pointed at the bread.

"A loaf?" she said. "Anything else, dear man? There's cheese, if you want; apples, sunflower seeds. . ." Her eyes roved across the stall as if she too were uncertain about what was on sale.

"This is my breakfast," Keith said, "and yesterday's dinner – and lunch."

She was instantly concerned. "Oh, dear man, eat all you can." She produced a paper bag and rammed in a loaf and three apples, pausing to hew a thick tile from one of the yellow bricks; cheese. "For that you get tea, too," she said, taking his coin, and turning to the animated pyramid beside her. "Hi, Streph, I pay you later in radishes. Give the dear man tea."

Streph, who was manning barrel and samovar, passed over a steaming tin mug. "Have a frog, dear man," proffering the basket. "Have two."

Keith took a frog out of politeness and clipped his teeth on one of its toenails, recalling the flat leathery thing on the hardware stall. Possibly that too was some kind of desiccated amphibian, an edible crocodile?

"Good, eh?" Streph said, with pride.

"Incredible. May I take the cup and sit down to eat? I'll bring it back."

"Of course." Streph laughed. "Of course you will bring it back. Where would you take it?"

He had feared that the sight of money might attract beggars, but no one pursued him as he made his way to the Registan where he sat on a bench in the formal garden by the parched fountain, and stared at St Vasili's Cathedral. There he had dreamed of meeting tall golden-haired robed figures who promised to meet him again, here in this very town. But if they were awaiting him, expecting him, where were they? One thing seemed very sure, they were not locals, neither Sturyat not Qantoumi. The only tall fair person he had seen so far was Lt. Kijé's sidekick, Fitzgibbon, who had shown no signs of knowing who he was. And no one showed any signs of wondering what he was doing here.

Keith attacked his breakfast. The cheese was as hard as Parmesan, but full of flavour; the bread, firm on top, was moist and warm inside; the apples, though withered and soft, were sweet. As soon as he broke the bread sparrows appeared around his feet. He sat drinking the tea and taking alternate mouthfuls of bread, apples and cheese. From childhood he had always expected abroad to be properly foreign; exotic plants, not grass and dandelions, orchids growing in the street, carboniferous trees, bright-plumaged birds; and yet here he might have been sitting in any park in London, and only as his belly filled and chilled limbs thawed did he return to the fact that he was in Qantoum, on the edge of the desert that sang by night.

And there was the small matter of Szusko's bear, that poked about in people's offices. Had it come and poked him while he lay comatose from exhaustion on the steps of Control Point E?

He looked up and saw that the sparrows had been joined by two dogs that were sitting at a respectful distance. He tossed them some crusts. One dog was obviously just that, a thick-coated retriever type; the other, of decidedly lupine appearance, called to mind Maisie's friends. He shared the last of the cheese with them but retreated while they were eating it. Might they be rabid? Were not all loose dogs to be shot on sight?

He went back to the market, occasionally glancing over his shoulder to see the couple following at a leisurely pace, and returned the tin mug to Streph who smiled widely at him and said, "Dear man, I told you you would bring it back."

Keith pointed. "Tell me, is that a dog over there?"

"Of course it is a dog."

"No, the other one."

"Dear man, that is the dog's friend."

"I thought I saw a sign – all loose dogs—"

"To be shot on sight? Ha!" Streph encircled his nose with thumb and finger. "Excuse me." It must be an obscene gesture. "Dear man, that is a special dog, the dog of Major Vetchinkin. It went with him everywhere. He called it a . . . a mascot. Yes, that is the word. Then the sand got him. One night he is on duty, the next morning he is no more here. The dog grieves, dear man, it pines for weeks, then it too vanishes. We say to ourselves, it is faithful to Major Vetchinkin, even in death; his spirit calls to it from the desert and it follows him, but one day it comes back with a friend. Happy ever after. Dear man, why should we shoot them?"

"The dog's friend; it isn't entirely a dog, is it?"

"Who is entirely anything?" Streph said, obscurely. "Now, you will be going to the museum, no?"

How could Streph know this? Easy; everybody went to the museum.

"Take that lane, there, behind the Hotel Iskander. And have another frog."

He rattled the basket hospitably. The frogs rustled like potato crisps.

"I still have one, thank you."

"Ah, take another anyway. You never know when you might need a frog. They are good for the blood."

The lane behind the Iskander ran straight; on one side the concrete ramparts of the hotel, on the other, duck-egg-blue plastered walls topped with low flat roofs. The lane ended in a sloping street parallel to the market and on the opposite side was a brooding frontage of stone-coloured tile. A gothic turret reared up at either end with a classical pediment between them beneath which, in incised letters, ran the legend MUSEUM OF ANTHROPOLOGY. The entrance was a broad-stepped portico where a woman was swabbing the tiled floor with a mop, overseen by Lady Hooke who, when she saw Keith, turned and held out her hand, elegant as a duchess greeting guests at a garden party. There was no question of shaking the hand, he bent to kiss it, a little brown freckled claw like an old chicken-skin glove.

"We've already met, Lady Hooke. In the cemetery." As you do.

"I expect so. One meets so many people during the Season." Memory was perhaps not her strong point. She wagged a finger under the nose of the cleaning woman.

"Lizaveta, stand aside. Deaf as a bat, poor thing," she explained to him.

"I'm looking for the widow Fahrenheit."

Lady Hooke's lizard eyes showed a flicker of recognition. "Fahrenheit? Appalling little man. Went into the desert, so they tell me. Wouldn't be surprised if she didn't shoot him. *I'd* have shot him," she hissed. "Wouldn't be the first time."

"Not him – Mrs Fahrenheit." What was going on? A sand widow in a manner of speaking, Fitzgibbon had said. In what manner? Had she really shot her husband? But Lady Hooke was off again, humming her wolf song, her brief waltz with reality over already.

Keith trod carefully across the wet and shining tiles and entered the museum through doors of bronze, folded back against the walls. He had stepped into a small rotunda lit from above by a glazed dome. The floor, glistening from the recent attentions of Lizaveta and Lady Hooke, was laid with polished tiles in a sun-burst design. Three arches led out of the rotunda and in the middle of the sun-burst was a small finger-post with four arms. EXIT pointed at his chest, ARCHAEOLOGY to his left, REFRESHMENTS to his right and straight ahead, THE ZHERDIN COLLECTION. It was the Zherdin Collection which had brought him here – without it he might have been in Gantheaume Australia by now – so he would at least pay his respects. He wondered if he were meant to pay an entrance fee as well, but the little desk to one side of the entrance was unmanned.

The central arch led directly into a gallery with a pitched

glass roof where the sun was gaining just enough height to pierce the few dusty panes that had not been boarded up. Lamps hung at intervals from long chains. On each side of the gallery stood display cases with a row of glass-topped cabinets running down the centre. A brief look round made one thing clear; his impressions of Prince Andrei Zherdin, deduced from *The Rover's Monthly*, had been mistaken. Acquisitive he might have been but this was not loot, rather the scavengings of an international car-boot sale.

The shelves were dim and dusty and so were the exhibits, each labelled in faded copperplate writing on small rectangles of white card. They were modest fossils, stone tools, ceramic fragments, simple weapons and artefacts of bone and metal, each meticulously tagged with its date of discovery and place of origin. Prince Andrei had been no kleptomaniac, these things had been chosen, amassed slowly in a spirit of genuine if naïve inquiry for, quite clearly, he had had no idea what most of them were. He could identify his fossils, name his weapons, make an educated guess at the pottery, but one whole case was devoted to curiously-shaped lumps of porous grey rock – *Black Sea Coast 1872*; another housed pale floating things in sealed flasks – *Viscera? Harbin 1850*; bottled spiders and a hideous mixed pickle of brains and tumours – *Uncurated Jar*. Here were eleven small blackish shucks in a pillbox: *Possibly warts shed as a result of the Miraculous Touch of Saint Athanasius of Smyrna 1847*; *Reputed tooth of Aurangzeb, Agra 1863*.

The drab exhibits continued; shrunken heads, three of

them, disturbingly similar to the fruit in the market, and a perforated skull, *Possibly a victim of Genghiz Khan*, but there again, possibly not.

One long glass case in the centre housed a dried and contorted creature, propped on its elbows, with many ribs and a mangy crest of fur running down a spine that terminated in a stout scaly fish tail with fins. *Believed to be a mermaid caught by Aino fishermen off Saghalien 1869*. Head to head with this horror was a whole human corpse, Setsemhotep III, mummified, unwrapped, lying shrunken, shrivelled, exposed, with his head tipped back, black lips writhing away from the small black teeth like rows of seeds. The grave-robbers had been and gone, seized the treasure, forced open the priceless sarcophagus, tipped out the worthless mummy to be retrieved by the dogged Prince Andrei, trudging in their wake, doomed to pick up the debris of history.

Even his big game was small: turtles and unambitious sharks, four-legged chickens, a two-headed sheep, misshapen stuffed squirrels with too many toes, deformed frogs, deformed eggs, a catalogue of nature's near-misses.

Keith had worked his way round to the entrance again, beside which hung an elaborately framed collage of mouse skins, mounted on velvet to represent a copy of Leonardo da Vinci's *Mona Lisa*.

"The work of Prince Andrei himself." A woman was standing at his elbow, in the archway. "He devoted his last years to breeding the mice especially. He was very particular about the colour."

She was tall, fair, her hair in a thick plait hanging down over one shoulder of a long blue smock that almost touched the ground. Could she be. . . ?

"Have we met before?" Keith said.

The woman looked him up and down and said firmly, 'No, but we've been expecting you since last night."

"Expecting me?" *We'll meet again. . .*

"Since Kijé brought your luggage over. Keith Chapman? I am Ernestine Fahrenheit."

The widow. "Are you the curator?" he said.

"In a manner of speaking."

In a manner of speaking she was the curator of the museum. In a manner of speaking she was a widow. But she was unequivocally beautiful, powerfully beautiful, and close to twice his age, alas.

"Lieutenant Fitzgibbon said you could fix me up," he said, beginning to wonder exactly what Fitzgibbon had had in mind. "About somewhere to stay."

"Ah, yes; well, as to that, anyone could fix you up. You could fix yourself up."

"It's a question of cost."

"No," Mrs Fahrenheit said, "it is not. All you need is a hacksaw. Come along to the bar and we'll talk."

As they left the Zherdin Collection they collided with Lady Hooke. She looked graciously upon the widow Fahrenheit and winked, grotesquely girlish.

"Ah, Daphne, I do believe you've found a young man at last." She swept on.

"Daphne?"

"Some subaltern's sister I expect, from 1945," Mrs Fahrenheit said. "She's been here so long, known so many people."

"So she told me."

"All those hundreds of names and so few of us left to pin them on."

"Alzheimer's?"

The widow paused. "I don't recall knowing anyone. . ."

"No, no, it's an illness, when the mind goes in old age. It's very distressing."

"I wouldn't say that Maisie seemed very distressed, would you? We call it dotage."

They had crossed the rotunda and followed the finger-post marked REFRESHMENTS, down an unlit corridor, but when Mrs Fahrenheit opened a door at the far end the light that poured through it met the light from the rotunda and he saw that the walls were lined with maps. Elaborate lamps hung from the ceiling. On the wall by the door was a single brass switch. He thought of the enormous number of street-lamps and last night's darkness, the needless gloom of the tunnel where they stood, and it crossed his mind that there was no electricity in Qantoum; no electricity, no heat, no light, no computers, televisions, telephones. . .

In the Refreshment Room three long windows framed the sunlit street and eight metres above them rococo nymphs ogled goitrously on a painted ceiling. The room was spacious, on two levels: a terrace on which they were standing, with small café tables and chairs and a piano at one end, then steps led down to a kind of well where there were benches and long boards on trestles. To one side was a bar, a real bar, with polished glasses and bottles.

Mrs Fahrenheit went round behind it and took out two unlabelled brown bottles. "Beer?"

He looked at his watch. It was 9 a.m. Why not? "Thank you."

The bottles were sealed, not crowned, and the beer exploded in a golden froth as she poured it. He sat at one of the little tables looking out into an empty street of shuttered windows and padlocked doors. He saw what she had meant about the hacksaw.

The widow Fahrenheit joined him with the two glasses, sat down and folded her arms on the tabletop. "Now," she said, "before we find you somewhere to stay you can tell me what you are doing here."

He did not care for the tone of her voice: suspicious, not unfriendly, but suspicious.

"I tried to tell Lt. Kijé, but he didn't seem to want to know. Lt. Fitzgibbon didn't even ask."

"Poor Fitz," the widow said, obscurely. "Kijé is another matter, of course."

"I met someone else in the market . . . Streph. Even he didn't want to know."

"Why should he? Streph is a Sturyat. He doesn't care who you are, what you want or why you are here. People have been invading and annexing and conquering this region for centuries. Sooner or later they all go away again. The Arabs came and went, the hordes came and went, the British came, briefly, and went, the Russians came and went. Which is why the Sturyat call them visitors, an approximation of their word for people who come in without asking and leave without saying goodbye."

"You're not a Sturyat?"

She gave him a forgiving look. "There are visitors who stay. Never mind about me, what about you? You told Kijé you were a tourist."

"Why do you think I'm lying?"

She enumerated the reasons on her fingers. "Tourists move in large numbers, they have cameras. They make reservations in hotels. They make complaints. They require chemist's shops and post offices. They arrive in aeroplanes. The English ones carry quantities of sliced bread with them. Tourists do not come to Qantoum."

"You can't get here by air."

"Quite," the widow said. "There is a military airstrip but nothing could land on it now. To reach Qantoum takes many hours travel in a railway train and then a long walk from the junction."

"Thirty kilometres."

"So you are not a tourist."

"I read about the Zherdin Collection in an old magazine. I was curious—"

"You could see better collections in Europe. Do go on."

There was nothing for it; she would have the truth out of

him sooner or later with her unwavering gaze and her potent early-morning beer. "I had a dream."

"Yes."

"It wasn't exactly a dream, it was a Near Death Experience."

"A what?"

He was aware again of that sense of dislocation. She might know his every secret, his very thoughts; but there were, all the same, things that she did not know of: Alzheimer's Disease, a Near Death Experience.

"I was in a car crash. I almost died – perhaps I did die – but I was resuscitated." He watched her for one of those syncopated moments when she missed his meaning. "This is quite common."

"Raising the dead is common?"

Just such a moment. 'It is these days. A lot of people have Near Death Experiences. They find themselves hovering above the body – "

"Yes. That is common."

It might be, too, here. " – and then they enter a kind of tunnel and at the end of the tunnel is a beautiful place, a garden, and they meet all the people they knew and loved who have died. Everyone is pleased to see them, welcomes them, sometimes Jesus is there too, then a voice says, 'No, not yet. You must return,' and they wake up, usually in hospital."

"This happens only to people who believe in heaven?"

"I don't think so, though they all do afterwards. But it was different for me. I didn't go to a garden, I didn't see Jesus. I was in a square with a fountain and a building with long steps, and the people who were sitting on the steps were pleased to see me, but I didn't know any of them. And then somebody, something, dragged me away, and one of these people said, 'We'll meet again in Qantoum'."

At last she looked surprised. "You died but you did not go to heaven, you went to Qantoum?"

"*No.* I woke up again. I *had* been resuscitated. When I got out of the hospital I tried to find out where I'd been. I was sure there must be some significance, you know, if everyone else goes to heaven—"

"Or hell?"

"I don't think hell is an option. I mean, I thought there must be some reason for me being sent to a place I'd never heard of – and I hadn't ever heard of it. It took me ages to find out if Qantoum even existed. In the end I came across it by accident, in a magazine. But I thought there must be a meaning to it, some kind of revelation, that I'd been shown a vision of Qantoum because I was meant to come here."

"You think you have a divine purpose? I would not tell that to Lt. Kijé."

Was she laughing at him? "I didn't think anything; I didn't know what to think, but once I knew that the place I'd dreamed of was real I had to find out. I couldn't even be sure if I'd got it right till yesterday, when I walked into the Registan, and saw St Vasili's, the building with the steps. It was what I had seen in my dream."

Behind him he heard the door opening, followed by the scuffling sound of someone dragging something heavy. The widow Fahrenheit said, "Thank you, Zayu. Just leave it there, would you?"

One of the Sturyat came through the door, in reverse, hauling his backpack. He – no, it was surely a woman – she was relatively lightly clad for a Sturyat, in a long grey garment like a cavalry greatcoat and a round felted hat and, bent over the backpack, she resembled a dung beetle with a particularly heavy load. As she turned to shove it against the wall he saw her face surrounded by curls and tangles of dark hair that escaped from under the hat.

"Thank you, Zayu," the widow Fahrenheit said again. It was an unambiguous dismissal. Zayu leaned on the doorpost and took off her hat, revealing level dark brows that so nearly met over her nose that she appeared to be scowling, but the scowl was all in the eyebrows. Beneath them her expression was neutral.

"Is that him? The tourist?"

"The tourist, yes it is. We are just discussing something."

Zayu continued to lean on the doorpost in an attitude not quite of dumb insolence but of dumb non-cooperation. She appeared to be in a position of subservience to the widow and evidently considered this to be the widow's headache, not hers. Although shorter than Mrs Fahrenheit she had a kind of grace, lolling there with the skirts of her ancient coat falling elegantly from the hip, the hat dangling from the hook of her index finger. She showed no hint of recognition when she looked at Keith; it was hard to tell if she even was looking at him, but he could have sworn that he recognized her, or someone very like her, the creature of his dream that had dragged him from the welcoming people on the steps and sent him hurtling earthward again.

At his back he felt the widow's displeasure. "I shall need you in, say, half an hour, Zayu." For some reason she could not say "Go away" and for some reason Zayu was not going. They stared at each other over his head.

Finally Zayu said, "I am going to the market. I shall come back in an hour," and went out, closing the door quietly. The widow exhaled furiously but said nothing.

"Does she work here?"

"In a manner of speaking. As generations of visitors have discovered, it is not a Sturyat habit to take orders. Unfortunately they do not take hints, either. Now" – the widow tapped the tabletop sharply – "you want somewhere to stay?"

He had expected further interrogation on the subject of his previous visit to Qantoum. "Don't you want to know the rest?"

"There is more?"

"Not *more*. But don't you find it strange? I do. I'd never heard of Qantoum, I'd never seen it, and yet I dreamed—"

"Memory plays strange tricks," the widow said, "and not only on people like Maisie. Had it occurred to you that you might once have seen a photograph? You read about us in a magazine, after all. This was a place of some importance. Before the Russians subdued the region this part of it was known as the Qantoum Khanate."

She might be right. He might have seen a magazine, *National Geographic*, one of those books with sepia photogravures of exotic foreign places. After all, the Qantoum of his dream was in far better shape than the Qantoum of reality, but that did not account for Zayu. He could never have seen a photograph of Zayu. What little peace of mind Mrs Fahrenheit's common-sense diagnosis offered him was counteracted by the thought of Zayu. He did not want to confide too deeply in the widow, not just yet.

He said, "I expect you're right. But it took me a long while to get here. I'd like to stay a few days and see the place properly. So where can I stay? Where do people live?"

"I live here," Mrs Fahrenheit said, "in the museum. Fitz and Kijé live, after a fashion, at Control Point E. Lady Hooke lives at the Sogdiana Serai in a suite on the third floor, but few people would care to risk joining her. The top storey is missing and it is haunted. Maisie of course does not notice. Most people live in the streets between here and the Registan. The Sturyat live where they have always lived, beyond the citadel. The choice is yours. All you need is a hacksaw."

"Why is everything so bolted and shuttered and locked up?"

"Visitors always intend to return. Deep in their minds, I suppose, there lurks the fear that if they just leave without securing everything against the possible depredations of the next gang, their departure will be seen as a disorderly rout. A leisurely round of locking-up, even under mortar fire, gives an illusion of being in control. So, choose your door. Take the

Iskander, the Gorki, the barracks, any one of a dozen consulates, the station, though you may find it draughty. When Fitz and Kijé feel the need to let off steam they go down there and shoot up the signs. They've taken out a number of windows, too."

"What about St Vasili's?"

"You want to live in a cathedral? You have delusions of grandeur."

"No, I meant why is St Vasili's shut up?"

"For the same reason that the mosque was shelled, perhaps."

"What do the Muslims do? This is a Muslim country, isn't it?"

"In a manner of speaking. I doubt if Islam would countenance what goes on at the moment. However, there are very few Muslims left here. The Sturyat are not Muslims."

"Christians?"

"No, nor Hindu nor Buddhist. It is their own peculiar religion that they brought with them from wherever they came. The rest of us, I am afraid, have rather given up the notion of a Supreme Being who sees each sparrow fall. No one would object if you were to move into St Vasili's but it might alter their opinion of you. The Sturyat would suppose that you thought you were a god, since they know that certain persons regard it as God's house. You would find them very kind, very tolerant, as they are to Maisie. Do you want that?"

"I don't want to live in the cathedral," Keith said, "or in the station, or the barracks. Just a room – in a place where there are people. I'd pay for that."

"Then you had best wait here. Sooner or later everyone comes to the museum, for a drink, for food. I begin to serve lunch at noon. Ask anyone, you'll be shown a place to live."

"Is there anywhere I can telephone – just to let people know I've arrived safely?"

She looked as close to laughing as she had done before. "No," she said, gravely, "there is nowhere. Nowhere closer than Iskanderabad, at any rate." He did not ask if she had heard of satellite phones. "Now, I have things to do. If I do not see you before you leave Qantoum, be sure to come back here tonight. We were quite disappointed when you did not arrive yesterday evening. Everyone comes to the museum."

"So they keep telling me. Why?"

"There is nowhere else to go," the widow Fahrenheit said.

Three

He sat a little longer, looking out into the sunny dusty street where no one passed; he examined the ceiling with its elephantine nymphs. Zayu did not reappear. Keith did not want to think too much about Zayu. He inspected the unlabelled bottles behind the bar and wondered what kind of home-brewed hooch they contained. Still no one came into the Refreshment Room.

He opened the door and walked down the shadowy corridor to the bright bowl of the rotunda, the finger-post at its centre with the fourth arm that pointed to the Archaeology Gallery. Like the Refreshment Room, it was at the end of an unlit corridor and he had to find the door by touch, but the large faceted brass handle turned easily in his fingers. On the other side was sunlight and, directly ahead, greeting him with the frisky grin of its kind, was a human skeleton. It was hanging from a hook on an iron frame like an anatomist's specimen, but before he could take it in a sound in the corridor made him turn to see something bulky advancing upon him from the rotunda, a furry silhouette against the sunshine.

He felt electric pains in his hands; his palms sweated; Szusko's bear, poking about? The creature spoke.

"Tourist?"

It was Zayu. At that moment he might almost have preferred the bear.

"Yes. I'm just looking around." He moved out of the doorway, into the gallery. She did not follow him. "You work here, don't you? Can you show me around?"

He was only making conversation but she said, "No. I do not go in there. I think you want somewhere to live."

How did she know that? She had left the Refreshment Room before they had begun to speak of it. Walls had ears.

"I'm just killing time till someone comes to show me a place to stay."

"I can show you a place to stay."

"With your people – the Sturyat?"

"No, in the Old Town. Fetch your luggage," she said, and waited for him in the portico while he went down to the Refreshment Room to collect his backpack. From the open door of the gallery the skeleton continued to smile at him.

Zayu led him across the street and into an alley a little below the lane he had come down earlier from the market. There was no room to walk abreast so he followed her silent back. They had been going for several minutes round a series of the right-angled corners that had so misled him last night before he ventured to ask, "Will anyone mind if I stay in the Old Town?"

"Why should anyone mind?"

"Well – me being an alien."

"All visitors are aliens." Including, he supposed, although she did not say it, the people who had put up notices about other aliens. Pointless to argue that he was not a visitor. He *had* arrived without asking, but he would not leave without saying goodbye.

"Do you know Lt. Kijé?" he asked. It was difficult holding a conversation with the back of her head but she would not turn round.

"Of course I know him."

"And Fitz?"

"Yes."

"Which army do they belong to?"

"There is no army."

"I can see that. Which one *did* they belong to?"

"All armies are the same. There was the Yueng. Fitz was with the Yueng."

It sounded Oriental, or else might be some bunch of bandits calling themselves a Liberation Army. This image did not quite seem to fit the languid lieutenant.

"I was not grown then. It was many years ago, seven, I think. They came for a little while, to keep the peace, they said. Visitors. When they began to be shot they went away again."

"But Fitz stayed? What about Kijé – and Acting Captain Tcherk?"

For some reason her stride faltered. "Tcherk? Tcherk was dead long ago. I was a little child. The sand got him. All they found were his clothes and his rifle. And his boots." She stopped suddenly, turned round and hitched back the skirts of her coat. "These are the boots of Tcherk."

He had never expected to see the boots of Tcherk. The original owner must have had smallish feet, for a man. "Why have you got them?"

"I have the rifle also. He was my father."

"*What?*"

She thought he had misheard and repeated, "Tcherk was my father," before turning to lead the way along another alley.

"And was *he* with the Yueng?" As soon as he said it himself, aloud, the word became comprehensible. "Did they wear blue berets?"

"The UN, yes. Tcherk was not one of the UN. I do not know what kind of a visitor Tcherk was."

"But your mother—"

She replied carefully, without turning round, "Captain Tcherk did not ask my mother if she would bear his child."

They had, all this while, been passing between the duck-egg-blue plastered walls with their little shuttered windows. At every corner a flight of stairs went up the side of the buildings. Zayu stopped at the foot of one such flight and jerking her head upward said, "Here."

"What is it?"

"A place where you can stay. Where there are people. I live here myself. When you have seen it you may prefer the house of Vasili."

She must have overheard every word they said, in the

Refreshment Room, every word that had passed between him and the widow. He looked for some sign in her face, but it gave nothing away, that curious combination of smile and scowl. He thought of Streph and the others in the market-place who had seemed to smile in pure friendliness, but with their hats on he had not seen those eyebrows. And he had not known then about visitors, visitors such as Acting Captain Tcherk. The sand had got him, had it?

Zayu ascended the steps which turned at the top, ending at a low wooden door. She nodded to him to enter so he had only an instant to take in the view of what seemed to be acres of sun-baked flagstones; a great floor paved with rooftops. Then he ducked in at the door behind Zayu and she closed it after him.

It was so dark that his eyes were marbled with flat green slabs, the imprint of the sunlit roofs, but when they faded he saw a small room with a fretted window; dapples of light were visible through oiled paper. Zayu was already disappearing down a square hole by the wall, nimbly descending a slatted staircase with no risers. He followed more cautiously, into an identical room, by which time Zayu had opened a door and he saw he was in a space perhaps three metres square with a dirt floor and a ceiling so low that his hair brushed the rafters. It had no furniture but in one corner was an iron cylinder that might be a stove.

Zayu was standing outside in a courtyard with a doorway in each of its four sides. In the middle was a low brick coping spanned by a winch from which a rope hung down.

"You have your own well here," Zayu said. "Is this what you wanted?"

"Who else lives here?"

"I do."

"Where?"

She pointed across the courtyard. "Over there."

"And who else?"

"No one else."

"Your family?" Was that tactless, given the circumstances?

"My stone is in the house of Theps. I go there some-times."

"Your stone?"

"My soul stone. It is kept in the house of Theps. That is my family, all the stones in the house of Theps. The others. . . Others are not there."

He remembered the dismissive words of Lady Charlotte Crow. *They have set up the bones of their ancestors and laid down the stones wherein they keep their souls.*

"Where are they then?"

"Not where they ought to be." With a boot of Tcherk she touched his backpack where he had dropped it on the floor. "That rolled-up thing is your sleeping mat?"

"Yes."

"At night, lay it in the upper room. Close down the trap-door at the top of the stairs. Fasten the door."

What lurked in the deserted town by night that must be kept out, apart from Maisie's wolves, Szusko's bear? Who? "Who am I trying to keep out?"

"Do you not seal your houses at night where you come from?"

"Yes, but. . ." Yes, but I come from an advanced nation with one of the highest crime rates in Western Europe. "Is that a stove? What do I burn in it?"

"Why burn?"

"For heat?"

"Put on more clothes."

"Cooking?"

Suddenly she laughed, finally fathoming the pit of his ignorance. "Come with me to the house of Theps, at sundown. We eat together."

"What about the museum?" Everyone goes to the museum, the widow had said. There is nowhere else to go. Apparently everyone did not, and there was.

"You may go to the museum."

"Can I eat with you and *then* go to the museum?"

"As you please, but be here when the sun goes down and I will be waiting."

She began to walk towards the door of her house.

"Zayu, wait – can I call you Zayu?"

"What else would you call me?" She seemed genuinely puzzled.

"If we eat at Theps's place . . . do I pay?"

"You do not pay, you bring."

"What can I bring?"

"Tonight, nothing. You are a guest." Not a visitor. "After that, we will think of something. If you stay." She turned again.

"Is there a key?"

"There is no key, there is no lock. Only visitors have locks." Didn't they just? "We, the Sturyat, go in and out. Where we cannot go we do not go." So why seal the house at night? "You will be quite safe. But if you wish to be safer you may set up the bones – if you have bones."

While Keith was adjusting to that she vanished and he looked up only just in time to see the door closing, to hear the click of a falling latch.

There was no exit from the courtyard; he would have to leave and enter through the door in the upper room, and recalling the labyrinth of alleys lying beyond it, wondered how he would ever find it again if he left it. He would have to mark the route or lay a clew of thread. He closed the door and went upstairs.

Later on, he thought, he would go out and try to get his bearings, but for now he would settle in, unroll the sleeping-bag and rest. He was still achingly tired after last night spent in the doorway of Control Point E. He was about to lie down but he knew that if he did he would never get up again. He ought to unpack, air the clothes he had brought with him, look out a few socks for barter, as Fitzgibbon had suggested. He opened the backpack and delved through the strata, shaking out the creased garments, jeans, sweaters, shirts, underwear, the useless adaptor, the emergency rations he had so badly needed last night. He could use those as polite contributions to this evening's dinner party. Everything was just as he had packed it. At the back of his mind had been the assumption that Lt. Kijé would have searched it, but either he was extremely methodical, which seemed unlikely, or he had not bothered.

Now that his eyes were accustomed to the gloom he saw hooks in the rafters and arranged his clothes on them in festoons, like giant roosting bats, reserving the folding coathanger that his sister had given him for his one good shirt and the chinos he had brought along for socializing. Then he lay down at last on the sleeping platform and gazed up at his dangling wardrobe. Clothes do furnish a room, he thought drowsily, as his eyes began to close.

Light blinded him. The door had swung open and someone stood framed in the entry, arrested in the very act of entering, and frozen, one hand extended flat to ward off whatever might be coming the other way. A voice cried out in an unfamiliar tongue. Keith rolled off the platform and stood up. "Who is it?" He clutched a boot. There was nothing else to defend himself with.

"You have put up the bones." It was Zayu.

He was still stupid with surprise. "Bones?"

"The hanging things."

"No, no. Those are my clothes."

He saw her relax. "I was going to my house. If the bones had been up I would have gone the other way."

"Oh yes. The Sturyat go in and out." Of each other's houses, apparently.

The door closed again. She was on the inside, and without giving him another look disappeared through the trap and down the stairs. He did not lie down immediately but squatted on the edge of the platform, pondering her possible reasons for returning so soon. Had she expected to find him asleep or absent? If there was any searching to be done it would more likely be Zayu who did it.

If he stayed here would he be continually intruded upon by passing Sturyat? Lady Charlotte's words came back to him again. *They have set up the bones of their ancestors.* Perhaps he ought to get himself some bones; they might have a few to spare at the museum. But did other Sturyat come here, or was it only Zayu who lived here and not among the rest of her people beyond the citadel? Zayu, who was not wholly of the Sturyat, daughter of the rapist Tcherk whose boots she wore, not out of filial piety he suspected, but because good boots were not easily come by.

She had his rifle, too.

But the widow had not *warned* him about Zayu.

But the widow did not know he was with her. Zayu had found him somewhere to stay, very close to her own home, on her own initiative. Even if she meant him no harm, she was taking an interest in him. He wished he knew how much she had overheard of that conversation in the Refreshment Room, and what she had made of it.

When he woke the courtyard beyond the little window was in shadow. He selected fresh clothes, and went down to the well to draw water. There was nothing to put it in so he gritted his teeth and poured the icy water over his head and fled indoors again. How could people survive here without heating? The Sturyat looked as if they were built for it and did not seem the kind for whom washing was a priority, but what of the Qantoumis and Europeans? Hanging with the natives was all very well but he might have to make other arrangements. The water drained into the earthen floor of the courtyard. Perhaps it was a crime to fling water about like that. Oasis or not, Qantoum could not afford water to waste, surely. He must be less free with it in future, and if he stayed more than a few days he must get hold of receptacles, a basin and jug. They might sell them in the market.

Remembering how darkness had caught him yesterday he checked his watch, alarmed to find that he had slept for seven hours; still, there ought to be a full ninety minutes of daylight left. He went out on to the flight of steps and looked across the vista of flat roofs. This cluster of buildings must be slightly higher than the rest, but the others were identical except that on some stood empty plant containers. On tiptoe he saw that his own roof was one of these; three big clay pots clustered near the edge. He could heave himself up without too much effort, but there must be a regular way. He would investigate later.

Instead he went down into the alley. He brought a felt-tipped pen and as he walked he marked each corner with a discreet circle at shoulder height so that even if he became lost he could retrace his way to the house. He became lost very quickly, and turning thoughtlessly at a junction, mistook a blemish on the wall for one of his circles. Qantoum Old

Town could not be all that large, he had after all traversed it eventually last night, but the alleys crossed and redoubled and with no landmarks to guide him he became more and more confused among the endless duck-egg-blue walls. Then he remembered the roofs. Beside him a flight of stairs like his own rose up to a door, but unlike his own continued beyond it. He went up, pausing to look in at the door and, finding only a vacant room, proceeded to the roof.

There was nothing up here except a number of dead birds, but the adjacent roof was a little higher and familiar; three big clay pots, also a bench and a small shelter with a ragged cloth hanging from it. He had been walking in circles. He was next-door to his own house. He could descend to the alley and try again, but far quicker, probably safer, was to jump across the intervening alley and make his way down from there. The alleys were narrow, this one less than a metre. He needed only a short run-up and he was back where he had started, looking down on the steps that led to his front door.

But there must be a regular way up and down, as with the house he had just left and he walked round the edge of the parapet. On the third side he came to what he was looking for, the head of a flight of steps that led to ground level with a door on the next stage. As he passed it curiosity overcame him; could this be Zayu's door? He knocked. There was no answer. He turned the handle and pushed. It swung inward and the draught of its movement set something swinging that hung beyond the dark rectangle of the doorway, a long narrow cloth bag with a geometric pattern woven into the fabric. He put a hand up to steady it and felt hard narrow things inside, and at the bottom, a hard rounded thing, the size of a melon. Very slowly be brought up his other hand and with all his fingers palpated the bag as delicately as a doctor with a frail patient.

This was a very frail patient indeed, a jumble of ribs, teeth, femurs, vertebrae and cranium. Zayu had set up the bones of her ancestors.

When they met in the courtyard at sundown he did not speak of bones. Zayu, still kitted out for a cavalry charge, had not dressed for dinner. He hoped that the way might lead through her house but she conducted him into one that lay on the fourth side of the courtyard, up interior stairs, through a trapdoor, and out on to another flight of steps, down into an alley. They were walking in single file again and night was falling swiftly, down here between the houses.

At least he had his torch this time. "Zayu, how shall I ever learn to find my way around?"

"Can you not find your way around your own town?"

"Yes, but our streets are wide, they're all different. They have names."

"The visitors give names to streets, you will have seen. We do not need names. We know where we are going."

"I don't."

In the course of the conversation they had rounded half a dozen corners.

"Zayu, wait. I'll never find my way back."

"But you wanted to live here. What did you think you would do?"

"I didn't know it would be like this. All I know is, my door is at the top of a flight of steps. I could never find it again. I tried this afternoon."

"Then you did find it again."

"By chance. It could be this flight – or that one, back there—"

"No, it could not."

"Well, no, literally it couldn't. . ."

The alley had ended, not in a street as he had been expecting, but in an open space. What little light remained showed him, on one side, the water tower and the broken remnants of Qantoum Industrial; on the other, the watch-towers of the wall that began by the cemetery, the old citadel. Here, where they stood, was the settlement of the Sturyat. Some of it seemed to be rough pasture, some of it under cultivation, in strips, like allotments. Zayu set out across them with unerring tread, as she had threaded her way among the alleys, making right-angled turns in the thickening dusk in which he heard, at a distance, the song of the desert.

"Why are you stopping?"

He hurried to catch up, afraid of stomping on someone's unseen vegetables. "I was listening to the sand."

"There is no sand. We are walking on earth."

"No – the desert – the singing."

"That is not the sand that sings."

"Yes—"

"No. They are the voices of those who died in the desert, those who have no soul stones. They have become one with the sand and are lost for ever. Only those who are mad stop to listen, they hear the voices calling, 'Save us,' and they run out into the desert and after a time their voices are joined with the others. All are lost, all lost."

"Is that what happened to Fahrenheit and Major Vetchinkin?" She did not answer. "And Acting Captain Tcherk?"

They were coming to the edge of the gardens. Here were more walls, the ruins of the fortifications perhaps, where the Khans of Qantoum had held out against Khiva and Kokand. Inside the walls dark angular shapes could be discerned. They were heavy circular tents, he saw, as Zayu guided them through an open gateway big enough to admit an elephant. The tents were pitched in a kind of compound formed by the broken walls; flaps were drawn back and inside each a small cooking fire flickered, the smoke escaping through a hole at the top. The Sturyat sat around their hearths in family groups – men, women and children – the first children Keith had seen, from staggering toddlers to teenagers. As he passed he thought he saw them smile in the firelight, friendly and incurious.

At the fire burning inside the biggest tent a man sat cross-legged on a strip of carpet. Zayu headed straight for him.

"Theps," she said.

Theps looked up benevolently. "The tourist?"

"His name is Keith," Zayu said. Who had told her that; the widow?

"Kleith," Theps said experimentally. "Kfeit . . . *Keith*." Finding that he could get his tongue round it he said again, "Keith, sit down, dear man. Eat with us."

"Cheers," Keith said, and folded himself down between Theps and Zayu. "This is very good of you."

"No," Theps said. "While there is food all are welcome."

"Is it your house I'm staying in?" Keith asked. Better get that out of the way as soon as possible. A little matter of rent. . .

"*My* house?"

"Do you own it?"

"Ah, you are thinking like the visitors. They find a piece of air; they put a wall round it. They say, 'This is my air.' They put a lid on top so that the air cannot get out. Then they sell the air."

"Well, not exactly. It's the land they sell."

"One cannot sell the land upon which the people walk."

"Then why do you – thank you." Someone had passed him a bowl of stew, lumps of meat and dumplings bobbing in dense liquid. "Why do you build houses, walls?"

"We do not. We have our *kibitkas* to keep cold air from warm air. To keep wet air from dry air. To keep out things in the night from the people. These are not our walls. Anyone can build a wall, a roof. If that house is empty, dear man, live in it. It is not mine. It is not owned."

"So I could live in any house?"

Theps gestured towards the Old Town. "The visitors have trapped much air, and the air is still there. The visitors have gone. Unless someone has set up the bones of his ancestors you may pass through any door. Why are you not writing this down?"

"Why should I write it down?"

"When visitors eat with us they write things down in little books. This is well known. From the time of the Crow woman and Lordayka, the visitors, the little books."

A voice on his left chipped in morosely, "The Soviets had tape recorders."

"Yes, the tape recorders. Now they too are gone, dear man. The Sturyat remain."

"I'm not a visitor," Keith said, fervently. "Believe me, I'm not. I came here to Qantoum because I had a dream—"

At his side Zayu gave him a violent nudge in the upper arm with her elbow, so that he almost dropped the bowl, and muttered, "Not now."

"What?"

"Dreams. Not now, not here." She was urgently insistent. Theps was being elaborately unconcerned, an urbane host overlooking the gaffe of a boorish dinner guest. A gaffe; a taboo?

"I dreamed of travelling to this part of the world," he amended hurriedly. "Something I'd always longed to do. Suddenly I had enough time, money."

"Dear man, you are welcome whatever the reason," Theps said. "Eat our food, drink our beer." He held out a jug.

It was time to contribute. Keith brought out his block of Kendal Mint Cake. Theps received it gravely, unwrapped it, broke it in pieces and passed it around the circle. More beer was poured. The stew was greasy, rich and filling. When the pot was empty it was removed and the fire burned brightly. He began to feel at home, accepted. Zayu suddenly stood up.

"Now we go."

"So soon?"

"Come away."

He stood also. Theps and his family nodded and raised their hands amiably in farewell, seeing nothing sudden in the abrupt departure. There was no more to detain him, nothing for it but to rise and follow Zayu, mumbling his thanks to Theps, although it was clearly unexpected and unnecessary.

As they crossed the compound he saw that the tents, *kibitkas*, were quiet. One might have expected singing or dancing after good food and beer, but even the desert was subdued now.

Zayu was making full speed ahead through the vegetable plots.

"Why did we leave so suddenly?" Had there been some subtle social nuance that he had failed to catch?

"We had finished eating. There was no Spelling."

"Spelling?" He hurried to catch up with her before they were forced into single file by entering, as they must, an alley.

"That is what you call it."

"Zayu, I don't call it anything. Remember, I don't know anything about this place, about your customs."

"Spelling is when we talk, when we tell things."

"Is that why you shut me up about my dream?"

"Yes." She sounded pleased that he had been so quick on the uptake. So dreams were not to be spoken of lightly.

"Don't you want to know about it?"

"Not here, not now. Now we are going to the museum."

"Why?"

"That was what you wanted."

"No, not any more. I want to go home."

"Where is that?"

"Not London, the house, the place you showed me this morning."

"Oh," she said, "that is good. Because you must not go away yet."

High walls engulfed them, but he looked up and saw, spectrally sketched in the starlight, the outlines of a watch-tower. A minute or two later they turned along a lane; there were railings, a gate.

"I know where we are. This is where Lady Hooke feeds the wolves." He looked through the railings and wondered if he only imagined lean grey shapes among the tombs.

"I said you would soon learn your way about."

"This is easy. It looks different."

"No."

He could not have tolerated these flat contradictions from anyone else, but if he were not learning his way about he was learning that there was no profit in debating perceptions. Zayu navigated like a homing pigeon. His insistence on landmarks must be incomprehensible to her. On what other levels might they fail to think alike, thoughts winging past each other like misaimed darts?

At the top of his steps she said, "No bones?"

"No bones."

She opened the door and walked through his room to the trapdoor.

"Thank you for this evening."

"How?"

"Thank you for taking me to the house of Theps."

"I go to the museum early. If you like I will show you the way."

"No, I must learn my own way about. Zayu, why do you go to the museum?"

"Someone must look after it."

"I thought the widow and Lizaveta did that."

"One of *us* must look after it."

But you aren't quite one of "us" are you? he thought. Or one of the others, come to that.

He heard doors open and shut, footsteps, another door. Peering through the oiled paper he searched for a light in the little house opposite, but saw nothing.

The room was not quite as cold as he would have expected, perhaps after having had the sun on the roof all day, but it was dank and chill now and he writhed swiftly into his sleeping-bag. He was not sleepy; tired but not sleepy, there was time now to review all the things he had meant to think about this morning. How far away Leyton, how far away the hospital on the flight path into Heathrow. He had spent his first full day in Qantoum and already he felt as if he had been here for ever. It was not what he had expected, but he was forgetting exactly what it was he had expected; armed police; prohibited areas? No, nothing like that. His expectations had been as fluid as oil, of Timurid splendours such as he had seen in the guidebooks, supplanted by grim Soviet architecture, rolling steppe subjugated by endless cotton fields? No, not that either. These things had spooled through his mind like a video loop. He had expected a town full of people, where he would pass unnoticed. Nothing could have prepared him for this eerie echoing ruin. His departure for Qantoum had been almost as dreamlike as his original visit. At what point had it ceased to be a dream?

His thought turned again to what he might be able to write about it. Not another *Footsteps of Genghiz Khan*; he would have a different tale to tell. Had he taken the widow's advice and waited for one of her clients to show him around, he might even now be sipping tea in the Refreshment Room. Instead, on his own initiative, he had found a native house, eaten with the Sturyat and, if he had interpreted Zayu correctly, would be welcome to visit again, and tell them of his dream. No doubt the widow had reason on her side when she ascribed his experience to the sight of an old photograph, but that did not explain his certainty that he had seen Zayu in his dream, that she was the figure who had appeared from nowhere to drag him away across the Registan, back to the tunnel, back to life, saying, "No. Oh no. Not here. Not now. Come away."

Almost asleep he woke with a start. These were the exact words she had spoken this evening, at Theps's fireside, when he had started to talk of his dream.

"Not now. Not here." And then as soon as was decent, "Come away."

He sat up in the chill darkness. This must be more than coincidence. He could no longer rely on memory, especially as he was no longer sure that his memory was as reliable as he believed it had once been. He must start to write things down, and if by day they looked like ravings, well, at least he would have a record of them.

Tomorrow he must go to the market and buy candles, or tallow, or whatever they used for artificial light here. For now he would risk running down the battery of his torch. He had two spares, but he had not counted on the nights being so dark (*Lighting is often switched off between 10 p.m. and 6 a.m. in Iskanderabad*, the guidebooks had cautioned; they had not mentioned Qantoum at all so there was no opportunity to point out that the lights were never switched on) and he had not counted on staying. True he was permitted three visa-free days in Iskanderistan and he had been advised that he might safely extend this to a week on payment of a fine minuscule by Western standards, but he had never imagined that there would be anything to stay *for*. He had envisioned himself walking into town, searching for the square, for the building with the steps, failing to find it and after seeing a few sights, clearing out again. He knew now, sitting there in the absolute darkness, that he never truly had believed that he would find what he had come looking for.

He had positioned the torch near his head in case he needed it in a hurry, should some wandering Sturyat barge in during the night, confident of the absence of bones. How many of them used these alleys and houses? It could be embarrassing: supposing you were merrily getting your rocks off? He would have to find himself some bones.

Balancing the torch on top of the backpack he took out his writing block and began to scribble urgently.

I am living among the Sturyat, he wrote. It was not strictly true, yet, but he would make it true. *If there was a purpose in my coming to this place I think I shall learn of it from them. Already what I foresaw is coming true. I no longer believe that what I experienced was a dream. In spirit I have been here before, and I have met with at least one person who confirms this.*

I saw the Registan of Qantoum and I saw a Sturyat girl. The Registan is as I saw it and the girl is Zayu who has picked me out and made me known to her people.

In fact the Registan was not quite as he had seen it and the third element of his dream, his experience, was as yet unaccounted for: the black sun. He had seen Qantoum at a time of total eclipse, and the woman who had risen from the steps had promised that when he returned to meet her it would be under a black sun.

That was something he ought to have checked on before he left home. There was a total eclipse of the sun due later this year, on 11 August, and he had intended to be in Cornwall to see it, the first total eclipse visible from England since 29 June 1927. Did Qantoum lie on the path of totality? But *his* eclipse would fall on the cusp of the Millennium. It was mid-April. Could he illicitly extend his stay in Iskanderistan for another eight months to make his rendezvouz in the Registan with the tall golden-haired, long-robed woman who had promised to meet him there?

He would go to a Spelling with the Sturyat, and it might be that they could tell him who she was, why she was waiting.

But as soon as he thought of the tall, golden-haired long-robed woman he began to see the tall, golden-haired long-robed figure of the widow Fahrenheit, with her thick blonde braid, her smock, her calm eyes, her deadly rationalism.

His elation ebbed. She too had said she would see him again, tonight, at the museum. He ought to have gone there, if only to explain what he had been doing, that he had found somewhere to live. She might be worried; twice he had failed to show when expected.

In the morning he would go there immediately, but he would be careful what he said. He did not want to be reasoned out of this, the only thing in his life so far that had had any significance. He was here in Qantoum for a purpose. He must remain until he had discovered what it was.

Four

By day the Sturyat settlement was not as he had imagined it. He left the house early, determined to learn his way through the labyrinth and chart paths to the market and the museum. Knowing now that the houses belonged to no one he took the felt-tipped marker and made large arrows and detailed notes on the walls and corners, as he rounded them. All the same, the first place he emerged was at the edge of the settlement.

In the early morning sunlight he saw that his impression of allotments had been wide of the mark. Here had once been gardens, orchards; what Zayu had been sidestepping last night were irrigation ditches, now dry. The strip cultivation must have been imposed by the Sturyat, for beyond the vegetable plots was a great pasture, bounded by the citadel on one side and the remains of Qantoum Industrial on the other. Goats and sheep grazed here, attended by small children. Chickens scratched and strayed at will. The smell of wood smoke hung in the air.

He sat down on a baulk between two plots and opened the map that Lt. Kijé had given him. It was a flimsy thing, apparently printed on wallpaper off-cuts taped together and it had been folded to display only the town centre. Keith laid it on the ground to open it fully and discovered for the first time the full extent of Qantoum, but not a great deal of information. The Industrial district was marked, and a power station – that accounted for the street-lamps – but not the open space where he was kneeling. There was no indication at all that people lived there, it was simply included anonymously in the red line that bordered what the map called the Old Town, a featureless polygon of white paper, bitten into by the market and Museum Street. There were, he saw, more ways of subjugating people than by actively oppressing them. To the map-maker the Sturyat did not even exist. Their pasture was of no more consequence than the other, larger expanse of white paper, the desert that lay beyond the skein of borders.

Even the desert was not quite so empty. At the far end of town the railway line did not stop at the Central Station but continued to a long rectangle that ran NE/SW. It had no name but could only be an airstrip.

He folded the map. If there was a power station there must once have been lines of communication to the outside world. Now there was not even a telephone link, assuming that the widow Fahrenheit was telling the truth. No telephones, television, computers, radios, nothing. How did these people keep in touch, heliograph? Last night he had decided to stay on; he ought to tell people where he was, something more personal and exact than the facetious e-mail. Sooner or later people might worry, when he failed to come back. Even his family might.

He thought of those strange elisions in his conversation with Mrs Fahrenheit. It must be like that with everyone. How did they keep up? They did not keep up. They did not know that the whole world was gathering itself to greet the Millennium in eight months' time, that there might be any special significance in his vision. No wonder the widow talked of photographs. But then, he recalled, he had not mentioned the black sun to the widow.

"This is a good place to sit. There is a fine view."

An elderly Sturyat had approached and was beaming at his side.

"Yes," he agreed. "Yes, it's a great view."

"In the old days we used to sit here and watch the shells fly across."

"Shells?"

"Mortar shells. They were thrown in the air, right over the town, to hit things far away. But then, one day, a new kind, one that knew where it was going. It would fly very low, that one, and go round corners seeking its prey."

"What was the prey?"

He pointed in the general direction of Qantoum Industrial. "Whump! Whump! Whump! Whump! And over there, the place where the electric came from."

"It wasn't the earthquake, then – that caused the damage?"

"Dear man, the earthquake, it was only a little shiver."

By their standards, perhaps. Force 5 by Richter, as he recalled. "So who was firing the mortars?"

"Who knows?" the Sturyat said, his smile becoming even wider. "They did not hit us. Visitor fought visitor. In the end, they all went away."

"Were many killed?"

"No. Only visitors."

Keith took the path below the citadel, past the cemetery, and went down the lane to the market, in search of breakfast and perhaps utensils. As he reached it people greeted him. He was becoming known. The woman at the bread stall hailed him and asked if he wanted the same as before. Streph offered tea and frogs before he could ask. At what he thought of as the Lada stall the welcome was more restrained. The stallholder was not a Sturyat but one of the European Qantoumis, red-haired, long-nosed and suspicious, but he sold Keith a jug, plate, mug and basin in thin light alloys, and three candles. At the next stall which offered mainly industrial swarf, nothing seemed to have been purchased since yesterday and the flat leathery thing was still there. He picked it up and turned it over, balancing it across his palm. It was almost weightless, stiff and translucent although not transparent. It had a dried-out feel to it. At one end were two ragged protruberances.

He turned to the stallholder, a Sturyat, wondering if she might be someone he had met last night at dinner. "What is it?"

The stallholder shrugged. "Sometimes we find them lying on the ground."

"What do you use it for?"

"Not for anything, dear man. It is just there. You could put things on it," she added helpfully. "When it snows the children slide on them."

"We call them leathers," said the red-haired man next door.

Put things on it; in his lower room were two bricks angled out of the wall as if to support a shelf, only there was no shelf. This thing would serve very well, and when he left he could take it home as a keepsake, conveniently light and odd enough to be interesting. The stallholder smiled as he carried it away.

He piled his other purchases in the basin, intending to take them straight back, or as straight as he could manage, to the house, but glancing up Market Street towards the Registan, he saw the sun shining full upon the dome of St Vasili's. There was time for another look. There was time for everything.

He walked the perimeter of the square, past the Hotel Iskander, the cinema, trying to work out where he could have emerged from the tunnel; it could only have been in the same place where he had arrived on the first day, along Oktyabrskaya with its view across the central garden to the remains of the Ensemble, its shattered tiles and decapitated minaret. He had glimpsed it through trees in his vision, entire, undamaged he was sure, but what about the statue?

What about the statue? What statue? Now he was certain, in his dream, there had been a statue, something grotesquely huge. There was no statue now, but on the eastern side of the

Registan was a massive granite plinth, three, four times his height, twice longer than that. It could have supported an equestrian figure, something as long as it was high. Had he seen a photograph, as the widow suggested, or had he been here before? Had he seen Zayu before? It was becoming harder and harder to remember exactly what he had seen in his vision, what he had seen yesterday, what he saw now; one image overlaid another.

To whom would Qantoumis raise an equestrian statue? Genghiz Khan? Alexander the Great? He had passed this way. Quite likely Qantoum had been founded by Alexander the Great, one of his watering holes, and originally named Bucephalopolis in honour of his horse.

He put up his shelf, whatever it was, and arranged the mug, plate and basin on it. It could not support the weight of the water-filled jug which he stood on the cold stove. Now he felt properly settled in. He had a base, an address, somewhere to retreat to. When people asked where to find him he could tell them, or would be able to when he had worked out the name of his alley. The fact that Zayu had no name for it did not mean, he was beginning to realize, that it didn't have one. But knowing that he had a home to return to gave him confidence; now he would visit the museum.

Following his mural instructions, watching the angle of the shadows, making inspired guesses, he found his way to Museum Street. The doors of the building stood hospitably open and from the other side of the street he could see right in through the rotunda to the Zherdin collection where Lizaveta was running a feather duster over Setsemhotep III.

In the Refreshment Room Mrs Fahrenheit stood behind the bar and some of the tables were occupied. A couple of elderly men sat pensive over tankards and a rampart of dominoes. One of them was accompanied by a bulky figure in heavy furs which leaned affectionately against him: Szusko and his bear. By the bar stood Lt. Fitzgibbon.

"Pint?" Fitz said.

"Let me get it."

"No, no. Take a seat." They might have been in a pub. Keith sat down at a table near the window, at some distance from the bear. It was not taking part in the game of dominoes. Perhaps it preferred canasta.

Fitz returned with tankards and the widow Fahrenheit who sat down beside Keith, her big freckled arms folded on the table.

"So Zayu has found you somewhere to live."

"A whole house. How did you know?"

"I asked if she had seen you and she was unusually eager to tell me more than I asked. I understand that you intend to stay for a while, and that you have met Theps."

"I ate with them all last night." Did he merely imagine a certain hostility, or disquiet?

"Well, I am glad to know you are safe. Until Zayu arrived this morning we had no idea where you were."

"I'm sorry." Had she been *worried*? "Zayu works here, doesn't she?"

"In a manner of speaking. I find her things to do—"

"And sometimes she does them," Fitz said.

"She doesn't seem to like it very much."

"No, but she can't keep away."

"If you *need* someone to work here—"

"You want a job? I don't, as it happens, need anyone. I certainly don't need Zayu."

"I must have something to do," Keith said. "I don't know how long I'll be here, but I don't have a lot of money."

"Join the club," Fitz said.

"I can't go on sponging off Theps, but there isn't really anywhere to cook at my place. Where *do* people go to eat? Where do you eat?"

"If you had taken my advice about the hacksaw you might have had a house with a kitchen," the widow remarked. "Among the Sturyat everyone eats with the – clan, I suppose you'd call it – in the compound of the headman, or woman."

"Well, you're our clan chief, aren't you, Ernie?" Fitz said. Keith felt almost shocked by his familiarity, but Mrs Fahrenheit seemed not to mind. "We eat here most of the time. Everybody comes to Ernie's."

Who were "we"? Keith wondered. "I'd love to join you," he said, "but that's my point. How do I pay? Can I earn? What do people do?" He turned to Fitz. "What do you do?"

"Do?"

"Your job. Don't tell me you get a monthly cheque from the Ministry of Defence."

Customers were entering; he recognized the red-haired

man from the market who kept the Lada stall. The widow rose majestically and returned to the bar.

"We have a little smallholding," Fitz murmured.

"We?"

"Me and Kijé. A little land. We grow food; sell some in the market. Bring the rest to Ernie. She's a wonderful cook."

"I'm sure she is. What does Szusko do? Is he a wonderful cook? Has he got a smallholding, a market stall?"

"He's the coalman."

"Qantoum has a coal merchant?"

"You ought to look round a bit more," Fitz said. "Down by the marshalling yards there are coal stacks, coke stacks, and what's left of the power station. If you go out to Industrial there's still bottled gas, oil, kerosene, tanks of the stuff. Szusko has a cart, takes orders, delivers to the door."

"And the bear helps him?"

"Not a lot," Fitz said. "There's a sort of system here, I think they have it at home, like earning points for doing things and exchanging them for other people – er – doing things."

"Lets."

"Let's what?"

"No, that's the system you're talking about. Paying for things in kind. How could I get into it? What could I offer?"

"Will you be here that long?"

"Well, yes, I think so, unless anyone wants me to leave." The only means of force he had seen so far had been Kijé's pistol on the filing cabinet. *How could I keep you out?* Kijé had said. He was sure there must be ways if anyone could summon up the energy to do it. "Yesterday you said I could barter spare socks. Do you want any socks?"

"Oh, well, I didn't know you yesterday."

"You don't know me now."

"Didn't know you'd be staying. I'll have your socks if you want but I expect you've got more money than you think."

Keith fanned a hand of Iskanderistan *sum* notes. "So how much is this lot worth, then?"

"That should keep you going for a bit. They're seventy to the pound. Is that all of it?"

"Not quite," Keith said guardedly, reluctant to impart too much information at this juncture.

"You won't starve. If you want to earn some of it back you can help me and Kijé with deliveries. I mean, you probably *will* get it back, literally. There aren't any banks here," Fitz said, earnestly, as if Keith had been expecting a branch of the Natwest. "What goes around comes around. There's a ten *sum* note with blue paint on it that turns up every few weeks. Come and see our place, anyway."

The Refreshment Room had filled up while they were talking. The dog and its friend were lying in the sunshine beneath a window, the bear reclined near by. Fitz gave it a friendly slap as he passed, on the shoulder, and it rumbled with pleasure. Keith supposed it was pleasure.

Now that its clients were in the museum the streets were as empty as they had been at sundown. Control Point E squatted at the crossroads, blinkered behind its slatted blinds.

There was no one in the office either but the H–M drawer of the filing cabinet was pulled out and a stack of mildewed box files lay on the desk. Fitz opened the top one. It was packed with freshly-cut mushrooms.

"Good crop," he remarked. "We sell these to the Sturyat. They haven't got around to cultivating them yet, they have to wait for autumn." He closed the lid and went through to an inner room. Keith had been imagining a kind of bedsit but it was stacked with seed trays and flower-pots; gardening tools were arranged neatly round the walls.

"I thought you said – Kijé said – you lived here. Mrs Fahrenheit—"

"Oh, do us a favour," Fitz said. "We don't live in this bit. The whole town to choose from and you think we'd live in a checkpoint?"

At the end of the room a door had been knocked through. He opened it and admitted them to a long corridor lined on one side with doors and on the other with windows.

"It looks like a school."

"It was."

"It says *Gimnaziya* on the map."

"Gymnasium. That's what they called a secondary school round here."

The corridor was one side of a square, built around an inner garden. As in his own courtyard there was a well in the middle. Unlike his the area was the size of four tennis courts and every centimetre of it was under cultivation. In the far corner was a figure moving slowly with a hoe: Lt. Kijé.

"You gave him a turn, the other day," Fitz said as they went down the corridor. "Rolling in like that and demanding to be interrogated. He couldn't make out what you were up to."

"I thought he was on duty. I told him I was a tourist."

"I know you did. He immediately began to wonder what you really were. Journalist? Spy? Travel writer? Loony?"

"This place seems to have been a hot-spot for travel writers. Have you ever read *In the Footsteps of Genghiz Khan* by Lady Charlotte Crow?"

"It's in the museum. No, I haven't read it."

"I told Mrs Fahrenheit why I came here."

"Something about a dream, wasn't it? Imagine, dreaming of Qantoum."

Fitz led the way into the garden through a pair of double doors.

"I tried to tell Zayu," Keith said, 'but. . ." He stopped himself, feeling as if he were betraying a confidence, that to discuss Zayu with people who were not exactly her friends was a breach of trust. She had not asked about the dream; he had volunteered the information, and she had not wanted to hear it. It was that reluctance that he seemed to be guarding.

"It ought to be hoofprints, really," Fitz was saying.

"Eh?"

"*In the Hoofprints of Genghiz Khan.* I don't imagine he *walked* here."

The smallholding run by Fitz and Kijé was not unlike the vegetable gardens of the Sturyat, neat rows with grass paths between them, pruned trees, vines. Kijé saw them coming and straightened up.

"It's Keith," Fitz said, needlessly. "I'm showing him round."

"Yes?" Kijé said. His amiable expression hung on the blunt features like a mask. He was uneasy; not suspicious, uneasy.

"What are you doing here?" Keith said, without thinking.

"Weeding," Kijé said, with a childlike simplicity that was not at all childish.

"No, sorry to ask, but I can't help wondering why you're here at all."

Kijé, leaning on the hoe, did not answer but Fitz, grinning again, unbuttoned his tunic and hitched up the singlet he wore under it, revealing two small purple knots below his ribs, then turning to exhibit corresponding craters of scar tissue at the back.

"Missing in action," he said. "Believed dead of wounds. Show him yours."

Kijé reluctantly loosened the buttons at the neck of his shirt. His wound was under the collar-bone, dark, discreet and probably near-fatal. If it had not punctured his lung it must have been a very close thing.

"Oh well," Keith said, and scraped back his hair to display the narrow pink ribbon that zigzagged from his left ear, across his hairline and over his scalp.

"Machete?" Fitz asked.

"Mercedes; M40."

Kijé blinked. "Is that a gun?"

"It's a motorway," Fitz said. "Car crash, yes? Shunt. Oh, the old M40. They had the road up at Gerrard's Cross when I was last there."

"It's still up," Keith said.

The two lieutenants were fiddling with buttons again after the impulsive intimacy that had led them to exchange injuries, although Kijé, Keith thought, would have preferred to keep quiet about his.

"Tea?" Fitz said, unexpectedly ladylike. "I'll bring it out."

"I'll help you," Keith said, turning to follow him, unwilling to be left with the disconcerting Kijé who silently returned to his hoeing. He wanted a closer look at this unlikely household.

The kitchen looked as if it had once been something else, a laboratory for instance, but it had a sink with taps and wooden draining board and an industrial-strength gas stove.

"Running water?"

"Not since they took out the pumping station," Fitz said cheerfully. "I should have warned you, don't drink any water without boiling it first. Not that the pumping station was much use. There was hardly anything to pump."

"I thought this was an oasis."

"Oases have to get their water from somewhere. The underground streams have gone the way of the Akdarya."

"The what?"

"The river; bled dry to irrigate the cotton. It used to flow into the Amudarya. Now it dries up before it even reaches the canal and the Amudarya doesn't even reach the Aral Sea. I've learned an awful lot since I came here," Fitz said, with mad enthusiasm. Had he forgotten *why* he came?

"So how do they water the cotton?"

"They don't," Fitz said. "Have you seen any cotton? There's plenty of water to go round now, of course. Almost everyone's left."

"What does your stove run off?"

"Propane, at the moment. When the bottles run out we call for Szusko." He lifted the kettle to test its contents. "Fetch down that tin, would you?"

"You don't grow your own tea. . . ?"

"It's not PG Tips, you know," Fitz said, arranging tall glasses in holders. "Some sort of local leaf – not sure it *is* tea . . . *tastes* like tea. Kijé yearns for lemon. He's got some trees started in the greenhouse, from pips. Could take years."

"You've got a greenhouse?"

"Not as such. We took one of the rooms on the south side, nice big windows, a stove."

"You didn't really answer my question just now," Keith said. "Zayu told me you were with the UN Peacekeeping Force. Why did you desert?"

"I didn't desert," Fitz said. "They went without me. I was missing presumed dead, remember."

"Where did you go while you were missing?"

"The museum."

"Everybody goes to the museum."

"Ernie's got some amazing cellars underneath, proof

against anything except a direct hit. Not that anyone was aiming at the museum, you understand. It was the Industrial sector and the marshalling yards they were after; and the airfield. Mind you, they buggered up the road while they were at it, and the consular district, the barracks . . . mind you I can understand the *barracks*. . ."

"Who did?"

"Don't ask. Half the time we didn't know who was firing or why. Fighting's been going on for centuries on and off, but it's only recently that anyone's hit what they were aiming at."

"The Cruise missiles?"

"Coming from all directions." The kettle began to bubble. Fitz plucked it from the stove and poured boiling water.

"What about the Sturyat?"

"Kept their heads down. That's what they're good at."

"Did they get to shelter in Ernie's cellar?"

"Wouldn't go near it. Seemed to think it wasn't necessary to shelter. And oddly enough it wasn't, most of the time. You know how they got here?"

"Trapped in a territorial dispute, according to Lady Charlotte."

"Yes, but that was in the late 15th century," Fitz said. "They say they were guided here for a special purpose. I think they're still waiting to find out what it was."

"Five hundred years is a long time to wait."

"They're patient people, the Sturyat. That's what the name means, in their language, people who wait. I'm not sure what they're waiting for, to be honest. Some kind of Messiah, perhaps. There's nothing to stop them folding their tents as it were and stealing away into the night."

"Anti-personnel mines, maybe," Keith suggested.

Fitz looked stricken. "Oh Christ, I forgot to warn you."

"You mean there *are* anti-personnel mines?"

"Along the old border strip . . . ought to have said something. Didn't Kijé? Kijé should have. . ." Maintaining his guilty mumbling Fitz placed the three glasses on a tray with a plate of what looked like bridge rolls, and started for the door. "Desert's full of them, of course, but do you know, ever since I came here, I've never seen a Sturyat step on a landmine. They know their way about."

"So I've noticed," Keith said.

"The earthquake didn't get them either."

Kijé was waiting for them in a room that had the look of a student house, easy chairs in grubby cloth covers, a coffee-table and two sofas, one an enormous overstuffed thing with a quilt thrown over it. All through the tea break Fitz kept up a running monologue on the Sturyat, the museum, the mine-field. Kijé said nothing at all. Keith wondered how they managed when they were alone together.

Fitz tidied the tray. "If you want something to do you could take the mushrooms to Ernie," he said to Keith.

Keith, who had been planning to make his excuses, agreed. He was faintly put out when Kijé mumbled, "I'll walk a little way with you."

In the office the smell of damp was powerful, the rich rotting scent of mushroom compost. Keith marvelled at the height of a delusion that could have made him think that this was a functioning army post. Dust covered every surface, the window was grimed behind its blind. Yellowing notices curled away from bulletin-boards. Still, it was not much worse than their sitting-room. The fact that he himself had lived like this until very recently was not the point. These two were not students. Anything was endurable, enjoyable even, if you knew it was going to end. No one was going to be a student for ever. What was the future here?

"Take the top three boxes," Fitz said. "You'll be at the museum tonight?"

"Yes. I really will make it this time. No one was worried, were they, when I didn't show?"

"He thinks you were missing a treat," Kijé said, as they walked the sunny length of Oktyabrskaya towards the Registan.

"How did you two meet?" Keith said. "Same regiment?"

"We weren't in the same regiment," Kijé said, with the ghost of a smile. "We met in the museum."

He imagined them colliding in front of Setsemhotep III. "Viewing the exhibits?"

"In the cellars. When the shelling was bad Mrs Fahrenheit allowed people to shelter there. She had a kind of hospital."

"You met in the hospital?"

"Yes. We were found wounded and brought there."

"You were wounded together?"

"We shot each other. We weren't even in the same army."

There was no answer to this. Friendship might have blossomed under stranger circumstances.

"The museum's down there." He pointed to a turning on the right. "I'll leave you here. We'll meet later."

They parted, but after a few paces Keith stopped and stared after the receding figure of the lieutenant in the misleading remains of the uniform he evidently wore for work; gardening, not waging war. He was as affable now as he had been at their first meeting when he had good-naturedly posed as a military authority to keep a stranger happy, but there was a marked difference in his demeanour. The stranger was no longer so strange, and Kijé had become unaccountably shy.

On the other hand it seemed increasingly likely that he had a certain amount to be shy about.

Five

At the museum lunchtime had come and gone. The air in the corridor that led to the Refreshment Room was thick and savoury, reminding Keith that he had eaten nothing since breakfast but one of Fitz's salty bridge rolls. The three women had the room to themselves; Mrs Fahrenheit tidying up behind the bar, and Lizaveta, treading heavily between the tables, towing a small trolley on which she was stacking plates. Zayu, in her hat and coat, was wiping tabletops with a damp cloth, the world's most improbable waitress. Woman? He had assumed she was a woman, but it was hard to tell. She might be a large little girl. When she saw him come in she inclined her head and continued swabbing. Lizaveta smiled. She was not, as it turned out, deaf. That was simply a cunning plan for dealing with Lady Hooke. The widow looked up from the bar.

"Mushrooms."

"How did you know?"

"I recognize the box files. Are you going into business with Fitz and Kijé?"

Was she joking? "Just helping out. Fitz told me the exchange rate. I've got more than I thought."

"We don't really need money at all," Mrs Fahrenheit said. "Bottletops would do as well, but old habits die hard. People like to keep track of their transactions. Do I pay you for the mushrooms or Fitz?"

"Or Kijé."

"No, the mushrooms are Fitz's enterprise. Kijé is allowed to cut and water them, I believe. How is the sightseeing going?"

"Sightseeing?"

"You are posing as a tourist."

"Not *posing*. Actually, there is something I want to see: the Archaeology Gallery."

"Go ahead. No one will disturb you."

She lifted the box files and went through a door behind the bar. The smell of cooking became stronger, it must be the kitchen. As he left the room he saw Zayu watching him from under her hat.

The Archaeology Gallery was more than twice the size of the one that housed Prince Andrei's pickings and the second thing he noticed was the striated light draped over the cabinets like pale cloths. The skylights were protected by a grille of thick metal bars.

The first thing he noticed was the skeleton. There was something obscene about the way it stood naked in front of the door, confrontational, horribly open for business. *Are you looking for a good time, dear?* In fact it was only the first of a procession of skeletons lined up between a double row of display cases; from the back a bear, a tiger, a wolf, a Baluchitherium, some kind of horned beast – antelope or gazelle, he could never remember the difference – a great ape, and *Homo sapiens*.

At the far end of the gallery was a bookshelf. Information was what he was after but in his guise of tourist he set out methodically to inspect the exhibits, down one row of display cases, up the next. Prince Andrei had assembled his treasures from over a wide area, from as far afield as Egypt, always assuming that he had found Setsemhotep III *in situ* and not picked him up cheap in a bazaar in Kabul. What had been signally absent from his collection was anything picked up in the vicinity of Qantoum.

That omission had been made good by those who followed him. Case after case displayed local artefacts; musical instruments, pottery, mosaics, prayer rugs, embroidery, metalwork. Keith had been right about Alexander the Great. There were trays of coins all bearing the conqueror's pouchy profile.

The rear wall was devoted to the town's relatively brief Soviet history; medals, military buttons, paintings to celebrate the Solidarity of Labour, household gadgets and a heroic refrigerator with a cooling unit that looked like a small oil refinery.

He came at last to the books, about ancient Turkestan in general, and Qantoum in particular. Arranged alphabetically they began with *In the Footsteps of Genghiz Khan*, by Lady Charlotte Crow; beside it *Russia in Central Asia* by George Curzon; *From Caspian Sea to Hindoo Cush* by Lazenby, Lord

Dacre; *Turkestan* by Eugene Schuyler. Lord Dacre's tome was almost 8 centimetres thick, leather-bound and generously illustrated. On the title page it stated, *Some notes on the Nomadic Peoples of Central Asia with engravings after the author's own sketches.*

It was extremely heavy. Keith opened it on a sloping ledge and settled down to examine it. Lord Dacre, writing in 1882, was very free in his opinions about the Nomadic Peoples of Central Asia, and even more candid in his illustrations. Kazakh, Kirgiz, Man-stealing Turkoman, Tajik, Uzbek, Uighur, Durgan, Tartar, all might have been assembled from Central Casting – "Get me steppe-type nogoodniks." He loathed them all impartially and let it show, but he reserved his basest contempt for the Sturyat, upon whom he descended with his little books.

What is one to say of the culture of these people? They write not, neither do they spin, clothing themselves in the detritus of their masters. They do not paint, nor work in clay, nor carve, nor embroider or knit. Having no written language their oral converse is such that they can scarce be described as having a spoken language either. Existing as parasites on the fringes of whatever power holds sway in Qantoum they seem not to have developed socially since the day upon which, in their tradition, they found themselves stranded on this oasis. In order to ensure their subjugation the Qantoum Khan, Khura, confiscated the stones which they carried about with them and in which, they primitively believe, reside their souls. When they proved resistant Khura Khan gave orders for the stones to be hidden in some desert fastness, promising their return at a later date in exchange for obedience. Upon the Khan's murder in 1503 the whereabouts of the stones was lost and the Sturyat have remained sullenly ever since, on the fringes of the town, awaiting, with inane optimism, the return of their souls. Various punitive regimes from Mussulman to Tzar have attempted to absorb them, wipe them out or drive them away, but for close on 400 years they have maintained a stubborn presence, never numbering more or less than a few hundreds. Successive generations have practised the civilizing arts upon them in vain. They remain unresponsive, uncommunicative, unmoving and unmoveable.

What little information one can extract on the subject of their traditions suggests that they believe they came into Asia on a boat or ship, leading certain anthropologists to conjecture that they debouched from the Ark which, being traditionally located upon Mount Ararat implies that their origins lie in Armenia; however, their looks belie this. They do not share the stature and complection of the Central Asian hordes, or the Sogdian heritage of the Tajiks, but neither do they resemble the peoples of the Southern Caucasus, being pale-skinned, blue eyed and with distinctively heavy brows.

What little can be deduced of their religion does not bring to mind the practices of the Hebrews. They seem to have no god or sensibility of a Supreme Being, and no form of worship, nor church, temple nor shrine. Such soul stones as they retain are kept in the house of the clan headman of whom there are three. These stones are not gathered locally and it would appear that the Sturyat believe in a form of multiple occupancy, since the supply is never replenished. At their apologies for ritual gatherings they foregather in a circle about a fire and tell interminable stories, often touching upon their "time among the stars", for although versed in no arts or sciences themselves, and evincing no interest in the arts and sciences of others, they nevertheless entertain the preposterous conceit of being astronomers.

They do not intermarry with other tribes but irregular unions do occur. The products of these, while fully accepted by the Sturyat, also maintain a position on the fringes of their enclosed society, apparently arbitrating between the Sturyat and the powers that be.

Zayu, he thought, product of an irregular union.

There followed a number of engravings of Sturyat tribesmen, uniformly villainous with the Kirgiz, Tajiks and Uzbeks. Their mode of dress had not changed in the intervening century. They ranged across the page, squinting, leering, pyramidal. Only one, "A Sturyat Maiden", was hatless, exhibiting Zayu's beetle brows. The next page showed a vista of Qantoum in happier times, with the porch of the madrasseh looming over the Ensemble, and the minaret towering above the madrasseh. Lord Dacre had seen the Registan of his vision; he had not seen the statue.

There followed further observations on degenerate Sturyat habits.

A curious feature of the area is the prevalence of large dry husks of obscure provenance. Qantoumis call them "leathers", although they appear vegetable rather than animal, and aver that they are in some way associated with the Sturyat, who deny this with some vehemence as if they consider them to be unclean. In truth they have only one taboo but this they observe with the utmost rigour. Much property is held in common and they pass freely in and out of each other's dwellings even at moments of such intimacy as any civilized person or indeed Hottentot, would hesitate to intrude upon, but when they wish to exclude visitors they "set up the bones of their ancestors". Their funerary customs are unexceptionable, burial following decease within twenty-four hours, but after an interval the bones are disinterred, boiled and placed in cloth bags, which are kept by the immediate family. When they wish to discourage entry or passage the bag is hung in the doorway of the tent or "kibitka" and their obser-vance of this prohibition is absolute. They have a superstitious dislike of keys which seem to them to represent an insult to their integrity, but they will not pass the bones of an ancestor, once set up.

Given the similarities between their regard for ancestors and that of the Chinese, it may well be that like the Mongol hordes before them they hail from the east, beyond the Taklamakan Desert, Mount Ararat and the Ark notwithstanding.

Here ended Lord Dacre's interest in the Sturyat. There fol-lowed a few pages more of derogatory comments about Qantoum and its garrison, at that time the troops of the Tzar under General Asimov, after which he turned his bilious attention to the Man-stealing Turkomans.

Even in the light of Victorian disdain for uncivilized peoples who fell short of the requirements for being Noble Savages, the Sturyat seemed to attract more than average dislike. Either they had changed or attitudes had changed. Had some good-humoured forebear of Streph presumed to address Lord Dacre as "dear man", or pressed unwanted frogs upon Lady Charlotte? Uncommunicative, unresponsive, sullen, degenerate; Keith had found them to be none of these things, but then he had not sat asking impertinent questions, writing the answers in a little book.

He replaced Lord Dacre's fulminations and walked slowly up the second aisle. Several of the display cabinets were empty, but still bore labels, handwritten like the ones in the Zherdin Collection. *So-called soul stones of the Sturyat Nomads. 1903.*

Was this what Zayu had meant when she said that her stone was in the house of Theps but that others were not there? Khura Khan had taken the stones to ensure good behaviour and they had been lost in the desert. But at some point they had been here, in the museum. Why did the Sturyat not simply walk in and retrieve them? Or had they retrieved them and these empty cabinets were the result? But Zayu had hinted at stones still lost. Did she mean the ones sequestrated by Khura Khan, or was it that the stones had been removed from display, not by the Sturyat but by some-one else, and were still missing?

He was back beside the skeleton. It hung across the aisle from a storage chest, shoulder high, holding fifteen drawers. He tugged at a lower one and it slid out revealing the contents to be layers of those curious flat husks that the locals called leathers, one of which he had bought, only that morning. Each was neatly ticketed, *Unidentified object supposedly held sacred by the Sturyat Nomads of Qantoum. Possibly once used as armour on limbs.*

These were in better condition than his own specimen, their colours ranging from dingy cream to mottled ochre, all translucent, like tortoiseshell, near-weightless, with the twin protruberances at one end, like the eyes of a toad, or a snail's emergent horns, or two tiny tits. Supposedly sacred? But the woman at the stall had said she had no idea what it was.

According to Lord Dacre they were virtually unclean to the Sturyat. Children used them as toboggans. He was using his as a kitchen shelf.

Zayu stood in the passage, a metre or so from the open door, staring at him from the gloom, no, not at him, at the dangling skeleton by his side. He recalled her earlier refusal to enter the gallery, and Lord Dacre's derisive comment on the single taboo of the Sturyat. Someone had set up the bones.

He attempted a light laugh. "Zayu, I don't think it's there to keep you out."

He gave it a nudge and it swung on its hook. Zayu leaped back and flung out her hand.

She said, "Prinzander!"

"I thought all his stuff was next door."

Zayu's voice trembled and came faintly. "This *is* Prinzander."

"Oh my Christ," he said, stepping away from it but thinking at the same time, Why is it more horrible now that I know its name? And, "*Why?*" he said, meaning, Why hang him up in his own museum? But he knew why; the one unbreachable taboo. Had Zherdin thought of it himself or had someone else decided that his skeleton could be put to good use.

He stepped swiftly out of the room and closed the door. In the dark passage he could hear Zayu breathing, shallow distressful gasps.

"Who put it there?"

"I don't know, but why does no one take it down? It has no

rest day or night, it hangs there always on guard. None of us would treat the bones of an ancestor so."

"Why don't you ask Mrs Fahrenheit?"

The next gasp was a snort. "As well ask the Hooke woman."

In the rotunda Zayu kept her head bent. He could not see her face.

"There are no stones in there, Zayu. When you said that not all the stones are where they should be, did you mean they were here in the gallery? Because they aren't. They were once, but they've been moved."

"We know that. But I think they have not been moved far," Zayu said.

"Still somewhere in the building? Have you looked?"

"They will be guarded," Zayu said. "In Prinzander's room there are things to keep me out."

"Setsemhotep and the mermaid? This is a museum, Zayu. There are museums all over the world full of things like that. People go to look at them."

"Not the Sturyat," Zayu said, as if he had implied that the Sturyat were given to sightseeing tours. She changed the subject abruptly. "Where will you eat tonight?"

"They seem to expect me to come here."

"It does not matter. But soon there will be a Spelling, then you must eat again at the house of Theps."

"And tell you about the vision? I could tell you now."

"No," she said, "all of us together."

*

When he left the house that night he carried his torch and, retracing his pictograms, reached Museum Street without taking any wrong turnings. The museum seemed to be in darkness but an oil lamp burned steadily in the portico. As he went up the steps and down the corridor he heard voices, bursts of laughter, the notes of a guitar being tuned. He opened the door.

The room was a warm bath of light from a dozen oil lamps and candles, and filled with people, sitting at the tables, leaning against the bar. No one noticed him enter except Mrs Fahrenheit who raised her hand, and Lady Hooke in a rook-feather boa, who graciously inclined her head in his direction. He took this as an invitation and went to the table where she sat alone, from choice, he surmised.

"Good evening, Lady Hooke."

"Maisie, darling. Do sit down."

"May I get you a drink?"

"How kind. Gin sling. *Lots* of gin."

He took up her glass, actually an earthenware tankard, and eased his way towards the bar, wondering, as he went, where everyone had come from and who they were. He recognized the red-haired stallholder and several others, including the guitarist who sat on the steps that went down into the well of the room, between a man with a violin and a woman clasping a button accordion. The fourth member of the group was Fitz, perched on a nearby table with a large flat drum in his lap.

The widow Fahrenheit leaned across the bar as he

approached. "Did you enjoy your visit to the Archaeology Gallery?"

"It was very interesting." He had a number of questions to ask her but did not want to have to shout. "Lady Hooke would like a gin sling."

Mrs Fahrenheit brought out a bottle and broke the seal.

"That's gin?"

"According to Maisie. And another for you?"

"How much?"

"Two *sum*. Don't bother, I'll start a tally for you, much simpler. Yes?"

A man farther along the bar claimed her attention. Keith took the tankards and began his return journey. Lizaveta, who had swapped roles and was now a customer, waved to him from where she sat with a slender young man who looked slightly familiar; strange to think he was already beginning to know people. Keith set down the tankard in front of Lady Hooke who raised it coyly to him before drinking, and made no reference as to the contents. Gin sling.

"Excuse me, Maisie." He edged between the tables towards the one where Fitz was sitting, but before he could reach him Fitz picked up the drum, slung it under his arm and began beating it with a paddle. The fiddler stood up, drawing his bow as he rose, and the other two players pumped and plucked in accompaniment.

Keith did not know the tune. The overall effect was of Klezmer, thumping, compulsive; people began to stamp in time to the music and beat on the tabletops. The music accelerated, harder, faster, two men vaulted on to the long table and began to dance along the length of it, kicking and twisting to the percussion of the crowd. The board bucked between its trestles, under their weight, but they kept their balance. One of them was Lt. Kijé, out of uniform.

The performance ended with a crash, then silence for a few seconds that erupted into applause, laughter and a surge towards the bar as Kijé and his partner sprang down among their audience who cheered and slammed their palms together, except for Lady Hooke who sat languidly batting the fingers of one gloved hand against the other.

Keith, who had begun to think that Fitz remained upright only with extreme difficulty, could scarcely credit the transformation, or the frantic dancing of Lt. Kijé, who was drinking from a beer stein the size of his boot. Next to the accordion player, a hairy face yawned revealing several centimetres of teeth: the bear again. Near by, the dog and its friend were lying asleep, paws interlaced, beneath a table.

"Come and join us!" Fitz bawled above the din. He had passed the drum on to someone else who, with the guitarist, was belting out a melody with strange Oriental cadences which Keith took to be a local air and only subsequently identified as *The Orange Blossom Special*. The fiddler joined in. The accordion player hefted her instrument and the bear, disturbed, arose grunting and shouldered its way into the crowd, apparently heading for the bar.

"Are you dancing again?" Keith said, when he reached Kijé. Kijé looked up, cold sober. Whatever elation had kept him going up there on the table had fled. He looked tired and strikingly unfestive. It was only then that Keith took in fully the fact that although the room was roaring with life and good-fellowship, there were barely fifty people in it.

"Later," Kijé said. He sat down on the steps, in shirt and trousers, just another man with nothing of the official about him.

"Is it always like this?"

"Like what?"

"A party."

Kijé looked round at the mêlée as if assessing the situation for the first time. "It's dark outside."

"I know."

"The Sturyat have one way to keep the dark at bay. This is ours."

Someone else was on the table now, bowling up and down in a striped jellaba like an escaped spinnaker. A hand reached down to Kijé, he pretended not to see it, the owner skittered away, returned, two hands this time, making a pantomime of tugging in the air. Kijé stood up, shrugged, and sprang on to the table with the unenthusiastic determination of a man embarking on an assault course. The jellaba, its work done, parachuted to the ground and left Kijé on the table in sole possession. He folded his arms grimly and began to stamp in a rhythm at odds with the *Orange Blossom Special* hora. After a while the musicians took the hint, adjusted their playing and when Kijé was satisfied he began to dance again. The audience resumed its desperate roaring, the racket increased, and the bear was coming back again. Keith saw candleshine on its claws.

At the door he turned for a last look, at the dipping shadows, the nymphs on the ceiling jiving in the flare of the smoking lamps, the clapping upstretched arms, Kijé strutting and spinning on the tabletop. Across the room the unhappy eyes of the widow met his.

Outside the air was smooth and cool. He paused on the steps, reeling from the rush of oxygen to his lungs and listening to the sound of fifty people trying to feel like a crowd of five hundred, five thousand; keeping out the darkness.

For ten days he kept to himself, stocking up with provisions in the market and eating in his little house by the light of candles. Now he knew how rich he was he splashed out: a dozen candles which, being made of sheep's tallow bought from the Sturyat, stank; a couple of woollen blankets, a thin mattress to reinforce the sleeping-bag. Summer was coming but the nights were cool. A word with Szusko brought him coal and wood for the stove although it involved a tense journey guiding Szusko and his cart through the alleys with the bear grumbling behind them. He would have liked to ask Szusko about the bear, but the old man was not chatty. He seemed friendly enough but he had no small talk. The bear answered to Marfa.

Keith ate alone in the lower room, by candlelight, with the stove creaking in the corner, writing up his diary and waiting for the call. It would not do to be whooping it up at the museum on the very night that Zayu decided to announce that he was required at a Spelling, and he was not sure how often he wanted to witness Lt. Kijé's nightly exhibitions of folk dancing.

The little room was becoming almost cosy. Sooner or later he would have to do something about communicating with home, his last effort having been a postcard from Frankfurt, two weeks ago. It might have been two years. Still, no one would be worrying yet; no more worried than they had been when he first took off. No one was going to come after him.

Home; this was home now. He had been sent here, drawn here. He must stay to find out why.

The Refreshment Room was pleasant enough by day. He called on Fitz and Kijé at the gymnasium once or twice, and, returning down Market Street one afternoon, enjoying the air that grew warmer by the day, he saw Zayu standing by Streph's tea wagon.

"I am waiting for you," she said, when he halted to fend off the offer of a frog. She fell into step beside him. "You will eat at the house of Theps, tomorrow."

"Is there a Spelling?"

"Yes. Always at full moon. You may tell us about your dream."

"What happens at a Spelling?"

"You will see."

Six

The compound of the house of Theps looked very different on his next visit. One big fire burned in the middle and the Theps clan sat round it in a huge circle, perhaps two hundred of them. And this was only a third of the Sturyat population. Keith thought of the little group in the museum, dancing and singing to keep the darkness at bay. If the Sturyat turned on them they would not stand a chance.

The atmosphere here was cheerful but serious and very quiet. Food was eaten in near silence, served by children who vanished while it was eaten, reappeared when the meal was finished to gather up the bowls, and faded away again.

"Children must not be out in full moonlight," Zayu said. "It brings madness."

"How old are you, then?" he asked.

She answered proudly, "In one month, fourteen years."

People sat pressed close together to keep the circle from spreading too far. This then was the apology for a ritual gathering that Lord Dacre had imagined scornfully to be a rudimentary religious ceremony.

When the last child had slipped away into the shadows and the moon hung like a gong above the citadel, Theps looked round the gathering and held out his hand palm uppermost, a clear invitation. An elderly man stood up and spoke in a resonant voice, words that were obviously a recitation, as if reading from scripture. He had uttered several sentences before Keith noticed that he was speaking neither English nor Russian and that Zayu, at his side, was translating in a fluid undertone.

"All are welcome. All are welcome to speak. We do this to remember the old time, and to prepare ourselves for the time that is to come. For how shall we return if we forget what we are returning to? Now, I, Gresk, will stand aside, so that others may speak. All are welcome."

Gresk retreated and his place was taken by a woman who began a recitation of her own. Zayu's translation resumed.

There was a man, and he took a woman for a wife.
And the woman brought to her marriage one brass pot, one red carpet,
One old blanket, one new blanket,
One cushion, two spindles,
And a basket, and a ladle
And a fat-tailed sheep.

And the man wanted food so he said to the woman his wife,
Kill the fat-tailed sheep.
The woman said to her man,
If we kill the fat-tailed sheep

There will be meat tonight, and meat tomorrow,
Meat the night after and the night after that.
But after the fourth night there will be no meat.

And the man said, What of it? I want meat now.
But the woman was prudent. She did not kill the sheep.
She waited until the man was asleep
And cut off his left leg below the knee.
With the left leg she made stew.

When the man woke up he smelled the stew,
He was hungry, he called for food.
He did not notice that the woman his wife
Had cut off his left leg below the knee.

The next day the man said to the woman his wife,
Bring me more of the stew you made of your fat-tailed sheep.
But there was no more stew.
So while the man slept,
She cut off his left arm below the elbow.
With the left arm she made another stew.

When the man woke up he smelled the stew,
He was hungry, he called for food.
He did not notice that the woman his wife
Had cut off his left arm below the elbow.

The next day. . .

Zayu broke off and muttered, "This is a very long story. Can you guess what happens?"

"She cuts up her husband bit by bit and he is so greedy he doesn't notice that he's eating himself?"

"Yes. In the end he eats his own head."

"I see. Is this meant to be a funny story?"

"It is very funny," Zayu said solemnly.

"No one's laughing."

"We will laugh when it is over. Everyone knows how it will end."

"Do you always tell old stories?"

"There are no new ones to tell, unless a stranger comes among us."

"Me, for instance?"

"I have spoken to Theps. You will Spell next."

"It's not a funny story."

"We may think it is," Zayu said.

"Will they understand?"

"Yes, hush. Now we reach the part where he eats his manhood."

She did not translate, to his relief, wishing to spare him pain, perhaps, but he became aware of a joyous, pent-up excitement coming to the boil around the circle. Zayu joined in again.

. . .did not notice that the woman his wife
Had cut off his head.
And when the man had eaten his head the woman said,
Will you take more stew? but the man did not answer.

So then the woman took up the brass pot and the red carpet,
The old blanket, the new blanket and the cushion,

The two spindles, the basket and the ladle.
She said to the fat-tailed sheep,
Come, little sister, let us find another man.

The audience exploded into laughter, arms waving, rocking back and forth, hooting and clapping. The woman, still on her feet, smiled complacently. It must be the way she told it.

Keith, knowing that it was his turn next, wished he could have been preceded by something a little less exciting. He could not imagine that the clan would settle down after this to hear a stranger recount his experiences in a foreign language. On the other hand, it would be a new story; but did they *like* new stories?

The applause subsided, the woman returned to her place. Theps held out his hand towards Keith. Zayu nudged him forwards, and he crossed the circle to Theps's side where he stood and surveyed the crowd. All he could see was the fire, flickering redly now, and the glint of flamelight on eyeball and cheek-bone. He felt, rather than saw, that Zayu had left her place and was hunkered down behind him. That gave him confidence. He began.

"My name is Keith Chapman. I come from England. Thank you for letting me speak. A year ago I had not heard of Iskanderistan, I had not heard of Qantoum. I had not heard of the Sturyat, forgive me. Then I was in a car crash—"

To his right a hand was raised. "What is a car crash?"

Zayu smacked her palms together. "Ladas."

"Thank you."

120

"The car was hit by a lorry – big Lada – and the driver was killed. I died too, but—"

Another hand went up. "Excuse me. You are dead?"

"No. We call it a Near Death Experience. My heart stopped beating. But I was brought back to life—"

"Thank you. This we do, also."

It seemed wise to simplify things. "While I was dead I had a vision. It seemed I left my body and rose up into the air. I found myself travelling down a tunnel towards a strange light. This happens to other people. They find that they have gone to heaven, a beautiful garden, where they meet friends and family who have died. They are welcomed – as you have welcomed me," he tossed in, politicly, "and the person is happy and wants to stay, but then a voice says, 'No, not yet, You must return,' and they wake up and find themselves in hospital."

He paused, in case anyone wanted to know what a hospital was, but no one interrupted.

"This didn't happen to me. When I came out of the tunnel I found myself in a square – a Registan, *your* Registan – with big buildings all round it, and a fountain in the middle. One of the big buildings had steps in front and there were people sitting on the steps."

Gresk was on his feet. "Were they Sturyat?"

"No, they were Europeans, tall, fair. But when I went to speak to them someone who was, who I think was – I mean, now I *know* it was one of the Sturyat, told me to come away, that the time was not right. Then one of the people on the steps said, "We will meet again in Qantoum at the end of a thousand years," and I woke up and found I was still in the — the Lada. Until that time I'd never heard of Qantoum. When I came here I told this vision to the widow Fahrenheit and she said that perhaps I had once seen a photograph." He paused.

"We know 'photograph'," Zayu muttered sulkily behind him.

"Well, when I got out of hospital I found out about Qantoum and decided to visit it. That is why I am here. I came because I wanted to find out about the vision. If any of you can tell me I shall be very grateful. Thank you for listening."

The applause was less rapturous than it had been for the fat-tailed sheep, but it was enthusiastic, all the same. As it died down he began to walk to his place, but discovered that Zayu was holding him back like a doorstop.

Gresk had risen again. "We are glad to know of your vision. Later we will tell you of the meaning, if there is a meaning."

He bowed. Keith bowed. Zayu relaxed the pressure between his shoulder-blades and pulled gently at his arm. They walked back to their places.

By the time they had arrived someone else, who Keith recognized as the woman from the market who sold him cheese, was standing in the Spelling place.

There was a woman and she had twin sons.
One of the sons was a man-child,
And the other son was a goat.

Things were getting back to normal.

*

Under cover of the applause and laughter that followed the adventures of the goat-brother he murmured to Zayu, "When Gresk said 'later', did he mean later this evening or later this – this week for instance?"

"Not tonight. It will take time to discuss it. Are you now going to the museum?"

"Of course not." Did they think him so boorish? "I wouldn't miss this for the world." It seemed the right thing to say, if not strictly truthful.

The fire was now little more than a smouldering pyre. He looked across it and saw that Gresk was deep in conversation with three others, including Theps, although another story was under way concerning the misfortunes of a man who, while drunk, mistook a quail's egg for his soul stone, carrying it around with him until the chick hatched, leaving the owner with the impression that he must be a quail himself. In the meantime his daughter had boiled the soul stone, thinking it to be an egg, until it shattered.

Keith had been prepared to roar with laughter; the story had struck him as at least amusing, but the audience was subdued, rocking back and forth quietly with stifled sobs. One or two people were wiping their eyes. Boiling your soul stone was evidently no laughing matter.

Another week passed. He began to fall into a routine, breakfasting in his house, visiting the museum by day, more to keep up appearances than anything, dropping in on Fitz and Kijé once or twice, delivering produce to market.

Under any other circumstances he would have been making friends by now, but he was held back by the thought that there was coming a time when he might have to take sides. The Sturyat had been deprived of their soul stones, the stones were hidden somewhere in the museum, under the care of Mrs Fahrenheit, who for one reason or another would not return them. His immediate sympathies lay with the strange collection of misfits and deserters who clung to a kind of life in Qantoum where no one troubled them because no one knew they were there, because Qantoum was of no further use to anyone, even as a place to wage war. But sympathy might turn out to be something he could not afford.

Mrs Fahrenheit had not taken his vision seriously. The Sturyat, it seemed, were taking it very seriously indeed. The longer he waited to discover its meaning, the more important that meaning promised to be. When he was at the museum he took care never to mention the Spelling.

One evening as he sat writing, Zayu walked into his room unannounced. She no longer looked for bones.

"Come with me to the house of Theps."

The compound was busier than before, the families eating around their cooking fires outside, now that evenings were warmer. By Theps's tent a number of women and children were talking. Zayu ignored them and approached the tent, pausing only to look inside the flap, for bones, before calling out, "We are here," and Theps replied, "Enter."

He was sitting on a carpet, among cushions, with three

other people, one of them Gresk, and motioned them to sit down. He began without preamble:

"There is something we have to know before we go on. Did you tell us all of your dream? Did you conceal anything, or forget? Do not be alarmed, but we must know, because if you told us everything then perhaps the widow is right and you are remembering a photograph."

"I left things out," Keith said. "I was trying to keep it simple."

"Tell us one thing you left out."

What had he left out: the trees, the statue, the light?

"There was a black sun."

The four men looked at one another. Theps said, "Then we have been waiting for you."

"In fact," Gresk added, "we sent for you."

"You sent for *me*?"

"Not by name," Theps said. "We regret, we did not know the name of the one we were calling. But the time is coming when we await a wonder in the heavens, and we send out many calls."

Keith, envisioning a celestial telephone exchange, waited for the next bit.

"This is the first time anyone has answered."

"We take a stone," Theps said, "and send a soul to call the chosen one."

"Whose soul did you send?" He could not help looking at Zayu.

"Since our stones were taken from us the few that remain

must house many souls," Gresk intoned. "We send them westward and eastward for it is well known that when the time comes for the All-High to call us home many will come from the east and many will come from the west to meet under a wonder in the heavens. Then the souls of our ancestors will join with the bones of our ancestors and the Sturyat will return to the place they came from. We have been waiting many years and seen many wonders, and always we have been disappointed, but now the time is near."

"How do you know?"

"Because you have answered our call."

"But you said many will come. I came alone."

"Others will follow you," Theps said. "Before our time, many came from the east, and since then, many have come from the west and north, but of all of them, you are the first who knew he had been sent for. Prinzander was not sent for, or Lordayka and the Crow woman."

"You know about Lord Dacre?"

"He had a little book."

"He wrote a big book. But he didn't know much about you, none of them did."

"He did not ask, or else we lied to him," Theps remarked cheerfully. "Visitors know only what we choose to let them know."

There was a short silence.

"Now I am here, what should I do?"

"I think you have already done it," Gresk said. "You are

not the one we are waiting for, but others will come because of you."

He felt like John the Baptist, *not that Light, but sent to bear witness of that Light.*

"At the end of every hundred years," Theps said, "we wait for the sign that we should depart and return. Your black sun foretells the wonder in the heavens, the sign we have been awaiting. Before the year is out, many will come from the west and many from the east."

"There's an eclipse due in a few months."

"Our sign will come to us at the end of the year."

"Do you want me to stay till then?"

"I think you will stay."

It was one of the silent others who had spoken, for the first time, a very, very old person. He was not sure now if it was a man.

"We are glad that you are here," Theps said, belatedly cordial. "Eat in my house whenever you wish, or in the house of Khlev, or the house of Senkh." He indicated the people on either side.

Zayu tugged Keith to his feet. He bowed awkwardly and followed her out of the tent flap into the cooling air of the evening. Here and there the red embers of fires rippled as the light wind passed over them.

"Now you know why you are here," Zayu said. They walked across the compound and out into the pasture. The moon had not yet risen and the sky dripped stars, close enough to touch. As they crossed the vegetable gardens a light ahead of them seemed to drop from between the arms of Cassiopeia and tumble earthward. Keith found that he had flung out his hand as if to field it.

"Did you see that?"

"Yes."

"Go and catch a falling star. . ."

"You cannot catch them. They are far away."

"It's a poem: *Go and catch a falling star, get with child a mandrake root.* I never understood before. I've seen shooting stars, never a falling star."

"Shooting? Arrows?"

"Meteors. They go across the sky very fast – sometimes they leave a trail. Sometimes you could swear that you hear them. They're bits of rock, debris—"

"They are the souls that do not come to earth, the fast stars. These days there are also slow stars. We think they watch us."

"They do watch you, Zayu. They're called spy satellites."

"And also there are the stars that blink red and green and hum as they go. We see them by day, they draw long lines in the sky—"

"Those aren't stars."

"No," she agreed, with perfect gravity. "Aeroplanes. Some of them lay eggs on the wing."

They walked on. He said, "Zayu, when you first saw me in the museum, did you recognize me?"

"No. Visitors are all very alike."

"I recognized you," he said. He waited for her to react but

she kept walking, out of the gardens, towards the watch-towers. "Remember I said, at the Spelling – that people who think they visit heaven are called away by a voice saying, 'No, not yet.' What I didn't say was, it was you."

"What was me?"

Now they were in the alleys again and he was addressing the back of her head.

"In my vision it was you who told me to come away, I'm certain of it. As soon as I saw you in the museum, with my backpack, I recognized you. Are you sure you don't remember me?"

She stopped at a corner and faced him. "If they used my soul stone I would not have known about it."

"You mean, they send out a soul without asking the owner?"

"How can they ask the dead?" Zayu said, walking on. "You heard Gresk, one stone may house many souls, the living and the dead. Perhaps it was a dead soul who came to fetch you. Perhaps my soul went with it. I do not know."

They had reached the foot of his flight of steps. He followed her up. "Zayu, what is going to happen when the Sturyat reunite the bones and the souls?"

"Gresk told you, we shall return where we came from."

"What about the missing stones?"

"The stones that were taken from us will be returned."

He opened the door and ushered her in. She made for the staircase.

"Zayu, wait. Those stones that were taken by Khura Khan and lost in the desert? Are they the ones you hear crying at sunset? Will they be left behind?" He heard her reach the bottom of the stairs. "Why does the widow want to stop you leaving?" The door thumped shut in the lower room.

He lit a candle, settled himself among his bedding and began to write it all down. At first it seemed ridiculous, he was overcome with embarrassment and crossed out large sections, but conviction drove him on, the conviction that, however unlikely it seemed, it was all happening. He *had* almost died, had seen his vision of Qantoum, had journeyed to it, recognized the figure in the vision, and now knew that there was no coincidence in it. He had been summoned. He was the forerunner of great events, a catalyst. The Sturyat would take back their soul stones and resume their wanderings. He thought of them, described them, waiting out the years, with mounting expectancy as each century drew to a close, doomed always to disappointment when the longed-for sign failed to materialize. At last the sign had been revealed to them and it was *him*. He was it.

He wanted to talk to someone about this. He could try knocking on Zayu's door, but he doubted if she would answer. She had said all she wanted to say.

There were always the Qantoumis at the museum. What were they going to make of all this? Ought they to know? Theps and Gresk had not sworn him to secrecy, had taken no steps to prevent him from cantering straight off to the museum and spilling the beans, telling the sceptical widow Fahrenheit that she was wrong, that he was not here in Qantoum by chance but as. . .

As what? The forerunner of some kind of liberation movement? Who were they expecting to come out of the west and east?

No one at the museum ever mentioned soul stones. No one had ever warned him about the Sturyat. No one had any idea that they were waiting for a reason to move on again, and that now they had their reason.

Then there was the matter of the black sun. They were not awaiting the August eclipse and he had not known of another, due at the end of the Millennium. Was their wonder in the heavens an eclipse at all? Lord Dacre had written of the Sturyat's preposterous conceit of being astronomers. Did they have astral knowledge far in advance of Western astronomers?

He looked at his watch. Only just after ten; he had expected it to be later. The museum would be open for business, the arthritic joint would be jumping. It was hardly an ideal time or place to strike up a conversation about the paranormal, but someone might be glad of a quiet chat. He had to look at things from both sides now.

The moon, in its last quarter, hung over the Old Town. The museum was strangely dark. He was struck by the silence. Where was the music, the lights? The great double doors were shut.

But the museum never shut, everyone said that. He looked at his watch again, still a little after ten; the battery had failed and he had no idea of the real time, of how long he had sat in his room, writing his account of the Sturyat and their wandering souls.

The only light was the little lamp that burned in the portico. He crossed the street, encouraged by that small gleam, and touched his hand to the door on the right. It swung inward, the doorway gaped, there were no bones. The bones were farther in.

The moon illuminated the rotunda and the horrors in the Zherdin Collection, but the corridor to the Refreshment Room was in deep shadow. On his left the way to the Archaeology Gallery was as densely black, but as he crossed the floor he sensed, rather than heard, a presence, and—

"Don't move." A voice came out of the darkness. "I have a gun."

"Kijé?"

"Did you close the door?"

"Yes. What's all this with the security? Who are you going to shoot?"

"You, if you don't stand out of the line of fire." The shadows in the corridor shifted and Kijé walked into the moonlight, holstering his pistol as he advanced. "Anyone else out there?"

"No, what's going on?"

"I could ask you that. It's after two."

"My watch has stopped."

"Wind it up."

"The battery's gone."

"Ah, micro-technology. I still have to wind mine. Which is how I know what the time is and you don't. If you want to talk let's go and sit on the steps."

They went out into the portico.

"Were you expecting someone?"

"I hope not."

"Then why not just bolt the front door?"

"Erna insists that the museum should never be closed. If the worst comes to the worst, people will need a refuge."

"And what worst are you expecting?"

"You cannot imagine," Kijé said impressively, but spoiled the effect by adding, "Come to that, neither can I."

"So there's always someone on watch here?"

"In the small hours. Sometimes Fitz, Usman, Vlodya. . ." He named the nameless, the museum crowd.

"What are you guarding?" Fragments of information picked up here and there over the last few weeks began to move together like iron filings to a magnet, chaotic but converging into a pattern. "The bones are set up, aren't they?"

"You know about the bones?"

"And the stones." He bit his tongue. Let Kijé do the talking.

"I'm not guarding the galleries. Anyone who comes in has to cross the rotunda."

"Suppose they come through a window? What about the roof?"

"The windows are shuttered. I have taken care of the roof."

"What's going on here?"

"I thought you might be able to tell me that."

"Me? I'm a stranger."

"Yes, and you came for a strange reason."

"You've been talking to the widow – or Zayu." What would Zayu have told him?

"To Erna Fahrenheit, of course. Only the Sturyat call her the widow. I would talk to Zayu, but she doesn't speak to me. What does she say to you?" Getting no answer he went on, "The Sturyat don't like to be out of their *kibitkas* after dark. When they hear the desert singing – it's like a curfew."

"So what makes you think they'll come busting in here in the middle of the night? I suppose it's the Sturyat you're sitting up for."

"Or their emissary. They have been here for five hundred years, waiting to leave, they say. Generation after generation has been preparing for that moment."

"So what's stopped them?" It was a leading question. What did Kijé actually *know*? "And what's your problem? There's only a few hundred of them."

"And scarcely a hundred of us, all told."

"Now, yes. But there've been whole regiments here."

"If the Sturyat think they can get their soul stones back who knows what will happen? They're awaiting a particular moment. When that comes perhaps the bones and the darkness will hold no more terrors for them."

"The stones are still here then? What about the stones that were lost?"

"I have read the Dacre book," Kijé said. "Khura Khan took the stones and had them buried in the desert. Things buried in the desert move. What is it you think archaeologists do?"

"You mean the stones that were in the display cases are the same ones – dug up."

"It's very likely; don't you think?"

"But Zayu told me – the singing sand – they believe it is the voices of lost souls."

"Not *their* lost souls," Kijé said patiently. "The souls of those they have driven into the desert. You could call it their guilty consciences."

"How drive?" His image of the genial, hospitable Sturyat underwent a convulsion. Even Lord Dacre had not called them homicidal.

"It is said," Kijé murmured carefully, "that Acting Captain Tcherk went into the desert, also Professor Fahrenheit. Many men went. The administration had a fund to support the wives of men who went into the desert."

"Sand widows."

"Yes, but women would claim to have lost their husbands to the sand even if they had died some other way."

"Lady Hooke thinks Mrs Fahrenheit shot her husband."

"In her more lucid moments she thinks I am Nikita Khrushchev to whom I bear not the slightest resemblance. Also, he has been dead for about thirty years."

They sat side by side on the steps. Somewhere in the silent pile behind them, Keith thought, were the soul stones that Khura Khan had hidden in the desert, where they had remained for centuries until archaeologists, happily ignorant of their significance, had brought them back to Qantoum and placed them in the gallery to lie tantalizingly out of the reach of their owners; who had been prepared to wait . . . until. . .

And for centuries numerical inferiority had prevented the Sturyat from making any attempt to recover their stones, but should they want to flex their muscles, the Sturyat were the masters now. Could they be planning some kind of a coup?

Keith realized, while Kijé spoke, that he himself was in possession of far more knowledge than either the lieutenant or the widow; perhaps more than Theps and Gresk. He was getting it from both sides. Whose side was he on?

"How big is a quail's egg?"

"What?"

"How big is a quail's egg?" He had been imagining soul stones as large, a double handful, the size of ostrich eggs. How big were they, in fact; and how many?

"Is that a riddle?" Kijé sounded riled.

"No . . . something I saw in the museum," he lied. "Sorry, how long do you have to stay here?"

"I don't *have* to stay."

"Do you want me to wait with you?"

"Not if you are going to ask riddles. What are you doing here, anyway?"

He had not prepared an answer to that, having come to the museum under the impression that it would be humming with life. "I didn't realize how late it was. I couldn't sleep. I just assumed there'd be someone here."

"There is."

"Not you. I meant, in the bar. Like the other night."

"There's a limit to how long we can keep that up," Kijé said.

They sat on.

"How long have you been doing this?"

"Since the fighting ended, the earthquake. People began to leave here when independence broke out; before the fighting; more after it. The Akdarya's dried up – have you seen the Aral Sea? Ships beached a hundred kilometres from the water."

"Why don't you go, too? You weren't born here, were you?"

"There are people here I cannot leave."

"You could all go somewhere else."

"Become nomads, you mean? Can't you see us trekking across the desert, Lady Hooke, Szusko, the bear?"

"You don't have to go into the desert. Twenty miles the other way is the railway."

"To Tashkent and Iskanderabad, Moscow, Teheran. We should be very welcome."

"What do you think is going to happen if you stay here? What do you think is going to happen if the Sturyat get their soul stones back? What does it matter if they go away again, it sounds as if it might be a very good thing."

"It would, but they want those stones first."

Keith thought of the railway, twenty miles, four hours' walking. Then he could sit at the junction and wait for a train. He could go now, while it was still dark; no one would notice. But it was not still dark. A thin blue pallor diluted the moonlight. Beside him Kijé was developing an outline. Keith stood up.

"I'll see you later. Will you need any help today?"

"Need?" Kijé said, destroying in a word any thoughts he might have had about being useful.

He stood up and stretched and Keith heard the door open and shut behind him as the lieutenant went inside. He still thought of Kijé as the lieutenant. Fitz was just Fitz; impossible to imagine him as a leader of men.

He had not noticed how cold and stiff he had become, sitting on the tiles for so long. A few birds were calling experimentally in the pasture of the Sturyat, perhaps in the little smallholding that Fitz and Kijé shared. Fitz and Kijé who had come within a hair's breadth of killing each other and were now inextricably committed, in partnership, or brotherhood or love, and with a large measure of patience on Kijé's side.

The dog and its friend trotted past, the friend slightly ahead, the dog matching it pace for pace, united by chance, happy ever after, Streph had said. On that first afternoon when he had happened upon Kijé in Control Point E and mistaken him for the Officer of the Day, the mistake had been compounded by the sight of Kijé's pistol on the filing cabinet. Subsequent revelations had led Keith to forget the pistol, even when the widow had described his going down to the station to shoot up the signs with Fitz. But Kijé not only had a gun, he was prepared to use it. Zayu had Tcherk's rifle. What kind of an arsenal did these people have access to? This had been a war zone. The Red Army had been here once. The UN had been here once; God alone knew who else.

The dog and its friend reached the top of the street and turned right into Oktyabrskaya. Keith crossed over and entered the lane behind the Hotel Iskander to go home and think. A night spent trying to extract information from Lt. Kijé had taken his mind off the Sturyat's plans for his immediate future.

Theps and his colleagues had interpreted the dream. Either they were right and he had been summoned by supernatural forces or the whole thing really was a coincidence, if not as prosaic as Mrs Fahrenheit's suggestion. He had a choice, to stay and see where the Sturyat soul-searching would lead him, or to pack his belongings, roll up his sleeping-bag and make ready to leave as soon as night fell.

He could no doubt leave by broad daylight. Had he not reported to Control Point E as an alien he might have entered Qantoum unnoticed. There was nothing to stop him turning round and walking straight out again. Kijé had not retained his passport.

But now he was known. He might be observed. He might even be watched. The Sturyat elders might be displeased by the hasty departure of their – what was he to them? John the Baptist? Prophet? Fall guy?

"I think you will stay," Khlev had said.

If he went it must be by night, perhaps leaving some clothes artistically scattered on the edge of the desert, near Maisie's wolf sanctuary, to imply that the sand had got him.

What *had* happened to Professor Fahrenheit?

Kijé took his responsibilities seriously; not just to Fitz but to Mrs Fahrenheit, Lady Hooke, the Qantoumis in general, the museum crowd in particular, the motley crew; as if he were in some way to blame for the situation they were in. Perhaps he was. He showed no sign so far of feeling responsible for Keith; and Keith had no ties to the museum crowd. If he stayed in Qantoum it would be to see how the prophecy was fulfilled, to see many come out of the east and many come out of the west.

He would stay. He had to stay. If he went away now he would be denying everything that had happened, everything that he had chosen to believe in, everything that had chosen him to believe it.

Part Two

Seven

Summer drew on. Keith was becoming accustomed to the place, to the silence, the seclusion, but not to the heat. He had never imagined such heat. The Qantoumis seemed to go into a kind of reverse hibernation by day, venturing out only towards sunset, otherwise clinging to the meagre creeping shadows. The Sturyat went on as usual, impervious to heat, shedding a layer or two, hanging on to their hats. Their stalls in the market became gaudy with gleaming piles of fruit and vegetables, augmented by contributions from Fitz and Kijé, whose nightly vigils were now much shorter, along with the nights.

In the evenings the museum festivities spilled out into the portico and continued into the small hours to be slept off during the heat of the day. Keith could hear them as he sat writing on his outside steps in the evenings. Sometimes he joined in; on several occasions he ate first at the house of Theps; once at full moon he attended another Spelling and heard again the tales of the goat-brother, the man with the quail's egg, and the fat-tailed sheep. There were no new stories and he was not asked to repeat his own. He did not know if he were being taken into Sturyat confidence. He took no one into his.

On his way back from the Sturyat settlement he sometimes detoured past the citadel and sat on the observation tower, watching the passage of the moon in its quarters and crescents, once, unforgettably, rising out of the desert like a golden scimitar in its waning phase; and the stars, fast and slow, the aircraft that by day scored white abrasions in the sky's skin, and reminded him of where he had come from. Had he set a limit to his excursion, named a time when he expected to be home, there might have been questions asked by now, but no one was waiting for him, no one was looking for him. No one had followed his farewell message. Maybe no one cared.

Once or twice he could have sworn he heard a car engine, far away, and half expected headlights to sweep the streets, but no one drove into Qantoum, and the motor, which never came closer or receded, died in the silent night.

One morning, strolling home from the museum at dawn, he was mounting the steps to his door when a voice close by said, "You have been followed."

He spun round, but there was no one on the steps behind him, no one in the alley. The voice, it was Zayu's, said, "Not down there."

He looked up. She was standing on the roof, right above his door.

"What do you mean? Where?"

"Come up."

"How?" He knew how, but she did not know that he knew. He had never told her of his early reconnaissance.

"Go through my house. I have steps."

It really had not occurred to her that he might have discovered this by now. He ducked in at his door refraining, just in time, from asking if she had removed the bones. He was not supposed to know what she kept hanging in her doorway. If she'd neglected to remove them, that was her lookout. She had, after all, invited him in. He sprinted down his stairs, aware, as he crossed the courtyard, of Zayu like a bird on the roof, racing to reach the door before he did. As he went up her staircase he heard the door above opening, an urgent shuffle. When he arrived in the upper room there was no trace of the long cloth bag.

"This way."

He followed her up the outer steps to the roof. The sun was still below the horizon but the air was clear and the sky brilliant.

"You did not know of this – the roof?"

"No." She believed him, evidently, and walked briskly to the place above his own rooms where she had been standing when he came along the alley, right up to the parapet where she pointed dramatically over the rooftops, the museum, the barracks and the northern reaches of the Industrial sector. The plain, featureless, stretched infinitely. He saw nothing.

"See?"

"No." She shrugged impatiently – he was spoiling the big scene – and drew something from under her coat, a case on a leather strap. Out of it she took a pair of high-powered binoculars and slapped them impatiently into his hand.

He tried to speak gently, but her short solid figure in its long coat so reminded him of Napoleon. "Zayu, I think Sturyat have keener eyesight than" – he almost said humans – "Europeans."

"Look along the railway line."

He raised the glasses and adjusted them. Even with the powerful lenses it was some time before he could make out anything except the receding track. Then he saw them, two, three figures, moving between the rails. He supposed they were moving. He supposed they were approaching.

"You have been followed. Remember what Theps said: others will follow you from the west."

He had been very happy with the prophecy as a prophecy. He was not at all sure that he wanted to see it realized. "How did you come to spot them?"

"I come up here every morning. And many times during daylight."

"Since I first came?" She nodded. "I don't suppose they are following me."

"Of course they are following you. Why else would they walk to Qantoum?" She strode away and raised a hand to prevent his following her. "Stay here. Watch. I am going to tell Theps."

He remained on the roof, straining to see what she had seen without the binoculars. This was surely superhuman vision. He had better wait until she came back, but there were others who ought to be told, or warned: the widow, Lt. Kijé, the keepers of the refuge who did not know what they were keeping the refuge against. Warned.

Zayu returned, still running.

"What did Theps say? What happens now?"

"We are to wait. We are used to waiting."

"You're not going out to meet them?"

"If they are the ones we are waiting for they will come to us."

"They may go to Control Point E. I did."

"Then they will walk on down the wide road until they come to the Registan. Then they will see the market. People will be expecting them. Or perhaps Fitz will send them to the museum. And I shall be expecting them there. I go now."

"I'll walk with you." It would give him time to think. He had to decide how much to tell Mrs Fahrenheit about this new development in Sturyat travel plans, without betraying Theps, although the man had not sworn him to secrecy. And on the subject of warning, how about warning those three travellers who could be the first of the many from the west or could equally be here by coincidence; warning them of what they were about to enter.

And he was jealous. This might be a madhouse but it was *his* madhouse; one way or another he had been directed to it. He did not want to share it with anyone. His best hope was that they were genuine tourists, on a package holiday, *In the Footsteps of Genghiz Khan*, fourteen nights, flight inclusive, single supplement, who would stop only briefly, rubberneck among the Sturyat, take photographs, look round the museum and go away again. He could ask them to post letters. They might have sat-phones, lap-tops.

"Zayu, when you get your soul stones back, what will happen?"

"We leave."

"That's all?"

"I do not know of anything else."

"Why don't you just *ask* for them?"

"Ask the widow?" The answer as before. "As well ask the Hooke woman."

"I know Khura Khan confiscated – stole them, he took them to keep you all in line, I suppose, but no one is keeping you in line now."

"In line?"

"Making you do what they want."

"No one makes the Sturyat do what they want."

"They made you stay."

She did not answer immediately. "Only while we wait. The visitors thought they were making us stay; we were waiting. If the ones from the east and west had come sooner we would have taken our stones back already."

"In spite of Prince Andrei?"

"Prinzander has not hung there very long."

In Sturyat terms, no he had not, but before him there had been armed men to keep the Sturyat in line, and since. Now there was only a handful of non-combatants and Lt. Kijé. Did Zayu know how Kijé spent the hours of darkness, or why? If she did know why it was possibly more than Kijé did.

"So why don't you or Theps or one of the other head-men—"

"The others are women."

"Oh, right, well, why doesn't someone just go to Mrs Fahrenheit and say, 'We'd like our stones back, please'."

"Why should we have to ask?"

"She might not know you want them," he said, foolishly.

They had reached Museum Street. "She knows," Zayu said.

The portico presented its normal face of domesticity. Lizaveta was polishing the brass door-plates while Lady Hooke looked on.

"Good morning, Maisie," Keith said.

"Good morning, Mr Asquith," Lady Hooke said, tranquilly. She did not speak to Zayu or stand aside, but her look was unmistakable: *Peasant.* However far her mind wandered it remained anchored to its place in the class structure. She would never confuse Zayu with a brigadier's daughter.

Zayu, treading round Lady Hooke with equal disdain, disappeared into the museum. Keith walked on very slowly up the street to Oktyabrskaya, and along to Control Point E. The little office was unlocked but empty. He went through the back room where the tools were kept, through the door into the long corridor of the gymnasium, pausing to look in at the rooms that Fitz and Kijé used as their living quarters. In his bedroom Kijé's boots lay on the floor but the bed was empty. He must be somewhere about, but there was no need to go searching. It would be a couple of hours before those three ambling beetles made it even as far as the Central Station.

Most of the other doors were locked since the rooms beyond them had no windows nor, in some cases, ceilings. Fitz was not at home, either. Having been up all night Keith was desperately tired now. How to keep awake until one of them showed up? It was 6.30. Kijé had found him another watch, a railwayman's heavy-duty timepiece which went very well when he remembered to wind it. He strolled along to the greenhouse which would be a furnace later but was still cool and airy, sat at a vacant bench and took out his writing block.

What had begun as a diary and degenerated into purple descriptions of Qantoum, with feebly humorous sketches of its inhabitants, had become a kind of exercise book in which he tried to make sense of events as they unfolded. At the back he had begun to make a list of known facts.

1. I came to Qantoum because I had a vision of the place although to my knowledge I had no idea it existed.

2. Mrs F. suggests I was remembering a photograph. She may be right. As I saw it, Qantoum was in quite good nick (statue ????) not like it really is now, therefore:

3. I was seeing the past not the future, but:

4. I am certain Zayu was in my vision.

It was a while since he had written that. He was by no means so certain now. At what point had he started to call his dream a vision?

5. *The Sturyat believe that they keep their souls in stones. They say they have waited in Qantoum for 500 years because they are expecting a sign that will tell them it is time to move on. They think this sign will come at a time of an astronomical phenomenon.*

6. *Could this be my black sun? They say not. They call it a wonder in the heavens but it doesn't seem to be their wonder in the heavens.*

7. *At least twice since the Sturyat came here the stones have been taken away, the first time by Khura Khan. After they were discovered in the early 20th century by archaeologists they were put on display in the museum. They are not there now.*

8. *The Sturyat believe they are still somewhere on the premises guarded by Mrs F.*

9. *Who does not admit to this. But Kijé organizes a guard on the museum. Zayu keeps an eye on the place by working there.*

10. *The Sturyat believe that I am the sign that they have been waiting for, that I am the first who will come out of the west. As they say, when many come out of the west and many come out of the east they will return whence they came and unite the souls of their ancestors with the bones of their ancestors.*

11. *This is no sillier than believing in the prophecies of Nostradamus.*

12. *Why doesn't Mrs F. give the stones back? What is she afraid of? What does she think the Sturyat will do?*

It had in fact occurred to him more than once to ask her this himself, but the lurking suspicion that she found him and his vision ridiculous had stayed his tongue. It was not solely regard for Sturyat confidences that had led him to keep quiet about their faith in him as a forerunner of momentous events.

What Kijé might say was beyond his powers of imagination. He wrote underneath:

13. Three strangers are arriving from the west right now.

14. Who is going to come out of the east (in the footsteps of Genghiz Khan?)?

He fell into a doze thinking about it. When he woke it was after nine o'clock. He looked again at what he had been writing. *Footsteps of Genghiz Khan. . .*

Footsteps. He looked up. "Fitz?"

A voice spoke. "That's what it says on the map." The footsteps, the voice, were outside on the street. The windows were too high to see out of. He was about to climb on one of the tables when another voice joined in.

"It's not a nuclear test site, is it?"

Laughter. It was the visitors. They were English.

"Clear skies in winter. There'd be a great view."

French . . . American? He was out of the door and half-way across the garden before the thought caught up with him. Clear skies in winter . . . a great view . . . a great view of what?

Entering the tool room he heard the door of the office being opened. He had left the communicating door ajar, and squinted through the gap. Filing into the office were the three strangers. Hanging behind the door was the camouflage jacket that Fitz wore in the garden. Kijé's peaked cap lay on top of a pile of seed boxes. Keith shrugged himself into the tunic and pulled the cap on, listening to the remarks on the far side of the door.

"They don't look as if they're going to be very fussy."

"Don't you believe it. These guys can be real bastards."

He had a split second in which to decide whether or not to be a bastard.

"Do we ring a bell?"

Not a bastard; firm but fair. He pushed the door fully open.

"Good morning."

The three turned to face him, young, cheerful, eager to please and hoping that he had not overheard them.

"We've come to report."

An echo from the past; he realized how Kijé must have felt, confronted with himself, uttering those very words, except that Kijé had rather more claim to being the genuine article and rather more reason to be surprised.

"Certainly. One moment, please." He needed time to think. Kijé had produced a form from – where? Mushrooms in the filing cabinet . . . top drawer of the desk. He opened it. The drawer was full of loose bullets but they were lying on papers. He drew out the pad of forms from the back and laid it on the desk. Fortunately a pen was parked there already, Kijé's old and enormous fountain pen that looked like a pocket version of the R7 rocket.

"May I see your passports?"

They had them ready, one limp purple EC document like his own, one Canadian, one old blue UK hardback. William Woodbridge, Jacques Bordeleau, Anthony Soames. Still playing for time he sat down and began to copy random details on to the forms, aware of the three shuffling nervously on the other side of the desk.

"Just run your eye over that list of communicable diseases, would you?" He scrawled a signature across the circle where Kijé had drawn a face.

"What is the purpose of your visit to Qantoum?"

The one with the UK passport, Anthony Soames, spoke for the rest. "We're touring Uzbekistan. I'm in energy systems – down from Kazakhstan on holiday. Bill's between jobs, taking a year out. Jacques is a photographer. We met up in Shakhrisabz."

Not from the west, exactly. . .

"But we're all amateur astronomers."

"Oh."

"I don't suppose you've heard of the Eclipse of the Century," Soames said and then, aware that this might sound condescending, added hurriedly. "That is, you probably call it something else here. There's this extraordinary story going around the Internet – that's a sort of global communications system – that there will be a total eclipse of the sun on 1 January in the year 2000, the first day of the next millennium."

"Really?"

"There won't be, of course," Woodbridge said. "You've only to calculate the moon phases to see that, but it's supposed to be visible only from Qantoum, which nobody's ever heard of – "

"In the West," Soames butted in, tactfully.

" – and it's amazing how many people believe it. There are half a dozen Black Sun websites."

"Full of quasi-mathematical gibberish to explain an eclipse that can't possibly *be* an eclipse," Soames said. "As we were going to be in the area we thought we'd check the place out."

So he was going to be followed by astronomers, was he, and no eclipse. . .

"To be honest," said Bordeleau, the French Canadian, "Westerners are poorly informed about Central Asia."

"They are?" Who did they think he was, for Christ's sake, sitting here on the edge of a post-Soviet earthquake zone, speaking perfect English? It was wonderful the effect an officer's cap could have. He riffled through the passports again. Like him they would have the three visa-free days almost one of which would be taken up by travelling. Unlike him they would be leaving.

"Would you mind telling me where you have been for the last four hours?"

That shook them.

"You were observed." If they were to be here for only 48 hours they were unlikely to discover who had observed them and how. Let them imagine a vigilant sentry if they liked. He liked it. "You were seen approaching Qantoum at 5 a.m. I have been awaiting your arrival."

Bordeleau looked the most shifty. Keith knew what they had been doing: taking photographs. Of what, rubble?

"We've been walking slowly," Soames said. "It's very hot."

"And going to get hotter. 35 Celsius at midday," Keith said.

"That's why we travelled overnight. Then we sat down and had something to eat."

"Where?"

"Station platform," Bordeleau said. "There didn't seem much point in waiting for the coffee shop to open."

A joke. He permitted them a wintry smile.

"That was when we saw the sign about reporting here."

"Ah, yes, well, you have probably noticed that there is great devastation due to the earthquake in 1994 – and civil unrest before that. There are few amenities. The road and the airstrip no longer function. On no account go into the desert, there are land-mines. If you are looking for the town centre I can give you directions. When you leave, which will be in about 48 hours, I believe, return here for your passports. Here are your permits."

"We're only staying one night. Can you tell us about accommodations?" Bordeleau asked.

"For one night there will be no problem. May I suggest you leave your luggage here until you have arranged for somewhere to stay?"

Soames and Woodbridge slid out of their backpacks with enthusiasm. Bordeleau hung on to his, mumbling, ". . .a lot of equipment."

"It must be heavy," Keith said. "I can assure you, it will be quite safe." He intercepted an eloquent look between Soames and Bordeleau. *Don't argue with him. He might turn nasty. If he wants to search it, let him.*

He ushered them out of the office and down the steps. "Continue along here. This is Oktyabrskaya, October Street, named for the glorious revolution of 1917. At the end is the

Registan, a public square, and leading from that, the market. I recommend that first of all you visit the museum, down the first turning on the right after this one. There are some interesting antiquities and good catering facilities. The proprietor will advise you about accommodation. You may take photographs," he added, to Bordeleau, "but ask the permission of the populace first."

"Are they Muslims?"

"No." Keith had been thinking of the Sturyat. Usman would not care who took his picture. "They have a local religion. They believe that visitors from the west are divinely sent. If you meet a girl called Zayu she may show signs of expecting you. This too is part of the religion."

They moved off. Soames paused and said, "You speak excellent English, Captain Tcherk."

He had forgotten the name-plate by the door. Oh, what the hell, why waste time explaining. "Thank you, Mr Soames."

Keith went back into the office and looked at the passports, marvelling at the way they had meekly handed them over to the authority of – what? Kijé's hat. The three faces stared back at him. Woodbridge, the youngest, was in colour, blue-eyed, russet hair; Soames blond, even in black and white; Bordeleau older, darker, thick hair, high cheek-bones, not unlike Kijé. He put them into the back of the drawer, under the ammunition. Now he would have to find Fitz or Kijé to explain what he had done, although not yet why he had done it.

So far, so good. The astronomers were not a threat and he had another fact to add to his data. He took out the note-pad and wrote again:

15. It seems likely that the only people who will come out of the west are astronomers and nutcases.

16. Will it be astronomers coming out of the east?

At the back of his mind a frivolous voice was singing *Three Wise Men* to the tune of *Three Blind Mice*. Three Wise Guys: he had to smile a little at their assumption of his ignorance, kindly explaining the Internet to him; and recalling it, stopped smiling, seemed to experience a kind of undoing in his head, as of two stuck-together pages peeled apart to reveal forgotten information. *Half a dozen Black Sun websites.*

Soames had learned about Qantoum on the Net. Back in March, when he had surfed it himself, he had discovered no reference to Qantoum, had remarked, in fact, that if Qantoum were ever to feature on the Internet he would have to be the one who put it there. He had done nothing of the kind, but now the words of his farewell e-mail returned to him, deliberately vague, deliberately ambiguous, deliberately teasing: *Keith has gone to Qantoum to find the black sun at the end of a thousand years.*

The Net was awash with paranormal speculation, conspiracy theories, elaborate predictions about millennial phenomena. He had sent eleven e-mails. It would have needed only one recipient to introduce his black sun in order to start a snowball of disinformation rolling. Two of them could have triggered an avalanche. Woodbridge, Bordeleau and Soames were sceptics. What in God's name would happen when the lunatic fringe came to Qantoum for the Eclipse of the Century?

The outer door of the office opened suddenly and Fitz came in, whistling. When he saw Keith behind the desk he stopped and stared.

Keith recalled what he was wearing: Kijé's cap and Fitz's tunic. He removed them both. "Look, sorry, had to act on the spur of the moment." He dodged out and hung the tunic behind the door, dropped the cap on the seed boxes. Fitz went on standing by the desk.

"What were you doing?"

"Just what Kijé did for me, being official for people who wanted officialdom. Did you meet anyone on Oktyabrskaya?"

"Maisie, orf to the Mess, don'tcha know?"

"No one else, no strangers?"

"Like you?"

He deserved that. "I'm sorry, I had no right – but I had a reason, Fitz, really I did." He would have to tell him *something*, and once one thing was told the rest might follow. It would be easier than telling Kijé.

"Look, Fitz, you haven't been out of circulation so long that you've never heard of the Internet, have you?"

"No. I mean, yes. I know about it."

"When I left London I e-mailed some friends—"

"You did what?"

"Electronic mail – via computers. I said, *Gone to Qantoum to find the black sun at the end of a thousand years.*"

"What's that when it's at home?"

"An eclipse, a total solar eclipse. There isn't going to be one."

"Then why did you say there was?"

"I dreamed it. I never imagined – oh, never mind. My message has got on to the Net, it's gone global. These guys who were here just now, the ones you didn't see, arrived the same way I did. They're astronomers, they'd heard about this mythical black sun and came to case the joint – that's their luggage. *They* know there'll be no eclipse, but others may follow who don't know, or don't care. Dozens, hundreds, maybe. Out of the west."

"You could hardly approach from the east," Fitz said. "People don't."

"Fitz, have you any idea why you guard the museum at night?"

"Not just me. We take turns, sort of keeping an eye on the place. Have to, Ernie won't lock up."

"Why not? Isn't that the obvious thing to do? The place is built like a nuclear bunker anyway."

Fitz sat on the edge of the desk. "We're very isolated here. That's putting it mildly. No real way in or out, no communications. If anything happened, people would need somewhere to go, quickly."

"Something like an earthquake?"

"It survived the last one."

Keith gave up. Either Fitz was genuinely obtuse or he was being deliberately opaque. Kijé, by no means obtuse, knew far more than Fitz, because he listened to what he was told, or the widow told him more, or someone had. Fitz was unmoved by Sturyat prophecies or else absolutely ignorant of them.

"Well, sorry about taking your coat," Keith said.

"That's all right. Why did you come here? Kijé's probably asleep."

"I . . . just dropped in to see if anything needed doing."

"Do you want some tea?"

"No thanks. I need to talk to Mrs Fahrenheit."

Fitz did not ask why. He came round the desk and opened the filing cabinet, drawer A–G.

"Hello, girls," he said to the mushrooms.

Eight

K eith did not go immediately to the museum. His lightning impersonation of an army officer had left him no time to wonder what would happen when he next ran into the three astronomers. "Ah, good afternoon, gentlemen, I am now a tax official. Give me all your money." He ought not to have taken their passports. Kijé had not taken his. All he had wanted to know was what they were doing in Qantoum. Now he wanted to keep an eye on them.

They ought to be easy enough to identify at a distance: Woodbridge and Soames in cotton trousers, stout boots; Bordeleau in a plaid shirt and jeans; all three with baseball caps. They were far more conspicuous than he had been when he arrived, dressed against the cold. People looked much more alike in winter.

He did not see them in the Registan, but among the throng around the market stalls he noticed a white cap, a glint of gingery fuzz. People would not be there for long; before the midday heat struck the museum crowd would withdraw to the Refreshment Room, leaving the Sturyat to man the stalls for each other's benefit. By two o'clock even they would have departed. It might be as well to collect his astronomers now, while he knew where they were, and conduct them to the museum himself, but he ought to speak to Mrs Fahrenheit first. Let them buy their souvenirs – Lada distributors? – while he warned her of what was going on.

Lizaveta was alone in the Refreshment Room, setting tables. When she saw Keith she nodded him towards the bar, where Mrs Fahrenheit was emerging from the kitchen.

He said, "Where's Zayu?"

"I should like to know that myself," she said. 'She came in this morning but I've not seen her since about nine."

"You're going to have visitors."

"In what sense visitors?"

"Tourists."

"Say what you mean."

"Foreigners. Three men walked into town today, they really are tourists, two Englishmen and a Canadian. Zayu saw them walking along the railway line this morning. I met them at Control Point E. I told them to come here for lunch."

"What a coincidence," Mrs Fahrenheit said, calmly. "For years no one comes near Qantoum. Three months ago you arrived – and now three others."

"It isn't a coincidence. There's something I didn't tell you about my vision of Qantoum. The whole thing seemed to happen during a total eclipse of the sun. When I left home I put a message" – certainly she wouldn't know about e-mail – "on my computer, that I'd gone to Qantoum to find the black sun at the end of a thousand years. Now it seems people are taking it seriously, but there isn't going to be a black sun, an eclipse. These three know about astronomy. They came to find out what's going on. They're quite sure about it. But you know that I go some evenings with Zayu to eat at the house of Theps? I've been to their Spellings, too. Their story-telling sessions."

"They are a little more than that," Mrs Fahrenheit said.

"So I discovered. They invited me to speak, so I told them about my vision."

"I see." Her tension was palpable. Her arm was resting against a tray of bottles and the bottles trembled in sympathy.

"They interpreted the vision, the headman – and women. They say they sent out a soul – they seem to do it regularly – and they believe this soul fetched me here. You must know about their prophecy – you *do* know. That they are waiting for the sign that will tell them it is time to move on. I am that sign."

She said nothing. The bottles continued to chime.

"When that time comes they'll want their soul stones back. You know *that*. Many will come from the east and many will come from the west, and now these three, from the west. And the Sturyat think my black sun represents a celestial phenomenon; but there isn't going to be one. That is, there won't be an eclipse."

The bottles were silent. The widow composed herself.

"I cannot imagine what will come out of the east," she said.

"Why won't you let the Sturyat have their stones back?"

"Who says I will not? So, you are John the Baptist, are you?"

"That's what I thought." She raised her eyebrows. "I mean," he amended hurriedly, "that's what *they* seemed to think."

"And you preferred that to my suggestion about the photograph? Ah well, I can see that John the Baptist must be more exciting. I wish you would go and fetch your astronomers. I think we should talk."

He went back along the lane feeling chastened. She had not said very much. She had not needed to say very much.

The market was emptier now and among the few people left he could not see the three strangers.

"Dear man, how you do walk about," Streph greeted him, as he came up to the tea wagon.

"What do you mean?"

Streph made piston motions with his elbows. "Always so fast, one place to another."

"Force of habit." He smiled weakly. Streph was right. Qantoumis did not hurry; he should not be hurrying himself. He must look to them quite frantic.

"A last mug?" Streph tilted the samovar.

"No thanks. Have you seen any visitors?"

"Visitors?"

"Like me. Foreigners."

"Have a frog," Streph said, also from force of habit, Keith thought. "I saw one I had not seen before. I sold him beer."

"What about the other two?" The widow's apprehension tweaked his memory. He took a frog and set off along the lane behind the Iskander, making an effort to walk slowly, conscious that Streph might be watching him.

Gradually the Refreshment Room filled with its regular customers. The astronomers did not appear. Keith moved discreetly from table to table, questioning, "Did you see. . . ?" Everyone had seen them. Usman had sold them a cucumber. No one knew where they had gone.

"They were taking photographs," Usman said.

"Winston would *never* have allowed it," Lady Hooke observed.

Fitz and Kijé rarely put in an appearance at lunchtime. Keith was not anxious to see either of them, particularly not Kijé. Candid was not a word he would have used to describe Kijé, but the Russian could be punitively forthright. He did not want to know what Kijé might think of his ridiculous charade this morning. For the first time he was hearing a small voice in his head which said, "You should not be doing this."

Without saying anything to Mrs Fahrenheit he left the room and went back to the market. It was deserted now. He took the lane to the cemetery, walked north along the border, back past the Ensemble to the Registan, along Oktyabrskaya, white hot, cruelly silent. Control Point E was locked. Either Fitz and Kijé were out or they did not want company. If it were his company they did not want he could not blame them. He would try the museum once more, then the Sturyat pasture.

As he went down Museum Street he saw Mrs Fahrenheit standing in the portico.

"Have you seen them?" They spoke simultaneously, but before either could answer, someone began to scream. Keith and the widow froze in shock, she in the act of moving from one step to the next, paralyzed. The scream did not end with that first shriek. It rose and fell like a klaxon, terrified, mindless, slashed into the white silence as if with a flint. When it stopped he could still hear the red streak of it in his head.

Mrs Fahrenheit completed her step and leaned on a pillar for support, one arm clenched round it. Behind her Usman reeled out of the doorway.

"What was it? Where – ?"

"Market? Old Town?" Mrs Fahrenheit said. "Not far. Close." Usman took off, at a run.

"That was a woman," Keith said.

"No cause for comfort," Mrs Fahrenheit said. At her side Lady Hooke appeared, gibbering and pointing. Mrs Fahrenheit led her gently indoors again. "You had better go and find out," she said, over her shoulder. "Find your astronomers. If it was a woman who screamed it may have been a man who caused it."

He searched for the rest of the day, in the Old Town, ranging the alleys, retracing his steps through the Registan, the market. He went back to Control Point E where the door was now open. Fitz and Kijé were not there but the three backpacks stood against the wall. The passports were still in the drawer.

Guilt drove him through the heat, through the cemetery, along the citadel wall, into the Sturyat pasture where he began to be seriously worried. There was no one about, even the children had vanished. The tents were sealed and silent, the goats and sheep browsed unsupervised. He approached Theps's compound, but even from over the closed gates he could see, hanging in the entrances to the tents, long cloth bags, pendulous, non-negotiable. The Sturyat were not At Home. This discovery sent him back to the Old Town, his own house and his neighbour's. The bones were up and Zayu was not there.

He had searched in all the familiar places, now it was time to try the unfamiliar. He looked in at the museum, drew a blank and, leaving, took the road to the consular district for the first time since he came to Qantoum.

This area had taken the full force of the shelling, or the earthquake; he had not yet learned to tell the difference. Maybe the quake had finished what the shelling had begun. What appeared on the map as a broad crescent was a wasteland of cracked asphalt punctuated by dead trees, dead lamp-posts, fallen walls, imploded buildings. He could imagine what it had been, an oasis in an oasis, leafy suburb now blasted into dereliction by Act of God, or the acts of men like Kijé and Fitz.

Beyond the ruins he could see the roof of the railway station, the shuttered eye of Control Point E at the intersection, and to his left the implacable bulk of the barracks. The road would take him there, but between two garden walls a sign pointed a path to the Central Station. If he went there he might retrace the route taken by the three men as they had entered Qantoum only hours ago. There might be something that they wanted to see again, although he could not imagine what; perhaps Bordeleau wanted to take more photographs.

The path, littered with debris, was passable. It brought him out into the station forecourt where he had had his first sight of the town. He walked through the swinging iron gate, crossed the platform and dropped to the track, where he turned to look back at the bullet-scarred signs. At first he had suspected a massacre; then, after meeting Fitz and Kijé, laddish high spirits fuelled by the widow's light ale. Now he was not so sure. He had imagined them skittering along the platform, taking pot-shots. Kijé was no pot-shooter. Next time he lost his rag and started firing Keith wanted to be at his side, not in front.

He walked along the rails, passing beneath the bandy legs of the water tower beside the barrack station. Now he was coming among the shattered warehouses and factories, the cranes and gantries. Some of the plant was old, pre-WWII, he estimated. Some of it, uncorrupted in the dry air, was still brightly painted. Cotton, King Cotton, Comrade Cotton was what they had dispatched from here, cotton that had exhausted the river and left Qantoum to wither away. There must have been heavy industry too, similarly strangled.

The sun was very close to the western horizon: the day had fled past him unnoticed. He walked on as far as the board-walk at Qantoum Industrial, and sat on it, watching the sunset over the plain, the colour leaching from the mountains. Far and faint he heard the sand singing, the voices of lost souls, the guilty consciences of the Sturyat. The memory of the jagged scream ripped across it. Who? Why? How many more coincidences could he take? Near Death Experiences, prophecies, bones, soul stones, eclipses that were not eclipses; all could be put down to Fate rolling dice. But three men vanished in broad daylight and that terrible scream. . .

Let it be coincidence. Let them be at the museum when he got back, drinking with Fitz, dancing with Kijé on the table, taking photographs.

Let them turn up tomorrow.

Hardly knowing where he walked he ploughed into the scratchy darkness of Qantoum Industrial, glittering fitfully in the starlight. There was a half moon but it was already on its back, slipping westward. If he went to Control Point E to wait they might return for their passports in the morning. Maybe they did have satellite phones and were already calling for help. Maybe they were not lost at all but holed up some-where with Zayu, regaling her with tales of marvellous technological advances in Europe in which she would have no interest whatsoever. Maybe they were being entertained by Theps, writing things down in little books while he merrily lied to them. They would resume their tour tomorrow, rejoin the train, return to Uzbekistan; go home.

He did not believe any of it, could not. He might have done had it not been for that dreadful scream, and the sequestered tents of the Sturyat where the ancestors kept their vigil.

Ahead of him against the stars, an enormous shape reared up out of the broken skyline like nothing so much as a foot on the end of an out-thrust leg, kicking up at an angle of 45°. He stopped and reassessed it. It must have been there already, he had not seen it until he looked up; some kind of lifting gear, a jib, a gantry, a toppled pylon.

It *was* a leg with a foot on the end of it. Wading through underbrush, stumbling on stones and rubble, he approached it. Several metres from the foot the mass was balanced by an outflung arm, terminating in a fist with a single pointing finger. In between, a torso, another leg buried in scrub, a second arm, bent back. The great thing was walking furiously, gesticulating violently, three-quarters supine and going nowhere. He knuckled it; metal. It was already cool; not stone cold, bronze cold. He walked the length of it and discovered the head lying its own arm's length beyond, hollow and gaping at the neck. It was face down, but he did not need to see the features to identify it. This was the figure that had occupied the plinth in the Registan, not equestrian but pedestrian, striding forward into the glorious dictatorship of the proletariat, pointing at the dawn of world communism. He did not need to see the face; the size of the thing alone told him that he would recognize the balding head, narrow eyes, jutting beard of V I Lenin.

The Father of the Revolution pointed unhelpfully at the stars. Keith knew where he was, he knew where Qantoum was, but in this perilous wilderness he did not know how to get from one place to the other. It was a hot night. He threw a few stones into the yawning neck in case something malevolent was roosting inside, made a kind of nest between the shoulders and lay staring at the wheeling sky. He saw his dream again; there had been no statue, he had superimposed it after he saw the plinth in the Registan, as he had superimposed Zayu's face on the creature who had dragged him away; put into her mouth words she had not spoken. The widow had been right; it was all a trick of the light.

By daylight he could see his way clearly enough, charting his path by the dome of St Vasili's. He came out of the scrub at the edge of the pasture where the livestock were already at work, eating. It was early, only a few children about, but heading for the market he saw Streph ahead, wheeling the tea wagon, and slowed down, made a brief detour, to give him time to reach his pitch and set up for the day. He did not know why, it seemed to be instinctive. He would prefer to talk to Streph with others around him.

The place was as usual, cheerfully busy, or at least maintaining its appearance of cheerful busyness. If the Qantoumis were a little subdued they were too few to depress the atmosphere.

"Tea, dear man?" Streph greeted him.

"Thank you." He waved away the frog basket.

"Bread? Cheese?" The trader at the next stall, the one he now thought of as the Goat Woman, leaned across. "Great happiness today, dear man. Zeze, wife of Streph's son, gave birth to twins yesterday. Two strong boys."

It was on the tip of his tongue to ask, "Was one of them a goat?" But he surmised that this might be regarded as in bad taste. There again, it might be taken as a delicate compliment, but he was running no risks this morning.

"Is the mother well?" he said.

"Very well, well rested," Streph said. "But oh, a long labour, a long hard labour. We should give thanks that you and I shall never know such labour."

"Ah, a scream to tear the heart out of the body, a soul out of a stone," the Goat Woman said, happily. "But that was at the last."

Neither of them asked if he had heard this scream. He drank the tea, purchased fresh bread, thanked her, congratulated Streph and walked on, up the street, across the Registan towards Oktyabrskaya.

So that's what it had been, the shriek of a woman in the last stages of labour with twins.

No, it had not. But nor was it the cry of three men *in extremis*.

He was sure he was being lied to. They had not waited for him to mention the scream and ask about its source, to find out, indeed, if he had heard it. A woman in childbirth, that was their story, they would stick to it. And if he asked to see the babies, well, they must have a few around the place. It was possible that a woman had given birth yesterday, but that scream – no. That had been terror, not pain.

Control Point E stared at him, unblinking, through its single window. The door was unlocked, so one of them at least would be at home, the other at the museum. He ought to have gone there himself, to tell the widow that he was still alive, not that she had shown any indication of caring whether he were or not. But she had been as alarmed as he by that scream. He went in and sat down at the desk. The insidious worm of hope was gnawing at him again. At any moment now they might come into view, from the station, from the consular district, from the Registan, three abreast like the Musketeers, swaggering down Oktyabrskaya.

He slid his hand into the drawer. The passports were still there; he did not want to look at them, at the three trusting, innocent faces. They might, for all he knew, be muggers, rapists – he would have been entitled to ask, wearing Kijé's hat – contaminators of a public water supply. They might be spies, gunrunners; but they had trusted him. They had been innocent in the face of his duplicity.

It was close to eight-thirty by his watch. He wound it and wandered restlessly round the desk to the door. They were leaving today, Bordeleau had said. They would never contemplate a four-hour walk to the junction at this time of day. How long could he bear to wait? His eyes ached from looking into the bright street; he closed them, and saw instead a garish green negative of the crossroads. Opened them and could not see anything for the glare, but he thought he heard footsteps and ran down into the road. Along the shallow curve of Oktyabrskaya three men were walking, one short and fair, the other taller, the sun shining through his gingery hair. The third was between them, sturdy, dark. He could not believe what he was seeing, his night of horror and despair had been for nothing. They had not vanished, they were alive, walking vigorously. The scream had been of a woman in the agony of childbirth. They were coming to collect their passports, then they would go away.

He knew that he ought to be sitting officially at the desk but he could not help himself and started along the street to meet them; but they were still a hundred metres distant when he faltered and slackened his pace, gazing at the three men in sick dismay; Woodbridge and Soames. The third man was Lt. Kijé.

Nine

H e stood in the roadway, unable to take another step. All his fears returned in a physical surge, the scream reverberated in his head, that mad incontinent braying.

They were within speaking distance now. He said, "Where's Bordeleau?" and felt wordless air leave his throat. "*Where's Bordeleau?*"

Kijé said, "They have lost their friend. What do you know about it?"

It was the voice of authority.

"I don't know anything. I saw all three of them here, yesterday, in your office. I've been looking for them ever since."

"We got lost," Woodbridge said, "stuck in that maze of streets in the dark."

"That was later," Kijé said. "We'll go through it all in a minute. Come in, please."

They were back at Control Point E. Woodbridge and Soames followed Kijé up the steps, into the office. Kijé said, "Wait here, Keith," and ushered the two men into the tool room. The farther door opened and closed. After a few minutes he came back.

"What have you done with them?"

"Handed them over to Fitz who will make them tea and find beds for them. They are exhausted. Now, what did *you* do with them?"

"I was here yesterday when they came in. I sent them to the museum." He found himself shivering with relief as he spoke. That *was* all he had done. Apart from taking the passports he had done nothing more than Kijé had done to – for – him on his arrival in Qantoum. Ought he to have accompanied them? No. Why should he? No one had accompanied him; he too had been lost. But that scream. . .

Kijé sat in his chair, frowning, Kijé as he must have been once, before orders posted him to Qantoum, before Fitz shot him, before he shot Fitz and took to market gardening. "What were you doing here, anyway? Tell me what happened yesterday. Begin at the beginning."

"Did you hear the scream?"

"The beginning."

"When I went home yesterday morning Zayu called me up to the roof. She'd seen some people coming along the railway line – like I did." Only as he said it did he wonder if she had seen him too, that first day, and had been awaiting him at the museum. "I haven't told you about my dream—"

"John the Baptist? I know about that."

"What she saw was people coming from the west. I came from the west. The Sturyat are waiting for others, and from the east. We both saw these three. She said she'd wait for them at the museum but I decided to get in first and see who they were, so I came along here. I guessed they'd do what I did . . . the notice about aliens. Look, before I left London I put a message—"

"Yes, yes, I know about your computer."

"God knows who's going to follow me. They'll be coming to see my eclipse and there is no eclipse. Has Mrs Fahrenheit told you all this?"

"Up to the point where you – *look*." Kijé wrested control of the interrogation again. "The beginning."

"I came here – to tell *you* about them." Again, that shiver of relief at having done, having meant to do, the right thing.

"I was here."

"I know you were, I saw your boots. But I didn't see *you*. I went round to the greenhouse, looking for Fitz. I must have dozed off – then I heard these, these astronomers on the road outside, so I nipped back to the office. I was in the tool room when I heard them come in. They seemed harmless—"

"Why shouldn't they be harmless? They weren't in a tank."

"They were looking for someone to report to."

"So you pretended to be me."

"Not really. In fact they thought I was Tcherk – like I thought you were. I just did what you did. I mean, when I first rolled in that day, why didn't you tell me what was going on here?"

"I tried to."

"Why didn't you send me away?"

"I wish I had."

"Yes, but you went through the motions of being Officer of the Day."

"You seemed to expect it."

"I did. They expected it too. And I wanted to know why they were here, who they were, no harm done. I went on being Acting Lieutenant Kijé. I said they could get food in the market but the best bet was to go to the museum. That way I thought we'd all meet up sooner or later, you, me, Fitz, the widow, Zayu. Anyway, they went off, quite happy. I saw one of them later in the market. Usman sold them a cucumber. Then they vanished. I spent the whole afternoon looking, and the evening. Then I got lost round by Lenin."

Kijé almost allowed himself to smile. "You wouldn't be the first."

"So I spent the night out there. I'd hardly slept for 36 hours."

"*Now* the scream."

"Yesterday afternoon, when I couldn't find those guys in the market and they hadn't shown up for lunch I did another tour round town. I'd just got back to the museum when we heard this terrible scream. We couldn't tell where it came from – it went on and on. And I couldn't find anyone – the market had closed, all the Sturyat tents were fastened, and the bones were up. And I still couldn't find *you*. Where were you?"

"We missed each other, that's all. Erna's story tallies with yours."

Keith felt a transient resentment that Kijé should even consider that it might not. "But didn't you hear the scream?"

"We're almost a kilometre farther out here,' Kijé said. "You can't hear the desert from here, either."

"That wasn't the desert screaming."

"I never said it was."

"Your turn." Keith felt he had allowed Kijé to play detective long enough.

"My turn for what?"

"To say what happened, what you know. I've been out of my head looking for them, wondering how they could just disappear like that. Then you just turn up with them—"

"With two of them. Continue to be out of your head."

"Do they say what happened?"

"The short one, Soames? Soames; he says that after they left here they walked to the Registan, Jacques was taking pictures all the way – Jacques is the one they have lost?"

"Yes. He's a professional photographer."

"They looked all round the Registan, went to the market, bought some food – not just Usman's cucumber. They stocked up. That's why they weren't at the museum for lunch. Then they went to the cemetery to have a look at the desert."

"*I* warned them about the land-mines."

"Yes, well . . . they admired the view, then went along past the citadel, Jacques still taking photographs. They ended up in the Sturyat pasture; men digging, women cooking, children tending livestock, everything as usual. They sat and talked to people, got invited in for tea. Jacques asked if he could take photographs; they said yes. After a bit the others noticed he'd gone but they were not too worried. Once he started shooting he was apt to wander off – but he didn't come back. The Sturyat said it was nothing to be concerned about; this is a small place. They said he would probably make his way to the museum.

"So, they set off, but they got into the Old Town, and were lost. Then *they* heard the scream. They were sure it was somewhere close by. They ran to find out."

"Did they think it was Jacques?"

"No, he has a deep voice, they said. This scream was a woman, they said, as you did. But the more they searched and called the more lost they became. They climbed on a roof, saw St Vasili's dome, but they could not find a way out of the alleys. Then the sun set. They got into an empty house and rested for the night. In the morning they finally got to the edge of the Old Town by jumping from roof to roof. They went to the market, were led to the museum. They were sure that Jacques would turn up by daylight, but he didn't. That is where I met them this morning. I have been helping them to search, asking questions. No one knows where this man has gone."

"Did you ask the Sturyat about the scream?"

"A women birthing twins, they say."

"That's what Streph told me; his grandsons. Do you think it is true?"

"It might be," Kijé said. 'But Keith, you've seen this

Jacques Bordeleau. You have spoken to him. Do you think he could have attacked a woman?"

"How can I tell by looking?" Keith said. "Actually he looks rather like you – more like you than the others do, that is. Would you attack a woman?"

"For five hundred years the Qantoumis have been looking at the Sturyat and learning nothing."

"One of them, do you think?"

"I do think. There are so few women amongst *us* it could only have been a Sturyat, but I cannot think why – unless he provoked someone."

"What do you have to do to provoke a Sturyat? Could he have been snapping something he shouldn't have done? That first day I was here – suppose I'd disappeared. Would you have been worried?"

"You did disappear," Kijé reminded him. "No, I wasn't worried. Perhaps I would have been if, say, by the second night there had been no sighting of you, or if Streph had appeared with your shoes to say that the sand had got you."

"You didn't warn me."

"Warn you about what? The Sturyat are accustomed to waiting. It takes a long while to insult them."

"But once insulted they respond with extreme prejudice?"

"Let us just say the desert is very discriminating. It seems to get the right people -- by Sturyat reckoning. This Jacques Bordeleau—"

"He's like the other two, quiet, polite. He's a Canadian, for Chrissakes. People *like* Canadians."

"To the Sturyat a visitor is a visitor. Canadian doesn't mean anything."

"What are we going to do?"

"First we had better find out what *they* are going to do. They cannot return within the limits of their visas, obviously. They were asking me if I could fix things with the authorities. I had to explain – how long did it take you to work out the situation here?"

"What makes you think I've worked it out yet? I suppose I began to get an idea when I realized there was no electricity, never any electricity."

"Your astronomers asked me if they could telephone."

"I hoped they'd have a mobile, I wanted to borrow it."

"They may have, but it won't work here, and there are no land lines. One of the advantages of this place is that it exhibits no signs of life whatsoever, in the electronic sense, which is the only sense now, I suspect."

"A satellite phone would." Kijé looked blank. Electronics had overtaken him. "What do you normally do in situations like this?"

"There *are* no situations like this. Anyway, I am not the police."

"You're giving a good imitation," Keith said.

"No one asked you to come here," Kijé said. "No one minded, but you were not invited. What the Sturyat call a visitor."

"I thought that word was reserved for people like you."

"Me?"

"I take it you arrived uninvited, with a few others."

"But we haven't left without saying goodbye. We cannot go."

"Like the Sturyat."

"You believe what you want to believe," Kijé said. "It is possible the Sturyat remain here because they are waiting for a sign. It is equally possible that they have been using the soul stones as an excuse for not going. They could have left once Independence was declared. As I recall, the British Government was one of the first to recognize the Independent Republic of Iskanderistan. It isn't like Chechenya. There is no oil, no pipeline, no mineral wealth. Soon no water. After the first upheaval, troops sent in to prop up some democratically elected hooligan, there was no more than token intervention. Qantoum was very much on the edge of things after the first few months. No one cares what becomes of the Sturyat, they may go or stay. If they choose to stay it will be nobody's fault. If they go, it won't be your doing."

"You don't believe in the soul stones."

"I believe they exist," Kijé said. "For all I know, they are coprolites. Now, I wish you would go and find Zayu."

"You want me to bring her here?"

"Don't be silly," Kijé said. "She never comes here; she will not come now. But you seem to have struck up a friendship, of a sort."

"You want me to ask her about the scream?"

"These men spent an afternoon with the Sturyat. They

may have met her. Bordeleau may have met her; see what happens. I'm not in charge," he said, helplessly. "No one is in charge. This is what anarchists dream of."

Keith took the back streets to the museum, meeting no one but the dog and its friend pursuing their private patrol of the town, as much in charge as anyone. In the Refreshment Room business went on as usual. If word had spread that of the three strangers who had arrived in town one had mysteriously vanished, no one seemed at all concerned about it. People were eating, talking, drinking; the bear basked under the window. Zayu collected plates.

Mrs Fahrenheit beckoned him over. "Beer?"

"Please."

"You've seen Kijé?"

"Yes. You know what's happened?"

"No, I do not. The man has disappeared. His friends came here this morning, very distressed. But none of us knows what has happened."

"When did Zayu show up?"

"This morning, as she always does."

"Last night?"

"She never comes here after dark."

"Have you asked her about the scream?"

"No. Lizaveta brought news of the twins from market. I asked Zayu about them, woman to woman," Mrs Fahrenheit said, unsmiling. "She tells me that mother and sons are doing well. 'A hard birth then?' I said. 'That's all over,' she said. 'Now we forget.'"

"Kijé wants me to – I'm not really sure what he does want," Keith said. "'Find Zayu,' he told me. He seems to think she'll talk to me."

"If you go to your house, sooner or later you will see her. She won't talk to you here. But *I* want to talk to you, whether this man turns up or not. In the Archaeology Gallery, this evening."

In the Archaeology Gallery, beyond the bones. He went back to his house and waited all afternoon, patrolling stairs, courtyard, roof, but Zayu did not come home.

While he waited for Mrs Fahrenheit, Keith returned to the bookshelf, at the back of the gallery. Tucked in at the very end, Z for Zherdin, was a slim volume by Prince Andrei himself, a modest description of his *Kunstkammer* and a few observations on the area. The prince was out of step with his fellow-authors; he liked Qantoum, he liked the locals, he liked the Sturyat. He regretted that there were so few native Qantoumis left, their religion disregarded by the Russian administration, their mosques falling into disrepair. He was concerned that the Aral Sea was drying up.

The book had been written towards the end of his life. How had it ended?

Keith went to look at the skeleton. It seemed to be intact, there was no dent or cavity in the skull, the ribs were undamaged, and yet. . . There was no reason to suppose that Prince Andrei had met anything other than a peaceful end, and yet. . .

He read the label, neatly lettered like all the others. *Homo Sapiens Male Caucasian*. It said nothing about Prince Andrei.

The widow came in, dressed as she had been when he first saw her, as she always was, in the long blue smock, her yellow hair plaited and tacked up behind in a heavy chignon. Everything about her was heavy, unshakeable. She would endure. With her ever-open museum as a comfort and a refuge she seemed to him, as she stood in the doorway, the lodestone that held the whole ramshackle place together.

"You look puzzled," she said.

"I was just thinking, there's nothing to say that this is Prince Andrei."

"Tell me something," Mrs Fahrenheit said, "what do you and Zayu talk about?"

He considered this. "We don't talk *about* anything. We don't have conversations."

"You don't pass on information?"

"I don't have any information."

"Likewise, you have nothing to tell *me*."

"I can see what you're getting at. Where do my loyalties lie? With me, mainly, at the moment. I told you why I came here, why the Sturyat think I came here. And you've told Kijé."

"Do you believe everything they tell you?"

"Theps said they lie to people who ask them questions. Why should they lie to me?"

"Why not? They lie because that is what they do. It seems to them perfectly logical, not reprehensible. They have no word in their own language for untruth. However, they do have a blind spot. They know that we do not think as they do, but although they understand that visitors also lie, the Sturyat are not very good at knowing when they are being lied *to*. If a lie fits their way of looking at something, they accept it."

"What has this to do with Prince Andrei?"

"This is not Prince Andrei. Who told you it was?"

"Zayu."

"Quite. The Sturyat may have excellent reasons for fearing the bones of Prince Andrei. I have no idea. Nor have I any idea who put the story about in the first place, but it suits me to keep it going. The sand got Prince Andrei, and yet his bones have reappeared in his house. These, therefore, are especially terrible bones. I believe that this poor creature has stood proxy for him for a century. Are you going to tell Zayu?"

"She wouldn't believe it."

"Probably not, but will you tell her?"

"No."

"Good. Now let us talk." She leaned against a cabinet. "If they had arrived earlier, in the 13th or 14th centuries, the Sturyat would have been wiped out very probably, by the hordes, which were in any case mainly made up of other nomads swept up in the move westward. I cannot imagine that the Sturyat would have made acceptable warriors, but by the time they arrived the party, as I think you would say, was over. Timur-i-Leng had been in his grave for almost a hundred years. The nomads of Central Asia were settling on the oases; Qantoum was nothing more than that, remember. The Sturyat would have moved on had it not been for the matter of their stones. I would guess that the Qantoumis had numerical parity. If the Sturyat were causing trouble the confiscation of the soul stones was quite likely an attempt to avoid outright slaughter. Khura was more scholar than warlord, which is probably why he died young. It was not meant to be a long-term solution. The stones no doubt would have been returned, had he lived. So the Sturyat settled in to wait.

"They waited for four hundred years, then the stones reappeared in an archaeological dig, and ended up in the museum. The Sturyat started to take an interest in the place in 1899 or thereabouts – and there must have been some version of Zayu here even then. And they are convinced the soul stones are still here. They aren't."

"I thought you refused to give them back."

"I know you did. You were wrong. You know, in the time you've been here, it is quite amazing the number of questions you have not asked. Did you think the Sturyat would tell you all you needed to know? The stones were removed in the 1920s – when Stalin came to power. It was a humanitarian gesture, I guess; you can imagine what would have happened to the Sturyat if they had suddenly decided to move on. The stones are not here, that's all I know."

"Why do you stay?" Keith said.

"You do not ask why I am here at all, Keith, running a café-bar with a museum attached to it, two hundred kilometres from civilization. Do I look like a woman who ought to be happy in a place like Qantoum?"

"You could say the same about any of your customers."

"Not quite, some of them really are Qantoumis, natives. Otherwise, you're right. People do not come to Qantoum from choice, they end up here, when there is nowhere else to go. Some of them are stateless. Some, Szusko, Usman, have attachments, some have families. You know about Fitz and Kijé. Lady Hooke is adrift; she will never make harbour."

"How did she get here?"

"And have you only just begun to wonder that? Sir Mortimer Hooke was an eminent British diplomat and anthropologist. He was also spying for the Soviet Union from 1945 onwards. He fled to Moscow in 1954 and Maisie joined him a year later. How they ended up in Qantoum, God knows. Maisie lives in the past, she has to. London circa 1935, I would guess."

"I thought he was an officer."

"He was. A colonel in the KGB. The sand got him."

"Along with Major Vetchinkin."

"That was quite recently. Hooke went in the late 70s. Before my time."

"You had a husband," Keith said, hesitantly.

"Friedrich," Mrs Fahrenheit said. "He was the curator. We never knew what he had done to deserve this posting."

"Did *he* know where the stones were?"

"If he did he never told me. He would have done, I think, had he seen the sand coming."

"The sand got him?"

"The sand got him. I inherited nothing but ignorance, and the museum. I don't even know *why* the sand got him, possibly the Sturyat belief that he did know where their stones were but would not say. Then the civil war broke out. I opened up the cellars as bomb shelters, then a hospital, after Qantoum General was blown up.

"Then the earthquake came. It seemed to me after the dust had settled that everyone had gone: the militias, the Russians, the UN. The only ones left were the ones you see here every day, who have nowhere else to go. And the Sturyat.

"I was in the Zherdin Gallery one day when one of the Sturyat girls appeared in the doorway. I was surprised. The Sturyat never go into the main part of town, not even the Registan. The market is the extent of their travels. She said she wanted to work for me. I didn't need her, I had Lizaveta; I said I couldn't pay her very much but she said that didn't matter, that she wanted to work in the museum. She was only about ten or eleven; I thought it was a childish fancy, although the Sturyat don't go in for that kind of thing and they marry young. It was Zayu, of course. She's not a full-blooded Sturyat, perhaps you knew that, and traditionally they use people like that as go-betweens. It was no whim; she didn't grow out of it, and after a while I realized why she is here. She's looking out for the stones, but, poor child, until she came here she never knew that a museum was so full of bones.

"I began to wonder then what lengths they would go to; after Friedrich, I mean. So I moved in here, and I never leave. Fitz and Kijé help me guard it and Zayu haunts it. Sometimes I'm tempted to move these bones to the front entrance, that would keep her away, but it would be like a declaration of war. At the moment we preserve a kind of armistice. But if your dream is the beginning of their exodus there is no telling what they may do to get their souls back. I did not know that your dream would mean anything to them. I am a rationalist. You may have noticed."

"So was I, once." He tried to remember his former self, the one who had lived for twenty years believing that what you see is what you get, who had died and risen again.

"So what will you do?" Mrs Fahrenheit asked. "Accept that you are an instrument of supernatural intervention or. . ."

"Or?"

"You could always leave."

"I had thought of that."

"Unlike the rest of us, you *can* leave." She noticed Prince Andrei's book, where he had left it lying open. "Are you looking for something?"

"Clues, I suppose. I read Crow and Dacre, and Schuyler, but he doesn't visit Qantoum. I wondered what Zherdin had to say about the Sturyat."

"He found them friendly, hospitable, not very intellectual, but congenial companions. Lady Charlotte thought they were degenerate, ignorant and pacifist. Lord Dacre found them irreligious, dirty, superstitious and given to large ideas about astronomy. The word no one uses is ruthless."

"I think Kijé's been hinting at it."

"They have been in the minority for a long while," Mrs Fahrenheit said. "Now for the first time since Khura Khan's day they are in the majority."

"What do you think happened to Bordeleau?"

"God knows – that scream – "

"The twins. Do you believe it?"

"I have been here a long time," she said. "I believe nothing."

Someone was coming down the corridor from the rotunda. Fitz looked in.

"Any news?" Mrs Fahrenheit said. "The missing man?"

"We're going to search Industrial," Fitz said. "Are you coming, Keith?"

"Sure. Where are the other two?"

"Resting at home." The words conjured visions of chintz and lamplight, a suburban semi with a privet hedge, a bird-bath in the garden and a name-plate by the front door: *Dunkillin*. "Kijé told them not to go out. I think he frightened them."

"I wouldn't have thought that was necessary," Mrs Fahrenheit said. "Go ahead, both of you. Be back before dark."

Ten

The shadows were already lengthening. Fitz, unusually concentrated, led the way, not through the Old Town but towards the consular district.

"Are we going along the railway line?"

"No, through the barracks is quicker."

"Why Industrial?"

"Kijé's taking it sector by sector. We've done the marshalling yards."

"Have you spoken to them, Soames and Woodbridge?"

"Tony and Bill," Fitz said. "Yes."

"How are they taking it?"

"Badly. They keep on about that scream. Pity they heard the scream."

"They could hardly miss hearing it."

"But it's given them the wrong idea. They think Jacques must accidentally have insulted one of the women. I keep telling them, the Sturyat aren't like that."

"Aren't they? Why do you spend all night guarding the museum?"

"Oh, the stones and bones thing," Fitz said, airily. "This has got nothing to do with stones and bones."

Their footsteps echoed among the high walls of the barrack blocks. In places they were walking through tunnels.

"How can you tell? Suppose this guy barged into someone's tent and ignored the bones?"

"It wouldn't be the first time." Fitz sounded unconcerned. "They're very tolerant. If it was a genuine mistake they'd forgive him."

"Would they?" Kijé must find Fitz something of a liability, at times.

Keith had been expecting silence in the Industrial district, but the place was alive with purposefully moving figures armed with sticks, both Qantoumis and Sturyat. No one spoke but all bashed energetically at the dry vegetation, like reapers with scythes. Precariously balanced on the jib of a crane, which he had scaled like a ladder, Kijé was directing operations, clinging to the metalwork with one elbow, pointing and gesturing with his free hand. Slung over his shoulder was something Keith had not seen before, an AK47 assault rifle.

At the foot of the crane Theps was standing, grave, arms folded, staring out from beneath the brim of his felt hat.

"This is a great grief," he said to Fitz.

"It's good of your lot to come out and help search," Fitz said.

"It casts a shadow upon all of us," Theps said.

You old liar, Keith thought, and was shocked to find

himself thinking it. He turned and looked up along the crane's jib.

"Don't try to come up, you'll have us both over," Kijé said. "This thing is held together by rust. Fitz, get along to the turntable and work back."

Fitz blundered away, tripping over concealed rubble and metal. Theps, to Keith's relief, went after him. Kijé looked round and down.

"I have an outer circle moving inwards and an inner circle moving outwards," he said.

"Do you think it will work?"

"If he's here."

"Do you think he is?"

"I have to do something," Kijé said. "I have to be seen to do something." The crane groaned warningly. "Look out, I'm coming down. What will I land on?"

"Just grass."

Kijé let go of his perch and plummeted, four metres, giving at the knees as he hit the ground, rolling over to rise in one movement, gripping the rifle.

Paratrooper, Keith noted, abstractedly.

"Did you call the Sturyat out?"

"Not directly. I made it known that this was a matter of grave concern. Their response has been magnificent," he added.

"Do you think they really don't care?"

"Of course they don't care. Why should they? One visitor gone missing – they've seen massacres. They know how to keep a sense of proportion. And a visitor, after all, scarcely counts as human."

"What do you want me to do?"

Kijé turned, smiling thinly. "I want you to be here. You are John the Baptist, no? No one will do anything he shouldn't while John the Baptist is watching."

"You don't trust them, do you?"

"Watch my back. If I were you I'd go and stand on a great man's shoulders."

"You what?"

"Vladimir Ilyich, he won't mind. He too is out of his head. Over there, beside the generator shed. I'll wait here, till you're ready."

Keith set off in the direction of Kijé had indicated. When he looked round he saw him still standing, backed against the ruined wall. He had, Keith noticed, put on the relics of his uniform, boots, cap, tunic, willing himself unwillingly into a role he must have thought or hoped he had escaped for ever; Officer of the Day, the man in charge. Who was he trying to persuade? All he needed was the Kalashnikov. No one was going to argue with that.

He found himself back where he had been last night, at the foot of Lenin. He climbed up the inside left leg, over the hip and on to the torso. From the shoulder he could see the head, one ear visible. A hoarse cry made him look away.

All around, in a double circle, the scything figures halted, lowered their sticks and looked towards the voice. Fitz was still knees-upping through the bushes, the school nerd looking for a lost cricket ball in the long grass. After a moment he too sensed that something was happening and stopped. Kijé left the shelter of his wall and advanced into the open, hurrying to meet a slow-moving stooped person who was coming the other way from the Sturyat pasture. It was Gresk, holding his arms stiffly before him at waist level. Something was draped across them, something that also had arms, legs, but no substance, limp, dangling. For delirious seconds Keith thought that Gresk was carrying an empty skin.

Kijé was running now, the two met only twenty metres from Lenin's foot. In the utter silence that had fallen over the waiting searchers, over the wasteland, voices carried. Kijé took off his cap. Keith could not see his face.

"Oh, my friend," Gresk said, "it is the madness, the desert madness. He must have heard the voices of the lost souls crying, 'Save us!' and run to join them. He is lost. This is all that remains."

Kijé said nothing. He held out his own forearms and Gresk gently spread the empty garments over them. The old man joined his hands beneath his bowed chin and murmured a few inaudible words, before laying a consoling hand on Kijé's unresponsive shoulder. Then he walked back the way he had come. Wordlessly the Sturyat began to follow him; the two circles warped, became a funnel, a wavering line that wove among the weeds and masonry. The shadows absorbed it, as though it was a runnel of water soaking into dust. As they disappeared a dozen people, the Qantoumis, detached themselves and left by a sharply divergent route. In a few minutes there was no one but himself, poised on Lenin's shoulder, Fitz waist-high in scrub, and Kijé standing where Gresk had left him, with the clothes hanging from his arms.

He looked up as the other two approached and said, "The sand got him."

"Bordeleau?"

"You saw him, Keith? Are these his clothes?"

Even in the fading light he recognized the green plaid work shirt, the indigo denims.

'Yes. He went into the desert? I warned them."

"About what?"

"The land-mines."

"This wasn't a land-mine," Fitz said. Appalled, he was fingering the shirt. "You know what they say, men fling off their clothes and run out into the desert. Oh God, that poor bastard. His first night here – what do we tell his friends?"

Kijé was neatly, madly, folding the garments.

"That is what we tell his friends."

"Well," Fitz sighed, "I suppose there's no point in hiding the truth from them." Kijé looked at him incredulously, swore under his breath and began to walk towards the barracks.

Fitz and Keith followed. Kijé said nothing for some while, then he spoke decisively. "Fitz, take the clothes and get back to the others. Explain what's happened. Console them. *Keep them there*. Whatever else you do, keep them there. Tomorrow they can go and meet their Sturyat friends and have tea and hear the proper condolences. But tonight, keep them in."

"Fair enough. Will you be at the museum?"

"Yes, and Keith can come with me. Stay at home, I'll come for you all in the morning. Do you understand?"

"Yes, sir," Fitz said, without irony.

He parted from them at the gate of the barracks.

"Can you trust him?" Keith said. "To keep an eye on them?"

"Trust him? Yes, I suppose so. But it is best that the news of Bordeleau's death comes from someone who believes what he is saying."

"You don't think he's dead?"

"Oh, he's dead all right."

'The sand got him."

"Fitz is an idiot," Kijé said, levelly. "Are you?"

"You mean, it *was* a land-mine?"

"No, it was not. Look at these nice clean clothes which have, I think, been washed."

The night closed down about them. Into the air rose the heartless harmony of the sand.

"I hate this place," Kijé said.

Night in the Zherdin Collection; Keith lay on a camp-bed which Mrs Fahrenheit had unfolded from a cupboard, sleepless in the moonlight, uneasily watching for movement, not so much from marauding Sturyat – Kijé after all was on guard only metres away with the Kalashnikov – but from the exhibits. The mermaid, propped on one elbow, was frozen in the act of stealthy advance. Setsemhotep III, head tipped back, mouth open, might at any moment emit a rasping snore and sit up.

Tomorrow – no, it was long past midnight – later today he must go back to his house and speak to Zayu, before she started for the museum; catch her on the roof. For all he knew she could have been ransacking his possessions. What proof had he that Zayu and the Sturyat really believed that his arrival foretold their departure or had they been calmly lying to him while they prepared some horrible fate for him? Why should they? What had he done? What had Bordeleau done? What had been done to Bordeleau? He had not even cried out. A woman had screamed and Bordeleau had vanished. Bordeleau had vanished into the desert having flung off his clothes and fled into the darkling sands. It was Fitz who first told him of such things; Fitz who believed in them. Kijé did not believe.

He fell asleep at last when the moon withdrew from overhead and Prince Andrei's foundlings merged with the shadows. Sometime later he heard a muffled explosion, started up, knew he had been dreaming of land-mines, and slept again. When he fully woke the gallery was illuminated by the dawn twilight, and he got up, sweating and stiff. What wouldn't he give for a good night's sleep in a real bed with a real mattress and pillows. Perhaps he should move into the Sogdiana Serai with Lady Hooke and her spooks. How did Kijé manage to stay awake through his vigils?

He walked down the gallery to the rotunda and looked along the corridor to the Archaeology Gallery, where a motionless heap was huddled against the door. Kijé had solved the problem of staying awake by falling asleep. Keith began to tiptoe away, not wanting to witness his shame and annoyance when he woke up.

The front door of the museum was opened by a violent shove and Fitz tumbled in followed by Bill Woodbridge. In the time it took Keith to turn his head and see them, Kijé was on his feet and running down the corridor.

"Tony's gone," Fitz said. "Bill woke up – early – empty bed – found a window – "

In the dawn's early light the four of them stood there each supposing that he looked as ghastly as the other three, unshaven and red-eyed, sallow and grey-lipped with fatigue.

"Take it slowly," Kijé said. "Tell me – no, not you, Fitz; Mr Woodbridge, Bill. Fitz, go and wake Erna and tell her we need coffee."

Fitz sprinted away. It was the first coffee that Keith had heard of in Qantoum. He surmised a carefully hoarded store, laid down against emergencies. This was an emergency. Doors thumped in the distance.

"Come into the bar," Kijé said. They followed the way Fitz had gone, into the smoke-cured atmosphere of the early morning Refreshment Room. Kijé sat down at one of the tables near a window, leaning his rifle against the wall. From his pocket he drew a flat dented tin and took out a nasty-looking cigarette, another item from a dwindling hoard, Keith thought. He had not seen Kijé smoking before and as the fumes caught the back of his throat he was grateful.

"Go ahead, please."

"Where's the other guy: Fitz?" Woodbridge looked round distractedly.

"He'll be back."

"He told us the most incredible story—"

"You thought so, did you?"

"What, that it was incredible?"

"I *learned* English," Kijé said, "with a dictionary. I mean, did you not believe it?"

"I could believe anything. Fitz came back last night with Jacques's clothes and said they'd been found at the edge of the desert. He said people can be driven mad by the sand singing and that they fling off their clothes, rush out into the darkness – never seen again. We heard the sand singing when we were on the roof. *Weird* – but not maddening. Do you really think that's what happened, he just took off?"

Keith said nothing. Let Kijé conduct this inquiry. He was good at it.

"What did you do after this?"

"Tony wanted to go straight out, comb the desert. Fitz said we couldn't do anything in the dark – best wait for morning. He was being tactful," Woodbridge said, "but it was quite obvious he believed that that was what had happened."

Kijé inhaled significantly.

"Fitz went to lock up. Tony said how could we just stay here as if nothing had happened? I said we'd best sleep on it, we were dealing with serious darkness here. He kept arguing that he'd slept all afternoon. I said we needed all the rest we could get. *I* was dead tired, I crashed out – I think Tony was asleep before me. You could have let a bomb off in my ear and I wouldn't have known."

Keith felt a foreboding prickle down the back of his neck and glanced at Kijé who was engaged in picking a small thorny twig out of his tobacco and did not look up.

Woodbridge went on, "I woke up about an hour ago. Tony wasn't there. Thought he'd gone for a slash, but he didn't come back. I went all round the building, up the stairs, not a sign, then I went into that greenhouse place, the window was open. So I went and woke Fitz; we had another search. Then we came here. Do you think the sand. . . ?"

"No," Kijé said. "The sand sings only at sundown; it's the change in the temperature that causes it."

A rich smell of coffee, redolent of long-lost civilization, was seeping into the room. The door behind the bar opened and Mrs Fahrenheit came through carrying a tray of mugs, jugs, loaves. Fitz followed, bearing a caterer's coffee pot steaming at the spout.

She came up the steps to where they were sitting and set down the tray.

"Sometime, I hope, we may meet in happier circum-stances," she said to Bill Woodbridge, as she laid out the mugs and food. Keith, his guts roaring and his nerve-ends yelping urgently after caffeine, made a supreme sacrifice.

"I want to ask you something," he muttered to Kijé.

"Bring your coffee," Kijé said, swiping a mug for himself

and getting a quick fix from the steam. "Please excuse us," he said. "There's something we have to check out. We'll be back in a moment." He rose, picking up the rifle, and started for the door, Keith following.

"Better be quick," Kijé said in the rotunda. "Lizaveta and Maisie will be here soon. And Zayu, perhaps. One of us must talk with Zayu – well, what is it?"

The caffeine was surging through Keith's veins. He felt almost cheerful.

"Did you hear anything last night – well, early this morning? Between two and three, I should think."

"What sort of a thing, mice?"

"An explosion. I thought I'd dreamed it – land-mines on the brain – but now I'm not so sure."

"I heard nothing."

"You might have been asleep."

"Never."

"You were asleep just now, before Fitz crashed in. I went down the corridor to find you. You were out of it, Kijé. They could have let a bomb off in your ear, as Bill said. That's what reminded me."

"Are you sure?"

"That you were asleep?"

"No, I believe you. The explosion."

"I *wasn't* sure, like I said. I assumed I'd dreamed it. But if that fool's gone exploring on his own, who knows? In the dark, in the desert. . ."

"I don't even want to think about this," Kijé said.

"We've got to go and look. He might be lying out there now – people don't always get killed by land-mines, they lose limbs."

"Don't tell me about mines," Kijé growled.

"Fitz said the Sturyat don't step on land-mines. Can't we get one of them as a guide?"

"Fitz has been told by the Sturyat that the Sturyat don't step on mines. We could put it to the test."

"Send one out in front, you mean?"

"And avoid the place where he goes up in smoke, you mean? How cynical you are becoming."

"I didn't mean that. I just thought we could ask one of them to help. What about Streph?"

"Streph the grandfather of twins? Look, Keith, till now the Sturyat have put up with us as they have put up with thousands before us, because they had no choice. Now they have decided that this particular cycle of events is at an end. They can do what they like, will do what they like, probably they are already doing what they like. Imagine, Streph agrees to help us. He leads me out into the desert. He is charming, as always. 'How warm the sun feels,' he will say. 'Summer is here. See, the apricots are ripening. Put your foot just here, dear man, it is perfectly safe.'"

"Then what *are* we going to do? Do you think I'd be safe? You said last night that they wouldn't do anything to you while I was watching."

"And five minutes later Gresk arrived with Bordeleau's clothes. I do not *think* they will harm you, but I wouldn't swear to it. We don't even know what they did to Bordeleau. I'll go out and look on my own. I have a metal detector."

"*A metal detector?* You've been treasure hunting out *here?*"

"The army issues them," Kijé explained, very slowly, "for locating mines. Tell me, Keith, assuming that this Soames is dead, what will happen when news gets back to his own country? Here are two young men gone without trace."

"I don't know," Keith said. "People disappear abroad all the time. The Foreign Office says it's doing all it can . . . anyway, Soames has been working in Kazakhstan. I don't think anyone even knew they were here."

"It would be happiest for us if no one ever knew that they had been here." Kijé drained his mug. "I'll go home" – that comfortable word again – "and pick up the metal detector."

"Will you be safe on your own?"

"Out there I shall be safer on my own. But it is possible that you did dream of the explosion. Soames may walk in safely at any moment. After all, you do have vivid dreams," he said. "Do what you can for Woodbridge. Make sure Fitz keeps him out of the sand. If he wants to search elsewhere, one of you must be with him. You haven't spoken to Zayu yet, have you? That is your detail. I'll see you later."

"I hope." Keith watched Kijé leave, rifle slung across his back, off to find Tony Soames, or what was left of him.

I didn't come here for this, he thought.

Zayu was coming up the steps.

He had not spoken to her for two days, almost to the hour, when they had parted at this very place, she to begin her

day's work at the museum, he to Control Point E; both awaiting three men from the west.

"How are the twins?" he asked, evilly.

"They are well. You would like to see them?"

Was this a bluff? Should he call it?

"Sometime, yes. How is their mother? I hear she suffered
greatly."

"It is over now. She forgets."

He studied her as they spoke. She was wearing her hat.
Her face was as unrevealing as ever, but he could swear that
her composure was shaken; that she knew his questions were
loaded.

"You know what has happened, don't you? Those three
men we saw from the roof that morning, you know what's
happened to them?" He half expected her to say, What three
men?

"The sand got one of them," Zayu said, as one might say,
"It's warm today."

"Yes, the sand got one of them, and now another has disappeared. Doesn't that bother you? You were so pleased
when you saw them coming, the first strangers from the
west."

"There will be more," Zayu said. "They were only the
first."

"Aren't you upset? They'd come so far; it was your soul
stones that had fetched them and one is already dead and
another is missing. Did you actually *see* them?"

"On the roof with you."

"No, afterwards, once they had arrived. They spent half the day with you, taking photographs—"

"I did not see them again," Zayu said. "I came to the museum, you were with me. But they did not come here so I went to my house. Then Zeze was in labour and I went to the tent of her man to help. I did not see the visitors. I am sorry. But there will be others."

He followed her down the corridor to the Refreshment Room. Fitz and Woodbridge were still sitting over coffee.

"Zayu, this is the third man, Mr Woodbridge," Keith said.

"The one who has not vanished?" Zayu said cleverly. She went to the bar, taking off her hat and coat as she went.

"Have you seen her before?" he said to Woodbridge.

"I don't think so. They all look alike – the hats and coats, I mean."

"Where's Kijé?" Fitz said.

"I'll tell you in a minute. What are you going to do?"

"That rather depends on him."

"He suggests you go home or look around a bit. Tony may have gone back to Control Point E," he pointed out reasonably, calculating that, moving at speed, Kijé would have been home and away again by the time they arrived. "Let's just clear up before we go."

"Zayu does that," Fitz said. "Don't spoil her simple pleasures."

"Take the coffee pot," Keith said, firmly, sweeping the remains of the breakfast he had not shared on to the tray. As they went towards the bar he said, quietly, "Kijé's gone out minesweeping, looking for a body. It's just possible that Soames went into the desert last night to search for Bordeleau. Maybe not, maybe he has gone back to your place, like I said; don't mention mines to *him*." He nodded towards Woodbridge.

"What are you going to do?"

"Some research of my own. Whatever else you do, stick with him."

Eleven

He wished that Mrs Fahrenheit could have heard his conversation with Zayu. She must know her better than he did, well enough at any rate to interpret her staggering callousness. She might have been speaking of a missed bus. There'll be another one along in a minute.

He ought to have told Fitz where he was going, so at least someone would have an idea of his whereabouts should he fail to appear later. But Fitz, who thought no ill of anyone, who did not, in fact, appear to think at all, might mention it in anyone's hearing; in Zayu's, for instance. It would not do for Zayu to know where he was going.

He took a circuitous route to his house, but went straight up the steps and jerked the door open. All was as he had left it, his bedding rolled, his clothes hanging, his pack strapped and buckled. Someone could have searched it but why would anyone bother? From Zayu's remarks he was beginning to suspect that John the Baptist had served his purpose. He had arrived, there was no need for him to hang around. When

Khlev had said, "I think you will stay," she had simply been stating a fact.

He crossed the courtyard and entered Zayu's door. The trap at the head of the stairs was open. He went up and sat on the top step, waiting for his eyes to adapt to the gloom, turning from the little bright dapples beyond the lattice in the window. The first thing he saw was the long cloth bag hanging in front of the door. Apart from the vigilant ancestor there was nothing else hanging except the binoculars on a nearby hook. A flat thin mattress lay on the sleeping platform, and beside it stood a solid wooden box, half a metre along each side. Facing him was a narrow brass hinge about ten centimetres down, denoting the depth of the lid. On the far side, where lid met box, his fingers discovered a metal hasp, fastened with a bar but not locked.

It opened easily enough, the lid sprung by the pressure of what was inside. He turned it back, fully open. The whole lid was wadded with a thick quilt. He took it out and ran his hand through the layers. Nothing was concealed in it but he was not at all sure of what he was looking for. Some signs of Bordeleau? He had not dared to articulate that, even to himself. Gresk had given Kijé only the shirt and trousers. Bordeleau had been wearing a cap, boots; he must have had underclothes. Still, no one claimed to know the precise details of what sand-maddened men flung off before they ran out into the desert.

One thing was without doubt, however. Bordeleau was a photographer. The bulk of his equipment was in the backpack at Control Point E, but he had been taking photographs when he disappeared. "We know photograph," Zayu had said.

The next item was a sheepskin, roughly cut into a jerkin, under that a flat brass bowl, a ladle, a square bag made out of a rug, what were they called? Kelims. These were resting on a felted blanket. Zayu's voice, her droning translation of the funny story, was in his head. "There was a man and he took a woman for a wife, and the woman brought to her marriage one brass pot, one red carpet, one old blanket, one new blanket, one cushion. . ." Here was the cushion, stitched into a square of ikat silk. This was Zayu's bottom drawer, the bedding and utensils collected against the day of her wedding. He took out one more thing, a little box containing a horn spoon with a carved handle, and set it aside, heavy with self-disgust, as if he had been rifling a woman's handbag, digging out the small intimacies that were not his to see.

Damn Kijé and his suspicions. But it was not only Kijé's suspicions that had sent him here.

He swept the bottom of the box with his fingers; there was nothing else except a scattering of dry aromatic twigs. If anything of Bordeleau's had survived, it was not here, and he began methodically to replace the items, putting them back where he best remembered finding them. As he closed the lid he recalled that Zayu possessed one other thing, to his knowledge; something that would not fit into a square box; the rifle that had belonged to A/C Tcherk.

Where would she keep that? He investigated the sleeping platform but by no means could he find an opening. The torch would have been useful in this half-light, but there was no time to make the journey back to his room; she might enter at any moment. The ceiling seemed to be the same as his, the rafters close together with small regular logs fitted between them. Right against the wall there were no logs. The woven reed that lined the ceiling was clear of the rafter, leaving a convenient shelf. His hand encountered something lying along it. It was only a little way above his head but he lifted it out with extreme care, knowing what it was before he saw it: an assault rifle, very like the one that Kijé had suddenly taken to carrying, lagged in cloth, carefully oiled.

He stood with it resting across his hands. It was no secret that she owned it, she had told him herself. Did Kijé know? Did Kijé want to know? Were there not enough unasked-for responsibilities piling up on his shoulders? Quite likely she did not regard it as a weapon but rather in the light of a keepsake or – more grisly thought – a trophy. He slid the swaddled weapon back into its cache above the rafter. Did she have any ammunition for it? The butt had snagged against something else lying farther along, jammed against the aperture at the very end, where the rafter entered the wall. It came down with a thud: a camera.

Had it been hidden? Was the rifle hidden or was it stowed tidily on the rafter because it would not fit into the box? We know *photograph*. It couldn't be hers, could it? Did the Sturyat know *hiding* or did they, she, rely on the bones to keep away prying eyes. Oh God, he prayed, don't let Kijé step on a mine.

He pushed the camera back into the place from where it

had fallen. If Zayu trusted in bones and believed him to be credulous, it was safe there and she would not know that he had been searching. He could get it out again when he needed it, but before he confronted her he wanted to see what she might let slip by accident. Better the Sturyat did not know yet what he knew.

All I need now, he thought, is to go back to Dunkillin and find that Woodbridge is missing too. Instead he went out, warily, and made his way to the citadel. The clay bricks were crumbled and cracked but enough remained of one set of steps to reach the ledge behind the embrasure and from there the observation platform of the northern watch-tower, where he had once sat to watch the moon rise over the desert. He was higher than he would have been on his roof and nothing interrupted the view. He could look directly down into the abandoned building lots, the neglected orchards, dry irrigation ditches, the little bridges, low walls, and then the gravelly dusty hillocks and the grey sand beyond. It was not the desert of his imaginings, a textbook vista of golden dunes. An undulating green film overlaid the stony soil.

At some distance, straight ahead, on a little hummock of pebbles and bushes, a man stood, head bent, weight on one leg, a study in active concentration. Then he moved, very deliberately, down the far side of the hillock. Kijé had not yet stepped on a land-mine.

Keith descended, walked along the border strip and skirted the cemetery, thereby reaching the Registan without passing through the market. He did not want to meet any Sturyat at the moment, to talk of twins, to listen to Streph and the Goat Woman with their carefully rehearsed commiserations. He seemed to hear Kijé's bitter mimicry of Streph and supplied his own version. "An explosion in the night? Oh, dear man, a great sorrow. Have a frog. My aunt blew up at dawn. It was very sudden. But I have other aunts."

By taking this way round he met no one but the charming family group of Szusko and the bear, the dog and the dog's friend. Szusko returned his salute with a friendly wave and walked on with his cart, leaving Keith to ponder the insane persistence with which the Qantoumis pursued their imitation of daily life. It was a good imitation; it had fooled him for several weeks. So far only Kijé had stepped aside from his role and reluctantly resumed the habits for which he had been trained. Keith respected his glum integrity. He could so easily elect to share Fitz's wambly optimism or refuse to accept the onus for what was happening; instead he was out there now in the desert, hoovering a minefield and looking for God alone knew what kind of horror.

Control Point E was open but empty. Keith stood in the doorway looking round the stifling office, Kijé's turbulent desk, the defunct telephone, Fitz's mushroom farm. It had not changed since he first saw it, yet he had not seen what he saw now. His eyes were opened. The soft woolly insulation that he had seemed to carry in his head since he left hospital had been cut away as cleanly as with a scalpel; how clear and cold his eyesight now.

He went through to the tool room, along the corridor,

towards voices. *You know nothing*, he reminded himself as he approached the open door. *You have not seen Kijé in the minefield. You have not found Jacques Bordeleau's camera.*

Fitz and Bill Woodbridge were, inevitably, drinking tea, Fitz on the divan, Bill sprawled on the sofa.

"Any news?" He scrambled to his feet when he saw Keith in the doorway.

"No," Keith said. "Look, whatever happens, promise you won't go off on your own anywhere." He had not meant to say that, but the sight of them sitting over mugs of tea in the midst of soft furnishings shocked him into vehemence. Colonials on the eve of Cawnpore. Aristocrats on the brink of revolution. Kijé, for whatever reasons of his own, allowed Fitz to remain in comfortable innocence, and Fitz in his turn would allow Bill to continue in the belief that there was someone in control. Kijé, meanwhile, was minesweeping.

"I was thinking of going down to talk to those Sturyat people again," Bill said.

"No, don't do that. Wait till Kijé gets back, he'll give you a – a debriefing."

"Where is he then?" Fitz said. "Thought he was coming here."

"He's looking along the border area," Keith temporized. "I've been in the Old Town." He could only hope that Fitz would remember, had been remembering, his injunction not to mention land-mines.

"He's not in the minefield, is he?" Fitz said. Bill, already white, turned green.

"Sit down," Keith said to him. "I warned you about the minefield when you reported to me yesterday. You know all about people going mad when the desert sings and rushing out into the darkness? Well, it's not just sand out there."

"I thought you told me not to mention—"

"You just did."

"Well, what's he *doing*?"

"He's got a metal detector. He's looking for traces of Tony Soames." That was an unfortunate turn of phrase. Traces might very well be all he would find.

"Do you think that's what happened to Jacques?"

"No, I don't." Not for one minute do I think it. "His clothes were intact; no bloodstains, were there?" Washed, Kijé had said.

"I can't *believe* all this is happening," Bill said, shaking his head.

"Are you staying?" Fitz said, getting up. "I'll go on down and see how Kijé's doing."

"You're not going to join him, are you?" Fitz in a mine-field?

"I know where it's safe," Fitz said, reminding Keith that he too must once have received some kind of initiation into the exciting world of high explosives. Whether he remembered any of it was another matter.

Bill Woodbridge watched him go. Sooner or later, Keith reasoned, it's going to occur to him to ask who the hell we all are, but Woodbridge seemed beyond curiosity or reason.

"It's a shame he'll miss Colney-Hatch," he said, fatuously.

"*What?*"

"He's looking forward to that. We're going to be witnessing some amazing phenomena."

"We are?" This man is probably dead, he's not going to witness anything.

"There's the August eclipse, and on 5 May 2000 the five major planets will be in alignment, and by then we'll be able to see Colney-Hatch."

"Which is?"

"Comet Colney-Hatch. You'll have a great view of it here. Tony kind of has a stake in Colney-Hatch. It was predicted by Avery Colney at Palomar, but a friend of Tony's actually located it: Bob Hatch. They'd been waiting for it. It last passed Earth in 1499, and before that in 999. People thought it foretold the end of the world."

"A five-hundred-year-orbit?" He was not well up in comets but he did not care for the sound of this.

"It might even have been the Star of Bethlehem."

"And what do people think it is this time?"

"You must admit it *is* significant."

"Of what, the Millennium? We didn't even start counting till the 6th century." Two of his friends are missing, almost certainly dead, and he sits here blathering about comets. "You don't believe it signifies the end of the world, do you?" He did say astronomer and not astrologer, didn't he?

"There's actually a belief that the planetary alignment will bring about the melting of the polar ice-caps and a massive global inundation," Woodbridge was saying. "Add to that this year's eclipse, and the comet, and the Eclipse of the Century—"

"Which you say won't happen."

"Well, basically, it *can't* happen, but people are getting odd ideas. They believe that the sun will dance, like it does when the Virgin Mary appears at Fatima, I suppose. And this is where they think it will be seen; somebody put it on his website and after that it went ballistic. And none of you knew about it?"

"About what?"

"The black sun. Colney-Hatch."

He dimly remembered hearing something about a comet before leaving home. And then there were the Sturyat, awaiting a wonder in the heavens, who had been waiting for five hundred years. Somewhere, not far away, a door opened and closed. It might be Fitz, still on his way out but. . .

"Wait a moment," Keith said. "Stay here." He ran down the corridor and into the tool room. Kijé was just leaving, with a spade. They looked at each other.

"I'll bury him," Kijé said, at last. "I left you a note." He pointed to the desk.

"Who – what was it?"

"A mine," Kijé said. "As to who, I suppose it was the man we have been looking for."

Keith walked past him into the office, opened the drawer of the desk and felt for the UK passport, noticing that the ammunition had gone. "Fair hair – him?"

"I think so."

"I'll come with you, you can't do it alone."

"It won't be the first time."

"Where?"

"Where he lies. Believe me, I can't bring it back. Don't argue. Where's Fitz?"

"Went out about five, ten minutes ago, to help you. Does he know his way around the minefield?"

"He barely knows his way around the garden." Kijé made for the door. "We must have missed each other. Stay with Woodbridge. You'd better break it to him that his friend is dead."

"Both his friends. He doesn't seem to grasp what's going on."

"He's not alone in that."

The door closed behind him, leaving Keith no chance to tell him how he himself had spent the morning, and what he had found in Zayu's roof.

In the living-room Woodbridge stood eagerly in the middle of the floor.

"Is it Tony?"

"Oh, God; no. You'd better sit down. I've got something to tell you." Woodbridge, seeing his expression, whatever it was, subsided on the divan. "Two things." There was no point in beating about the bush. "Tony's dead."

He anticipated an eruption of grief. Bill said only, "How do you know?"

"Kijé has found his body in the minefield. Bordeleau's

221

almost certainly dead too. This business of rushing out into the desert; no one ever comes back. Well, there was a dog. . ."

"It's a bit different with dogs, isn't it?" He sat without speaking for a few minutes. "I just can't take this in," he said. "It doesn't seem real. Nothing does, this whole place, not even you, sorry. And the guy with the gun. As if at any moment I'll wake up and find I imagined it all."

"I know the feeling."

"I guess it's shock. I mean, they weren't close friends, hardly knew Jacques at all, but they were good guys. If I really knew them I'd know their families, I'd be thinking, Oh Christ, I've got to tell his wife, his mother. . . I'd feel involved. I don't even know if they had mothers and wives. Jacques wasn't married. I ought to do something about a funeral, getting the bodies sent home."

"No. Kijé's burying Tony where he found him."

"That's terrible—"

"Bill, the other thing I had to tell you—"

"I thought you had. Jacques not coming back."

"That wasn't it. You've got to understand, there's no one in charge here, no authorities, no administration, just a bunch of left-overs; and the Sturyat."

"What are you, then?"

"Same as you, a visitor, a tourist. I've only been here since April."

"Why did you give us those permits, then; take our passports?"

"Isn't that what you expected? I came here the same way

you did; I saw the notice about aliens reporting to Control Point E, so I did. And I found someone I thought was the Officer of the Day, Acting Captain Tcherk."

"Just a minute," Tony said. "I thought you were Tcherk."

"There is no Acting Captain Tcherk. He's been dead for years. My name's Keith."

"I know. Keith Tcherk, I thought. So who did you meet?"

"Kijé; the one with the gun."

"What about the woman who runs the hotel?"

"Mrs Ernestine Fahrenheit. It's not an hotel, it's a museum. The hotel is the Sogdiana Serai, and its only inhabitant is Maisie, Lady Hooke, widow of a British spy, who puts out crumbs for the wolves. Qantoum is a ghost town."

"What about the Sturyat?"

What indeed? "Nomads, they settled here. I'll tell you about them some other time."

"Fitz has been keeping me here. I wanted to go down to their place and talk to them some more. One of them may know what happened to Jacques."

How right you are. "Don't do that, not yet. Wait until Kijé gets back. He'll advise you what to do next."

"I thought you said he wasn't in charge."

"Officially, no, but he's better equipped to take charge than anyone else." He's armed, for one thing. "Do as I say. Don't go wandering off on your own like Tony did." As he spoke he remembered what Kijé had said. That it would be the best solution to their problems were Woodbridge to disappear too. "How long are you staying?"

"In Qantoum? I don't know. We were only meant to be here one day. I've got to clear my head. I can't think straight at the moment."

"Get some rest," Keith said. "Where did you sleep last night?"

"I'm too tired to sleep," Bill said, but he got up and led the way along the corridor. "What *is* this place, a barracks?"

"It used to be a school."

"Thought it looked familiar," Bill said. "Funny, you go halfway round the world and end up in a place that looks just like Westlands, Sittingbourne. School's the same wherever you go."

He was beginning to ramble. Keith wanted him asleep before reality hit. "Is there anything you could take?" He recalled the widow's dictum on tourists: they require chemist's shops.

"Tony had a sort of medical kit. We all did, but his is a proper fitted one, he may have something."

Fitz had quartered his unexpected guests in what might have been a study. A heavy desk was pushed against the wall, the blind was drawn. On the floor were two sleeping-bags laid out on makeshift mattresses of blankets and curtains. One lay flat and tidy where the occupant had slid out silently to avoid waking his companion, sleeping a metre away, and crept from the room, to force open a window and make his way through the starry streets to his death among the mines. Keith could only guess at the thoughts that had driven him there. Loyalty to a lost friend? Hope that he might find him?

Suspicion that the truth was being kept from him? Almost certainly the last and certainly correct. The other bag was turned half inside out, witness to the speed with which Bill had left it when he woke and saw that Soames had gone.

The three backpacks, one open and spilling clothes, stood under the window. Bill went over to the other two, one still neatly strapped with its bedroll across the top.

"That's Jacques's. He's got most of his photographic equipment in it, he hardly bothered with clothes. That's Tony's. I don't really want to open it. Would you?"

Keith unfastened the pack, put aside the bedding roll and stared in, equally loath to fossick around in a dead man's private possessions. Fortunately the medical kit was on top, a professional square white box with a green cross on it. Inside were dressings, analgesics, antiseptic ointment, iodine tablets, rehydration powders, antihistamine cream, diarrhoea pills, insect repellent, a brown plastic bottle with a chemist's label on it. That small link with home, J Darcy & Sons, Angel Row, Nottingham, was unbearably moving. The writing was crabbed: *Mr A Soames. Phen. Barb. As directed.* He passed it to Bill Woodbridge.

"Take two and get to bed," Keith said. "Is this clean water?" There was a tin mug on the desk. Bill took it from him.

"Would you mind staying? Just till I get to sleep. Can't face being alone, right now."

"Sure I'll stay." He sat on the abandoned bed. Bill distractedly straightened the other and lay down on top of it.

"We're being a terrible nuisance," he said.

"No."

Nor is "we" any longer the right word. Nuisance does not begin to describe what you are being. But it's not your fault, it's mine. I should never have told anyone where I was going.

After a while the mumbling voice burbled into steady breathing. Keith watched a few minutes longer, then leaned over and shook the other man roughly; no reaction.

He went into the corridor and stood looking out over the courtyard garden from the open double doors. In his pocket was the little pill bottle taken from Soames's medical kit. How well-prepared he had been for the hazards of Central Asia – he had even packed malaria tablets – forewarned about all the health-hazards bar one: Qantoum.

Twelve

In the quiet garden small birds hopped and foraged along Kijé's neat vegetable rows. Then he heard voices, voices and footsteps, as he had done before; a number of people, a large number by local standards, passing in the street. Had Kijé been wrong? Were the Sturyat breaking their habit and marching on Control Point E?

Pausing only to look in on the sleeping man he hurried down the corridor through the tool room and out on to the steps of the office. A knot of people, two dozen perhaps, was coming up Oktyabrskaya from the station. At first sight they bore a distinct resemblance to the people of his dream, long haired, long robed, draped in gauzy cottons, but all of them were trussed into backpacks like his own, like the ones in the room where Woodbridge was sleeping. They had come from the west.

He ran out into the road, arms spread ridiculously, like a scarecrow, like a policeman on point duty, shouting, "No! Go back! Go Back!"

They shuffled to a halt, gaping at him. A voice in the mass murmured, "Heavy, man."

Someone at the front stepped forward. "Are you the pigs, man? Like, we understood there'd be no one here."

"There is no one here."

"Fine," someone else said. "Then No One won't mind if we come in. Great guy, No One."

"What are you looking for?" Keith said. "What do you want?"

"This is Qantoum?"

"Yes, but—"

"That's what we want. We're just following directions."

"What directions?"

"Come to Qantoum at the end of a thousand years and see the black sun."

"There isn't any black sun."

"We can wait."

The phrase mocked him. Qantoum was already a place of people who waited. "Why come here? There's one in Cornwall next month."

"Oh, you know British eclipses. English summer; heavy cloud; thunderstorms."

"Snow," a voice intoned in the mass.

"*Tempests.* Anyway, *this* is the Eclipse of the Century. We want a front seat, man. There's going to be large numbers. Throngs."

"There isn't going to be an eclipse."

"Now, the fat cats and the in-flu-ent-ial persons will be stacked up in the Tashkent Hilton, but the people will be here. We are the people. This is the People's Eclipse."

"There aren't any hotels, shops. No electricity."

"Heaven, baby."

"Did you walk from the junction?"

"Hey no, man. We flew."

"And what have you seen? This town is derelict. Didn't you notice? There's no one here."

"That No One again. Take us to him."

"*You're* here," the man at the front said, with a flash of lucidity.

"It's not safe. You don't know what you're letting your-selves in for. There's a minefield."

Not even that had any effect. They were on the move again, surging past him in a cloud of patchouli and herbal smoke. He could do nothing except skip alongside them, snapping at their heels like a terrier ignored by cattle. Instead he stood and watched their retreating backs as they pro-ceeded into the curve of Oktyabrskaya.

"Where are you *going*? What do you think you'll find?"

"Nirvana."

His immediate impulse was to forestall them, to get out to the border and warn Kijé who was either in the midst of his grave-digging or searching for Fitz. Dare he leave Woodbridge who had appeared deeply asleep but might wake at any moment, had perhaps only been faking and was planning even now to evade his minder?

He stared after the dwindling group. Musical notes drifted towards him. One of them had a guitar. He ought to have approached them calmly, diverted them, invited them into

Dunkillin for tea. If they followed Oktyabrskaya they would come to the Registan, where they would be observed by the Sturyat in the market, who would welcome them eagerly, matter-of-factly, more portents from the west. He could issue all the warnings in the world; they would respond only to the siren calls of the Sturyat. Perhaps the Sturyat knew they were coming. Neglecting her duties at the museum, Zayu might have been on the roof with her binoculars.

He went indoors and returned to the bedroom. Woodbridge was sleeping soundly, not faking. Suppose he did do a runner, would the loss of one more foreigner matter in the light of what was likely to come?

On the back of Kijé's note he wrote a message explaining Bill's whereabouts, and pinned it to the door of the tool room where Kijé would be sure to see it. He added underneath, *We have more visitors. Stoned out of their brains*. Then he left; there was someone in the museum who needed much more urgently to be apprised of the situation.

The Refreshment Room still smelled lingeringly of food and the rare insistent odour of the coffee they had drunk only a few hours ago, after Soames's disappearance was discovered, before his death had been confirmed, before Keith had found Bordeleau's camera in Zayu's roof.

The customers had left to go about their business, their impersonations of people with business to go about. The tables were cleared but unwiped, chairs pushed together in a perfunctory manner. Either Zayu's mind had been on other things or she had decamped, leaving Lizaveta to do her waitressing alone. A faint clattering caught his attention. For the first time he opened the door behind the bar. The room on the other side was a kitchen. The heat struck him, radiating from a sarcophagus-sized stove along one side, where large pans stood. A scrubbed wooden table of similar proportions filled the middle of the room. Beyond it, by a small, heavily barred window, Mrs Fahrenheit stood, sleeves rolled up, washing dishes in a galvanized tub that stood in a shallow stoneware sink.

She looked over her shoulder at him. "Bad news?"

"How do you know?"

"You carry it like a banner. What has happened?"

"Have you seen Fitz?"

"Not since he left with you this morning. Has anything happened to him?"

"I hope not. Look, there are things you ought to know. I have to be quick, I left Woodbridge alone. He's asleep, sedatives. He won't wake yet, but I ought to go back. First of all, Soames is dead."

"Who?"

"The second man. Kijé found his body in the minefield. He's burying him there. The other thing is much worse. After I left here this morning I went and searched Zayu's house. Where is she?"

"I have no idea. You took a great risk."

"Bordeleau, the Canadian, had a camera. It's hidden in her room. Whatever happened to him, she must know something about it."

Mrs Fahrenheit, carrying a plate between sink and draining board, halted in mid-movement, holding the plate aloft while suds dribbled down her arm.

"Does Kijé know?"

"I haven't had the chance to tell him. But there are more people arriving. I've just spoken to them."

She slowly inserted the plate into the wooden rack that overhung the draining board. "What kind of people? More astronomers?"

"New Agers."

"What?"

"Like hippies." She must have heard of hippies.

"Do such things still exist?"

"Neo-hippies. I tried to turn them back but they wouldn't listen. They've come looking for the black sun."

"Your followers," she said. "Where have they gone?"

"They were heading for the Registan – they'll meet the Sturyat."

"Who will greet them with open arms, no doubt. How many?"

"Twenty, two dozen, I didn't count."

"Twenty people can hardly disappear without trace, I think."

"I'm not bothered about *them*," Keith said. "It was you I was thinking of."

"I?"

"The soul stones. Can't you move the bones out front? You once said—"

"Let us see what happens," Mrs Fahrenheit soothed him. "Nothing happens quickly, here."

"That may change. What about Zayu; Bordeleau's camera?"

"Say nothing to her. Remember, the Sturyat are not good at recognizing deception, unless it is their deception."

"What do you want me to do?"

"Go back to what's-his-name, Woodbridge. Wait for Fitz and Kijé. If they come here I will warn them."

"But what about you?"

"Do not worry about me," the widow said. "Yet."

When he returned the note was still on the door, Woodbridge still deeply asleep. Keith sat in the office with the door wedged open, listening, expecting at any moment to hear the tramping of feet coming up from the station. He tried to remember the timetables that were stowed away somewhere in his luggage. Two trains a day in each direction; from the north, one that reached the junction just after noon, the one that he had caught; another arriving in the small hours which had delivered Soames, Woodbridge and Bordeleau. In between were two going the other way. On which had the latest mob arrived? They could have been floating along the line for hours. They seemed as indifferent to the heat as the Sturyat were. Let them boil their brains, if they had any.

When the footsteps came there were only two. Fitz stood in the doorway.

"You didn't blow yourself up then?"

"Where's Bill?"

"He's taken sleeping pills, he'll be out for hours. Fitz, more people have arrived."

"We saw them," Fitz said. He was carrying the spade and went through to the tool room to put it away.

"Where have they gone?"

"They didn't go anywhere. They're camping with the Sturyat."

"Did you speak to them?"

"No. We went up the watch-tower and saw them. Kijé's gone to tell Ernie."

"I already did that."

"He wasn't to know. He says it might be as well if we all go down to the museum tonight." Fitz walked behind the desk and opened the bottom drawer of the filing cabinet, T–Z. "Better get the watering done first."

Keith wondered what, exactly, Kijé had said to Fitz, and how he had said it. He had never overheard them talking privately to each other. Did Kijé adopt Fitz's attitude that everything was normal, as the only way to get through to him, or did he expend urgency on trying to pierce that bland exterior? Was there anything left in Fitz's battle-addled mind to react to urgency?

"Do you have any immediate plans?" he said.

"The watering."

"And then you'll go down to the museum with Bill?"

"Yes. Before dark."

"I'll see you there, then." He started to leave. "I've told Bill that Soames is dead. He didn't really take it in. Be careful what you say to him."

"Of course." Fitz looked on the way to being affronted. "I'm not stupid."

A worrying thought struck Keith. "Have you got a gun?"

Fitz was reaching for the watering can. "Kijé took it away."

His house lay as he had left it. Down below, the few utensils, his pathetic attempts at housekeeping, mocked him from the shelf. How snug his little future had seemed those short weeks ago; how pleased with himself he had been, settling in among the Sturyat, making friends, entertained by the charming eccentrics who haunted the museum.

From the pocket of his backpack he took the writing block where he had made his first patronizing observations about Qantoum, his attempts to make sense of what was happening. The timetables were in the same pocket. He was about to take them out when he heard a sound above him, footsteps on the roof. Zayu was up there, watching perhaps, always anxious to be the first to see strangers from the west. So long as no one comes out of the east, he thought vaguely, we are safe, but he was already on his feet, moving towards the inner staircase. He went down, opened the door into the courtyard, made his emergency exit through the house on the left and round to her staircase. Then he ran, stamping, up the first flight, and hammered on the door. "Zayu! Zayu!"

He heard her coming, across the rooftop, and was ready with a huge smile.

"Great news, Zayu. More visitors from the west."

"They are with us already," Zayu said, making a rare effort to recover her self-assurance. "They sit at our firesides. There will be a Spelling soon. We will tell them of our soul stones."

"But what of the others?" he said. "What of the first three who came out of the west? Kijé is burying one of them right now."

That shook her. She could not conceal it. She did not know what had happened to Soames, she thought she was talking about Bordeleau.

"How can he be buried? He went out into the desert. The sand got him."

"No, Zayu. A mine got him. He died early this morning."

He could see her mind working, writhing like a cut worm. Which? What? *How?*

"I'm not talking about the man with the camera, Zayu. It is the second man that Kijé found. But why couldn't he have found the first? If Bordeleau ran out into the sand he might well have stepped on a mine, but he didn't, did he? *Did he?*"

"The sand got him. He flung off his clothes. He ran—"

"Who saw him?"

"No one saw him. The clothes were found. No one ever sees – the sand sings in the darkness."

"And the rest of his clothes. Gresk brought a shirt and trousers. He was wearing more than that. He had a *camera*."

"The sand got him," Zayu muttered sullenly. It never crossed her mind that he might know where the camera was, that he had passed the bones and searched her room. But even as she lowered her head he saw her eyes flickering, teeth gnawing at her lower lip. "I never saw him," she said. "After on the roof, I never saw him."

"But you have the camera." He had not meant to say it, to say anything yet, but her obstinacy maddened him. *Anything I say three times is true.*

"I have no camera. Look!" She threw the door open. The dangling bones lurched in the draught. "What would I do with a camera? See, where is it?"

She swirled about the shadowy room, waving, pointing. Noting her panic he let her rant. For once he had the upper hand. He knew what she had hidden in the rafters; she did not know that he knew.

"May I pass the bones?"

"Yes. Enter. Search." She dragged aside the mattress from the sleeping platform and pulled out a loose plank. How had he missed that? "See? Put your hand in. There is nothing."

Content to play along he stooped and scythed his arm this way and that beneath the platform.

"See? Nothing. My box."

It was still standing by the platform. She heaved it over, opened the hasp, the lid swung and the contents flopped heavily out. She sprang on to the heap, stirring it like a pudding.

"I believe you," he said, standing up, and casually steadied himself by resting his hands on the rafter. His attitude, seemingly hanging from the beam, as if from a crucifix, drew her eyes in horrified fascination. There was something more here than guilt. The obvious Sturyat response to his questions would have been simple denial, the customary cold-blooded deceit.

"Where do you keep your gun, Zayu?"

"I have no gun. I do not bear arms."

"You told me you had your father's rifle."

"Ach, that. It is not here. It is with my stone, in the house of Theps."

He began to pat softly on the rafter with the flats of his fingers. He felt the loose flaps of sacking. All it would take would be a gentle nudge.

"You came here because we sent for you. Theps has given you food, you have spoken at our Spelling. Why do you talk now like a visitor?"

"Because you are treating me like one," he said, and making scissors of two fingers he gave the sacking a tweak. Bordeleau's camera pivoted, he saw it teeter with the tail of his eye, then it fell. Zayu leaped back against the wall.

"A rat!"

"No, it isn't a rat."

"A dead rat, stiff; see its tail."

For a second he almost believed her, almost believed what she claimed to believe. In the semi-darkness the camera might indeed have been a dead rat.

"It's a camera, Zayu. You know *photograph*."

"I know camera."

"Where did you get it?"

"I do not know how—"

"Where's Bordeleau?"

"I do not know."

"You do know!" He let go of the beam and hurled himself at her, pushing her back against the wall and pinning her wrists when he saw, as her coat swung open, the knife in her belt. "You killed him, didn't you?"

"I never saw him."

"You did see him. You killed him. I know you did."

He ought to have said it sooner instead of wasting time with questions. She collapsed instantly and hung from his hands, gasping.

"Why? What did he do? Did he attack you? Was it self-defence?"

"What is that?"

"Did you kill him to stop him killing you?"

"He had been sent to find me."

He propelled her to the sleeping platform and lowered her carefully until she sat on the rumpled quilt, crouching beside her, still holding her arms.

"Zayu, no, he wasn't sent to find you. No one sent him. He came with the others because he was curious about the black sun. If anyone is responsible for his coming here it's me, because I left a message to say where I'd gone; but it wasn't a message to *him*. It was sheer chance that he came."

"He was looking for me. Tcherk sent him."

"What?"

"I met him among the apricot trees. He spoke to me. He asked my name. I told it to him. He said that he had spoken to

Tcherk. He said Tcherk had told him that I would be waiting for him."

"That's impossible. Tcherk's dead. You told me so yourself, the sand got him, years ago. That means he's dead, doesn't it?"

"He is dead."

"But it wasn't the sand?"

"He had offended us. He had to die. The sand got him."

"I know, it was a terrible offence – the worst."

"But he was a visitor, he had no soul stone. So now his spirit wanders and seeks revenge. Then comes this man with a camera, who knows my name and tells me that Tcherk sent him."

"But *you* didn't kill Tcherk. Why should he be revenged on you?"

"He knew my name," Zayu repeated. "He said, 'Acting Captain Tcherk says you will be waiting for me.' So I cut his throat before he could take me to Tcherk."

The combined explanation hit him all at once. Soames being polite to an officer: *You speak excellent English, Captain Tcherk.* He had found it amusing, as no doubt Kijé had found his selfsame mistake amusing. But how could he begin to explain to Zayu?

"Have you ever been to Control Point E – where Fitz and Kijé live?"

"No."

He could not be sure even of that. "There's a sign on the wall, with Tcherk's name on it. It's been there for years. Those men thought I was Tcherk. I told them about you."

"He was sent by Tcherk." There was to be no arguing with her.

"Where is he now?"

"I do not know. In the ground."

"Who buried him?"

"I do not know. I cried out. Others came. I told them he was sent by Tcherk. They finished him."

"And won't *his* spirit wander the earth, seeking vengeance?"

"Yes, forever in the desert, crying at sunset. But we shall soon leave this place." She brightened. "Then Qantoum will be a place of spirits, wandering and howling in the desert like wolves."

"And where is Tcherk buried?"

"Tcherk is not buried." She stood up, disengaging her wrists, and went over to the door, pulling it open. The invitation to leave was unmistakable. He did not wish to decline it. As he went out past her she laid her hand on the hanging bag of bones. "Tcherk."

Keith sat in his room on the closed trap above the stairs and heard Zayu, light-footed on the roof, unburdened by fear or shame or guilt. She had lied about Bordeleau's death, as had Streph and the Goat Woman, because the Sturyat knew from long experience that visitors could bear very little truth. All his questions had done was to revive her fear of Tcherk, not fear of being found out. They were all going to go away, leaving their guilty consciences behind them. It was Kijé who had used the term "guilty consciences". He had been wrong about that. They did not feel guilty.

On the other hand, *he* did. If he left Qantoum now his conscience would accompany him, reminding him of how he had blundered in and upset the delicate balance of life maintained on the lip of a precipice. Bordeleau was dead because of his foolish impersonation, Soames was dead because he had gone to search for his friend, and they were both dead because of his ridiculous message that was now luring the innocent, the idiotic, the sceptical and the credulous alike to this godforsaken place. He could not walk away from what he had set in motion, leaving Kijé and the widow, Fitz and Maisie and Szusko and the rest of the Qantoumis to face the consequences. Whatever dubious reasons they might have for being in Qantoum, who was he to visit retribution on them?

He would follow Kijé's advice and sleep at the museum; and tonight he would have to tell Kijé all that he knew, starting with what he had discovered about Bordeleau and Tcherk, ending with the most ominous thing of all: that with the onset of the influx from the west the Sturyat were convinced that their time in Qantoum was drawing to a close. If others, never mind how, started arriving from the east, then there would be only one impediment to their departure: the failure to recover the soul stones which they believed unequivocally to be hidden in the museum.

When he arrived it was still quite early. The usual sounds of conversation drifted from the Refreshment Room. The accordion groaned companionably to the tentative notes of the guitar.

Keith went the other way, to the Archaeology Gallery. Yesterday, waiting for Mrs Fahrenheit, he had been reading Prince Andrei's contribution to the history of his adopted town. There had been a few pictures; he remembered seeing them as he leafed through it. It still lay open where he had left it, face down on the display cabinet beside the skeleton who was not Prince Andrei. Now he turned to the illustrations at once. Prince Andrei had not been a gifted artist but his portraits of the Sturyat were affectionate and thus a more accurate record than the surly low-brows depicted by the more skilled hand of Lord Dacre. Conversely, Lord Dacre might well have come closer to capturing the inner Sturyat, as it were. On the next page was a row of small dark roughly spherical objects, laboriously drawn and shaded with cross-hatching.

Coprolites, Kijé had suggested: fossilized shit. They certainly looked as if they might be fossils, trilobites, dinosaur eggs, even. That would fit the theory of an eastern point of origin. Dinosaur eggs had been found in the Gobi.

Prince Andrei had not thought so, however. He had simply called them what the Sturyat called them: soul stones. If he could get a glimpse of even one, by whatever means, he would at least know what they were looking for, might be able to organize a search, create fakes. For a time was surely coming when people would arrive in Qantoum who had no fear of bones. He knew now why the Sturyat were happy to lie to him. Prompted by Theps they must have supposed that he was to be the one who would breach the taboo on their behalf, and he had failed them. He had made no move. He had admittedly concealed their belief in him from the widow for a time, but they did not know that and probably did not care. They would care even less now that others were arriving. Find us our stones, they would say. Bones would be powerless, whoever that anonymous representative of *Homo sapiens* might be, hanging from his coat hook.

Kijé had come in and was standing behind him. "What are you doing?"

"Looking something up," Keith said. "Look, have you *any* idea where those stones might be?"

"No one has, particularly not I," Kijé said. "Why should I know? I came here to prevent a blood bath, so I was told. I'm not a historian."

"What are you, then?" Kijé did not answer. "I know what happened to Bordeleau. You'd better decide who else should know. Zayu cut his throat."

"He attacked her?"

"He didn't do anything, but he said that Acting Captain Tcherk had sent him to find her. He was just making conversation."

"Tcherk? What did he know about Tcherk?"

"Nothing. You remember that first day I came here, I thought you were Tcherk. He thought *I* was. He wasn't to know – and neither was I – that if Zayu met anyone who had spoken to her father in the last few hours she'd be scared witless. She thought the spirit of Tcherk had sent Bordeleau to fetch her, and she screamed. We heard the scream. Twins, remember? Perhaps he tried to calm her, or panicked and tried to shut her up, I don't know. But she killed him."

"How do you know that?"

"She told me," Keith said. "She says she doesn't know where the body is now. That may be true, but she has his camera."

"The sand got him," Kijé said, tonelessly. He walked the full length of the gallery and back before he spoke again. "That other one, Woodbridge, wants to leave. What will happen when he gets home? When it is known what has happened. I can't force him to stay, can I? How many dozens, hundreds are coming here to find your black sun? How many are the Sturyat expecting?"

"How can I tell?" Keith said, wretchedly. "I never expected *anyone* to follow. I thought I would come here, look around, go back."

"You ought to have gone back. I ought to have sent you back." He set off on another tour of the display cases. Keith had never seen anyone *thinking* so violently before; it was almost embarrassing to watch. He turned and stared towards the rotunda where Fitz and Bill Woodbridge were just coming in from the street. They went down the corridor to the Refreshment Room.

Kijé was back again. "What have you told Fitz?"

"Nothing," Keith said. "I've been running around all day looking for you, looking for him. And that's another thing; the bones that Zayu keeps hanging in her doorway: Tcherk."

"For a man ten years dead he exerts a powerful influence," Kijé said.

So early in the evening the bar was empty except for Fitz and Woodbridge, the latter still a little bleary-eyed.

"You still want to go home?" Kijé said.

"I must. Awful leaving Jacques like this . . . not knowing . . . can you arrange it?"

"Yes," Kijé said, becoming suddenly decisive. "You can leave tonight. When you return you may be fined for over-staying your three days, but not very much, by Western standards. Then you had better go to your embassy. I think there is one in Tashkent."

"Yunisabad," Keith said.

"God knows what they will be able to do; perhaps send a representative here. This is a dangerous region, still in fer-ment. I doubt if anyone will be able to do anything."

Keith, about to butt in, remembered in time that so far only he and Kijé knew the exact truth, the inexact truth. As far as Bill was concerned, both of his friends had vanished into the desert of their own volition. Probably that was indeed what had happened to Soames; better he went on thinking it of Bordeleau, also.

"You've all been very kind," Bill said. "And Kijé – sorry, is that your first name or your surname? Seems so formal. . ."

Kijé gave him an odd look, his bitten-back smile again. "Kijé will do."

"Like Morse."

"Eh?"

Mrs Fahrenheit joined them. "Have you come to any decision?"

"Mr Woodbridge is going back to Tashkent," Kijé said. "He has slept all day. He can leave tonight."

"According to my timetable, there's a train north at 3 a.m.," Keith said.

"And will you also be on it?" Mrs Fahrenheit said.

"No. I'm staying. How could I walk out on all this?"

"Very easily, I would have thought," Kijé said.

"I'll go with him to the junction. Then I'll come back," Keith said.

"Come and have something to eat," Mrs Fahrenheit said. "In the kitchen, you can be private there. Then go back with Fitz for your luggage."

Fitz and Woodbridge followed her through the door behind the bar. When it had closed behind them Kijé turned to Keith. "Why do you want to go to the junction?"

"We can't just leave him to it – not after all he's been through."

"Very thoughtful of you. Now, be honest, please. If you go to the junction with Woodbridge tonight, will you come back? Or will you get on that train to Tashkent?"

"I'll come back. Didn't I just say I wouldn't leave? I *will* come back."

"Then there's no point in your going. I'll do it."

"I'd rather—"

"No. You are quite sure that you don't want to go home?"

"Quite sure."

"Then don't argue. 3 a.m. – we should leave at 10. Walking will be easy in the moonlight. I can be back by 8 at the latest, before it gets too hot."

"I suppose *you* won't get on the train to Tashkent?"

"Is that a joke?" Kijé said. "Now, if I do not sleep, I shall die. Four hours. You and Fitz will have to watch here, tonight."

"Are you going to tell her – Ernie – about Bordeleau?"

"Yes. I'll leave you to fill in the details. Tomorrow, collect your belongings and move into the museum."

"Move in – to live? What about Zayu?"

"What about her?"

"She found me that house. She might be offended."

"She doesn't need to be offended," Kijé said. "Two days ago she killed an unarmed man because she thought he'd been talking to spirits. Then she went off to work as usual. Tomorrow she may kill somebody else, possibly you, if you give her what she thinks is a reason. Move out."

By 9.30 the bar was humming and thumping as it did on any evening. Keith wondered if word of the events of the last three days had got around; if so the hectic gaiety must represent a more determined effort than usual to keep out the darkness. Fitz and Woodbridge had gone to Dunkillin and returned with two backpacks.

"Whose?" Keith said, eyeing the second.

"We've divided up Jacques's and Tony's gear. I'll take back what I can – not the photographic stuff, it's too heavy. You'll have to look after it until someone comes to collect."

"Kijé can carry it to the junction," Fitz said. "There'll be someone to help at the other end; porters, you know. . ."

"You'd better go and wake him," Mrs Fahrenheit said. "He's in the cellar. Take him coffee, he'll need it. On the kitchen table."

Fitz went through the door behind the bar and returned a few minutes later. The widow looked up in alarm.

"What's wrong?"

"Nothing, Ernie, but he's dead to the world. It seemed a crime to wake him, he was up all last night and most of the one before. I'll go with Bill."

Mrs Fahrenheit looked doubtful. "Do you think that's wise? If he'd wanted you to go he'd have suggested it himself."

"He just wanted to save my poor old feet," Fitz said, foolishly. "Let him sleep, Ernie. He's curled up like a baby."

"Babies do not curl up," the widow said. "You are thinking of a foetus."

"I'll go," Keith said. "It was my idea in the first place."

"You stay put. I know my way about," Fitz said. "I *do*," he added, petulantly, seeing their faces. "Anyway, I've got this."

"This" was Kijé's pistol.

"Does he know you've got it?" Mrs Fahrenheit said.

"Of course not. I'll be back before he finds out. Are you ready, Bill? Look, Ernie's made us sandwiches."

They might have been going on a school outing. Keith accompanied them to the door. He would have offered to walk a little way with them, but with Kijé asleep, and in the cellar, he felt a kind of obligation to stay in the museum.

"Which way are you going?"

Fitz was putting on the second pack. "Through the barracks – quickest. Don't worry, I'll come straight back."

Keith shook hands wordlessly with Bill Woodbridge.

"I'll never forget how good you've been," Woodbridge said, leaving Keith with the thought that he was easily satisfied. He stood on the steps and watched them walk away.

Thirteen

For whatever reason the party broke up shortly after midnight. Keith sat on in the Refreshment Room, watching the stragglers leave, followed by the dog and its friend which, retaining the pack instinct, liked to be last out, herding the rest. Mrs Fahrenheit returned from seeing them out. He had been waiting all evening for a moment alone with her. She regarded him across the room from the doorway.

"Kijé told me."

"About Bordeleau?"

"And Zayu. Yes."

"What are you going to do about her coming here? She must have known I'd tell you."

"I do not think that will trouble her in the slightest." She leaned on the bar. "I ought to have woken Kijé myself."

"I don't know how he can sleep through that racket anyway."

"He's not slept much at all, recently, and the cellars are deep. But I think he will not be pleased when he finds out what Fitz has done."

"He likes to have his own way?"

"For excellent reasons, as you must know," she answered sharply. "As I said, if he'd wanted Fitz to go to the junction he'd have sent him."

"Well, he can't get lost, can he? All he has to do is follow the rails there and back." *He scarcely knows his way around the garden.* "Let Kijé sleep," he said. "I'll sit up tonight. I don't have a weapon, though."

"It doesn't matter. I myself don't expect a sudden attack. Kijé's the one who insists on sentry duty."

"He thinks I ought to move in here," Keith said. "Would you mind?"

"Not at all. I'm hardly short of space."

He went into the Zherdin Collection and sat on the folding bed, back propped against a display case, conscious of the mermaid, leering near by. Ought he to have accepted Kijé's invitation to leave? He could still scarcely be said to fit in here. His discovery of Bordeleau's murder and Zayu's part in it had left him reeling. Kijé and the widow behaved as though she had owned up to breaking a window. The revelation about what she kept hanging in her doorway had done nothing more to Kijé than provoke one of his peculiar half-smiles as if the joke was too esoteric to be shared with anyone else. Mrs Fahrenheit was more worried about what Kijé would say when he discovered that Fitz had gone walkies without permission than she was about the news that her waitress was a murderer.

He did not know what system of measurement was used here.

1 a.m. They must be more than halfway to the junction by now. He pictured them striding in the moonlight towards the rendezvous with the north-bound train. Surely Fitz would have the nous to return safely or did Kijé suspect that he would become confused and follow the line south, never noticing until, some days hence, he wandered into the concrete suburbs of Iskanderabad?

At intervals throughout the night he checked his watch. The train would be arriving now . . . now Fitz would be starting back, walking faster since he had nothing to carry . . . he'd be in sight of Industrial by now. . .

5.30. Down in the cellar Kijé must still be asleep. Keith had not yet seen the cellars and imagined him wedged between old tea chests and cobwebs. With luck he would not wake up until Fitz got back and he could do his own explaining.

He went along to the Refreshment Room and heard sounds behind the door to the kitchen. Mrs Fahrenheit was sitting at the table, elbows propped, drinking tea from a bowl which she held in both hands. She smiled at him through the steam.

"Where's Kijé?"

"Still asleep, I suppose. Fitz will be back soon. He can wake him up."

"That's what I thought." They shared one idea, at least.

"Pour yourself some tea." He sat down opposite her to drink it.

"Now," she said, "I think you mentioned moving in here. You would like to see the room?"

"I thought the Zherdin Collection."

"That will hardly do for every night. Prince Andrei had his own apartments here – he lived over the shop, as you might say. Would you like his rooms? You might have to share them, one day."

"If it turns out that everyone needs a refuge?"

"Possibly. Come along." She rose and led the way into the next room.

This was actually where she lived, it seemed; there was a bed, a walk-in cupboard with the door ajar, where he could see clothes hanging; a comfortable armchair, and shelves of books. On the window-sills a red geranium bloomed. The window was barred by an expanding grille and through the diamonds he could see into a small dank yard, the kind of place where people keep dustbins. It was stacked with coal, brushwood and a platoon of red gas bottles.

They went through and along a corridor with doors on either side.

"What are these?"

"Storerooms, offices; desks and files; exhibits that were not on display."

"Could the stones be here?"

"Once, perhaps. Do not imagine that I haven't searched. We are behind the Zherdin Collection, now." She opened a heavy door where stairs rose in darkness. Keith followed her up and she opened another door at the top. Like his gallery, Prince Andrei's quarters were lit from above, the cloudy light revealing a room lined with plan presses. Beyond it was another, smaller chamber, hung with spider webs and mosquito netting in about equal proportions. In one wall a small window looked down, not over the landscape outside but into the gallery from where, Keith assumed, the prince had kept watch over his collection.

"He was a soldier to the last," Mrs Fahrenheit said. "Inside all that netting is nothing more than a camp-bed. Perhaps you read in his memoirs that after years of campaigning in the most austere conditions – by which I imagine he meant a tent – he never again felt comfortable in a bed. Will you be comfortable here?"

"Yes. Very."

"Go and fetch your luggage, then."

He watched her leave, understanding why Bill Woodbridge had thought she ran an hotel. She would surely be happier running an hotel.

He walked through the still quiet streets, through the alleys to his house where, dark against the new morning, Zayu stood like a little statue on the roof, binoculars at her side.

"See anything?" he called up.

She looked down. "Not now."

That could mean "not any more" or "not yet". Fitz must have reached the Industrial sector already, and in any case, she could never have identified him at that distance, even with her superior eyesight and the glasses.

"But more will come," Zayu said. Yesterday's confrontation might never have happened, the discovery of the camera, the interrogation, the confession, the grisly whereabouts of Acting

Captain Tcherk; or, rather, it had happened and now something else was happening. Yesterday's events were of no further significance.

"Will I see you later at the museum?" he said.

"Of course. I will always come to the museum."

"Till when?"

"Till we return where we came from."

"I'll see you later, then," he said.

My first murderer, he thought as he went in at his door, but there was no vicarious thrill in it. As far as Zayu was concerned she had done what needed doing; the Sturyat had a long history of responding to expediency.

He swept his clothes together from their hooks and stuffed them into his backpack, rolled blankets and cotton quilt into the sleeping-bag. He went down to fetch the kitchenware he had bought in the market; Mrs Fahrenheit could make use of it. Then he slung everything about his person and went out quietly, not wanting to alert Zayu to his departure. Not that she was likely to care but he still felt a certain delicacy about walking out on her even if she were likely to knife him without a second thought if it should seem desirable.

He was halfway to Museum Street before he remembered the leather, the thing he had been using as a shelf. He would have to sneak back for it later; his arms and hands were full; but as he havered in the alley someone came round the corner ahead of him so suddenly that he almost dropped his armful of luggage. It was not a Sturyat, nor one of the museum crowd, but a stranger, neatly dressed in a light blue track suit with white stripes down the legs. He stopped in front of Keith with heel-clicking precision although he was wearing dusty trainers that squealed on the pavement.

"Good morning," he said. "I seem to have missed my way. I'd be glad if you could give me directions to the market-place. May angels guide you."

Keith stared at him, recovered himself and found his voice.

"Good morning. Yes. This way. Follow me."

The market was very close to where they were standing. Keith had forgotten how easy it was to become instantly lost in the Old Town. One alley, two corners, brought them out into the broad street where the traders were beginning to assemble. There was scarcely time to wonder where this apparition had sprung from, but he was not alone. Standing in a group were more track suits carrying identical shoulder-bags of the kind distributed by language schools. They might have stepped out of a tour bus. A young man detached him-self from the group and approached. He was dressed like all the others but had a transparent perspex crucifix hanging around his neck.

"Good morning," he said. "Thank you for delivering our brother. May I know your name?"

"Keith Chapman."

"Angels guide you, Keith. Are you here for the black sun?"

"No, I live here. And you?"

"We seek the truth," the man said, ominously. "I don't suppose you have heard of our organization, but soon the world—"

"How did you get here?"

The man looked faintly affronted. "In the only way possible at this moment in time. We took the train and walked from the junction."

"When did you arrive at the junction?"

"At 2 a.m., local time. It was an overnight train."

"Then you must have met – did you meet anyone on the way?"

"There was no one to greet us."

"No, I meant, as you walked towards Qantoum, did you pass anyone going the other way, towards the junction?"

"We met no one. Can you explain—?"

"Did you see anyone? Two men, carrying backpacks?"

"I told you, we saw no one, until we reached the main square."

"You didn't report to Control Point E?"

"We attempted to, but the place seemed to be locked up. I can assure you that we have all the necessary documentation—"

"I'm sure you have. Excuse me – speak to you later." He left the man standing and fled down the lane to Museum Street, staggering and blundering under his load.

As he reached the door Mrs Fahrenheit was crossing the rotunda. She did not see him until he dropped his pack on the floor. The jug, basin and mug rolled cacophonously in different directions. The plate spun. As she swung round he saw a look of hope in her eye that faded as she recognized him.

"Have you seen Fitz?"

"Is Kijé awake?"

She spread her hands. "He is angry, Keith. I've never seen him so angry."

"Because we didn't wake him up?"

"For letting Fitz go."

"Where is he?"

"Gone home. Five minutes ago – what's happening?"

"There are more strangers in town, in the market. They didn't meet anyone on the way. . ." He took off at a run. Let her work it out. He had to find Kijé.

From the top of Museum Street the long curve of Oktyabrskaya hid Control Point E. He slowed to a walk, anxious to find Kijé but reluctant to face him. Kijé angry was nothing special, but he kept his anger tightly buckled. He must have let the buckle out a notch, from what the widow had said in her distress. Keith, acknowledging himself to be the source of Kijé's present troubles, would have kept out of his way, but if he held back what he knew he would never be forgiven.

The door of the office was unlocked. Kijé was pacing the tiny space, three strides one way, three strides back, wheeling at the turn as if someone had tethered him on a short chain. When he saw Keith he stopped and stood breathing heavily. At last he said, "I suppose you think you were doing me a favour?"

"Me? How was I to know? You, Fitz, what difference did it make?" Kijé was grinding his teeth. His rage was fearful, but this was as far as he was going to let himself go. There would be no carpet-chewing. "I couldn't tell Fitz what to do. Why would he take any notice of me? Anyway, that's not why I came. Something may have happened. Fitz isn't here, is he?"

"No." Kijé was beginning to pay attention. "What has happened?"

"There's a whole new bunch of visitors in the market. They walked from the junction. *They didn't meet anyone.*"

"Who would they expect to meet?"

"Oh, Kijé. It's after 7. They ought to have passed Bill and Fitz on the way, but they didn't."

It began to sink in. "You mean they didn't see them? Are they like those others, stoned?"

"No, deadly respectable, religious. They were walking *up* the line. Fitz and Bill were walking *down* it. They *had* to pass each other at some point."

"How many did you speak to?"

"Only one. It makes no difference. You can see for miles out there."

"It was dark."

"Almost full moon."

"They must have turned back."

"Why aren't they here then? They'd have had to turn back within a couple of hours or this other lot would have seen them up ahead. They weren't at the museum. They aren't here."

"Cut through Industrial. . ."

"It won't work, Kijé. Even if they did turn back they'd be

here by now. What can have happened? What are we going to do?"

Turning from one catastrophe to the next, Kijé rallied.

"Go back to the museum and question them properly. I don't mean interrogation, just get more than one version. It's possible Fitz saw them coming, took cover, didn't want to . . . to. . ."

"Why should they hide? There's nowhere *to* hide out there unless you lie flat behind a bush."

"I know. Forget it. Did he tell you which way he was going?"

"Through the barracks."

"Right, I'll follow the line, see what I can find. Meet me at the Industrial Station when you've found out something. Go through the barracks as well."

"It'll be easier to cut through—"

"I want to know exactly the route you take," Kijé said. "*Exactly* the route. You may be watched."

"They may be watching for you."

"Well you know exactly my route too. One hour from now, Keith, at Industrial."

As he passed the open windows of the Refreshment Room he observed that there were far more customers than usually turned up for breakfast at the museum. When he entered the rotunda he saw why. Several of the blue track suits were in the Zherdin Collection, clustered round the miraculous shower of warts. In the Refreshment Room the rest of them were sitting at tables, eating, and chatting earnestly. It looked like the buffet at Paddington. Business seemed to be booming. Lizaveta was clearing tables, Zayu stood behind the bar – deal with her later. Meanwhile she was where he could see her. He scanned the customers, trying to identify the man he had spoken to before, but they all looked eerily similar, male and female, with neatly-cropped hair and plastic ID badges pinned to what he could only think of as executive track suits. They had a bespoke look about them; nothing simply fitted where it touched. Their trainers, though travel-stained, were Nikes. They were lean, fit, tanned, clean; their teeth white and regular as dentures.

He spotted the perspex crucifix and advanced. "I spoke to you just now."

"Why yes." The teeth smiled hospitably. "May angels guide you. I'd ask you to join us but we seem to have run out of chairs. I guess you are not accustomed to such large numbers."

"Not really, no. Just now I asked you if you met anyone on your way here."

"You did. And I explained that we saw no one until we came to the market. One of the salespersons told us we could eat at the museum. And here we are."

"This is very urgent," Keith said. "I know it was dark, but are you absolutely sure that you saw no one? I don't even mean met them. You can see for a long way on that track. As you walked—"

"We did not walk. We jogged. We jog for Jesus. We would

have been here sooner but we had a prayer meeting half-way."

"Eyes shut?"

"We would have noticed people passing us. In any case, we were stationary for no more than twenty minutes."

"So you would have seen anyone coming towards you, going away from you . . . hiding in the bushes?"

"I told you; we seek the truth; we speak the truth; we wreak the truth."

"*What?*"

"If we meet those who resist the truth, we wreak it – as one wreaks havoc," he explained, kindly. "Ask any of us, we will all tell you the same. We saw no one." He pointed to his lapel badge. "Brother Joel," he said. "We'll speak again. I shall need to know about accommodation. Angels guide you."

Keith walked to the bar, intercepting another track suit: Sister Alicia, by her badge.

"I'm looking for some friends of mine," he said. "Did you pass anyone while you were jogging from the junction?"

"I think you have already asked Joel that," she said, teeth glinting.

He wondered if he were up against some kind of a gestalt where they all tapped into each other's core consciousness.

"People see different things."

"We see the truth," Sister Alicia said. "Where the truth is, all perceive it equally – all those whose eyes have been opened. The truth is, we saw no one on the railroad. Angels guide you."

Mrs Fahrenheit came through from the kitchen with a tray of loaves.

"What is going on?" Keith said.

"They just came in and started asking for cottage cheese on rye and decaff, which appears to be a form of coffee with no coffee in it. As you see, they are eating *non* and drinking tea. People are wonderfully adaptable."

"Not this crew."

"They seem pleasant enough. Americans."

"Americans don't adapt. They bring Big Macs and Coca-Cola. You'll have golden arches over the door next."

"I remember when McDonald's opened in Moscow," Mrs Fahrenheit said. "Fast food. We queued for three hours."

"Ernie, listen, they came the usual way, up the railway line." He was aware of Zayu, apparently, but necessarily, occupied with a customer. "They didn't see Fitz and Bill. They'd have to have passed them, but they say they didn't. Either they're all lying, which seems fairly pointless, or the others never made it that far."

She set down the tray, heavily. "Fitz – lost?"

"Both of them. I told Kijé. The only thing I can think of is that they might have doubled back for some reason. He's gone down to Industrial. I'm meeting him there in half an hour."

Before he could stop her she turned to Zayu. "Were you up on your roof this morning? Did you see Fitz or Bill on the railway?"

"Who is Bill?"

"The man whose friends went into the desert," Keith said.

"No. I did not see." Zayu returned to her customer.

"These seekers of truth are going to have their work cut out with the Sturyat," Keith muttered to Mrs Fahrenheit. "This doesn't look good."

"Don't start worrying yet. Has Kijé forgiven us?"

"I don't know. You, I expect. I'm sure he has. What are you going to do?"

"As usual. Feed the hungry," she said. "When there is time to worry, I shall worry. There will be many more mouths. See, the regulars are beginning to arrive."

Just entering was Szusko, closely followed by the bear. In the ensuing consternation, Keith left.

He wanted to visit the market, enquire after the health of the twins, ask leading questions if only for the negative result of hearing lies, but he had promised Kijé to go through the barracks. "Watch my back," Kijé had said as they combed the Industrial wasteland for lost Bordeleau. From now on they would be watching each other's backs. How many backs would they have to watch?

The brick tunnels and chasms of the barracks generated their own darkness; it was like being lost in an endless underpass, but the only footsteps he heard were his, although he watched his own back, turning to look over his shoulder so often that he was proceeding in a series of tipsy gyrations, half dancing.

At the far side of Barracks Station he dropped to the track by the water tower. Qantoum Industrial Station was still some distance away but in the clear morning light he saw someone sitting on the boardwalk: Kijé. He hoped it was Kijé. Or could it be Fitz, Bill Woodbridge? He began to hurry.

It was Kijé. After a while he stood up and waved, a reassuring wave, he thought, not a warning, but he was passing the wreck of the industrial area now, the ruins, the bushes, the possibility of concealed watchers. Kijé was striding towards him, not running.

"Have you found anything?" Keith called, when they were within hailing distance.

Kijé replied loudly, oddly, "How good of you to come and meet me." Keith saw that he was carrying his rifle.

"Have you seen them?"

Kijé kept on coming, kept on shouting, waving with a lunatic cheerfulness.

"Not a sign of them! They must have got there in time after all!" When they were ten metres apart he lowered his voice and said, "Turn left and head for Vladimir Ilyich."

They simultaneously veered off the track, Kijé keeping up an over-loud, over-enthusiastic hymn to the efficiency of the railway. "Whatever else you say about Iskanderistan, the trains run on time."

"What are you talking about. Fitz caught the *train*. . .?"

When they reached Lenin Kijé vaulted on to the ankle and clambered rapidly to the shoulder. Keith sat on the unyielding waistcoat.

"What was all that shit in aid of? Why are we here?"

"For the view. Also I did not want to be seen turning back.

We have nothing to worry about. We have been seen not worrying. I have been heard not worrying. We will worry in private. What have you found out?"

"What is this about Fitz catching the train?"

"I walked along to Industrial Station, very casual, lost in thought. I have just seen something which catches my attention when who should come down the spur from the turntable but Theps himself. I take care not to notice him, naturally; I stroll to the boardwalk, sit down, with my back to what I have seen – not seeing it, you understand. I throw my coat over it and put down my rifle. I light a cigarette and a few minutes later I look up in surprise to see Theps coming alongside the platform.

"We greet each other. 'Where are you going?' he says, which in itself is surprising. Ordinarily the Sturyat do not care where we go, what we do. 'I am not going anywhere,' I tell him. This was clearly true, I was sitting down smoking. 'But last night two of our people went to the junction to catch a train. They left very late. I was afraid they might have missed it and would be walking back again, but as you can see there is no one coming or going.' The Sturyat do not know a great deal about trains or they would realize that people who miss a train they have walked thirty kilometres to catch will wait for the next one, not come home again. 'Ah, that is good,' says Theps, and for ten minutes we talk about nothing at all in a neighbourly fashion and then he went back the way he had come. He was not out of sight before I saw you, hence the extravagant welcome. So, you see, they knew that we had sent two people to the junction; they did not know that we expected one of them to come back. So they think that whatever happened here last night will remain undiscovered." Kijé was muttering now, in a frantic undertone. Keith broke in.

"What did happen here last night? What was it you'd seen?"

"It was under my coat. I did not want him to see it. I didn't want him to know I'd seen it. It had, after all, appeared in the dark. I don't think he knew it was there."

"*What was it?*"

"Blood," Kijé said, as though he thought Keith must have known all along. "Bloodstains, dry but still fresh. And on the little plants between the rails."

"No. Oh no."

"But yes. Do you think I cannot identify blood? I would guess that this is the last we shall hear of this matter; unless, next time the sand sings, Theps or Gresk will come to us solemnly bearing garments which they will have carefully washed."

Keith could not look at him. He would have cried, "Is that all you can say?" but it *was* all he could say.

"So, you understand," Kijé went on in his overcareful dictionary English, "it was very important to our well-being just now that we should be seen neither to be worried nor to be leaving. We are being watched, and if I had gone beyond the station very likely I should have got no farther. That's why we are sitting on V I Lenin. We can watch the watchers.

"I doubt if they knew it was Fitz," he added after a moment. "It was dark. Most of them can't tell us apart anyway."

"Kijé, I'm sorry. I'm so sorry." He reached out, unthinking, and took his hand. Kijé seemed not to notice, but his fingers crept away.

"He would have gone cheerfully to his death, not seeing the knife. I could never make him understand. And Woodbridge was in shock. He never knew what was happening anyway. But now the Sturyat feel safe again. The man who spoke to Tcherk is dead. The man who went to look for him is dead. The man who might have alerted outside interference is dead. Three dangerous people, by Sturyat reckoning, are no longer dangerous."

"If only we'd woken you up." Keith was thinking: Fitz is dead because he went with Woodbridge instead of me. I offered to go and Kijé wouldn't let me. Who is he hating more, me or himself? Me. I let him sleep while all this happened.

Keith said, "If you'd gone with Woodbridge, you would be dead instead of Fitz."

"Likewise you, if you had gone with him."

Keith had not thought of that. In spite of the warmth, Kijé was shivering.

"Something you must know. Woodbridge would have died anyway. Not where he did, farther along the track. How could I let him go back, knowing what he knew?"

"What are you saying?" He shivered too. He knew what Kijé was saying. "But if I'd gone with him. . .?"

"You also, if you had decided to go home. I should have met you both, on the railway . . . farther along. But you chose to stay."

"You'd have killed us both?"

"You would have gone home with stories of murder—"

"No."

"Ah, what would you have said about this interesting place? And Woodbridge – questions asked. What would that have brought down on us?"

"You would have killed *me*?"

"Better you than us. A hundred of us at least, maybe six hundred Sturyat."

"You want to save the Sturyat?"

"You want to see six hundred die for the sake of two?"

"Why should anyone die?"

"If people come here to investigate they will not come with flowers in their hands. Now, as far as anyone knows, those three men were never in Qantoum. They vanished in Uzbekistan. Let the Uzbeks take care of it."

"You're no better than Theps – Zayu – "

"Worse, I assure you, much worse."

"Yes. You'd kill your own side. What do you think will happen when all these other crazies arrive, looking for the black sun? There could be thousands. Won't they start wondering in Tashkent when all these people start getting on trains and never come back?"

"That won't happen yet."

"It's beginning to."

"The black sun, your black sun, will rise, set, whatever, in five months' time. By then we will have had time to work out how to survive. Iskanderabad may put a stop to it. Tashkent may put a stop to it. I had no time."

"You panicked."

"You can call it that if you like. But remember, please, in the end, I did not do anything. I was asleep."

He stood up and made his precarious way down the statue. Keith followed him, at a distance. Were they being watched? They skirted the peaceful Sturyat pasture where men and women tended the vegetables, picked fruit, and children played among the goats and fat-tailed sheep. Smoke rose gently from cooking fires.

"One of those bastards has my Makarov," Kijé said.

"Your what?"

"My pistol. Fitz took it."

"With all the fighting that went on here, they've probably got more than that."

"They prefer knives," Kijé said. "Quieter. If it makes you feel any better, they would have got me before I got Woodbridge."

The Joggers for Jesus had moved on. Kijé sat at his customary table, near the window, looking perfectly normal but emanating an aura of misery so powerful that within minutes the few remaining customers had also left, giving him a wide berth as if afraid that if they came too close they might turn black at the edges and curl up.

"Do you want a drink?" Keith asked, when they were alone.

"I want to get drunk, but this is not the moment. If you see Erna, tell her I'm in here, will you? Don't tell her anything else. I'll do that."

Keith left him slouched in the chair and went through the door to the kitchen. There was no one in it and no one answered when he knocked at the door of the private room behind. He hardly liked to go in, but the widow was not there. In the side corridor that ran alongside the Zherdin Collection he tried various doors. One on the left opened into the gallery, next to the two-headed sheep. In future he would use that as his own private entrance.

He went up the stairs to his new quarters. The mosquito curtains hung in folds and stirred slightly as he closed the door. From the window he looked down into the Zherdin Collection, and through the archway at his luggage still waiting in the rotunda where he had dropped it. After a minute or two Mrs Fahrenheit came into view through another door, almost immediately below him. He watched her walk slowly down the aisle, head bent under its heavy coronet of plaited hair, the blue smock hanging straight with regal simplicity from her shoulders. He almost fancied a train dragging along the floor behind her. She knew nothing yet, only that Fitz might be lost. She was never to know what Kijé had been planning. She never would have known; no one would. Kijé would have kept his horrible secret among all the others that haunted him. If ever a man had been hoist by his own petard it was Lt. Kijé, whose machinations had spectacularly back-fired and cost him his closest friend.

Suddenly he was standing in the archway. He was speaking. She looked up and saw him in front of her, and stopped. Kijé, still carrying his rifle, laid it across the cabinet containing the shrunken heads and the perforated skull, possibly a victim of Genghiz Khan. Keith could hear nothing through the glass; he needed to hear nothing. Kijé's desolation was plainly drawn in his stance, the droop of his head. Mrs Fahrenheit walked towards him, and took his hands. She put an arm around him, fingers pressing into his hair, and tried to draw his head against her shoulder, but he straightened up, spoke again, shaking his head; picked up the rifle and walked away, under the arch, out of the museum.

Keith moved away from the window and sat down, wishing he could comfort her, wishing, in spite of everything, that he could comfort Kijé, but he had no rights here, as her friend or his. He had forfeited any rights he might have had the moment he stood up at the Spelling and told the Sturyat why he had come to Qantoum.

Part Three

Fourteen

The mushrooms had become Keith's responsibility. Kijé could not bring himself to look at the filing cabinet, and Fitz's old camouflage jacket had disappeared from the tool room.

Kijé worked for two in the garden. He really did need Keith's help now, but neither of them was comfortable working alongside the other. Although there was much to say, they could not say it and they could not achieve the hours of companionable silence that had enabled Kijé to endure hours of Fitz's directionless blathering. Keith was uneasy alone with someone who, however disinterestedly, had been ready to kill him if it seemed necessary. Kijé was miserable in the company of the person he had been prepared to kill, in the absence of the one who had died instead. Keith, eyeing him nervously, called to mind the warning to skaters about ice: if it cracks it bears, if it bends it breaks. He waited for him to break, and hoped he would not be there when it happened.

Had it not been for this he would have offered to move in to Dunkillin, partly to ease Kijé's loneliness, partly for convenience. On the other hand it was better for him to be at the museum every night, whether he stood watch or not. And when he did not it was a comfort to know that one of the others was awake and alert in the Zherdin Collection, or the corridor: Usman the guitarist, red-haired Vlodya from the Lada stall in the market, Kijé himself with the AK47.

Occasionally, when Keith stepped out into the portico for fresh air, during the night watches, he could swear that he heard the car again, purring in the distance, but it never arrived. He put it down to passing aircraft.

One morning, delivering mushrooms to the Goat Woman who, with Streph, still hailed him like an old friend, he noticed that on the stall next to Vlodya's, the one where he had bought the leather, the Makarov, Kijé's pistol, was laid out among the sundry bits of metal. He tried not to look at it as he stood a couple of metres away, buying candles from Vlodya. Ought he to buy that too, and return it to its owner, or at least get it out of circulation?

"Where do you suppose that came from?" he asked, disingenuously.

"You can pick them up like eggs in a barnyard here," Vlodya said, wrapping the candles in a sheet of newspaper so ancient it was yellower than the tallow.

Vlodya, it seemed, did not recognize it. Didn't the Sturyat know that Keith might recognize it, that Kijé certainly would? Evidently not, but then they had had no idea that it was Kijé's own weapon. He paid fifteen *sum* for it, which might just as well have been fifteen shirt buttons.

The next stall along had been appropriated by the New

Agers. They lived in a tepee with yin-yang symbols painted on the sides, erected at the south-eastern corner of the Sturyat pasture. Several hog-backed benders grovelled round its skirts. The New Agers had metamorphosed into the Sundance Tribe and on the stall displayed artefacts of vaguely aboriginal provenance which they made on the premises: Native American dream catchers, clay figures of prehistoric astronauts and little fetishes made of saxaul twigs, shards of bark and feathers. The Sturyat seemed to like these and acquired them in quantities, as tourists in London buy plastic Beefeaters. A female Sundancer squatted in the dust beside the stall and played a backpacker guitar in a manner that caused Usman exquisite pain.

Having disposed of half of the mushrooms he took the rest to the museum, the pistol knocking about in the empty box file. He did not know if it was loaded, even, if the safety catch was on or off. It would be deeply ironic if it were to go off by accident and blow a hole in him.

As he turned down the lane behind the Iskander Hotel he saw the Joggers for Jesus on their vigorous way across the Registan, seeking the truth although, as far as he knew, they had made no attempts to wreak it. They had moved into the old elementary school on Vostok Street, which ran at a right-angle to Museum Street and was conveniently placed for meals. Thrice daily they appeared in the Refreshment Room, said Grace, ate wholesome food over which they conversed solemnly, consulting Bibles, said Grace again, and took off at the double. At intervals they could be seen jogging around

Qantoum in their blue track suits, chanting tuneless hearty litanies like rookie GIs, and never flagging, even in the fiercest summer heat. Kijé, mesmerized by their radiant orthodontics, called them The Teeth. They tittupped harmlessly around town on the toes of their Nikes and did no damage, although they disapproved of the Sundance enterprise culture, calling the native craftwork Implements of Satan. The Qantoumis, who had their own ideas about how Satan operated, allowed them to get on with it.

For one reason or another, probably the heat, no one had followed them; they had not been the vanguard of an influx from the west. With every day that passed and brought no more strangers Keith prayed that the rumour of the black sun had perished in the scorching summer. Perhaps the real eclipse, in August, had killed it. In Qantoum, as Woodbridge had predicted, they had seen only a partial occlusion. The Sturyat had ignored it, showing far more interest in the spectacular meteor shower that had peaked the following night in the dark of the new moon. But it was October now, the heat was ebbing by day, the nights were cooler. He imagined Zayu on her roof every morning at dawn, gazing westward.

In the Refreshment Room she stood at the bar, an unsmiling hostess. He had had to get used to her all over again. In the light of what Kijé had been prepared to do her impulsive act of self-preservation no longer seemed so frightful, but Kijé was paying with every day that he lived and Fitz did not. Zayu did not give a toss. Nor did she seem to care that Keith had moved out of the house in the Old Town.

"Good morning," he said to her, as he passed her on the way to the kitchen, and "Good morning," she replied, as if they were meeting for the first time.

Mrs Fahrenheit was at the stove and greeted him without looking up. He took advantage of her preoccupation to abstract the pistol from the box file and shove it into his pocket. "Mushrooms," he said.

"I remember the first time you brought me mushrooms," she said, straightening up to take them. "Do you?"

He did, it was one of the things he tried not to remember; his early attempts to belong, to be wanted here, to integrate himself, when his every instinct ought to have sent him back to the junction and the Tashkent train. What right had he to jeer at the Sundancers?

When he returned to Dunkillin – he could never now tell Kijé what he had called the place – he laid the pistol on the table in the living-room, with a note explaining how he had come by it. Kijé did not seem to be around, which was a relief. Neither of them would want to talk about the weapon or its reappearance. He watered the mushrooms and went out to attend to the small duties that had accrued to him, lastly checking the windows in the greenhouse which was coming into use again now that autumn approached. Kijé's little lemon trees were in there, poignantly hopeful.

He noticed that it was growing dark, too early, surely. When he went out into the garden he saw that the sky was no longer a limpid blue but hazed with clouds. He could feel, taste the moisture in the air, although rain was not yet falling.

He had forgotten that it rained here, and suddenly, passionately wanted to be out in it as if it might restore some part of himself that over the last weeks had been baked out of him.

Instead of going directly back to the museum he made detours and an unnecessary circuit of the Registan, until he felt the first drops on his neck and held out his hands, turned up his face to be slaked. At first a soft misty drizzle, the rain persisted gently and its silent fall stifled the song of the sand. It did not last for long, but it was a beginning, a sign of change, whatever that change might be. The light had almost gone now, he ought to be starting back to the museum. It would be a night of full moon and, he supposed, a Spelling, but nothing could be seen overhead. He must start carrying his torch again and wished he had it now as he made his way through streets unrelieved by even a glint of starlight, thinking how an English town would shine in the rain; the lean quivering reflections on concrete and Tarmac, glass and brick, the glitter and sparkle. Qantoum by contrast might have been draped in wet velvet.

In such blackness he could see, when only halfway down Museum Street, the light from the oil lamp that burned in the portico, long before he saw the lamp itself, and was moved to something like homesickness at the sight of lamplight on a wet night.

After that the rain held off for two days. On the third an unwholesome silence fell over Qantoum at midday, and above the plain a great greenish thunderhead drew itself up out of the southern horizon, top-heavy, overbalancing towards the town. As darkness fell it still hung there and in his room above the Zherdin Collection Keith looked up to see raindrops landing like gobs of spittle on the dusty glass. Below, Lady Hooke floated wraith-like out of the dusk, clutching a ragged bat's wing of an umbrella.

When he went down she was still there, in the rotunda, an iridescent toque of feathers clinging to her sparse hair and a conglomerate of flayed mammals hanging round her neck as if she had pillaged her wardrobe from Prince Andrei's cabinets. When she saw Keith she clasped her little chicken-skin hands and complained, "Darling! The most appalling people – the *noise* – can't *fathom* what Pavel Issurevich is thinking of. What is one to do?"

"What's the matter, Maisie? I'm afraid the bar is going to be a bit crowded for a time." Lady Hooke did not care for the Joggers. She considered them *loud*.

"The bar? Oh no, child. One is accustomed to the bar. Even the bear is a lady, which is more than can be said for its husband. But one's *hotel* is a different matter. It is, after all, one's home."

"The Sogdiana Serai, Maisie? Are the ghosts getting out of hand?"

"If it only were the ghosts. . ." She laid a claw on his arm and drew him relentlessly towards the street. He had no choice but to follow, short of picking her off him, finger by finger, like a gripping baby. Adhering thus she conducted him up Museum Street and into Oktyabrskaya. Whatever she had on her feet clicked and nattered on the pavement.

The rain cascaded about them as if aimed from a bucket. The umbrella flapped uselessly. As they came into the Registan he saw at once, even in the darkness, that all was not as it had been in the Sogdiana Serai, for the darkness was no longer total. In the hotel's many windows on the four remaining floors, lights were showing stickily behind the smeared panes. The great front doors stood open wide, revealing more lights, many lights, people moving busily in and out of doorways and on the broad sweep of the central staircase.

"Maisie! Who are they?"

"I don't *know*," she said, piteously. "I came back from feeding my little ones and the foyer was *heaving*, simply heaving with people. No manners, no breeding. One has been billeted upon before, we had the most verminous evacuees in '39, *sewn* into their underclothes. One has seen one's home requisitioned, but one always dealt with *orficers*, or the WVS. Oh, Jackie, what does it mean? Make them go away."

Distractedly he patted her arm and, now dragging her, still attached to his sleeve, mounted the steps. The foyer was alive with people none of whom looked even slightly familiar, heaving furniture about. They were all dressed in black like a conference of vicars. He thought vaguely of the mob storming the Bastille – but they did not seem to be looting. Rather they had the look of people who were settling in.

"Where is your suite, Maisie?"

She pointed a spiralling finger aloft and pronounced, in the tone of an embarrassed hostess, "I'm afraid the lift is out of order."

Two men were carrying a bed downstairs. Keith and Lady Hooke stood aside to let them pass, and were ignored. As no one seemed to be following they continued upwards and along the landing that ran round three sides of the stairwell in a gallery. Lady Hooke was in front again, twittering, reeling, as her heels snagged in dust-piled carpet. On the third floor they halted. As on the previous landings corridors ran into the darkness on all sides.

"Which is yours?" Keith said and found that he was whispering.

"Down here." The sharp little talons dug into his arm. This corridor was not in darkness. Several doors stood open to dimly-lit interiors.

"They seem to be moving in," Lady Hooke said. "One ought to speak to the management. Pavel Issurevich. . ." From the threadbare reticule on her wrist she drew a key that was still attached to a hefty brass tag, and opened a door with 349 on it. There were no lamps in here but Lady Hooke fumbled again, struck a light by some means he did not see, and held up a candle.

The smell of warm wax, perfume, dust, damp, mice, old age and paraffin quickened in the steadying flame. She lit a second candle from the first and set them both, fixed in wooden holders, on a sideboard. He had imagined that she subsisted in faded elegance surrounded by relics of the past life that furnished her fantasies, but as the light spread into the corners and up to the ceiling he saw a stockade of tea chests, packing cases, steamer trunks, all of them stuffed with trailing fabrics among which a squeaking, scurrying upheaval suggested that Maisie was not the only tenant. Flocks of dust dropped softly from the ceiling which was riven by a great black crack meandering through the moulded plaster like the Amudarya. The fifth floor, he recalled, was missing.

Lady Hooke doddered among the boxes to a curtained, pelmeted doorway and another light sprang up in the room beyond. Except for an enormous bed, piled with pillows and quilts, with a small pathetic trench down the middle where she must nest at night, the room was empty. Opposite the door a massive gilt-framed mirror reflected the two of them, dark in the doorway. Flanking it were two life-sized portraits in oils; the candle, trembling in her hand, gave them a horrid semblance of movement. On the left a tall soldierly type, touched with grey at the temples, wearing a red mess jacket with medals; on the right, a tiny vivacious girl with a nimbus of auburn curls about her head, laughing up at the onlooker from where she sprawled on a divan, tapering cigarette holder in one hand, the slack of a long string of pearls in the other: the notorious spy and his wife.

"M'husband," Lady Hooke said, gesturing with her candle. Sir Mortimer's eyebrows went up and down with sinister complicity. "Always claimed to be the sixth man . . . or the seventh . . . can't think who *she* is."

"Isn't it you?"

"One of his floozies, I suppose. Can't *imagine* how she got in here. Silly trollop. One lost count."

Either she really did think that the laughing beauty was

some tart her husband had had a fling with or, deep down, she knew it was her younger self and could not bear to acknowledge the girl she had left behind her.

"Oh Maisie," Keith whispered, "what a dish you were."

"You can go now," she said, turning on him. "Shan't need you again tonight. Don't *hover*."

A thud reverberated next door and flakes of plaster came down in a dusty blizzard.

"Maisie, you can't stay here."

"Don't tell me what I can and can't do, young man."

"But you'd only just got to the museum. You wanted me to come and see what was happening."

"Well, now you've seen it."

"All these strange men—"

"I'll lock the door. I survived the Great War, the Second World War, the Civil War. And Brezhnev. Take more than Carter Patterson to shift *me*."

"Maisie, I don't think—"

"Get out!" she shrieked and swung the candlestick at his head. This one was brass and weighted at the base like a knobkerrie. He dived through the living-room and out into the corridor. She pursued him, whirling the candlestick and moving at astonishing speed among the packing cases, while the shadows lunged over their heads. The door slammed on his heels; he heard the key turn and a muffled thump as some more of the ceiling descended.

At least she was locked in. She would be safe for a time, until he could find out what was going on here.

Opposite, the door of 348 was open. Keith put his head round it and immediately a woman, who was burrowing in a wardrobe, turned to confront him, at the same time making an elaborate sign in the air, touching various parts of her compass as if she were drawing a composite cross like the Union Flag.

"Good evening," he said. "Would you mind telling me what you are doing here?"

"Who asks?" she said, with a dramatic swirl of black robes.

"I do. I live here – I live in Qantoum. But there *is* someone actually living in this hotel. Who let you in?"

"Altaera."

Who? Not one of the Qantoumis; surely not one of the Sturyat. "Who is Altaera?"

"Our leader. Not our leader on Gaea, but in the next sphere."

Oh Christ, he thought. *Serious* weirdos. "Who is your leader on Gaea?"

"The Archon is in the Eleusynium. I can ask if he will speak with you. Follow."

She glided past him and into the corridor. Maisie's door remained closed, he saw as he followed her to the galleried landing.

"This way's quicker – if we're going down."

"Where there is a choice we elect to walk counter-clockwise to maintain the equilibrium," she said, without slackening her pace. "In the southern hemisphere the Equispherians go clockwise."

"What is an Equispherian?"

"We are all of us Equispherians here – not *you* of course," she added. "But I am not on a plane where I can talk of such matters. If the Archon is with us he will explain."

"I thought you said he was downstairs."

"The Eleusynium has been established downstairs. His Gaean body will be in it but he may be conferring with Altaera, in the Hypersphere."

"Which sphere are we in, then?"

"The Hyposphere. Please do not ask any more questions."

They had reached the first-floor landing. Proceeding counter-clockwise behind her he looked over the balustrade into the foyer. Black-robed figures were batting about, arms filled with computer screens and consoles. His guide led the way down the last flight and past the old restaurant where tables had been pushed back against the wall. Something resembling a pulpit was being erected at one end.

The woman stopped at the end of a passage where shrouds of mosquito net had been tacked up in front of a door. She looked round and said, "Tell me your name."

"Keith Chapman. Yours?"

"You may call me Phoenix Helen."

While he digested this she put her head through the drapes and knocked at the door. A gong sounded behind it.

"Wait here." She opened the door, dropped to her knees and crawled in. He watched her dirty bare feet creep under the netting like two fugitive rats. Low voices could be heard. Within a minute the rats reappeared and Phoenix Helen emerged backwards.

"The Archon is entering the Hypersphere," she announced, tottering upright, "but if you wish an audience you may return tomorrow morning."

"Thank you, I will. In the meantime, what about Lady Hooke?"

"There is no aristocracy in the Hypersphere, except for Altaera and his Archon. Beneath them, all are equal."

"She's just an old lady who lives here."

"She has nothing to fear from us. Altaera is all-merciful. We will expect you tomorrow, before noon. Phoenix Mary Beth!" Another woman was sashaying down the corridor. "Archon needs you."

"What's all this phoenix business?"

"Those of us who were men on Gaea take the name Sphinx. They have the answers to all riddles. Those who were women become Phoenixes. We shall rise in flame. Are you satisfied?"

"Not by a long chalk," Keith said.

"There is nothing you can do," Phoenix Helen said. "It is the will of Altaera."

He walked down the passage, losing her at some point when she resumed her orbit. In the foyer a bunch of Sphinxes was manhandling a sound system into the restaurant.

"There's no electricity here," Keith said, remembering the computers with pleasure.

"Altaera will provide."

Away from the unaccustomed brightness of the Sogdiana Serai the rain-sodden night was blacker than ever.

Disoriented, even in the breadth of Oktyabrskaya, he mistook a narrow lane for the entrance to Museum Street and in seconds was hopelessly off-course, as confused as he had been on his first excursion through the alleys of the Old Town. He switched on his torch to get his bearings, but it fluttered feebly and he hurriedly extinguished it. It might be weakened by the dampness but possibly the batteries were failing, now, when he needed them most. He must dig out his two spare cells and keep them dry.

The path beneath his feet was greasy and uneven, and he slipped at the foot of a staircase going up between buildings. His right hand slapped on to a chill hard step as he flung out an arm to steady himself. The left encountered something cold, smooth, soft, that moved under his fingers. He sensed, rather than heard, an overripe thud as it fell, or rolled, from one step to the next, a sensation of internal surging.

He sprang back in disgust, frantically scrubbing his hand on his coat, expecting a vestigial stickiness, an odour. He had an image of a plastic bag full of offal or rotting vegetables, but unable to see did not stay to look, although he had, even in the dark, an impression of whiteness. The torch beam stuttered and died almost as soon as he switched it on and he hurried away, still scouring his hand and envisioning an uncollected bin bag, festering at a back door.

It was only when he reached the museum that reason caught up with him, reminding him that no one in Qantoum put out the garbage in white plastic sacks for the binmen to collect.

With half of his mind he knew that there could be nothing like that lying around in the street; at any other time he would investigate, bring lights, fetch Kijé, but he and Kijé would have other things on their minds when they met.

The Refreshment Room was filling up but conversation was subdued and there was no music. It was eleven weeks since Fitz had played the drum and Kijé danced. People drank and talked quietly to one another. At the bar Mrs Fahrenheit leaned, arms folded, watching over her flock.

"Where have you been?" She looked gratifyingly concerned.

"With Maisie. We've got to get her out of the Sogdiana Serai. It's been invaded by lunatics."

"The Joggers?"

"Worse than that. Where's Kijé?"

"At home, I expect. Who are these people?"

"They call themselves Equispherians. They've got into the hotel somehow, about a hundred of them. It looks like they're turning it into some sort of temple."

"What have they done to Maisie?"

"Nothing, but she's completely lost the plot and locked herself in her room. She hauled me off to see what was going on, then forgot who I was – who she thought I was, and threw me out again. Some woman, Phoenix Helen, said she'd be quite safe, they meant her no harm. Maybe they don't but she can't stay there."

"Keith, Maisie has been through more than you can imagine – "

"So she told me."

" – and survived. She's a very durable old lady. How do you suppose she's lasted this long? Certainly we must get her out of the Sogdiana Serai, but not this instant. By tomorrow she may have convinced herself that your Equispherians are a visiting opera company."

"Maybe, but it might not just be them. I've got an audience with their leader tomorrow. I'll find out why they're here."

"I think we can guess that."

"Exactly, so who knows what else is going to come out of the west? It's only two months to the end of the year. I'd hoped this black sun crap had died the death, but now this mob have arrived – it's all starting again – the soul stones—"

"Keith! Enough. Out of the west *and* out of the east remember. Nothing has come out of the east."

"Yet."

"Nothing out of the east and no black sun. The equation is incomplete. If at the end of the year nothing has happened, the Sturyat will go back to doing what they do best: waiting."

He wished he could be so sure.

When everyone had gone home except for that night's guardian, one Makhmud whose pebble glasses suggested that he would not notice any interlopers until they had passed him, Keith went out again. The rain was easing but the heavy air was thick with the smell of trapped smoke from stoves and cooking fires. With the torch beam probing ahead of him he went up Museum Street and along Oktyabrskaya to the hotel. The windows were dark, the great doors secured again. He played the torchlight over them. Someone, Altaera perhaps, had been at work with a crowbar. There must be some other way in, at the back, but now, in the rainy night, was not the time to find out.

Instead of going directly back he retraced the route of his last journey, when he had mistaken the turning for Museum Street. It was scarcely more than an alley; he could touch both sides with outstretched arms. He found the flight of steps again; no bin bag; nothing; no trace; no sound except for the rainwater in the gutters. He made his way back to Museum Street and as soon as he saw the steady glow of the lamp in the portico, switched off the torch to conserve the precious battery. He was only a few paces from the steps when he stumbled, almost falling. The torch went flying. Something heavy, cold and soft lay across his foot and ankle. Once, when he was a child, swimming in the sea off Folkestone, a jellyfish had floated against his leg. The sensation was similar, but this had more weight, more substance, than any jellyfish. The image of the sack of offal returned. Gingerly casting about for the torch his hand discovered a gelid presence, firm to the touch but instantly yielding; that foul surge of energy again.

The lamplight did not reach so far but he thought he saw something move in the gloom, that same impression of pallor. Then his scrabbling fingers found the torch but the impact of its fall had loosened a connection. The night had swallowed whatever it was. He covered the distance to the steps in two strides and stood banging the torch against his palm and peering out into the night.

Whatever it was. . . What *was* it? His mental picture became one of a corpse, bloated in the rain; but whose? Even the insouciant Sturyat would be unlikely to leave a body lying in the street for just anyone to trip over, and in any case, it had not felt dead, it had seemed to move inside itself with pulpy ripples.

It lived.

Fifteen

The dust in his room had developed overnight into a moist bloom. In the absence of artificial light and heat Keith could almost feel moulds growing, yeasty spores on his bedding, his clothes, the mosquito nets, hanging with a mildewed phosphorescence in the dawn light that seeped through the murky panes overhead.

In the Refreshment Room Makhmud was reviving himself with hot tea before he went home. His eyes behind the thick scratched lenses were difficult to engage. Keith had never felt easy communicating with him and had not warned him last night of any chill slithering thing that might come up the steps. He had not mentioned it to anyone, telling himself that darkness had made a mystery of something unremarkable, but he said to Makhmud, "Was it all quiet, last night?"

Makhmud nodded.

"You heard nothing? Saw nothing?"

"What was to hear, to see?"

Keith did not know what hours the Equispherians kept but when the Joggers had left for their morning run he went out into the cool morning, the clean washed light. In the Registan St Vasili's dome shone as if polished. By the fountain, a girl stood, her arms clasped around the trunk of an elm tree.

He changed course for a closer look, thinking it might be a Sundancer in distress, but when he came near he saw she was a stranger and that she was in fact embracing the tree. Her head was tipped back and she was gazing up into the foliage, whispering a prayer or incantation. Drops of water fell on her upturned face. She did not see him.

The doors of the Sogdiana Serai stood open. He went in and accosted the first person he met, one of the women he had seen last night, Phoenix Mary Beth.

"I have an appointment with the Archon."

"Oh yes. You are Keith Chapman. Archon awaits. Follow me."

He felt obscurely uncomfortable that she should know his name, but he went with her down the passage to the door of the Eleusynium where Phoenix Mary Beth plunged to her knees and crawled beneath the festoons of netting. The gong sounded. An arm emerged, beckoning. He pushed through the drapes into a large room lit with dozens of small candles set out in intricate patterns on the floor. On a tumulus of cushions reclined a fattish middle-aged man stuffed into a white jump suit with a diamanté collar. For one incredulous moment Keith thought, *Elvis*? Phoenix Mary Beth crawled among the candles. He remained upright, by the door.

The reclining man gestured graciously. "Mr Chapman? I

am Archon. Phoenix Mary Beth tells me you want to ask some questions."

"I do, yes. I mainly want to know who you are, why you're here, how you got in and what about poor Lady Hooke? That's all, really."

Phoenix Mary Beth rose up on her haunches like a dog begging and muttered something.

"Oh, the elderly lady upstairs. I assure you, Mr Chapman, no one has molested her. No one will molest her. We, the Equispherians, do not molest, even unbelievers."

"Lady Hooke isn't an unbeliever. She's very old, very confused and this is her home. You come busting in here—"

"No one has bust in anywhere," Archon pronounced. "Before we left Anglo-Terra we made extensive consultations. Altaera directed us here."

"Via the Internet?" Keith could not help that.

"We do not scorn technology, far from it. The Net has been an invaluable vehicle of communication between the Equispheres, but Altaera is," he chuckled, "*beyond* that. *I* channel him."

Naturally, Keith thought. I should have expected channelling.

"Even here you must know that the end of days is almost upon us. In these latter years, Gaea – what you call Planet Earth – has survived to meet the Millennium only because of the united efforts of the Equispherians striving to maintain the balance of all matter. For decades we have sought to know where we should foregather to enjoy our final union with Altaera, in the Hypersphere, and it was given to me as temporal leader to bring the people here."

"To the Sogdiana Serai?"

"To Qantoum. But we continued to seek guidance even as we travelled and Altaera led us here. When the black sun rises on the last day we shall go to join him. Meanwhile we need a place to concentrate our energies."

"How did you get in?"

"The doors fell open before us."

With a little help from Altaera's divine crowbar. "And Lady Hooke?"

"We have no quarrel with Lady Hooke, but Altaera has given us this place. If she wishes to remain no hand will be raised against her."

"There are other people living in Qantoum," Keith said.

"The Sturyat."

"And others."

"We are a hundred strong and more are coming, the Equispherians of the south. We have already spoken with the Sturyat. We shall be welcomed."

"Do you mind telling me what will happen when the black sun rises?"

"In conjunction with the great comet we shall see the end of days," Archon said. "The light of the black sun will show us the path to Altaera who bestrides the comet like a colossos and we shall all be changed in the twinkling of an eye." Specks of foam appeared at the corners of his mouth. "Now you must leave. Phoenix Sheila will give you one of our videos."

"You may have noticed," Keith said, "that we have no electricity here."

"Altaera will provide," Archon said and wallowing, became one with his cushions.

Phoenix Mary Beth was crawling towards him, flapping her hand to indicate that he should leave. He backed through the mosquito nets and after a moment she joined him, rising erect as she left the Presence.

"What was all that about?"

"That is the Eleusynium where Archon can meet with Altaera in seclusion."

"I got that. But what's all this with the comet and the black sun?"

"Archon has spoken." Phoenix Mary Beth wheeled to the right, heading anticlockwise for the restaurant. Keith wondered if he should make another attempt to extricate Lady Hooke, but before he could reach the stairs he saw Szusko and the bear, standing in the doorway, both equally dazed.

"Szusko! What are you doing here?"

Szusko had taken off his hat and was twisting it in his hands, the universal sign of discomfort.

"They want fuel," he said.

"Come outside." Keith ushered him through the double doors and went a little way down the steps. The bear subsided against his legs. "What do they want fuel for? Light? Heat?"

"They say they can bring the electricity again," Szusko said. "They have a generator – I don't know where—"

"What does it run off?"

"Oil, they say."

"Tell them you haven't got any oil."

"But I've already told them I have."

"Tell them you've run out. How did they latch on to you, anyway?"

"Yesterday, Marfa and I, we were delivering gas bottles, in our little cart. These people came up from the citadel, chanting as they walked. It was like a funeral. They did not speak to me then, but when they found there was no light I suppose they remembered me. They said it is Altaera's will that I fetch oil for them. '*Fiat lux*' they said. They gave me this."

He held out a flat packet. Keith thought it was a book until he read the lettering on the back. *The Revelations of Altaera to the Congregations of the Equispheres. 93m PG VHS*. It was the Archon's video.

As he crossed the Registan Keith noticed that the tree-hugger had been joined by several fellow-enthusiasts, each clinging to his or her chosen trunk. Outside the cinema a couple of Qantoumis, on their way home from market, observed them from a safe distance, puzzled and pointing discreetly. Did they realize that, quite apart from the Sturyat, they were now outnumbered all over again?

Brother Joel passed him at a trot. "Dupes of Satan," he remarked as he went by. "Angels guide you."

You should see what's in the hotel, Keith thought.

Mrs Fahrenheit met him in the rotunda.

"Have you found Maisie?"

"No," Keith said, "but we ought to get her out. The chief loony has set himself up in a sort of boudoir, channelling a higher consciousness, surrounded by candles. Ernie, these guys are *trouble*."

"Which guys?" Kijé came in off the street.

"The ones in the Sogdiana Serai," Mrs Fahrenheit said. "You don't know? We'd better have a council of war. Come into the kitchen and leave the door open. If anyone wants serving they can shout."

She took her place at the head of the table which had been cleared and scrubbed. The boards were soft, almost velvety, from many scourings. The other two sat on either side.

"Shoot," Kijé said, quaintly.

"Lady Hooke came here last night and said her hotel was full of strangers. I wasn't too bothered, I assumed it was the usual hallucinations, but she dragged me off to see. There's about a hundred of them and more to come, they say. Some kind of a cult, the Equispherians, and they're turning the place into a temple or a shrine or something. They're led by a maniac who calls himself the Archon although he looks as though he thinks he's Elvis Presley—"

"Elvis Presley is dead."

"The jury's still out on that one. They believe they're in touch with someone they call Altaera who is riding in on Comet Colney-Hatch, as far as I can make out. They're millennnarians, think the world's going to end at sunrise on January 1st."

"So do The Teeth," Kijé said. "These people, have they threatened Lady Hooke?"

"No, worse, they're ignoring her. Archon says that Altaera led them to the Sogdiana Serai and made them a present of it. They're all over the place, ransacking rooms, shifting furniture, behaving as if Maisie's one of the mice. Have you seen her rooms, Ernie?"

"No, but I can imagine that mice would feature prominently."

"She doesn't understand what's happening, but she's flipped, Kijé. She asked me in, then turned and came after me with a bloody great candlestick. We can't leave her there."

"Perhaps if I called in a neighbourly way they would let me in," Mrs Fahrenheit said.

"Oh, they'd let you in. They'd treat *you* like one of the mice, too; we're an irrelevance."

"But what is so horrible about them?" Kijé said.

"Doesn't what I've described sound horrible enough? You haven't seen them. Their women go on all fours."

"When I came in you were saying: 'These guys are trouble'. That sounded worse than what you have described. People storming in and taking over – what's new? I've done it myself," he added, absently.

"It's not the way they behave to us, it's the way they are with each other. They've given up being men and women – I don't know exactly *what* they've given up. The ex-men are Sphinxes, the women are Phoenixes. I was taken to see Archon by Phoenix Mary Beth. She crawls about in front of him. That's just creepy. But on the way out I met Szusko. They want him to supply them with fuel. They've got hold of a generator, or brought one with them. They're going to start producing electricity, they're doling out videos. This is worse than Big Macs and Coca-Cola."

"Is Szusko going to oblige?" Mrs Fahrenheit said.

"I think so – he's not in a position to refuse. They'll lean on him. What are they up to?"

"Perhaps they just want light and heat," Mrs Fahrenheit suggested.

"They've got enough candles to light the whole of Qantoum, but they want electricity and they're going to have it. They want to show their videos. Who do they think they're going to convert – us? The Sturyat? And that's another thing, they didn't follow the rails to the station, they seem to have peeled off at Industrial. Archon says they have already spoken with the Sturyat, which suggests that the Sturyat came out to meet them."

"People with electricity can communicate over long distances," Kijé said. "They can send and receive information. Do these Equestrians have radios?"

"For all I know they're setting up a television station. It's Equispherians, Kijé. They've got some idea that the Earth is made in two halves that'll come unscrewed unless they take steps – literally – to keep it in one piece."

"Is that crazier than believing that souls can be kept in stones or that a virgin can give birth?" Mrs Fahrenheit murmured.

"No, and no crazier than believing that aliens are abducting one American in three and subjecting them to medical experiments in spaceships."

"Are they really?" Kijé said. "That would explain a great deal. I wonder why no one ever abducts Russians. You know, this will go down very well with the Sturyat."

"What will?"

"All of it. In their wildest dreams they could not have hoped for the kinds of strangers who are coming out of the west. The Sturyat, of course, have not had the benefit of a Western education."

Keith turned to Mrs Fahrenheit. "Is there a generator here, in the building?"

For some reason she exchanged a look with Kijé before answering. "This is a museum. There was never much call for a supplementary power supply."

"Didn't you run a hospital here?"

"In a manner of speaking. We still had a power station then. It was bombed. The General Hospital had an auxiliary plant but that was shelled before the power station. We heard a great deal about revolutionary missiles that could home in on military installations . . . the hospital, the mosque, the warehouses. How cotton burns. It seemed in the end when the power station went up that it was probably an accident, hit by a shell intended for the public library."

"They used bombers to take out the airstrip," Kijé said. "It was pleasantly old-fashioned. Tornados. Where do Tornados come from, Keith?"

"I only asked," Keith said, defensively, "because if people keep arriving in these numbers, Maisie won't be the only one who's squeezed out."

"Have I not always provided for that?" Mrs Fahrenheit said. "My ever-open doors. My sentries." She patted Kijé's arm. "And my cellars. Show him, Kijé, I have to go back to the bar."

"What about Maisie? Suppose she comes out of her room and starts swanning about looking for Winston Churchill?"

"Knowing Maisie she will find him. Go back for her later. While you are here you might as well see how to get into the cellars. I ought to have shown you before."

Kijé lit a small paraffin lamp and led the way into Mrs Fahrenheit's room.

"Three ways," he said. "One from the street which we sealed long ago. One through the Archaeology Gallery, and this." He opened the door of the clothes cupboard and pushed aside the hanging garments. Keith heard the sound of keys, then the lamp smoke flared back at him and a draught of cool air swept past his face.

"Twenty steps," Kijé said. "Quite steep. Handrail on the left."

Keith followed the light, seeing nothing at first but the ragged silhouette of Kijé's hair going down before him. As his eyes adjusted to the darkness he saw a vaulted ceiling, pillars, arches, like the crypt of a cathedral.

"We're under the Zherdin Collection," Kijé said. "Back there, beyond the steps, was the place where the coal was delivered. No one can get in that way now, but if necessary we might be able to get out. Follow me. We are beneath the rotunda; along here" – he moved from archway to archway – "is the corridor to the Archaeology Gallery. Here Erna had her hospital. Not much has changed since Fitz and I. . ." He trailed off and looked around him. "It seemed prudent to keep it ready, in case it was ever needed again. I believe we thought the town might be rebuilt, but after the earthquake hit most people went away, those who were left to leave."

"Except the Sturyat."

"Who regard themselves as immune to earthquakes. Who knows?" he said. "Maybe they are. They were not affected. I think they believe the museum was spared because their soul stones are in it."

"Are they?"

"God knows," Kijé sighed. "But the museum *was* spared."

All around the walls were low beds with pillows stacked, blankets formally folded on the mattresses. At intervals stood white painted cupboards. Keith tried a door; it was locked.

"Medical supplies." Kijé stood looking down at a bed. "Mine."

The low white cots, the dim lamp, the gloom; it reminded Keith of pictures of Florence Nightingale's hospital at Scutari. It was quite as primitive.

"Kijé – your wound – it nearly killed you, didn't it?"

"But not entirely, as you see."

"How did Ernie manage to save you?"

"Good nursing kept me alive. It was the surgeon who saved me."

"You had a surgeon *here*?"

"After the hospital was destroyed the survivors came here. We still have the surgeon. You know him quite well."

"No riddles, Kijé. I thought you didn't like riddles."

"Not a riddle. The surgeon who is a surgeon no longer, for one reason or another, is one of Erna's customers."

"The bear, I suppose."

"Close."

"*Szusko?*"

"A man of great courage. He was treating a casualty in the minefield. You will have noticed that he never removes his gloves. He has lost most of his fingers so he is justly proud of his dexterity with the dominoes. Part of his left foot too, but that does not interfere with his game. By then, thank God, Erna had learned enough to save him."

"But why is he peddling fuel around town?"

"The surgeon's mind went the same way as the surgeon's fingers. You might say the sand got it.

"This bed was Fitz's," he said. "We'll take the other door out, then you'll know both ways."

"I suppose it's no good asking where Szusko got the bear?" He followed the lamp to a second flight of steps.

"No," Kijé said. He was opening a door at the head of the stairs and they left the darkness of the cellar for the sunny charnel-house of the Archaeology Gallery. They had come through a door disguised as part of the panelling; fixed to the other side of it were the bookshelves.

"We can get in and out through Erna's cupboard," Kijé said, "but this door is exit only. No handle, see?"

"I never knew there was so much to this place."

"Dear man, you never asked," Kijé said waspishly. "Anyway, you have to admit that it is only recently that we could risk showing you anything."

"Didn't you trust me?"

"No," Kijé said. "As you seemed more than half-ready to believe that you were summoned here by a wandering Sturyat soul I thought it better to let you make up your own mind about where your loyalties lay – if you had a mind. I took your head injury into account. Did you?"

"Did I what?"

"Take your head injury into account."

At various times during the afternoon people reported that the doors of the Sogdiana Serai were closed. It was dark before Lizaveta brought word that lights were showing and people going in and out. Kijé arrived in a long military greatcoat that made him a dead ringer for the bear in a bad light, and offered to go and fetch Maisie to safety.

"Take Keith," Mrs Fahrenheit said. "Don't go alone."

When they reached the Registan the Sogdiana Serai was dark again, save for the foyer which was empty. They went up the steps and became aware that in the restaurant candles were lighted, concealed from outside eyes by the shutters. There was no apparent movement but the room and the foyer were filled with a low buzzing, as of a disturbed hive, the sound of a hundred voices at their unintelligible devotions. At one end of the room a pale elevated swelling indicated the presence of the Archon in his pulpit.

Hoping that the Equispherians were too rapt to notice them they edged round to the staircase and tiptoed up it. The buzzing died away as they went higher. All the doors were now shut, including 348 where Phoenix Helen had been digging in. Keith tried the handle gently but it was locked. Kijé meanwhile was urgently tapping on 349. There was no response. He went down on his knees and laid his face to the carpet to see under the door.

"Something's moving."

The door opened suddenly and Lady Hooke, resplendent in balding sables, teetered on high heels. She looked down, saw Kijé transfixed with surprise, still kneeling on the carpet, and kicked him briskly in the stomach.

"Voyeurrrrr!"

"Maisie, are you all right?"

"Dear boy." She held out her hand; Keith took it and she stepped regally over the prostrate Kijé who was trying to recover his breath.

"Where are you going?"

"To Maxim's," she said. It occurred to Keith that she had imagined the museum Refreshment Room to have been a classy nightclub all along.

"Maisie, wait." Kijé was crawling to his feet. "You can't stay here."

"I am not staying here. I am going out. Stand aside, you *insect*." She barely reached his armpit. "Hotel detective," she said in a loud aside to Keith. "Not the kind of person one needs to speak to. Send him away. Give him money."

"It's Lieutenant Kijé, Maisie. He's right, you really shouldn't stay here. There are some very undesirable types moving in."

"I cannot leave my things."

"You can come back for them. Just pack something for tonight."

"Estella can do that." She staggered off down the corridor. "Estella?"

"I suppose her maid," Kijé shrugged helplessly. "No doubt long dead. Has she left the key in the lock?"

"Yes, and candles burning. I'll put them out and lock up. You keep an eye on her."

Kijé moved off behind Lady Hooke. Keith scrambled round the apartment, stuffing random garments into a cracked overnight bag on the assumption that she was unlikely to notice what was in it, extinguished the candles and came out again, locking the door behind him and pocketing the key.

On the landing he paused and looked into the well of the stairs. Opposite, two floors below, Kijé was standing a little back from the balustrade, faintly discernible in the light that shone upwards. He saw Keith and crooked his finger.

Soundless on the dusty carpet Keith ran, leaping the stairs, until he reached Kijé. Together they leaned over the stairwell. Maisie, with agonizing slowness, had just reached the foot of the last flight. They watched her, foreshortened into a meandering scarecrow, cross the foyer without casting a look towards the restaurant where the Equispherians had ceased from buzzing and a potent silence obtained.

"What's the matter?" Keith hissed.

"There's someone in the doorway – came in and went out again – waiting on the steps – *there*."

As Maisie wavered out of sight somebody stepped in and stood almost beneath them. Truncated by their eyeline it was difficult to identify, but there was a familiarity about the hat, the scarf, the coat. . .

"A Sturyat," Kijé said.

The boots.

"Zayu."

She was going towards the restaurant. An asexual figure in black robes came out to meet her, making the elaborate sign, like someone mending a fishing net.

"A Sphinx?"

"Phoenix," Keith said. "More cloth in the robe."

"Phoenix Courtney," the woman said, obligingly.

"Zayu. I was sent."

"Welcome."

"I have a message for your headman."

"Archon. Say it. Archon may not be addressed after he has called on Altaera. I will speak your words to him."

"I said they'd get on well," Kijé remarked.

"There will be a Spelling in nine days. Gresk invites you."

"We will be honoured to come."

"I will fetch you after sundown. You will eat in the house of Theps."

"We will be glad to share your bread, but Archon may not eat, he is fasting."

"Fasting!" Keith snorted. "He could give Henry VIII half a tonne."

Zayu had turned and left without speaking again.

"They are going to a Spelling, are they?" Kijé said. "Then so are we."

"Spellings are held at full moon. We've just had one. This must be special. Do you think we'll be invited?"

"No, but suitably disguised we may pass unnoticed, if numbers are great enough. It seems they will be great."

Such cloak-and-dagger proposals came oddly from Kijé, but these were odd times, and it was the first sign of animation that he had shown in a long while.

As they spoke the Equispherians had issued out of the Restaurant and were processing round the foyer, in an anti-clockwise direction, heads bent.

"What are they doing?"

"Maintaining the equilibrium. We can sleep easy, the world won't fall apart tonight, so long as the Australians are going the other way. Oh bugger, they're coming upstairs."

"This way," Kijé said, and withdrew down a corridor that led off to the right.

"Where's this go to?"

"Fire exit."

"You know your way around, don't you?"

"Yes," Kijé said, tersely. "It's a push-bar, we can't shut it – just hope they don't hear and come to investigate. Push it to, behind you."

They came out into a darker darkness, on a resilient metal platform, a handrail at hip height.

"Where are we?"

"Fire-escape. Tread carefully, it's unsafe." Kijé's voice came from knee level. He was already on his way down. "It comes out in the alley beside St Vasili's."

Keith, groping for the rail, followed more slowly.

"There's another landing halfway down. Watch out for—" The last word was a startled gasp. Keith heard a clatter of boot heels on iron, then nothing; then a thump far below him. And again, nothing.

Sixteen

He made his way to the half landing, whispering, "Kijé. *Kijé*," stuttering with shock. He thought, in his confusion, that there was something on the steps ahead of him, but the platform was empty. Kijé had gone over the railing.

Crouched on the landing Keith tried to see what horror lay at the foot of the walls, but it was like staring into a well. Still half aware of the unfastened door above him and the Equispherians beyond it, he called again, "*Kijé!*"

After a while he heard soft stumblings and swearing from below, and shuddering with incredulous relief continued his descent, gripping the rail and feeling for each step with his foot, lest he trip on whatever had overturned Kijé. There was nothing in his way but the treads were slippery.

Kijé was on his feet, testing joints and long bones.

"Are you all right? What happened?"

"I'm all right. I don't know how. I must have fallen six metres. I landed on . . . I don't know . . . it was soft. . ." Kijé's voice too was ragged with fright.

"How did you fall?"

"There was something on the stairs. I don't know, it felt like a bolster, but it was moving. I thought it was moving. Did you feel it?"

"No, not this time. But the other night, in the street – something in the dark, pale and damp. I thought it was a garbage sack at first, but afterwards, I thought it might be alive."

"That thing I landed on – it seemed to burst on impact. I can't see – feel – "

"We'll come back in daylight and look."

"I don't think I want to know."

"I do. Let's get out of here now."

"It *did* burst – my coat – soaked – oh, this is horrible."

Whispering, they waded through the rubble and undergrowth between the buildings to the moonlit oasis of the Registan. Kijé was limping and massaging his neck.

"Are you sure you're not hurt?"

"Of course I am hurt, I had three high-velocity bullets in this shoulder. But not injured. Let's go and drink Erna's beer and decide what to do next."

"I'm surprised you haven't got any vodka put by."

"I have, but I am keeping it for the very worst of times."

"Which haven't arrived yet?'

"Often I think they have, but every time I tell myself, No, Shura, leave it. There may be worse to come. So far, I have always been right. Today I saw a woman over there, by the fountain, making love to a tree."

"I don't think that's what she was doing. It's a form of worship. What's that?"

A discordant racket was reaching them along an alley: human voices, half-singing, half-chanting; an asthmatic instrumental undertone.

"The Teeth," Kijé said. "Another form of worship." He stopped and leaned against a wall. "I think I'll go home, after all. My head hurts."

"I'm not surprised. I'll take you back."

"There's no need. I know the way home."

"I'd rather make sure that you get there. You had a hell of a fall." It had been hard enough to knock his own name out of him at that unguarded moment.

At Control Point E, Kijé hauled himself up the steps by the handrail.

"Are you going to be all right?"

"We shall know in the morning. Come and see if I'm still alive. Now go back to the museum and make sure that Maisie arrived safely. Erna will be worried about us – don't tell her what happened. She'll worry more."

Keith had forgotten about Maisie, about everything in fact except the incident on the fire-escape. He was not looking forward to the walk ahead of him, but the moon was rising now and he could see where he put his feet.

It had been Kijé's turn to sit up that night, a fact that had understandably slipped his memory. Keith took his place, first checking that Maisie had made it back. She was in the kitchen, bending Mrs Fahrenheit's ear about the overnight bag which he had, he now remembered, dropped on the fire-escape.

At dawn he retired to his room above the Zherdin Collection and slept until mid-morning, and then went out. His first instinct was to go straight to Dunkillin and make sure that Kijé had survived the night, but there was something he wanted to check on beforehand. He looked in at the Refreshment Room to tell Mrs Fahrenheit where he was going and set out for the Registan. The tree-worshippers were not at their stations but among the yellowing leaves Keith could see that sundry rags and ribbons had been attached to the branches, stammering and snapping in the autumn breeze. The sun shone on the dome of St Vasili's and the doors of the Sogdiana Serai were shut. Thank God they had got Maisie out. He saw no one at the windows as he approached and picked his way along the canyon between the walls of the hotel and the cathedral.

The fire-escape zigzagged up the side of the hotel for three floors. Above that the earthquake had dislodged it and it jutted from the wall in a series of elbows. He searched the ground beneath it but found nothing except Maisie's overnight bag. Then he went up the first flight as far as the landing where Kijé had pitched over the handrail, noting, as he climbed, that the fire door was still ajar.

He leaned over and looked down. Kijé had said he landed on something that had seemed to burst. Keith had in his head the image of a small water-bed; he had been looking for rubberized fabric or plastic. Finally he made out the indistinct presence of something lying where he had already looked, which he must in fact have stepped on. It was diaphanous, draped over the grass and stones like nothing so much as a sheet of particularly thick cling film. How had he missed it? Then he realized that while he had been searching, the sun had moved round and now shone directly between the buildings. The thing was becoming more visible as he looked, like a developing photograph, acquiring a yellowish tinge.

He went down again and examined it; when he tried to pick it up it poured over his fingers in a way that was reminiscent of mercury, but without breaking up. It was simply impossible to grasp, like liquid silk; soft, disgusting. On the other hand, it wasn't going anywhere. He could get Kijé to come and look at it later.

Instead of returning to the Registan he went on down the side of the hotel. At the back of the building was a high-walled yard, and the cathedral extended beyond it. He struck out to the left into the startling normality of streets lined with small, derelict clapboard houses in little gardens. He had explored the area only once or twice in the early days, but he knew that the route would bring him to the road that ran alongside the gymnasium, where Control Point E stood on the corner of Oktyabrskaya.

He went through the office to the corridor and looked out of a window. Kijé was in the garden, turning the earth with a spade, pausing at intervals to rub his neck and shoulder. That fall last night ought to have broken one or the other since he had obviously landed head first; what could it be that he had landed *on*?

Kijé looked up and saw him. His face was pale and

bruised-looking, but he waved and came over to meet Keith at the door at the corner of the garden.

"Should you be digging?"

"I don't want to get stiff – stiffer." He rotated his left arm. "I've done for now, but we are going to need every scrap of food we can produce." Keith, walking down the corridor behind him, noticed that he was still limping. "What do you think our friends at the hotel are planning to live on?"

"Planning? I don't know if they *plan*. Altaera will provide, I expect. Which means, on past form, that they'll take anything they want."

"Erna is feeding The Teeth, but they pay only in money, which is quite useless. The Sundancers are living off the Sturyat. The tree-lovers? They eat twigs, maybe. I'll be interested to see how long the Sturyat will be happy to feed their many from the west if numbers increase at this rate. I wonder if they have a word for parasite. Well, we shall learn something at the Spelling."

"You're still set on going?"

"How else do we find out what is happening? Qantoum is never mentioned on the news bulletins. I used to be very happy about that but—"

"News bulletins?" Keith said. "What news bulletins?" Kijé's consternation was delicious. *Gotcha*, Keith thought. "What news bulletins?"

Kijé went into the tool room and put his spade meticulously where it was meant to be. Keith came up behind him. What else was he going to let out?

"You've got a radio, haven't you?" Kijé turned round. Keith stared into his eyes.

"What's the matter? Don't do that."

"Just checking to see if you're concussed. Something's been shaken loose. What about this radio?"

"I run it off a car engine."

"Not that thing outside?"

"No, this one is garaged. The reception is terrible. Sometimes I can't tune in for days."

"Tune in to what?"

"Radio Iskanderabad, the BBC."

"The BBC? What do you listen to, *The Archers*?"

"Who? No, the World Service. Someone has to know what's going on."

"Don't you tell anyone else? Don't they want to know what's happening?"

"Believe me, they don't," Kijé said. "Neither do I, come to that. I keep Erna informed. Don't talk about this, please."

"I've heard the car – I wondered what the hell it was. Look, I'm not joking, I think you are concussed. Your eyes are wandering."

"I'll sit down for a while." He went into the office and sank into the chair behind the desk, propping his head on his hand. "We were talking about the Spelling."

"Never mind that. We've got eight days."

"We can go as Equispherians. They dress in black, all alike. They wear hoods."

"Only the women – Phoenixes."

"Very well, we will be Phoenixes, in hoods. We are not going to speak, after all."

"I'd shave if I were you. Have you got anything in mind for our drag act?"

"Excuse me?"

"Dressing as Phoenixes. Do you have any long frocks in your wardrobe?"

"Erna has a cloak. She's as tall as I am."

"We can't both get into Ernie's cloak. But Maisie has boxes and boxes of stuff, clothes, curtains, bedspreads. That fire door is open – or it was just now, and I've got her door key. She need never know. She probably wouldn't notice anyway."

"Do you want to go and look now?"

"Not really – there was something else I wanted to show you, but I don't think you ought to be going anywhere."

"What did you want to show me?" Kijé, instantly alert, brought his eyes into focus. "I am not concussed. What is it?"

"I'm not sure. I think it's what you fell on last night."

"Describe it."

"I can't, and it's changing all the time."

Kijé stood up. "We'll go now. Let's take the back roads, and see this thing before it changes so much we don't recognize it."

They went out into the street. Keith said, "What did you think it was?"

"I was not making detailed observations," Kijé said. "At the time, while I was falling, I expected to die. I did not take in what was happening. I thought it must have been a mattress, thrown out of the hotel, but it felt like one of those rubber floating things."

"A lilo."

"Yes, but full of water, not air. It seemed to give way as I hit it. And there was nothing to be found, was there?"

"There is now. And you ran into something on the fire-escape – that's why you fell."

"I thought it was a bolster – you know, the picture in your head? Something long, round, soft . . . but not soft."

"Yielding?"

"That's it. But it happened so fast. I am going down the steps, there is suddenly something round my leg as if I am *wading* into it, like thick water." Kijé was reluctantly reliving his experience.

"Do you think that what you fell *on* was what you fell *over*?"

"I don't think it came down with me."

"No, I meant, the same kind of thing. After you fell I heard something moving on the steps, something going down. I was looking over the rail, trying to see you, and when I followed there was nothing there, but the steps were wet. It wasn't raining."

In the time Keith had been away the sun had moved on and the fire-escape was in shadow, but before they reached it he could see the outlines of the thing that before had had no outline. It was still transparent, but had developed a waxy sheen, the colour of congealing fat; it did in fact seem to be congealing, no longer draped over the ground but still pliable, conforming to the contours beneath like a pancake, ragged at the edges, although it was more oblong than round.

Kijé gave it an experimental prod and his finger left a dint that vanished as they watched.

"It's shrinking," Keith said. "It was over a metre long when I last saw it. And it's still changing. An hour ago – not even that – you could hardly see it except where the light caught it. And I couldn't even get a grip on it, it sort of *poured* over my fingers. Have you seen anything like it before?"

"No," Kijé said, gratefully. "Never. Look, it's still impossible to handle. It has no friction."

"More than it had before. Shall we leave it here and see what happens? If you're right, that thing you fell on that burst – this may be it. A kind of skin."

"A skin of something alive?"

"I hope not. You mean the thing on the fire-escape?"

"And the things you said you had met in the dark, that you took for garbage sacks. If this is what I landed on it has certainly shrunk. It broke my fall almost completely, only my right foot struck the ground. I am 1 metre 80. It must have been longer than it is now."

"You said it felt as if it was full of water. Perhaps it *was* full of water."

"I think it is changing as we watch," Kijé said. "Let's go to Maisie's now that we are here, and choose our robes, and then see what has happened while we are gone."

Holding the fire door open they looked along the corridor where they had fled the Equispherians last night. There were still only two sets of footprints in the dust. Kijé pulled the door shut but did not engage the bar. They walked down the corridor, hugging the wall in case one of the doors should open, and came out on to the first-floor landing. The foyer below was flooded with sunlight and roiling dust as the Equispherians swept and garnished. Keith noted, by their hoods, that it was the Phoenixes who did the housework. The Sphinxes no doubt had their minds on higher things.

Unobserved, he and Kijé edged round the landings, up the stairs, until they reached the third floor and Maisie's door. Keith let them in, turning the key in the lock behind them. In the fusty twilight Kijé tracked among the packing cases to where a faint rectangular glow indicated the window. He tugged a cord and the heavy curtains creaked apart, releasing a shower of dust, plaster and dark flapping creatures, large moths or small bats. They dived under a table while the debris of decades churned and drifted in sunbeams. All around them trunks and cases spilled fabulous cascades of furs, curtains, clothing, bedding.

When the air cleared a little they dived in and swam through the preposterous hoard, dredging shoulder deep among swathes of brocade and damask, linen, silk, velvet, satin, voile; surfacing like breathless pearl divers with jewelled purses, poison-green evening gloves, sweeping plumes, clocked stockings, scarves, beaded fringes, patent-leather pumps with the soles danced out. Keith came up clutching a tiny gossamer camisole and held it against his chest. Kijé, who had arisen beneath a devoré velvet stole that hung from him like a mantilla, snapped open an ostrich-feather fan.

"Insect!" he squealed, pirouetting on a blunt-booted toe. "That old bitch nearly ruptured my spleen last night. Give him *money*!" He reeled towards the bedroom and fetched up short in the doorway. "Who are they?"

"Someone's here?" Keith reached the door in two strides and found Kijé looking at the twin oil paintings that hung either side of the pier glass. "That's our Maisie – seventy years ago, at a guess; and that's her husband. The one in the middle's you."

"Aren't I lovely?" Kijé said, unconvincingly.

Keith adjusted the stole about his shoulders. "You are now."

Kijé flourished his fan and flounced girlishly in front of the filthy-looking glass. There followed ten minutes of heartless fun among Maisie's past glories, rampaging through an archive of 20th-century underwear. Keith, squeezing an arm into a peach tulle peignoir trimmed with moulting marabou caught sight, in the mirror, of Kijé trying on a corset, multiple suspenders jiggling, whalebones creaking, and recalled a cruel raid on his sister's lingerie drawer with a school friend, long ago.

Having been made to measure for Maisie the corset went halfway around Kijé like an apron. When he let go of it, it recoiled with a twang and shot across the room. There was a brief pause and then Kijé, who rarely allowed himself even

to smile, started to laugh, a hoarse unpractised rasp, dangerously loud in the dusty silence.

"Kijé, shut up. Someone will hear us. Stop it!" But having
started he could not stop. Weeks, months, years of self-control
had overwound his mainspring. The laughter escalated from
a manic cackle into a high-pitched wail as he backed up
against a wardrobe and leaned there, speechless and panic-
stricken, taking in air in long helpless whoops, on and on
and on. Tears were beginning to leak from the corners of his
eyes.

Keith, who had never seen anyone in hysterics before, took
a swing at him and ducked away as the wardrobe, under
stress, groaned feebly and began to tilt sideways.

"Stop it. Shut up. If you don't shut up I'll hit you." He
advanced again, crabwise, one eye on Kijé, one calculating
the wardrobe's angle of declivity as the door began to drop
open and a lifetime's collection of coathangers fell out. He
drew back his arm for a really definitive slap but before he
could land it the pile of bolsters and quilts stowed insecurely
on top of the wardrobe, overbalanced and began to descend
in an avalanche of epic slowness, smothering the dreadful
laughter in a snow drift. The air was full of little feathers.

Keith went to the door and opened it a crack. Nothing
stirred in the corridor. If the Equispherians, three floors
below, had heard the outburst, they must have assumed it
came from the Registan. He relocked the door and turned
back into the room. Kijé had dug himself out and was kneeling among the coathangers as if praying, with his face hidden

in his hands, overwhelmed by delayed shock and, Keith guessed, bitter humiliation. The presence of the absurdly feminine velvet stole, still hanging round his neck, threatened to crown his embarrassment. Bending to pluck it away Keith felt the other man flinch at his touch and remembered how Kijé had withdrawn even from Mrs Fahrenheit when she had tried to comfort him. It was his own awful pride that had brought him to this. The kindest thing would be to creep tactfully away, to pretend that it had never happened; to go and sit on the fire-escape until Kijé recovered his composure and came out, poker-faced and sardonic as usual. Then they could go and have lunch. Keith knelt down, put his arms around him and pulled him back against the tumbled bedding which shifted accommodatingly under their weight like a welcoming third that embraced them both. Kijé, already taut as a lute-string, tensed to a quivering rigor and Keith, looking downward, saw his eyes widen with alarm at the prospect of further indignities.

"It's all right. It's all right. It's all right." He ought to be out on the fire-escape. He had wanted only to console, to be consoled. It was not all right, he should not be witnessing this. "It's all right. It's all right."

Kijé whispered hesitantly, "Do you like men?"

"Oh. Oh no. Not that way." He stroked the greying, dusty hair. "You?"

"No."

"Not Fitz?" He had to ask.

"No, not Fitz." He caught his lower lip between his teeth

and began to cry quietly. Keith felt the shuddering body relax, the trusting weight of a head on his shoulder, a clenched fist unfurl against his neck. Then his eyes engaged with the knowing smirk of Sir Mortimer Hooke through the bedroom doorway.

What a pity, said Sir Mortimer's roguish eyebrows. What a shame you can't love each other. What a *waste*.

Keith transferred his gaze to the crack in the ceiling and lay staring upward while Kijé wept in his arms, a weary monotone that sounded as if he had been at it for hours without hope of respite. The feathers still fell around them.

When they stood up they moved apart shyly, making clumsy attempts to tidy up, and both desperately trying to think of something to say. Keith stuffed the coathangers back into the wardrobe. Kijé recovered the corset and folded it back into its box with a deal more respect than he had whipped it out.

"Isn't this what we need?" He was holding up a voluminous cloak with braided fastenings and a loose, lined hood.

"Perfect, but it's grey."

"It won't be when we get the dust out. But it only reaches my knees. I need something long. Try it. You're shorter."

"Not that much shorter. We'll need skirts. Just take an armful of anything black – or grey – and we'll sort it out at the museum." Keith upended one of Maisie's suitcases and they packed it with clothes and curtains, each looking up now and again to see the other watching him covertly. They were in a most unseemly hurry to leave.

At the foot of the fire-escape they paused and sidled up to the thing, the skin, mattress, whatever it was. In the last hour a further transformation had taken place. It was growing darker, mottled, gristly almost, curling up at the edges and now very easy to handle, being almost rigid and almost weightless. It had shrunk to something the size of a cricket pad. At one end were two ragged protruberances.

Kijé picked it up and held it to the light. It was no longer transparent, but translucent, like parchment.

"Have you seen one of these before?" Keith said.

"They turn up all over the place, but they're usually cracked or broken. The best ones are in the museum. That chest in the Archaeology Gallery is full of them."

"'Unidentified objects supposedly held sacred by the Sturyat nomads of Qantoum. Possible once used as a form of armour on limbs.' When I first came here there was one for sale in the market. I bought it and used it as a shelf. That was before I knew it was supposed to be sacred."

"Supposed by whom?" Kijé said.

"No one seems to know what they are: leathers. How come you've never come across a live one before?"

"You've only found two." Then he said, "*Live?*"

"All right, in a fluid state. But you've been here for years. Has nobody ever mentioned them before? Aren't there any local tales of itinerant lilos? Don't the Sturyat have a funny story about a man who married a plastic bag full of water?"

Kijé turned it this way and that. "If this thing was alive I killed it by falling on it, from a great height. It saved my life,

I'm very grateful. But in seven years here I've never seen one of those things before. Now we come across three, maybe four of them in, what, two days? Where are they coming from?"

"Is it the rain that brings them out?"

"The whole region gets rain storms at this time of year. Spring and autumn. You saw the desert bloom in spring, perhaps these also come from the desert."

"But what *are* they?"

"Not lilos, not plastic bags. Let us take this one back with us. The next time it rains we can make an organized search. That is, we can watch where we put our feet."

Kijé picked up the leather and tucked it under his arm like a skateboard. Keith collected Maisie's overnight bag from where it lay, under the iron stairs, and they walked demurely across the Registan.

"Don't say anything to Erna," Kijé said abruptly.

"About the – *them*?"

"About anything."

Seventeen

Keith began to accompany Lizaveta to market in the mornings. She could manage perfectly well on her own but now that Kijé sent everything he grew to the museum Keith needed an excuse to visit the stalls he no longer delivered to. It was an opportunity to see who, or what, had arrived in town since the previous evening.

The weather continued dry. There were no further queasy encounters in damp places and oblique enquiries among the Qantoumis produced no response. No one had seen anything strange; no stranger, that was, than Brother Joel and his Joggers, the Sundancers, the mute etiolated people who haunted the trees in the Registan like dryads. The Equispherians remained in the Sogdiana Serai. If they were growing impatient with Szusko's failure to deliver oil they were making no move to go after him. Possibly the presence of the bear gave them pause for thought.

On the morning of the Spelling Keith went with Lizaveta as usual. If any enmity were developing between the Qantoumis and the new arrivals both sides took care to conceal it. Business was booming. Vlodya had even sold some of his Lada parts. The Goat Woman waved cheerily. Streph greeted him as usual.

"Tea, dear man? Have a frog."

He bought his tea, some bread and cheese from the Goat Woman and stood among the crowd to eat, drink and observe. Who, among these friendly, generous, kindly people, had ambushed Fitz and Woodbridge, would have killed him had he been there, would have killed Kijé who had been ready to do the same thing himself? It was a carousel of possibilities that he tried not to ride, but it went on turning.

"Dear man!" Streph bellowed. "All is well! You remember my son's wife? Here are the babies."

A young woman was carrying two small children, the famous twins. Even to Keith's inexperienced eye one looked considerably older than the other.

"See, fine boys. Growing like kids."

They would indeed have to grow like kids to have reached that size in fourteen weeks. Keith inspected them gravely, congratulated the mother, he supposed it was the mother, and handed back the mug. Had Zayu ever told them all that their bluff had been called? Scarcely worth mentioning, really. What could he do about it?

That evening he stood in the kitchen doorway with Kijé and Mrs Fahrenheit, looking over the bar to the warmly domestic scene beyond. The Teeth had eaten and retreated to their tabernacle, or whatever name they had given to the elementary school, and the regulars were at their regular tables. It looked as safe and cosy as an English pub on a rainy English evening.

"The rain I could do without," Kijé said. He had an assortment of dark fabric rolled under his arm.

"It isn't heavy. You will not dissolve," Mrs Fahrenheit said.

"It's not that – " Keith began, but stopped himself at a warning look from Kijé. They had stowed the leather in the cellar and she was not yet aware how they had come by it.

"We ought to leave," Kijé said.

"Already?" She looked alarmed.

"Already. We planned to arrive at the last moment, but I think we might go to the citadel first to see what's happening. Ready, Keith? Will you make us coffee when we come back, Erna?"

"Be careful," Mrs Fahrenheit said, and hugged his shoulder; then unexpectedly did the same to Keith. "Be careful."

"Yes, Mum," he said, smiling, but felt tears pricking.

Lady Hooke was in the rotunda. "The Boat Race. . ." she said vaguely as they went past.

"The what?"

"All these *people*."

"She thinks there will be a boat race?" Kijé said as they crossed Museum Street.

"The Oxford and Cambridge Boat Race, a great sporting event in England."

"I've heard of it. It must be all of forty years since Maisie saw one."

"She doesn't have any trouble with forty years. It's forty minutes that floors her."

They crossed the market and went down the lane past the cemetery.

"Is Maisie still putting out crumbs for the wolves?"

"I don't think so."

"Were there ever any wolves?"

"Who knows? In Maisie's head. Dinosaurs too, maybe. Let us be very quiet from here on," Kijé said. "Go to the citadel, get dressed, walk to the pasture and wait. If the Equispherians are eating with Theps they will be here soon. We follow them in. If they are joining them for coffee as it were, we will just have to wait."

"Why are you walking so slowly? Do you think we are being watched?"

"No – I don't want to step into – against – on anything."

"A lilo? They're pale. They catch the light."

"What light? I wish it would rain or not rain. I hate this wet air. Take care on the steps."

On the observation tower they changed into Phoenixes. Mrs Fahrenheit had tacked and basted Maisie's cloaks and skirts on to lengths of curtain, so they each had a long black shift and a hood with various flapping attachments that approximated to Keith's approximate memory of Phoenix Helen's outfit. He was grateful for the extreme darkness. It would disguise any shortcomings in the costume and ensure mercifully that they could not see themselves or each other.

"Do you hear anything?" They peered down over the wall, straining to see.

"Feet on grass. They are in the pasture already."

Not a light showed in the Sturyat compounds, but on the western side of the pasture an undulating ribbon of candles was beginning to make its way around the perimeter. Something pale and portly was leading, a little ahead of the rest.

"They are leaving?" Kijé whispered.

"No; they go anticlockwise, remember?"

"That thing in front – one of our lilos?"

"That's the Archon."

The procession was now moving along the southern side, and the unpleasant buzzing they had heard in the restaurant rose up again along the length of the line.

"Are we going to tag on the end?"

"Not till the last moment. The ones at the back will know that there should be no one behind them. When we get inside we had better sit among the Sturyat."

"But they know us."

"Our faces will be hidden. The Equispherians know each other – oh, wait."

Someone was carrying a flaring torch across the pasture. It plunged like a meteorite and a roaring flame sprang up as a sizeable fire was kindled in the centre of the space. By its light they saw that from the shanty town that now clustered around the tepee in the south-eastern corner, people were emerging in large numbers.

"The Sundancers are joining the party," Keith said. "It will be bedlam in there.

"All to the good, whatever bedlam is," Kijé said. "Let's get down there and join them. They won't know a Sphinx from a Phoenix."

"Or an arse from an elbow. Now what – "

The gates of Theps's compound were opened, but no one went in. Instead the Sturyat were coming out, and at the same time people began streaming from the other compounds.

"They are going to meet in the open, around the fire," Kijé said. "Fate is on our side, for once. We'll go round the edge. By the time we get to the south side they will all have met in the middle. No one will notice."

It was to be no mere domestic Spelling; the whole tribe was turning out. The Equispherians had changed course and were spiralling towards the fire. The Sundancers mingled promiscuously with Equispherians and Sturyat alike. Keith was mainly struck by the fact that the original two dozen had swollen to a hundred or more. People from the west were no longer passing the railway station but being intercepted, welcomed, redirected by the Sturyat lookouts at Industrial. How many more, of other persuasions, had been going in unnoticed? There was a splinter group, following a tall cloaked man in a high-crowned, broad-brimmed hat, carrying a staff.

"In this chaos," Kijé observed, "we might have come as ourselves. But keep your hands hidden." He drew his own large, dirt-ingrained maulers into his sleeves. "We are meant to be women. Once the Spelling begins we do not speak unless we must."

"What counts as must?"

"If we need to leave immediately. Head for the Old Town, if so. You know your way about. They don't."

With their heads bowed they left the edge of the pasture and sat down on the outside of the circle. The Equispherians had stopped buzzing; even the Sundancers were keeping their voices down. Only the followers of the man in the hat kept up a nervous twittering. The Sturyat themselves were quiet but generating an electric excitement in their silence which infected the others. By the time Gresk stood up to speak the hush was palpable, hanging over the pasture like a low mist.

Sitting there in his ridiculous disguise with Kijé shrouded beside him, Keith remembered his last words and took comfort in the thought. There was one place, outnumbered and outmanoeuvred though they might be, where he would have the advantage. He knew the maze of alleys, the short cuts, the steps, the roofs. For once Kijé would be reliant upon him. To his knowledge, the Sturyat, apart from Zayu, did not know the Old Town, and as he thought it he saw her, standing a little behind Gresk, ready to translate.

"We are the Sturyat," he began. "We are the star-born. We have had the promise of the All-High through many years that when the end of time is accomplished, our star will return and we will follow it. For we were sent forth in a ship, and when the ship came to land, we, the people, sat down to eat, and when we had eaten one rose and said, 'How shall we remember the old time and the old place?' And another said, 'We shall remember the old place thus: Make a circle about a fire and the fire shall be our star until our star returns.'" His voice deepened, became more resonant. "For many years one has stood here as I stand and remembered the promise of the All-High, and we have waited for the call to go home. We have sent out souls to bring us a sign, and the sign has come among us, that many shall come from the west and many shall come from the east and our star will return. Many have come from the west, and now many will come from the east also. When our star returns we will rise up and claim our heritage."

Gresk stepped back out of the light. Khlev took his place, immeasurably ancient, leaning on a stick. Zayu propped her up on the other side and spoke for her as the old woman mumbled in her ear.

"When we came to this place we set up the bones of our ancestors and made honourable places to lay down our souls. But the ones who ruled here stole our souls away. Another brought them back and they were put shamefully for all to see in the house of Prinzander, but then they were taken away again and hidden again. And so, those without soul stones took our soul stones and to this day they remain hidden from our sight. But when the many from the west join with the many from the east the soul stones *will* be restored to us, and our star will return and we will follow it."

On this ominous note she ended and Zayu guided her back to her place. The rain was falling in earnest now, but no one seemed to notice. Where Khlev had stood was a thickening of the darkness, amid it, something white: the Archon, surrounded by Sphinxes.

"People of the star," he declaimed, "people who wait; your star is coming to guide you home. Soon it will be seen in the east, and your all-High, known to us as Altaera, will call us to him. When the black sun rises on the morning of the end of days, the star will hang above it. Already we may see it coming. Soon it will be here. Mankind calls it Comet Colney-Hatch—"

"Comet Galadriel!" a voice volunteered from the circle.

" – but we know, as you know, that it is the dwelling of Altaera. We too will be going home. Believe me, O star-born Sturyat, we of the Equispheres will restore your soul stones to you."

A curious sound arose around the fire, perhaps a thousand voices, the buzzing of the Equispherians, random hoots and yoicks from the Sundancers and over all a Nurembergian roar of triumph from the Sturyat. Under the row Keith risked muttering to Kijé, "Do you realize what this means?"

Kijé did not answer but touched his arm, warningly, for the noise subsided as suddenly as it had arisen. The man in the mutant fedora, dressed, he now realized, as Gandalf, had stood up beside the Archon.

"Middle Earth will unite with these believers to restore your stones to you."

They were joined by the leader, if they could rise to anything as concrete as a leader, of the Sundance Tribe.

"Hey, you guys. Peace. Your star is our star. You go, we go. You shared your bread with us, now we'll settle accounts. You want your soul stones back, count on us. Whoever took them from you will give them back in peace and love. Count on us, man."

The variegated applause broke out once more. Keith, fascinated, felt Kijé nudge him sharply. About a quarter of the way around the circle, at three o'clock to their six, two Sphinxes had stood up and were counting heads, or hoods, looking all around them and then, fixedly in their direction.

"We leave," Kijé said, "immediately."

As they detached themselves from the circle the Sphinxes, as one Sphinx, stood upright and began to move, forgetting the Earth's equilibrium in the emergency of the moment, clockwise. The Archon was shouting, the Sundancers and the Hobbits, having no equilibrium to worry about, cut across the circle, across the embers in some cases, and joined the chase. As they had no idea who they were chasing they were fanning out in several directions, colliding with the Equispherians who were getting into their stride, and the greater numbers of Sturyat who were going nowhere.

Keith and Kijé had only a small start and they were losing the advantage, stumbling over the uneven ground and seriously impeded by the novel experience of running in long skirts. But they made the mouth of the nearest alley ahead of their closest pursuer, a lean and lolloping Sphinx. Kijé dropped back a pace.

"Get us in as far as you can. Stay away from the museum."

"They don't know we're from the museum," Keith said, but he turned right, then right and right again, clockwise, in the hope of further confusing the Equispherians. Whether or not it did, the footsteps behind them faltered and Keith pictured the leading Sphinx, disoriented, slowing down while the rest piled up behind him. He gripped Kijé by a handful of cloak, doubled back, turned right, dragged him up an exterior staircase and in at a door.

"Leave it open so we can see. Let's get this crap off."

Gasping for breath they tore at the robes to the sound of splitting seams and rending cloth.

"How did you lose them?"

"Wound them up – disturbing the equilibrium. But the Sundancers are out there too, and Hobbits."

"*Hobbits?*"

"Never mind. We shouldn't stay here, we're still too close to the edge. If they've got any Sturyat with them the doors won't keep them out. They'll go through any house without stopping – unless the bones are up."

"You lead the way, then. No more talking. If one runs, the other runs."

"The same way?"

"Yes – stay together. We must."

There were footsteps and voices outside, voices already angry. Keith, tweaking Kijé's shirtsleeve, tiptoed across the floor and fumbled for where he thought a trapdoor would be, found it and raised it. They slipped through and down the stairs, Kijé lowering the trap above their heads. Keith urged him across the courtyard, through the house opposite and out on to the exterior flight, in an alley that did not connect with the one they had left. They could hear the voices and the footsteps, only a few metres away.

The steps on which they were standing ran, as Keith had calculated, up to the roof. He put his mouth to Kijé's ear and hissed, "Can you jump?" Kijé nodded. Keith pointed upwards. They crawled up the half-dozen steps to avoid presenting an outline against the sky, and on to the roof where they lay flat.

"Why jump?" Kijé said.

"In every courtyard there's one flight that goes up to the roof – and down from it. If we can jump from roof to roof – if we *have* to—"

He was cut short by a heart-stopping shriek from close by, at ground level, followed by howls of fear. Kijé rolled back to the steps and lowered himself until he could squint round the edge of the wall. Keith, on elbows and knees, made a circuit of the roof. On the third side he located the source of the cry. Illuminated by the presence of two Sundancers, carrying flambeaux, the scene below was startling. The mouths of three converging alleys were impacted with a log-jam of people and several dozen were crammed into the narrow space immediately below him, those at the rear jostling to advance and escape from the pressure of others massing behind them; the ones at the front scrabbling to move back. Love and peace had been abandoned to terror and confusion. Voices were raised. Among the heads and flailing arms he saw black robes. The principal panickers were the Equispherians who had lost all sense of direction and were profoundly off-balance.

He looked back, saw Kijé peering over the top step, and waved him forward. Kijé came at a loping crouch and arrived just in time to witness the cause of the mêlée. Blocking the end of the alley was what seemed at first to be a wall of enormous pale sandbags, toppling slowly towards the people who were madly struggling to get away from them. They glistened whitely, wetly, in the torchlight, bulging, slopping over one another as they proceeded slowly but inexorably, blindly, senselessly, impelled only by an irresistible instinctive urge to go forward. A screaming Phoenix tripped on her robe, sat down backwards and was submerged as one of the things rolled over her.

People were clambering up steps and hammering on doors, unaware that they were unlocked. On this side no stairway reached the roof, but hands were appearing round the sides, groping for purchase, as the stronger climbed over the weaker to escape from the crush.

"Again, leave immediately," Kijé said, and before the first refugees could gain the roof they were back at the foot of the steps and in the alley.

"Where now?" Kijé said.

"Next flight, round the corner."

"And suppose round the corner comes—"

"We'll go through the houses, over the roofs."

"But I can't *see* – we may fall."

The fire-escape must still be fresh in his mind. "I won't let you fall."

They ran, from stair to roof to stair to courtyard to room to stair to roof to stair, until they reached the lane by the cemetery. The turmoil in the alleys was still audible but muffled by distance. They crossed the street and with unspoken agreement collapsed on to a brick coping under the mulberry tree to recover their wind. The tree, although losing its leaves, had broken out in strips of rag.

After a while Kijé took out his cigarettes and lit one.

"See," he said, "no wolves."

"Sod that. I'd rather meet a wolf than – Kijé, what *are* they?"

"Excuse me, do you ever smoke?"

"No, thank you."

"Don't you wish you did?"

"Yes, but I'm not starting with your floor-sweepings. Have you ever seen anything like . . . slugs . . . seals. . ."

"Walruses. Slugs the size of walruses. They have no horns."

"No, and no moustaches. But there's something at the front, sensory organs of some kind. They don't seem to know where they're going, but there's a front and a back. And when they dry out, the one you burst, the ones in the museum, there's two little sort of stalks."

"Whatever they are we should give thanks for them. We might have been trapped by that mob, otherwise. Who were just as senseless. They didn't know why they were chasing us; they didn't know who we were. The Equispherians said—"

"Didn't *say* anything. That word you used, mob. No thought, just impulse."

"They may be injuring themselves quite badly," Kijé said hopefully.

"But where do these things come from? They're like – just great bags full of water. Where's the nearest water? They can't be coming out of the wells."

"Can't they? I don't know what they can do. But the nearest running water must be eighty kilometres away."

"Kijé, think about this: you said, when you fell off the fire-escape, that in seven years you'd never come across such a thing before."

"True."

"And you'd never *heard* of such a thing."

"No, never."

"And the Sturyat never spoke of them."

"Unless they used a word I do not recognize."

"Look, you and I know, because we've virtually watched it happen, that these water-beds, slugs, walruses, whatever, dry out into leathers. *But nobody else does.*"

"Does that put us in a position of intellectual strength?" Kijé asked.

"No, but don't you see, no one we know has ever mentioned them. No one's ever said, 'By the way, Keith, watch out for the walking water-beds in autumn.' Lord Dacre wrote about leathers, but he didn't know what they were. Nor did Lady Charlotte or Prince Andrei, and *he* didn't just drop in and move on. He lived here. He knew the place."

"But never saw a water-bed. A decadent Western indul-
gence, the water-bed. There were no water-beds under
Socialism."

"Leave it out," Keith said. "You see what I'm getting at,
don't you? No one has ever recorded seeing them before, but
the leathers must have been around for over a century."

"Possibly five centuries."

"You're beginning to get it. The Sturyat have been waiting
five hundred years for their comet to come back. Suppose
they've been waiting for these – these *sacs* as well. Two five-
hundred-year cycles. The leathers are the ones left over from
last time."

"When they first arrived."

"The Sturyat are preparing to leave on a long journey;
into the mountains, up to a comet, I don't know. But this is a
desert region."

"And those things are full of water. Yes, I have got it. The
desert is in the east. Remember what Gresk said back there.
'Now many will come from the east also.'"

"We'd better go back to the museum, Ernie will be getting
worried. We've got to tell her what we've found out; not the
lilos, this Equispherian crud about the comet. Did you know
about the Sturyat believing that they'd arrived on a ship?"

"Yes. Noah's Ark, not a spaceship." Kijé stood up and
ground out his fag-end.

"Do you think we should go back to the pasture and see
how the Sturyat are taking the news that their water tanks
have arrived?"

"No. I didn't see any Sturyat in that mob that came after us, and we don't know how the ones who did see them will describe them. They are fairly indescribable and we haven't seen one by daylight yet."

"Do you want to? Perhaps they only come out at night."

"I think you are right; rainy nights. Now, we must go back and tell Erna – what's that?"

From behind the mulberry tree a spectral form glided past them and flitted away among the tombs like a white moth.

"Did you see – ?"

"One of those tree-huggers. Do you think she was listening?"

"Listening? I do not think she was even alive," Kijé said. "Now even the tombs are giving up their dead."

Eighteen

They sat around the coffee pot at the kitchen table. Keith let Kijé do the talking. His long measured sentences made the things he was describing sound marginally more credible. Mrs Fahrenheit listened with mounting incredulity and finally broke in.

"Tell me if I have understood you? The Sturyat did not come out of the Taklamakan Desert, they arrived in a spaceship. They have been waiting five hundred years for the spaceship to come back."

"That's the Gospel according to the Equispherians," Keith said, "but the Sturyat seem to like the sound of it. Gresk said they were getting ready to leave because their All-High had sent them a sign—"

"You," Kijé said, unnecessarily.

"Then the Archon got up on his hind legs and said that Altaera was the same as their All-High, and that the ship the Sturyat arrived on was the same as Altaera's spacecraft."

"Comet Colney-Hatch, on its five-hundred-year orbit," Kijé said. "So when the Sturyat leave the Equispherians will be leaving with them. Then old Khlev spoke. She said that all they needed now was their soul stones back. At which point the man in the hat—"

"Gandalf," Keith said.

"You know who he is?"

"I know who he thinks he is."

"He said that his people would be happy to take back the soul stones from whoever was withholding them. That means you."

"The Sundancers will help them; in peace and love."

"That means bloodshed," Kijé said.

"Then one of the Sphinxes noticed that there were too many Phoenixes round the fire, and we left, followed by a large number of people."

"But not as large as the number who stayed. There must be a thousand at least. Visitors from the west no longer follow the tracks to the station. The Sturyat wait for them at Industrial."

"You are sure they are all from the west; none from the east?"

"What is coming from the east may not be people," Kijé said. "There is something we haven't told you about. You know the leathers in the chest in the Archaeology Gallery?"

"Yes. I noticed you had one the other day."

"The ones in the chest are old. The one we brought in is fresh. We saw it develop. Erna, have you any idea what they are?"

"None at all. Nor had Friedrich. Even the Sturyat do not know."

"I think they do," Kijé said. "I think they have always known."

Keith said, "A few weeks ago it started raining for the first time in months. The night the Equispherians arrived I came across something cold, damp, in a lane near here. It was dark, I couldn't see anything, so I went back later to look. There was nothing there, but on the way back I tripped over one—"

"Tripped? How can you trip over a leather?"

"Wait," Kijé said. "I have fallen on one, and burst it. I thought it was a mattress full of water, but all we could find next day was a kind of rubbery skin. When the sun got to it it began to shrink and harden. After an hour or so it was what you saw me carrying, a leather."

"You are telling me," Mrs Fahrenheit said, "that these leathers are the dried remains of large creatures full of water?"

"I don't think there's much doubt," Keith said. "Tonight we actually saw them. After we got away from the Equispherians they ran into a great heap of these – water-beds."

"Water-beds?"

"Imagine a seal," Kijé said. "No flippers, no face, no head even. Imagine that instead of blubber they are full of water. They can move forwards but not, I think, backwards. They keep advancing, over each other, over anything that gets in their way. And they can go up stairs. They must be enormously heavy."

"What happened to these creatures when they met the Equispherians?"

"We didn't wait to find out," Keith said, "but listen: leathers have been around for five centuries, and there's no record of anyone seeing a live one before. But, say the Sturyat know what they are, what they were. They're going to travel through the desert, they'll need water. Gresk was saying this evening, those who come from the east will come *now*. Not people, these things. They've been waiting for the comet to come back and they've been waiting for these – these water-beds. And if they are what the Sturyat have been waiting for, out of the desert, out of the east, they're going to want their soul stones, too."

"They may dismantle the place," Mrs Fahrenheit said. "They may raze it to the ground. They will find nothing. I have shown Zayu everything that could possibly be a soul stone, and every time she has said, with a kind of weary contempt that I should be so foolish as to think I could deceive her, 'No, not that.' Not only do the Sturyat not recognize lies, they don't recognize the truth either. They will *not* believe that I do not know where their stones are. They think I am hiding them."

"Haven't you ever asked to see one?" Keith said. "So that you'd know what to look for?"

"Do you take me for a fool too? Of course I have – and was shown something that looked to me like a gallstone. They refuse to believe I do not know what a soul stone looks like."

"They have a story about a man who mistook his stone for a quail's egg. What does a quail's egg look like?"

"Cabinet 11F. Birds of the Southern Steppe."

"You asked me about quails' eggs once," Kijé said.

"I'd just heard the story."

"They are *not* quails' eggs," Mrs Fahrenheit said. They were all three becoming shrewish with fatigue.

"Prince Andrei drew them in his book."

"I doubt very much if they showed *him*. And he was dead before the buried ones turned up."

A little imperious voice in the shadows announced, "One needs one's sleep. One has slept through aerial bombardment, but to have to listen to below-stairs gossip – "

"Oh, Maisie, I *am* sorry." Mrs Fahrenheit, all passion spent, went towards the little creature in its trailing negligée. "Of course you need your rest. Come along."

"Who won the Boat Race, Maisie?" Kijé enquired.

"Can't find m'bed. . ." The voice tailed off as they went through the door.

"Where's she sleeping?"

"Ernie put her in one of the offices," Keith said.

"I hope she enjoyed her Boat Race," Kijé said. "Are the shutters up in the bar? Good. And I think the front door should be locked at night, from now on. Whoever sits up must be armed; not just me."

As they went out, Keith said, "Were you armed this evening?"

"Of course I was. Since you so kindly returned my Makarov I always carry it."

"Would you have used it?"

"I don't think so," Kijé said. "Who fires the first shot may lose the war."

"Is that what you would have used on me?"

"No, no," he said reassuringly. "We were trained to kill with our bare hands."

At daybreak they opened the doors of the museum and heard near by the combined shuffling and squeaking that identified Szusko, the cart and the bear. Keith went out into the street and watched their painful progress up the slope towards Oktyabrskaya. In the cart was an oil drum.

"I think the Equispherians are getting their oil at last," he said to Kijé."

"Yes, I told him to let them have a little – before they went looking for it. I wanted to see if they knew where it comes from and it seems they don't. A little is all he can manage. I don't think they will be in the mood to do much with it today, do you?" He came out into the portico, yawning. "I am going up to the garden to start shifting food. We ought to be laying in supplies, here."

"Are you expecting a siege?"

"Oh, a little one, perhaps," Kijé said. "Are you coming?"

"I'll be along later. I thought I'd pay Zayu a visit first."

"About soul stones?"

"It's worth a try."

"Is it? She will probably show you a woodlouse. Tell Erna what we are doing, where we are going, tell her exactly. There is no point in keeping things from her any more; anything we know, she needs to know."

The sun had not yet risen as he walked the lane behind the Iskander, keeping a weather eye open for late-retiring water-beds, lilos; they would have to find a name for them. Aquasacs. The fact that they had never been seen in daylight did not mean that they never would be, but they must shun sunlight. He had seen what sunlight did to them, once they were damaged. Where did the foul things go by day?

Had the Sturyat seen them yet?

He made a detour to examine the place where the visitors had, last night, met the other visitors, the collision between east and west. In spite of knowing better, he expected pools of glistening slime as might be left in the wake of a titanic slug, but the pathway was only damp after the rain. When he reached the site of the confrontation, however, there was evidence, although he could make little of it. The blue-washed walls were stained with tulips of smoke where torches had burned too close. Lower down they were smeared, smudged, abraded. He remembered the terror-stricken mob, clawing and jostling in the confined space, struggling to flee the senseless advance of the unknown horror. The relics of the panic were all too human: blood streaks, threads adhering to roughcast, a discarded shoe that lay in a slick of liquid.

As he bent to touch it his feet shot from under him and he landed on what felt like cold satin. Scrabbling to rise on the frictionless surface he knew what he was touching. One of the things had suffered an injury, been punctured, seared. He writhed away from it, pushing himself clear by kicking against the wall. In an hour or so, when the sun rose high enough, there would be another leather lying in the alley.

After that he went quickly up the steps, through rooms, until he came to the place where he had lived and, he supposed, Zayu still did live. He was on Zayu's stairs so he went directly to the roof, and there she was, standing with her back to him. He hesitated, unsure how to begin. They had never been exactly intimate, but until the episode of Bordeleau's camera they had never found conversation difficult. Was Zayu at all sensitive to atmosphere? The difficulty would be all his. It had taken her a matter of hours to recover.

She heard him, turned and motioned him to come forward, showing no unease at the memory of the meeting in her upper room. Possibly she had no memory of it, since, in her scheme of things, it no longer mattered. He had scarcely spoken to her since the morning when Fitz and Woodbridge disappeared. If he were to say to her, "Zayu, what happened to Fitz?" she would reply, "The sand got him."

"See," she said, raising her arm.

He saw. The railway line was dotted with moving figures, some single, some in groups.

"Soon it will be time to leave."

"When the many come from the east and the many come from the west. Who is coming from the east, Zayu?"

"The ones we have been waiting for. They are already here."

"Why are they here?"

"It is time." He was about to butt in when she went on, "It is not the first time."

"You've seen them before?"

"Not I. But when the Sturyat travel, they travel with them. We have been waiting for them to come back."

"So it's five hundred years since the last visit?"

"They are not visitors," she said, taking him literally. "This is where they come to breed."

"They're *breeding*?"

"Of course."

"How many – ?"

"Very many. When they go, as the star leads them, we shall go too, with those from the west."

He remembered why he had come. "What about the soul stones?"

"They will be returned to us."

"Zayu, please listen. They would have been returned to you already if anyone knew where they were. No one knows where to look. No one knows what they are like."

"Prinzander saw them. He drew them in his little book."

"Prince Andrei has been dead for a century," he said. "Anyway," he added craftily, "I don't think that what Prince Andrei saw were soul stones."

"No," she agreed cheerfully. "He saw little lumps."

"How do you know?"

"We do not show our soul stones."

"Then how the hell are we supposed to know what we are looking for?"

"Looking? The widow knows where they are."

"Zayu, she doesn't. Believe me, she doesn't."

Zayu studied him thoughtfully. He wondered, does she

think I'm lying, when I tell her the truth? He said, "Mrs Fahrenheit has searched all over the museum, many times. They are not there, but if they were she couldn't find them because she doesn't know what they look like. All she has seen are Prince Andrei's little lumps – his drawings. How big are they? What colour? If you can't show me one, at least tell me what they look like."

"Why should you care?" she asked, in a spirit, as far as he could tell, of genuine enquiry. She could not comprehend his concern.

"I want to help – remember how I came here. One of your souls brought me."

"But that was long ago. There is nothing else you must do."

He was not of as much consequence as even one of those bloated things basking in the rain.

"Nothing else I *must* do," he said, "but things I want to do. I want to help Mrs Fahrenheit find your soul stones."

"There is no need. They will be found."

"How?"

"Those who come from the west will find them for us."

He understood her scenario. When the time was ripe assorted Equispherians, Sundancers, Hobbits and, possibly, Joggers, would break into the museum, kill anyone who stood in the way and ransack the place. That was fine by her.

"They'll find nothing." It was like banging his head against a duvet; the smothering indifference. It did not even hurt. "Has any of *them* ever seen a soul stone?"

"Once the Sturyat showed Khura Khan the soul stones and he took them away. We shall never show them again."

"But we don't want to take them away, we want to give them back. Why should I want to see the museum smashed up, my friends attacked, killed?"

Choosing her words carefully, Zayu said, "The museum is a disgusting place. It houses the dead who may not rest. Every time I go into it I pray to the All-High to cleanse me. Soon I shall go there no more."

"Why *do* you go there?" He was moved by the dreadful daily sacrifice she had been making, entering a place that was a standing blasphemy to her.

"For the stones' sake."

"Oh, Zayu." Forget Bordeleau, Soames, Woodbridge, Fitz. Their blood was on his head as much as on hers. "For the stones' sake, show me one, just one. It needn't be yours. Show me a stone whose owner is dead."

"You were told," she said. "Our stones are few. We must share. I will show you mine, that is my mother's, and her mother's, and her mother's mother's also. I have no right to the rest."

"Shall I come with you now?"

"No. I will bring it here. Wait. If anyone learns of this I shall die."

He waited, listening to her footfalls die away. What had he let himself in for by trusting her? Would she return, would she return alone, or would she send others in her place? And if she did return would she bring her soul stone from the house of Theps or would she bring a substitute as Kijé derisively suggested? And if she brought the real thing, would she let him live to tell of it?

He turned his back on the railway and looked towards St Vasili's, the sunlight on the dome and beside it the sinister sight of the Sogdiana Serai with the cranky ladders of the fire-escape akimbo.

It was half an hour before he heard her coming back, alone by the sound of it, but he looked over the edge of the roof to be sure. She was alone, walking with almost ceremonial precision, one foot planted before the other, head bowed over some object that she carried at breast level, in both cupped hands. As slowly, she mounted the steps, giving him time to return to the place where she had left him.

Without speaking she sat down on the roof and began to unwrap her parcel. It was netted in woven twigs and as each disengaged, a tight wrapping of leaves began to spring apart like an opening bud. He stood close and watched until, without help, each furled leaf curled back to reveal a dark heart, a little cindery mineral heart.

"Do not touch it," she said, holding the twiggy nest with infinite care. "Our soul stones come as we do, from the stars."

He knew that at last she was telling the truth; it was a meteorite.

Back through the Old Town, where the thing, the aquasac, had reached the pancake stage, congealing in the sunlight.

Where before it had filled the alley from side to side, it was already shrinking away at the edges, but there was not room yet to sidle past and he could not bring himself to jump over it. He might land short. Instead he cut to the right and came out at the lower end of the market, already heaving with life in spite of the early hour and the cold. He was about to turn down behind the Iskander Hotel when he noticed activity in the Registan. Were the Equispherians coming to the boil? He went to investigate.

The Registan was full of people, assembling in the central square around the fountain, watched with a kind of vacant dismay by the tree-huggers. Luggage was piled in cairns. Several men had scaled Lenin's plinth and were hauling wooden beams into position.

"Is that a gibbet they're putting up?" Usman had followed him from the market.

"I think it's a cross."

"A cross is a gibbet," Usman said, accurately. "More Christians. Are they here for the black sun? What has that to do with Christ?"

"Nothing," Keith said, "but the Millennium . . . birth of Jesus . . . two thousand years."

"That is the symbol of his death," Usman said, jerking his thumb at the cross.

As the transverse bar was slotted into position a cheer went up.

"They have come a long way for nothing," Usman said.

They parted, Usman back to the market, Keith along the

lane behind the Iskander. He was almost past it before a movement caught his eye and he looked up. Someone on the first floor was opening a window. A mattress was flung over the sill. Who was in there, one of the people from the Registan? Or was this another group? They were coming in hundreds, surely no longer in response to his message. Surely the black sun, the Eclipse of the Century, which had become a grim joke among the Qantoumis, no longer had credibility anywhere else.

He arrived back at the museum as the Joggers were leaving. He nodded to them all, comprehensively, and went through to the kitchen where Ernie and Lizaveta were at work, paring vegetables. Kijé had just arrived with a sack of potatoes.

"Have you seen what's in the Registan?" he said.

"Yes I have. And there's someone in the Iskander, airing the bedding. Dozens out on the railway line – and I saw another of those things dead in an alley. Zayu says they are here to breed."

"You spoke to Zayu?"

"Yes I did. I asked her to show me a soul stone – said we couldn't hope to find them if we didn't know what they looked like. She argued, but in the end she fetched her own."

"What makes you think it was her own?" Kijé said. "Or that it was a soul stone?"

"Because it's the last thing you'd expect it to be. It looks like a bit of clinker."

"It probably is."

"No. She said it came from the stars as the Sturyat do. It's a meteorite."

"You believed her?"

"This time, yes."

"Do you think all soul stones are meteorites?" Ernie said.

"Why not, if they're all supposed to have come from the stars?"

"We are still no closer to finding them. There are no meteorites here."

"Zayu is sure they'll be found; by those who come from the west. You know what that means."

"Mayhem. They may destroy the fabric and murder us all, but if they still do not find the soul stones will the Sturyat go on waiting? If the numbers you describe keep arriving then there cannot be enough food in Qantoum to support them. Now, they may intend to live off the land, in which case they will shortly be practising cannibalism. On the other hand they may have provisioned themselves for a short stay, intending to leave on a particular day; when your black sun rises on January 1st."

"Ernie, don't call it my black sun. And when it rises as usual?"

"I cannot guess how they think. I am not at all sure that they do think. Even Brother Joel and his Joggers – they seem sane enough—"

"No they don't," Kijé cut in. "If they were sane they would not be here. I was not entirely joking about a siege, Keith.

Let's get back to work. These maniacs can eat each other if they like. We must take care of our own people."

The stove had been lit in the greenhouse. Keith lingered in its glow while Kijé made a last round to double-check window shutters and doors. There was little warmth in the late afternoon sun, but the sky was clear; no threat of rain tonight. Qantoum must have received a good proportion of its annual 30 cm the day the Equispherians arrived, the day the creatures, aquasacs, had embarked on their breeding season. The Sturyat knew they were here, Zayu had said so, but what were they doing about them; herding them in the pasture as they did their sheep and goats? How would they travel with the ghastly things? What would happen when the temperature dropped; would they freeze into mammoth ice-packs where they lay?

Kijé was waving from the far side of the quadrangle. Keith closed the greenhouse door and went round to catch up with him in the office where a paraffin stove was spluttering.

"Who's on guard tonight?" he asked as they went down the steps, past the name-plate that Kijé had daubed over indelibly. Acting Captain Tcherk had claimed his last victim.

"Vlodya."

"Are you going to come back here to sleep?"

"I think so. Why not?"

"I wish you wouldn't. Not alone, not at the moment."

"Which is worse: someone breaks in and slays me in my bed, or someone breaks in and steals food because I am not here? Why should anyone break in? If you are offering to guard me, please don't bother. Erna needs you more than I do."

"I wasn't," Keith said. "I expect you've got a few grenades stashed under the bed for emergencies."

"I expect I have – did you hear that?"

A lugubrious baying echoed towards them down Oktyabrskaya.

"The desert yodelling?"

Kijé gave him a withering look. "That was human – or what passes for human these days."

"It sounded more like dogs." As he spoke, the dog and its friend streaked round the corner, tails down and going like greyhounds. "Wolves?"

The sound grew more frenzied as they approached. Before they reached the Registan they could see a man standing on Lenin's plinth beside the cross, striding up and down waving one hand in a declamatory manner. The other hand gripped a loud-hailer.

"What's he doing?"

"Preaching a sermon?" Keith said. Along one side of the central square tents had been erected. Their occupants were kneeling in front of the plinth.

Kijé listened intently. "What language is that?"

"I don't know, you're the linguist."

"Yes, I am enormously gifted," Kijé said. "That is why I am ending my days in the armpit of Asia, surrounded by religious maniacs. It sounds like English – it could be German."

The voice was increasing in pitch and fervour. The people in the crowd were starting to join in and the motionless figures began to sway and wave their arms. Several sprang to their feet and went into convulsions, rolling on the ground, and their words fragmented into hooting and yelping.

"They're speaking in tongues," Keith said. "They believe they are divinely inspired."

"I don't think so," Kijé said, flatly. "This I have seen before. It is like the old standing ovations in the Politburo. No one dared to be the first to stop applauding and sit down."

Before he had finished speaking every other sound was obliterated by a tremendous stentorian roar from somewhere up in the sky. The congregation flung themselves flat, gazing up, open-mouthed, as if expecting the face of God to look down on them. Keith and Kijé clung to the wall in shock as the appalling row intensified, wave after wave of tuneless, toneless, meaningless noise, above which soared the tell-tale caterwaul of feedback.

"It's the Equispherians' sound system," Keith screamed. "That's why they needed the generator."

They looked up. Black loudspeakers were lodged in the first-floor windows of the Sogdiana Serai. The people in the Registan had seen them and, as one, turned on the hotel yelling imprecations, led by the preacher with the loud hailer. It was hard to make out any words but they appeared to be bawling, "God! Is! Love!" clapping their hands and stamping on the off-beat. On cue, round the corner, came the Joggers, hup, hup, hup, led by Brother Joel and shouting one of their paramilitary psalms: "Loving Shepherd of thy sheep! Keep thy lamb in safety keep! Nothing can thy power withstand! None shall pluck me from thy hand!"

The Equispherians had mastered the feedback and now the voice of the Archon boomed across the square, completely unintelligible. The Joggers were starting their second circuit of the Registan. All around, from the side streets, the Qantoumis were beginning to assemble, drawn out of their houses by the din, watching the warm-up to the Apocalypse.

Nineteen

It was several days later that Lady Hooke disappeared and several hours before anyone noticed. She had burrowed quite happily into the room that Ernie had given her, only complaining at intervals about the clothes that Keith had salvaged from the Sogdiana Serai. He soothed her by promising that he would return for the rest, hoping that she would forget, as she forgot everything else. Perversely, she remembered.

He was returning to the Refreshment Room one evening after locking up behind the last customer, when Mrs Fahrenheit said suddenly, "Have you seen Maisie?"

"This morning, before I went out. Is she in her room?"

"She may be, but I don't think she's been in here all evening."

Keith cast his mind back. Lady Hooke was a fixture in the Refreshment Room, holding her imaginary court at the same table, night after night. He simply assumed that she was there. She had not been.

He went through to the passage that led to his own staircase behind the Zherdin Collection. Maisie's door was closed.

He knocked and waited, discouraged by the thought that if he went in she would be sitting in her chair, insolent, arrogant, and dead. There was no answer. He went in.

In the few weeks she had lived there Maisie had managed to turn the bare little office into a smaller version of her suite at the Sogdiana Serai, like the results of an explosion in Selfridges, but she was not there, dead or alive. He went back to the Refreshment Room.

"No sign of her. Could she be in the cellar?"

"It's locked. I have one key, Kijé the other. He's looking in the galleries now." Mrs Fahrenheit slumped over the bar. "God help me, I didn't even notice. . ."

"Don't worry. I'll see if she's gone upstairs."

From the window of his room he saw the beam of a torch sweeping the Zherdin Collection. Setsemhotep III was eerily revivified for a second. He could not see who held the torch but guessed it was Kijé. Strange that the three of them, with so much to concern them, should be so concerned for one crazy old woman, but the thought of her alone, bewildered, benighted in the hostile streets, was unexpectedly upsetting.

They all converged in the rotunda.

"Erna, search thoroughly; if she is here you'll find her soon enough, but *don't go outside*. If she isn't here she's probably trying to get into the Sogdiana Serai after her clothes. We'll go and look – Keith – yes? Lock up behind us, you'll be alone here. When we come back, I'll knock like this" – he beat a little tattoo on the door – "don't answer to anyone else. Let them wait till we get back. We won't be long."

"Bring the torch. Is that my torch?" Keith said.

"It is. No, no lights. There's enough of a moon." He opened the door of Lizaveta's cleaning cupboard and withdrew a mop. "Do not dare to laugh. We may be glad of this."

Up Museum Street into Oktyabrskaya, the moon shadows lengthening in the roadway. The tents in the Registan were dark, but the cross was illuminated by a row of candles placed in little glass pots along its arms. No light showed in the Sogdiana Serai. The loudspeakers were dumb and the doors were fastened.

"Fire-escape," Kijé said. He was already on his way round to the side of the building, but proceeding with caution, testing the ground ahead of him with the mop. He took the iron ladder slowly. Keith, at his heels, looked up and saw no shadow on the door.

"They've shut it. Can we get up to another level?"

Kijé went to check the door. "Two more floors, but I wouldn't want to risk it. The whole thing might come away from the wall. Anyway, this one was open only because we opened it. There's no reason why the others should be."

"Can't we look?"

"No," Kijé said and blocked the way. "We cannot be spared."

"The cemetery?"

"At this hour?"

"She doesn't know what hour it is. She doesn't know what year it is. But that was the only other place she went to, wasn't it?"

"Was? No, we must go back. Search in the morning, Keith. We are so few, and getting fewer. Poor Maisie, we will do what we can, but not now."

In the morning Lady Hooke had not returned. As people arrived at the museum each was asked the same question. The answer was always the same. No one had seen her. Lizaveta brought word that she was not in the cemetery but that it was inhabited by the tree-huggers, exiled from their haunt in the Registan and now lurking among the tombs, worshipping the mulberry tree.

When noon came with no sighting of Maisie, Kijé put on his coat, announcing: "The Equispherians need more fuel, Keith."

"How do you know?"

"I have just decided. Szusko will need help delivering it. Once we get inside I can look around. Maisie may be there, and anyway, I want to see what is going on."

"You might be recognized," Ernie said.

"As what? They've seen me about, sure, one more stupid Qantoumi. They don't know we went to the Spelling. Whatever happens," he said, as he went out, "don't come searching for me."

After that, every time the door of the Refreshment Room opened they looked up expectantly. Kijé did not return. Once there were shouts and running feet in the street followed ten minutes later by a burst of rapid gunfire. Keith, in the kitchen with Ernie and Lizaveta, leaped up.

"Kijé?"

"He only took the pistol with him. That was a sub-machine-gun."

They waited for answering fire. The lack of it was the more alarming. In the Refreshment Room the remaining customers were emerging from beneath tables. The Joggers, who had not moved, were saying Grace.

"I'm going to look." Keith started for the door but Ernie seized his arm in an iron grip.

"Don't be foolish. We cannot tell what is happening."

"We'd be able to tell if I went to look. And Kijé's out there somewhere."

"He is better able to take care of himself than you are, than any of us. Go and unlock the cellar, we may need it."

She pressed the key into his hand. He went into the warm presence of her wardrobe and turned it in the lock. When he returned she had gone out to the Refreshment Room where Brother Joel stood punctiliously counting coins on to the bar top.

"Stay here," she was saying. "At least wait till we find out what is happening."

"We shall be quite safe," Brother Joel replied calmly. "We were led here in safety, no harm can befall us. We shall return to our tabernacle to pray."

"I beg you."

He raised a pacifying hand, as to an overexcitable child. "Attend to your own safety. We have no need to fear. Angels guide you."

The Joggers were leaving in an orderly manner.

"Let them go, Ernie." Keith put his hand on her shoulder. "If they want to get their heads blown off – " He could feel her trembling, not, he thought, at the likely fate of the Joggers, but in helpless reaction to the sound that must have aroused terrible memories. But when she spoke her voice was firm.

"We agreed. *We* go nowhere, any of us, unless the other two know of it. At least we know where Kijé is."

"We don't. All we know is, he isn't here."

"It is too soon to go searching. He said that we were not to search. He was with Szusko. At the worst – *Keith*, face facts – at the very worst, what we heard was the two of them being shot. It's not likely."

"Don't forget the bear," he said, bitterly.

"The people out there are less likely to fire on them than on each other. The town is now full of deranged strangers with wild beliefs; fiercely territorial. So far they have let each other alone, but space is running out, time is running out, food will soon be running out. What is more likely than that they will turn on each other – not for time or space or food, but for what they believe in? No war is more fearful than a holy war."

"I ought to guard the entrance. Where's Kijé's Kalashnikov?"

"Not here. I don't know where he keeps it and you, I think, do not know how to use it. Lock the door behind the Joggers and stay by it. You can look through the keyhole, it's large enough. Lizaveta and I will take candles down to the cellar."

He felt cowardly rather than prudent, behind the locked doors with one eye to the keyhole. He could see little, a rough oval of street, the building opposite, the mouth of the lane. If anyone were to advance from either end of Museum Street he would not know until they were directly in front of him. He waited for more gunfire, shouts, explosions, running feet; he replayed all the newsreels he had ever seen of war-torn anywhere. What actually happened when hostilities broke out? What did you do if your friends went out and never came back?

He heard feet, many feet, neither running nor walking, marching in step. A column of people passed in the street, northwards to Oktyabrskaya. They did not seem to be armed, or in uniform; they looked more like monks than soldiers. He dared not open the door to see where they were going for fear that there might be others behind them.

After a while a single figure appeared at the end of the lane; Kijé, unharmed as far as he could tell, but moving with caution. Keith opened the door and beckoned, but Kijé remained where he was for two or three minutes, looking both ways, and behind him. Then he ran.

"You heard the shots?"

Keith slammed the door and locked it behind him. "Yes. What was it?"

"Semi-automatic."

"I meant who?"

"I don't know who, they weren't shooting at me. Where's Erna?"

"In the cellar, getting it ready. Did you see that procession go by?"

"There's no one in the streets – except in the market, where everything is carrying on as usual."

"Are people buying food?"

"To eat where they stand. There is little to buy. What procession?"

"A bunch of people marching past. *Marching*. No one we know. What have you found out?"

"Have The Teeth gone? Good, fetch Erna, I'll meet you in the bar." He went down the corridor to the Archaeology Gallery.

"Just a moment!" Keith went after him, but the corridor was empty. The gallery door had not opened. In five seconds, Kijé had vanished. Keith went back to the rotunda. Daily Kijé revealed hidden depths but to date dematerialization had not been one of them. It was a waste of time to speculate. He went to the Refreshment Room where Erna and Lizaveta were clearing up, which brought to mind the fact that for the first time, to his knowledge, Zayu had failed to turn up for work. Perhaps, since she showed him the soul stone, she had decided to trust him to act upon the information. Or it might be that she no longer saw any point in coming to the museum; others would take over, now.

"Kijé's back," he said.

Lizaveta crossed herself. "I told you he could look after himself," Ernie said. "Has he found Maisie?"

"Didn't say – Ernie, he's just disappeared. Said he'd meet us in here, went down the corridor and vanished."

"Stairs to the roof," Mrs Fahrenheit said. The museum had even more hidden depths than Kijé.

She was in the kitchen, washing up, when Kijé returned with the assault rifle and a rucksack.

"You've got one of these, Keith. Empty it. In a few minutes we'll go back to the *gimnaziya*. It is time to start transferring provisions in bulk. I have the loan of Szusko's cart, but the fewer trips we make, the better."

Mrs Fahrenheit came out to join them. "You didn't find Maisie."

"No. I went to the hotel with Szusko and delivered the oil. The Equispherians did not ask where it came from. They did not pay for it. When Szusko named a price they said that the days were accomplished and that soon there would be no need of money."

"What did Szusko do? What did *you* do?"

"I stood in the doorway being a stupid Qantoumi, remember? Szusko said that his days were not accomplished and he would quite like to buy some food."

"And?"

"Same argument. Soon there will be no need of food. These people are more dangerous than any army. They did not stay to talk, they began walking in circles again and went into the restaurant. Where they started buzzing. I told Szusko that we would take care of him – I told him to come here, Erna."

"Of course."

"And the bear?" Keith said.

"Of course the bear. Then I went upstairs. Maisie's door was locked. I went in, I don't think she's been there. Nothing seems to have been touched, all as we left it." Remembering *how* they had left it, Keith caught his eye, and he blushed. "I came back through the market. No one has seen her."

"So they say."

"Why would anyone lie about poor Maisie?"

"Because they are Sturyat."

"Usman and Vlodya would not lie. And she is nothing to the Sturyat."

"She insults them regularly," Ernie said.

"They are accustomed to that. I am sorry, we cannot make Maisie a priority until we have taken care of everyone else. I will put the word around later, Erna, and tell them to prepare to move here. We'll meet this evening to discuss it. Will you feel safe while Keith and I go to the *gimnaziya*? I'll leave the pistol."

Ernie laughed. "Of course I shall not feel safe. But if there is any trouble Lizaveta and I will wait in the cellars."

"What will you do if we don't come back?"

"You will come back," she said, laying a hand to the side of his face.

Archon was broadcasting again. The incomprehensible rant followed them down Oktyabrskaya. Since he could apparently

keep it up for hours Keith suspected the involvement of a
tape recorder. It was hard to tell when they could never make
out any words. Even with the door shut it was audible inside
Control Point E.

"Have you listened to the radio, recently?" Keith said.

"Yes." Kijé was rattling about in the tool room but he
recited as if from memory: "There is growing international
concern over the numbers of people entering Iskanderistan
at a time when the country is known to be in a highly volatile
state, and disregarding warnings to avoid the region.
Representations to the authorities in Iskanderabad are meeting with little response and the outskirts of the capital are
currently under attack from militias which are fighting their
way towards the city centre with great loss of life among the
civilian population. The television station is in the hands of
insurgents. Foreign nationals are being advised to leave; several embassies have evacuated all but key personnel. The
train service from Tashkent has been suspended.

"In short," he concluded, putting his head around the door,
"the Government, such as it is, has other things on its mind
than Qantoum. I do not think they will be celebrating the
new Millennium in Iskanderabad. How are the mushrooms?"

"T–Z looks about ready."

"Cut them all but the buttons. We can come back from
time to time to keep an eye on things." He passed Keith his
knife. "Please use this only on the mushrooms. Have you ever
stabbed anyone, Keith?"

"No."

"Don't start with this. Wave it about if you like, but if anyone disturbs you, holler for me. Actually, I am using you as an early warning system. Lock the door," he added, as he went out.

Keith felt as crazy as Maisie, cutting mushrooms while the world collapsed around him. What good would mushrooms be when Ernie was trying to feed five thousand? The answer came upon the heels of the question. She and Kijé were preparing for a siege; anything edible would be of use. There might come a time when Streph's frogs would look appetizing.

He fitted the mushrooms into a box file, left them on the desk and went out to the garden where Kijé was swinging loaded sacks into Szusko's cart.

"How will you get that out? How did you get it in?"

Kijé wiped the sweat out of his eyes impatiently. "This was a school. You did not think that the only way in was through a military checkpoint, surely? It was built before the railway came here. Oktyabrskaya was not always the main street; the front of the building is at the back," he explained obscurely, "on Petropavlovskaya. Where are the mushrooms?"

"In the office. I thought we'd be going out that way."

"Fetch them. Bring the key."

He took a last look out of the office window. There were several people at the intersection; not people he recognized, Hobbits or Joggers or Sundancers; certainly not Sturyat; doing nothing, but in a concentrated manner. Keith took care not to disturb the blind and slid the key quietly from the lock, glad that Kijé had another exit.

Kijé was with the cart in the north corridor.

"I think this place is being watched," Keith said. "There are suspicious types out in the street."

"It will be dark soon," Kijé said. "Next time we'll come here at night. I think, all told, we can hold out for three weeks."

"You believe all this will be over in three weeks?"

"Your Millennium," Kijé said. "Isn't that why they're here, waiting for an eclipse that will not happen?"

"Some of them are waiting for a comet that definitely will happen."

"I begin to wonder. It has been mentioned on the radio. When are we going to see it?" He halted the cart in front of a pair of doors, picking through the assortment of keys he carried everywhere now. The doors opened into a spacious lobby with a tiled floor. Facing them was another pair of doors that evidently led out into the street.

"Which way do we go?" Keith said, as Kijé selected another key.

"Through the station and by the back streets. I don't want to cross Oktyabrskaya. Once we get near the museum we can decide; it depends who is around. We may have to leave the cart and unload it in consignments."

The Archon had shut up for the evening. The squealing of the cart's wheels sounded dangerously loud in the quiet twilight and the juddering of its contents on the uneven surfaces made it unwieldy, but they saw no one and reached

Museum Street without hindrance. As they neared the museum they could hear a roaring babble of voices that rose from the direction of the Sturyat pasture like a dust cloud; hundreds of voices; thousands?

With its shuttered windows the museum had a grim aspect; no light escaped to illuminate the street, but the lamp was burning in the portico, the door was open. On the other side of it Vlodya stood on guard with his own rifle. He moved aside while Kijé bumped the cart backwards up the steps like a pram.

The Refreshment Room was crowded as it rarely was so early, and not only with the regulars. Keith saw many faces that he did not recognize; there were even children among them. The Joggers must have decided to trust in their tabernacle at the elementary school. Ernie stood with Lizaveta at the bar. When Keith came in she walked towards him with suppressed urgency.

"Both of you?"

"Kijé's unloading. We had no trouble, but there are some odd characters about."

"Still, we are all here safely, except for Maisie. You've not seen—"

"No, but we've not had time to look."

"Tell Vlodya to lock up and come along here."

When they were all assembled, looking expectantly towards the bar, she stepped in front of it and addressed them. They heard her out in near silence, broken only by the low voices of some translating for others.

"The situation is this," she said, "the Sturyat are preparing to leave because they believe that the time they have been waiting for has come. The only thing that may detain them is the fact that they have not recovered their soul stones, which is bad news for us because, as you must know, they believe that these are hidden here in the museum. We cannot find the stones and we cannot tell what may happen. There are now many people in Qantoum who may take it upon themselves to make a last effort to find the stones. You can imagine what that will mean. One way or another, it ought to be resolved within three weeks. Our visitors are waiting for a total eclipse of the sun on the morning of the first of January; it is not going to take place. This will be a disappointment to them; we do not know how they will take it. The Sturyat are waiting for a comet; this is real. It will come. There are signs that already the visitors are quarrelling among themselves and more arrive daily. Soon they will be desperate for food.

"You have a choice. This building can shelter us all as it sheltered us before. For a limited period we can feed ourselves. Everyone is welcome, this is your place now. On the other hand, while the soul stones remain unfound, and I cannot imagine how they will be found, the museum may be a target. Up to a point we can defend it, but we are very heavily outnumbered, by perhaps as many as twenty to one. But again, we are not dealing with sensible people. They are unlikely to have a plan of campaign.

"So, I leave it to you. If you want to be with us, bring all that you value and as much food as you can, tomorrow. If you would rather take your chances outside, then do that. We shall never close the doors against you if you change your minds, unless we have to; but we may have to."

There was no sound except for a loud sigh from the bear. Ernie turned to Kijé who sat on the end of the long table where he had once danced. "Do you want to speak to them now?"

Kijé nodded. "How many of you have firearms?"

To Keith's surprise almost everyone raised a hand. Some of them raised the weapon in question, a mass salute of AK47s, Uzis, M16s, Armalites, mixed with old Bren guns, Lee Enfields, hunting rifles and a grenade launcher. Kijé surveyed this arsenal in some dismay.

"How many of them work?"

Most of the hands, and weapons, remained up.

"I would advise you not to use them," Kijé said. "Do not think that because you have a gun you are in a position of strength or superiority. We are dealing with maniacs; for all I know they have tactical nuclear weapons. Always remember the numbers – twenty to one. That is today. Tomorrow it might be fifty to one. Imagine, you are attacked, pursued, cornered. You fire in self-defence. You disable or kill. Fine, you are safe. It will not be you who suffers the retribution, remember that. For one of them it might be ten of us. Ten of them and we'd be wiped out."

Someone said, "Are you in charge, *Lieutenant*?"

"Unless anyone here outranks me," Kijé said. "No? Then

383

tomorrow do as Mrs Fahrenheit says. Bring all that you can here, food and bedding especially. Avoid confrontation. The door must be guarded in rotation from now on. Ramadan is beginning, I think. Those of you who are Muslims will not be asked to stand watch during the day, if you are fasting.

"One last thing. We have lost Lady Hooke. We have not seen her since yesterday. Has anyone. . . ?"

There was a curious reluctance to co-operate on this issue; no response at all, no shaking of heads or denials. People looked at the floor.

"I know she offended everyone, but she was, is, very old, very mad. She is alone. She has had no chance to decide whether to go or stay. Madder people than Maisie are living in the Sogdiana Serai. Have pity, forgive her. She did not know what she was saying to you."

"Yes she did. Only she never knew who she was saying it to," a voice growled near the door. "She despised us all; whether she knew us or not, she knew we were her inferiors. It caused no harm because, after all, what could she do? But why should we worry about the old hag? She will only curse us all over again."

"You can talk," someone else cracked in. "We all remember—"

"That is enough!" Mrs Fahrenheit smacked a bottle on the bar top. "How shall we survive if we quarrel amongst ourselves before we have even begun? No more of this. I do not think we shall see poor Maisie again, but if we do, let no one turn on her. Do not turn upon each other."

An apologetic murmur circulated. People shook hands, with embarrassed smiles, and pats on the back.

"Well done, Erna," Kijé said. "You have put down your first civil unrest. Can you handle them now?"

"Yes, but aren't you staying?"

"For a while," Kijé said. "I'll eat here, then I'll go back."

"Alone?"

"Of course alone. You think Keith should go back with me, and then I walk back here with him, then he walks back with me. . . ?"

"I meant Keith should go with you and stay."

"No, you need him here. Tomorrow, when people move in, perhaps he can be spared."

"It would be better if you both stayed here. What about the *things*?"

"The water-beds? Keith has a name for them: aquasacs. It's a dry night, and I'll know what to look out for. Don't worry about me, Erna. I'll carry my mop."

Twenty

The migration into the museum began. When people arrived for meals they brought with them bedding, cardboard attaché cases, boxes tied with rope, which they clutched suspiciously, reluctant to leave them, transformed overnight into refugees. They were distributed throughout the building in the cellars, in the empty offices. The hardier elements were given spaces in the galleries where they drew chalk rectangles on the floor, occupying them like fortified islands.

"We must trust each other," Mrs Fahrenheit said, but she gave them vacant display cases for storage and they concealed the keys about their persons.

"What about Maisie's room?" Keith said.

"We'll leave it for now," Mrs Fahrenheit said. "She may come back. Keith, she *may*. We have to believe that." She had brought up the folding cot from the Zherdin Collection and put it in Keith's room. "When we persuade Kijé to sleep here, you can share," she said. "Usman and Makhmud can go in the other room; they'll sleep during the day. They regard it as cheating but that cannot be helped, right now.

You had better sleep too. I suppose you will be with Kijé tonight, bringing food?"

Keith followed her advice and fell asleep with ease, waking in the early evening to find that a little snow had fallen, the temperature low enough to sustain a light and crunchy crust in the streets. When he went down, Lizaveta was spreading sand on the steps in the portico.

He had always associated snow with silence but when he and Kijé, who had come down to the museum for supper, walked back through the streets to the gymnasium, the midnight air was discordant with voices, singing, chanting, howling. The smell of smoke and cooking hung over Qantoum, air that had been so pure and calm now thick and loud. But they did not speak, fearing not the mass attack but the lone speculative watchers, until they reached the old front entrance on Petropavlovskaya, where Kijé remained for some time, with the door ajar, looking along the street until he was satisfied that they had not been followed. They did not have the cart this time, only the backpacks and burlap bags, which they filled at the clamps in the garden. Afterwards Kijé made tea and they sat in the office to drink it, in the smoking warmth of the paraffin stove which was the only light they dared allow themselves.

"What happens to the aquasacs in winter weather? Do they freeze?"

"How can I know?" Kijé said. "If they keep moving, perhaps not."

"I'll tell you something really strange. No one else has mentioned them."

387

"Are you suggesting we've imagined them?"

"There's nearly a hundred people in the museum – nobody has said anything. Why are we the only ones to see them?"

"We go to places the others do not," Kijé said. "Like the Old Town. And they come out only at night, in wet weather. It has been dry for days."

"Does snow count as wet? We've found them outside the Old Town."

Kijé was quiet for a while. "And where were they heading? Where have they all been heading? They don't come *into* town, they leave it."

"Then they're here already? They're not coming out of the desert, out of the east? Zayu told me they come here to breed."

"Since when have we believed what the Sturyat tell us?" Kijé said.

"It was the day she showed me her soul stone."

"If it was a soul stone."

They were walking back to the entrance lobby where the packs and sacks were waiting. Kijé was just closing the inner doors behind them when he stopped where he stood. "What was that?"

"I didn't hear anything."

"Wait." There was no time to protest. Kijé was gone, at a stooping run, absorbed in the shadows of the corridor. Keith, not daring to move, stood in the chill silence, listening for a sound, a voice, a footfall, a shot. Through the half-open door he could see out of the window opposite, where the stars lit the snowy garden in a monochrome chiaroscuro. Was that a bush, a barrel, a man? Had that shadow been there just now, lying between the potato clamp and the rubbish heap? *Kijé, come back.*

He came back.

"What was it?"

"I don't know. I thought I heard a door closing. I couldn't find anything."

"Who'd break in?"

"Equispherians looking for fuel? Teeth looking for food? Another gang of maniacs looking for somewhere to stay? Perhaps I imagined it." They stepped into the street. "Perhaps I am being overcautious. This cold should keep people indoors."

"Which way are we going back?"

"The quickest. With this load I don't want to make detours."

The eastern sky was paling, but the stars burned as fiercely. They were halfway along Oktyabrskaya when Kijé stopped, and gasped, and pointed. The view across the Registan was uninterrupted from here, and above the broken gateway of the madrasseh a new light was rising, as if racing before the following sun, a great hazy star with a forked and flaring tail.

"The comet," Keith said. They stood in the middle of the road, gazing at the Sturyat's promised sign. "Why haven't we seen it before?"

"It's been rising and setting in daylight, but every morning a little earlier. We've been indoors at dawn."

"The Sturyat will have seen it."

"Without doubt. They won't be the only ones. Now they really will be eager to leave."

"Isn't it beautiful?"

"Yes. I am glad I have lived to see it," Kijé said, leaving Keith with the disagreeable but probably unintentional impression that he did not expect to live much longer. "That truly is a sight to mark the end of a thousand years," he said. "By the way," he added, turning to walk on, "today, on the radio, I heard news from London, Keith. On 31 December the whole of Trafalgar Square will be closed off for the Great Millennium Domino-Toppling Record. How can a comet compete with that?"

When they had unloaded, Kijé disappeared immediately to his eyrie on the roof. Keith knew better than to ask him about it. No doubt, when the time was right, Kijé would tell him, show him. It might be where he kept his vodka against the day when he judged that things could get no worse. He had shown no symptoms so far of resorting to it on the quiet. Things could still get worse.

Keith stood at his window and looked down over the Zherdin collection, where the new occupants slept in rows between the cabinets in their chalk cubicles. They were getting up now. Privileged in his privacy he retreated from the window, ashamed to have been watching them in their enforced exposure, and went down to the Refreshment Room. The Joggers had arrived for breakfast. He waited in the kitchen with Mrs Fahrenheit and Lizaveta while they said Grace.

"What are you feeding them on?" he asked. "Sawdust?"

"It may come to that. I have explained to Brother Joel that supplies are running low. He says that God will provide."

"For them, maybe. What about everyone else? What are they relying on? Is there still food in the market?"

"I doubt it. Szusko reports that there are a number of videos on sale."

"I'll go along and have a look."

"Wait for Kijé to come down."

"No," he said. "Kijé may have other plans. I won't be long. Look, you know where I'm going. I won't go anywhere else, and we really do need to know about the food situation," he added, seeing her reluctance.

Szusko and the bear were watching the front door.

"What will you do if we are attacked?" Keith asked unkindly.

"We will close the door," Szusko said, with dignity. "I am prepared."

The market looked very much as it always did, at first sight. The Sturyat were at their usual stations but in place of the Qantoumis were crowds of strangers, not buying, not selling, but watching each other, it seemed to Keith, in spite of the bitter cold.

"Hi! Dear man; have tea. Have a frog." Streph was waving jovially.

Keith took one of each for old times' sake. The basket of

frogs was depleted. As he drank the tea Keith looked at the other stalls. The Goat Woman had no bread or cheese or apples. The fruit stall was bare. The only things on sale were the metal fragments and a number of video cassettes, arranged on edge, like dominoes. He was almost surprised to see that no one was offering leathers on the specious grounds that they would make good eating in an emergency, and with that thought there came to mind his conversation last night with Kijé, that had been interrupted by the sound, real or imaginary, that only Kijé had heard. The aquasacs were not coming out of the desert, they were here already. In what form were they here already?

There was no point in asking questions. No one was going to tell him anything. Were all lines of communication with the Sturyat closed, or would Zayu still speak to him? He had promised Ernie to go nowhere but the market; but he had not given her a route plan. He would take a long way home.

He strolled away from the crowds and into the alleys. If anyone followed him he lost them at once and made his way to his old house, approaching from Zayu's side of the building and climbing the steps to the roof. She was not there, but from her lookout point by the plant pots he could see the railway line, thick with moving figures like ants following a sugar trail. He descended, knocked on her door and opened it. The bones were not up, the bones were gone. She had gone. The room was empty. He went down the stairs, through the lower room and across the courtyard to his own door, pushing at it with great caution and squinnying through the crack. The leather that he had used as a shelf was as he had left it, balanced across the two bricks. Now that he knew what it was he recoiled from touching it, but even from the doorway he saw that there was something different about it. It had acquired a waxen, tripey opacity. He went closer and touched a knuckle to it. It was no longer stiff and dry; not moist, but with a kind of incipient elasticity.

The idea which had come to him in the market was forming itself into a loathsome theory that he could not wait to share with Kijé, if only to see the look on his face. He closed the door on the thing and went out through the adjacent house to an alley that would take him one way to the citadel and the Sturyat pasture, the other to the cemetery. There was just a chance that Maisie might have gravitated to her old feeding grounds, but only the impassive eyes of the dryads gazed back at him from among the leafless shrubs, the bedizened boughs of the mulberry tree.

He walked on along the borders, then turned left into the Registan, and there he saw her. By the steps of the Sogdiana Serai an upright little woman was sitting on a pile of luggage. Incredulously he approached. She was wearing a toque of violet feathers and a cashmere coat collared by a torrent of monkey fur. The spindle-shanks tapered to tiny cracked spool-heeled shoes with pointed toes.

"Lady Hooke!"

She turned, saw him, saw someone, and remarked petulantly, "One cannot get a cab."

"For fuck's sake, Maisie, where have you been?"

"Fort Belvedere; HRH and the Simpson creature. I see trouble brewing there. Porter!"

Keith surveyed the luggage: steamer trunks, suitcases, vanity bags.

"Did someone help you?"

"They were put out on the steps. The doorman, I suppose. I don't know who packed. *Staff*, no doubt. Taxi!"

"I'll carry all you need, Lady Hooke," Keith said. "We can get the rest sent along after us." Wherever "we" are going.

She stood up, selected two suitcases, an overnight case and a vanity bag.

"Come along, then."

"Could you carry something, Lady Hooke? I've only got two arms. Take the little one."

"Certainly not. No, don't leave it. One's jewellery. Bring that – and that one." She sallied towards the roadway, addressing the air. "Why employ someone who can't even lift?"

He picked up the suitcase, which was not particularly heavy, and the vanity bag which did not even leave the ground, almost dislocating his shoulder.

"Maisie, wait. What have you got in here?"

"Lower your voice, young man." She turned laboriously and tottered back towards him. "I told you," she hissed. "One's jewels. Do you want this riff-raff to hear? Never let them out of your sight, Mortimer said."

"If I carry this I can't carry anything else."

"Rubbish. Put your back into it."

"Maisie, why don't you just wait here for five minutes and I'll bring a cart – taxi." But she was off again. He put down the suitcase and, dragging the vanity bag, staggered after her.

At the museum Kijé was in the doorway, small-eyed with anger.

"*Where* have you been?"

"Where I told Ernie, the market. Wake up, Kijé. Look what I've found."

Lady Hooke shoved past him, treading on his foot, and entered the rotunda, hooting, "Ludovic! Ludovic!"

"Where has she been?"

"Spending the weekend with Edward VIII and Mrs Simpson. No wonder she can't be bothered with the likes of us. I found her sitting on the steps of the Sogdiana Serai waiting for a cab." He dropped the vanity case with a crash. "Can someone take a cart and pick up the rest of her rubbish?"

"We don't need the rest of her rubbish. Did the Equispherians throw her out?"

"I don't know and it's no good asking. She'll only blame the Bolsheviks."

"I'd always assumed she had rather a soft spot for the Bolsheviks."

"Maybe, but she's here and the rest of her luggage is sitting in the Registan."

"It can sit," Kijé said, viciously. "Look, I thought it was

understood that we don't go anywhere unless the others know."

"I told Ernie."

"Erna isn't me."

"Well, you weren't there to tell. You shouldn't have gone buggering off up to the roof. What do you do up there?"

"You've never been up?"

"No. I didn't know it was possible until you disappeared the other day."

"There are walkways, apparatus for cleaning the glass, and a fire ladder."

"That goes down to the ground?"

"It seems to, but I unbolted it long ago. Now it hangs by a thread. No one could get up it. You see why I was so wary of the one at the hotel. But it is a good observation-point, up there. Since the earthquake, one of the highest points in Qantoum, apart from St Vasili's. And if, by any chance, a mob does break into the museum, we'll have the higher ground."

"Literally."

Kijé turned and tripped over the vanity case.

"What the hell *is* this?"

"Maisie's rocks."

"Her what?"

"Diamonds. I'll put it in the Zherdin Collection for now. She says Mortimer told her not to let it out of her sight, but she's forgotten it already." Kijé declining to help, he pushed the vanity case in front of him and stowed it under Setsemhotep III.

"Well, what did you find in the market?"

"Streph is still selling tea and frogs. Everyone else is down to Equispherian videos. But I did find something odd."

"Really? How odd does something have to be these days to qualify as odd?"

"Oh, stop sulking. Something you said last night, about the aquasacs being here already, not coming in from the desert? Do you remember my telling you that I bought a leather in the market, months ago, and used it as a shelf? I've just been back to look at it and it's not – leathery any more. It isn't soft, but it's different. It seems to be swelling."

"You think maybe the damp air?"

"The air was damp after the rain, but the things still dried out anyway. That one you fell on, and the one that met the Equispherians. You've still got the one you fell on. Where is it?"

"Lizaveta found it in the cellar and uses it as a tray. It's still a leather. I saw it just now."

"But that one's dead. You killed it."

"Are you saying that yours is not dead?"

"It could be dormant."

Kijé's expression was all that he had hoped. "Dormant for five hundred years? And now it is coming alive again? Oh my God, this place is full of them."

They ran down the corridor to the Archaeology Gallery and the storage chest. Kijé tugged at the bottom drawer.

"Is it stuck? Try further up."

"No, not stuck. But whatever is inside – take the other

handle – whatever is inside is larger than it used to be. It's fouling the top."

They could only inch the drawer open gradually and squinting in saw that the contents, once flat and dry, almost two-dimensional, were thickening, imperceptibly, but enough to be expanding beyond the space available.

"You're right," Kijé said. "Something is happening to them."

"They're not as thick as my shelf."

"Perhaps being in here has slowed down the process. Does yours have access to water?"

"It's still up on the wall, it hasn't moved. Those aren't moving – are they?"

"Not yet." He shunted the drawer shut. "No, I was thinking, what I said about the damp air. They must be hygroscopic. Either this chest is strong enough to contain them until their breeding season is past, or they will go on swelling until they burst out of it."

"What are we going to do with them?"

"I think we ought to get them out of here while they are still light enough to lift. Take them to the pasture for the Sturyat, set them loose in the Sogdiana Serai. Leave them for now. We will keep a close eye on your shelf, Keith."

Keith said, "Why do you suppose the Sturyat have always pretended not to know what they are?"

"Aside from the fact that they routinely lie about everything? Because they knew that if they showed too much interest in them, they'd be taken away as well. Which is obviously what happened at some point. They also knew they'd come back again." He slapped the chest of drawers. "But these things are not coming out of the east."

"I can see that."

"So what is?"

Since people now had to walk only a few metres to their beds there was no hurry to leave the Refreshment Room that night. A kind of contentment had set in. There was talk of going out at dawn to view the comet.

"But I could not have rested easy with poor Maisie lost," Ernie said to Keith.

"Have you found out where she's been?"

"Asking is no good. Once she knew my name, Keith. Not any more. She has some notion that she has been with royalty. And she has got hold of liquor. She is sitting on her bed singing, 'Hark the Herald Angels sing, Mrs Simpson's pinched our King'. How many more times are you going to the gymnasium?"

"Twice should do it. Only twenty days to go."

"People brought more food with them than I expected," Ernie said. "The habit of hoarding dies hard, here. We shall survive. Try to persuade Kijé to stay here afterwards."

No more snow had fallen but the thin dusting had frozen where it had not blown away. Even in the darkness Keith appreciated Kijé's insistence on a different route for every journey. They encountered their own tracks only when they reached the corner of Petropavlovskaya. Kijé halted, pressed against the wall, and looked around the corner.

"Too many footprints."

Keith looked along the street. The snow was more churned up than their own cautious steps could have made it.

"People walking past. They don't lead to the door."

"Why should anyone walk past? Stay behind me – don't speak."

They edged along the wall of the gymnasium to the entrance, still locked as Kijé had left it last night, and crept into the lobby between the two sets of doors. Kijé was about to lock the outer ones behind them when he stopped.

"Do you smell anything?"

"No – yes – "

Kijé turned the key in the inner lock, opened the door a fraction and closed it immediately.

"Out!"

"You haven't locked it."

"*Get out.*"

They hurled themselves into the road. Keith started to go back the way they had come, but Kijé seized his arm and swung him round, plunging in the opposite direction, then struck out at an angle into tangled undergrowth. Very close someone opened fire with a sub-machine-gun. Keith heard the smack of bullets hitting masonry, then, as Kijé dragged him down flat into the scrub, an extraordinary suffocating gasp that seemed to suck all the air out of the air. In an instant every window of the gymnasium was illuminated and all other sounds were extinguished by an explosive roar as the building ignited from end to end. Glass shattered. Flames soared through the broken roof.

Kijé was on the move again, hauling himself by his elbows into shadow that seemed to withdraw as they pursued it. There was more gunfire, random shots, shouts; men screaming. They were out of the undergrowth, at the foot of black pyramids, the coal stacks at the edge of the marshalling yards beyond the station.

Kijé mouthed, "Don't move. You could start an avalanche. Wait."

They lay at the foot of the towering sierras that glittered in the oily orange blaze behind them. A small group of people was gathering in the flamelight along Petropavlovskaya, pointing, gesturing, apparently talking although no voice could carry above the sound of the fire. After a while the group dispersed into the darkness. The sight of a building alight, the sounds of men dying, were not of any pressing interest. It was a full twenty minutes before Kijé spoke.

"They only came to look. They weren't looking for us. I don't think anyone knew we were here."

"That wasn't meant for us?"

"If it had been meant for us they'd have waited till we got inside. Though if it *was* meant for us, somebody else walked into it first – broke into it."

"Last night?"

"Maybe. Whoever they were they've wiped each other out."

"But the shooting—"

"In the garden. They trapped themselves in their own ambush."

"What was it?"

"Petrol. I smelled it as soon as I opened the door."

The cloud above the gymnasium was spreading, glowing, stinking.

"How are we going to get back?"

"It ought not to be too difficult. We are dead. We'll follow the lines to the Barracks Station and go back that way. If anyone *is* looking for us there are plenty of places to hide. Give it another ten minutes."

At last they rose upright. Keith found that he was shaking almost too much to stand. His legs seemed to bend gracefully, like stems. Kijé nudged him firmly into action and treading delicately round the coal stacks they made their way over the network of lines and points at the end of the station platform, any sound they might make covered by the busy crackle of the burning building. Smoke occluded the stars.

"Who do you think it was?" Keith asked.

"Who wanted the fuel?"

"The Equispherians?"

"That is only a guess, but why not the Equispherians? The end of days is accomplished, I heard them say it. Why not The Teeth? Reason sleeps."

Halting often to make sure that no one was tailing them, they reached the Barracks Station and entered the brick passages. Keith could feel his heart beating, slow, leisurely almost, why was it not racing with terror? It was so hard, so loud, it filled his ears, it seemed to fill the whole tunnel, thump, thump, thump, thump, like an engine. Surely Kijé must hear it too.

Kijé did hear it. He stopped walking. In the darkness Keith sensed his shock.

"It's a gunship. A helicopter."

They waited in the reverberating vault while the thudding intensified, receded, returned, lower, louder, hovered and at last withdrew. When it was no longer audible they went out into the air that was foul with the smell of burning fuel.

"Sooner or later someone had to start taking an interest in what's happening here," Kijé said.

"Iskanderabad?"

"I would think so, but not necessarily. Those slow stars the Sturyat are so fond of watching can probably read the numbers on my watch. Then that inferno, after years of nothing but cooking fires. I wish I had got the radio out."

"What will happen?"

"How can I know? Fire; I did not expect fire. I didn't plan for fire."

"Plan?"

"The cellars; secure against blast, snipers, rioters – but not fire. You know about the Dresden effect? Saturation bombing: towards the end of the Great Patriotic War Allied aircraft dropped tons of incendiaries on the city of Dresden in Germany. It created a fire storm, a fire that fed itself. Thousands were incinerated but others died of suffocation where they hid in cellars. All the oxygen was drawn up by the fire to feed itself."

"Do the Equispherians know about the museum?"

"Know? Of course they know. How could they not know? We were at that Spelling. Any talk of the soul stones must include the museum."

"But they never come near it. They don't know what it's like. Would they know that people are sheltering inside?"

"That is what I am afraid they will know."

"I suppose they believe what the Sturyat have told them, that the stones are somewhere in it, stashed away by the wicked widow Fahrenheit. They aren't going to burn the place down until they've been over it with a fine-tooth comb."

"You speak as if they were rational. What was rational about what was done tonight? Whoever did it. Whoever they did it to. *Not rational*, Keith. Reason sleeps."

"Did you lose anything in the fire?"

"My home. I wish I had thought to bring the gardening tools away."

"The Control Point may not have burned."

"No. It may not."

At the museum Mrs Fahrenheit was waiting at the door.

"Don't do that again," Kijé said, brusquely. "Sitting target. Did you hear it?"

"The helicopter, oh yes. It had a searchlight. When I first heard it I thought perhaps more visitors, arriving by air; no, not true. I didn't hear it at first, I felt it; the thudding in the bones; the memories. But there's been a fire, we saw the glow. Did you—?"

"Lock the door," Kijé said. "There's worse than a helicopter. Tonight the *gimnaziya* was burned. We were very nearly caught in it – no, Erna, don't faint now. We weren't caught in it. We are here, not even singed. I think it was the maniacs from the hotel, they were the ones who wanted oil, but there again, by now, there may be others who know how to get it."

"Is it much damaged?" Mrs Fahrenheit recovered herself.

"I should think it is entirely destroyed," Kijé said, "along with those who set light to it. Tomorrow we'll know. I suspect it was the fire that brought the helicopter, but there is no telling now what may happen."

Keith, listening to the quiet exchange, was appalled by their terrible calm. Whatever shocks he had sustained tonight, they had seen far worse. Kijé had lost virtually everything he owned. She had almost lost him, but apart from her one unguarded stagger, they might have been discussing a minor traffic accident. And what of Kijé? Once already he had seen him break, because he could not crack.

In the same tranquil voice Kijé was saying, "This building will burn as well as the *gimnaziya* did."

"How did they fire it?"

"Petrol. The place must have been drenched. Kijé smelled it just in time."

"We can prevent that at least. With the shutters up there will be no Molotov cocktails through the windows."

"The roof." Kijé looked up fearfully into the darkness.

"How would they get up there? You unfixed the ladder."

405

"The first person up that ladder will probably die from the fall," Kijé said. "But there are other roofs. It would not take too much ingenuity to find a place from which to launch petrol bombs. This is the highest roof for some distance, but even someone on, say, the elementary school might manage it. Now, as Keith points out, they are unlikely to destroy the museum while the soul stones may be in it, but I say that only intelligent people think like that."

"Do we keep them out for as long as we can," Ernie said, "or do we invite them in and keep them searching for as long as we can?"

"I think the latter," Kijé said, "but we will not invite them in. Wait until they ask or demand. I have the beginning of an idea. Keith, it is time I showed you the roof."

The door where Kijé came and went was concealed in the panelling of the corridor. They went up by stages, Kijé's torch revealing doors, landings, access to places Keith had never imagined existed. How simple the museum had seemed once: the rotunda, the Archaeology Gallery, the Zherdin Collection, the Refreshment Room. And every inch of it to be searched and searched again.

The final staircase was little more than a ladder leading to a glass skylight. Kijé switched off the torch and they crawled out into a valley between steep slopes.

"We are above the Archaeology Gallery here," Kijé said. "Stay exactly behind me, tread where I tread. We'll go to the roof above the Refreshment Room. It is tiled and there's a flat area. Keep your head down."

Guided by the stars reflected off the sloping glass they clambered out of the trough to the foot of the northern corner turret. To the north-west the pyre of the gymnasium still burned. To the south-east a hundred small fires were glowing in the Sturyat pasture, then a patch of darkness, that marked the wasteland around Industrial and beyond that more fires in a huge encampment that was centred on the Industrial Station, tailing off along the railway line. Where ants walked by day, now fireflies came on in an endless beaded stream that must have been of equal interest to the helicopter pilot.

As Keith surveyed the distance Kijé was occupied with the nearer view, searching for adjacent roofs and calculating trajectories.

"From now on," he said, "someone up here day and night, but not Szusko. He'd never leave the bear. I am not adding to my woes with a bear on the roof."

Keith stared to the east. "It's almost dawn. See, the comet's rising. Every night a little earlier." Kijé was looking elsewhere. Propped against the parapet he gazed skyward.

"Do you know what is up there, Keith?"

"No." Was he going to turn spiritual at this most temporal of moments, to speculate on the space-time continuum and the hand of a Great Architect in the design of the universe. "Altaera's flying saucer?"

"I don't mean that. The turret; it's a water tower."

"It must be empty."

"It is. We are going to fill it."

Twenty-one

It was still early when Makhmud drew the bolts and let them out into the cold streets where the town lay smoke-bitter and eerily quiet. A few flakes of snow fell.

"Where are we going?"

"To your house, please. I want to look at the leather."

Keith led him through the alleys to the steps, and in at his door. They stood in the upper room, listening to the peculiar liquid sounds that came up the inner staircase, looking down through the trapdoor to where something the size of a pillow was rolling and flopping on its own axis, sloshing like a small concrete mixer.

"That's your shelf," Kijé said. "Let's see if we can pick it up."

"*No!*" But Kijé was on his way down. He skipped over the immature aquasac, stooped and threw his arms round it. It seemed to pour out of his grasp, switching itself from side to side as it went, the sheer weight of it knocking him off his feet. He fell against the door with the thing surging in his arms.

Keith bounded down and laid hold of it. The surface was

deadly chill and the pulpy interior, which he recalled from previous experience, had become a semi-solidified slush.

"It has no centre of gravity," Kijé complained, disengaging himself. The aquasac squelched to the floor, apparently exhausted, but even as they watched they could see that it was getting its strength back as ripples rolled from one end of its body to the other.

"What are we going to do with it?"

"With this one, nothing. Let's get out of here, back to the museum," Kijé said. Outside he went on, "Now we know how quickly they rehydrate once they start. Twenty-four hours ago, you say, that was a leather. Now, we go back, get our leathers out of the chest of drawers, and take them up to the water tank. Over the next two or three days they will grow. Then we can do what we like with them, blockbusting water bombs, fire extinguishers, reservoirs. If the Sturyat use them for drinking water, so can we."

"How do we get the water out?"

"Puncture them," Kijé said. "I shall enjoy watching them burst."

They returned across the lower end of the market where people were beginning to collect in clusters. There were no Sturyat among them. By this hour Streph and his tea wagon ought to be in position but his place between the stalls was vacant and the stalls remained empty. As they went by faces turned to watch them, blankly inimical, mute, until a woman sprang in front of Kijé and screamed, "Antichrist!", stabbing him in the chest with her finger. She wore a smiley-face badge on her lapel. Kijé stepped round her murmuring, "No, I assure you. . ."

"Why me?" he said, as they passed into the lane behind the Iskander.

"Perhaps you remind her of someone."

"I don't think so."

Makhmud opened the door to Kijé's knock. They went straight to the Archaeology Gallery and yanked open the bottom drawer of the chest. The leathers bulged out, nacreous, glistening with a sweaty dew.

"We're only just in time," Keith said, putting his gloves on again to handle one. "They're getting heavier."

"Fetch our backpacks, sacks, anything that will hold them."

"Why not a few helpers? There's enough of us."

"Oh, no." Kijé scooped out leathers by the armful and dumped them on the floor. "I don't want anyone else stampeding around up there." He slammed the drawer and tugged at the one above it.

"You said the roof had to be guarded at all times."

"We'll make up a roster: you, me, Vlodya, Usman, no one else. *Hurry up.*"

Keith ran up to Prince Andrei's room to fetch his backpack. As he was crossing the rotunda on his way back someone rapped on the front doors. It was the same rhythm that Kijé used as a signal. Someone had been watching them. He called out to warn Makhmud, but Makhmud was not there. He had been relieved by Vlodya who did not know that Kijé was in the building. He swung the door open and was confronted by Gandalf, supporting himself on a gnarled wooden staff, surrounded by Hobbits of assorted sexes and sizes. He advanced to the centre of the rotunda.

"My were-light is strong," he announced.

"His what?" Vlodya said.

"As it happens, nothing we have to worry about."

"None shall stay us." Hobbits swarmed in his wake.

"Of course not." Mrs Fahrenheit was sailing to meet him, all smiling composure. "This is an open and public institution. Please feel free to enjoy the exhibits."

Gandalf looked disconcerted. Keith hissed to Ernie, "Keep them out of the Archaeology Gallery. We're shifting the leathers."

She beamed at Gandalf and his retinue. "Do come and see the Zherdin Collection. This way – is there anything in particular that you would like to look at?"

Keith ran back to Kijé who was emptying the last drawer, knee-deep in leathers which flopped in spongy heaps all around him. He snatched a sack and began stuffing them into it.

"What's going on out there?"

"Gandalf and his Hobbits are being shown over the Zherdin Collection. Vlodya let them in by mistake. Kijé, hold on. How big is this water tank?"

"Very big."

"Enough to hold all these? We still don't know how large they can grow. You don't want them getting loose on the roof. Whale-sized water-beds. . ."

"I've been thinking – come on, you've got enough there – we can keep the rest dry in the stove till we need them." He set off at a run for the hidden entrance in the panelling of the corridor. "Come *on*. We've got to get those maniacs out of here next."

They scrambled up the steep twisting stairs, groping their way, Kijé sure-footed on familiar territory, far ahead. By the time Keith caught up with him he had the door of the northern turret open and was on his way up a ladder bolted to the side of the great galvanized drum that filled it. At the top he clung on one-handed and reaching over his shoulder to pull leathers out of his backpack like a longbowman drawing arrows from a quiver, posted them over the top of the tank. Keith heard them landing damply inside.

"Leave yours. Go down and see what's happening," Kijé said. "Why did Vlodya open the door?"

"He didn't know who it was."

"All the more reason not to open the door."

"Ernie's showing them round. It's all very civilized. They're only Hobbits, not Equispherians."

"Get back down and stay there. I'll join you when I've got rid of all these."

The Hobbits were still milling around in the Zherdin Collection. Mrs Fahrenheit saw Keith come round the corner and motioned to him. "They're behaving very well. No one has mentioned soul stones. They don't even seem to be looking for them."

"Now we shall depart in peace," Gandalf proclaimed,

gyrating in the archway. His followers streamed towards him. It struck Keith that there was something unwontedly co-ordinated about their movements, as though they were manoeuvring themselves into prearranged places.

"Vlodya, open the door," Mrs Fahrenheit said.

"No – wait!" Keith started forward. Vlodya hesitated, his hand on the key and Gandalf swung the staff at his head. Vlodya ducked and stumbled as the staff caught him across the shoulder, and before he could recover Gandalf had turned the key and opened the doors. The street was full of people. As the doors swung inward they surged up the steps and charged into the rotunda.

Vlodya had been smacked flat against the wall by the impact of the door. Keith cowered behind the desk where the force of the charge had knocked him. Mrs Fahrenheit had fallen but was already up and pulling Vlodya to his feet. The Zherdin Collection seethed with people, Hobbits, Sundancers, Equispherians, so numerous and close-packed that the heavy display cases at the centre of the room were being forced out of line. Glass cracked; the mermaid was suddenly afloat on a sea of hands; someone had Setsemhotep III by the ankles and was laying about him with the shrivelled cadaver. Gandalf could be seen everywhere, whacking cabinets and cupboards with his staff. More people were pouring in from the street, down the corridor to the closed door of the Archaeology Gallery. In the narrow confines of the unlit passage shouts were mixed with cries of fear and confusion.

Ernie and Vlodya were struggling to reach the Refreshment Room. Keith was closer to the door into the side passage but feared to draw attention to it. As he inched along the wall he looked up and saw a dark silhouette against one of the skylights. Kijé was still on the roof.

When he made it to the Refreshment Room Vlodya was just closing the door and held it long enough for him to slip through. Then he slammed home the bolts.

"Where is everyone?"

"In the cellar. Help me get the furniture stacked across the doorway. Anything. Everything."

Two of the men had come back through the kitchen and the four of them dragged chairs and tables against the door. There were already sounds of assault and battery from the other side of it. When everything that could be moved had been, they retreated through the hanging cupboard and down the steps. Keith, last to go through, found Mrs Fahrenheit at the head of the stairs.

"Keith – where's Kijé?"

"On the roof. He can look after himself. Lock the door. I'm going up the other way."

The sounds of demolition reached the cellars only faintly. In the light of a few candles the museum people sat or stood in petrified groups, faces turned towards the ceiling. Keith edged through them, stepping on unseen feet, brushing past the heavy pelt of the uncomplaining bear which sat with its head in Szusko's lap, to the foot of the stairs that led to the door behind the bookshelves in the Archaeology Gallery.

The room echoed with measured blows from the corridor. Even as he closed the bookshelf, knowing as he did it that he was cutting off his escape route behind him, the heavy door, which was in any case not locked, began to splinter and bow inwards. He flattened himself against the side of a display case and did not see the door fall, but he felt the air displacement as the mob crashed into the gallery.

The skeletons fractured like matchsticks. Now people were armed with femurs and long jaws full of teeth. The human skull came to rest at his feet, zipping across the floor like an ice-hockey puck. He thought of the leathers, the heaps kicked aside in the onslaught. People fell heavily as they skidded on them, to be trampled by others. Screams of pain chimed with the sound of splintering glass. At any moment someone might turn his attention to the case of carpets where Keith was sheltering, beautiful Bukharas, ripe for destruction. He was calculating how he might make it to the door when he saw a great wavering shadow against the wall. Kijé was monitoring the proceedings up there on the roof, he guessed, planning appropriate intervention, at which moment Kijé's boot came through the skylight, followed by the snout of his rifle.

Keith curled into a ball, arms round his head, and rolled under the cabinet. There would be a massacre, indiscriminate shooting into that heaving press. Kijé was forgetting his own advice; what retribution was he going to bring down on them?

The opening burst took out the refrigerator. Unnoticed and able to choose his target at leisure Kijé had aimed at the largest inanimate object. The noise alone in that enclosed space was enough to bring silence, then the mob turned, howling, and began fighting among itself for the quickest way out, struggling in the corridor, leaving the gallery with a wrack of debris as if a tsunami had passed through.

Keith crawled out of his shelter and looked towards the roof. Kijé had moved on. Seconds later another round of gunfire suggested that he was flushing out the Zherdin Collection. Keith picked his way through the wreckage, splintered woodwork, glass, bones, crushed leathers. The gutted cover of *From Caspian Sea to Hindoo Cush* by Lázenby, Lord Dacre, had fetched up in the doorway. He stepped over it and went down the corridor where the panelling was smashed to kindling, but darkness had hidden the presence of Kijé's door to the roof, and crossed the rotunda to the passage that led to the Refreshment Room. He could feel the bruised and buckled panels of the door, but the barricade had held. The cellars were safe.

He returned to the rotunda and stood where the finger-post had stood, surveying the Zherdin Collection; the stoved-in doors, smashed cases, the exhibits trodden to powder. Stirred into the ruin were the shredded remnants of clothes and bedding that their owners had entrusted to the locked cabinets. Down in the cellar they would still be jealously guarding the keys. The window of Prince Andrei's room, his room, had been kicked out and he knew that his own possessions had gone the way of the rest. By some perverse miracle the two-headed sheep had survived and stood where it always did, looking blandly up and down the room. In the middle of the floor lay a battered crocodile-skin vanity case.

He ought to secure the entrance. First he ventured out into Museum Street which was entirely deserted but littered with shoes, cudgels, bones, abandoned by the fleeing rioters. There was blood on the snow. From the foot of the steps the head of Setsemhotep III gaped up at him.

"Get inside, you fool." Kijé was leaning over the parapet. "Lock the doors. I'm coming down."

They met in the remains of the Zherdin Collection. Kijé stood without speaking, for the first time taking in the extent of the desolation, then he said hopelessly, "How are we going to tell them?"

Keith did not ask him who he meant, or what they had to be told. "At least *they* are safe." He could not forbear to add, "Why didn't you open fire sooner?"

"Sooner? I was in the turret, remember, I didn't know what had happened, was happening. I thought the Hobbits were still looking round. When I heard the noise I went to see; they'd started smashing up the Zherdin room. I went for the rifle. I tried to get down the stairs but by then the corridor was blocked – I couldn't open the door – so I went back up. Minutes, Keith; it was scarcely ten minutes, start to finish."

"I'm sorry. I didn't mean. . . Oh Christ, there's nothing left. *Nothing.*"

"The sheep," Kijé said, bleakly. "And that thing." He kicked the vanity case which barely shifted. "What did you say was in it? Maisie's bricks?"

"Her jewellery, she says. It couldn't be ingots, could it? I wouldn't put it past the old bat to be carting gold bars around with her."

"No, you said before; I asked you what was in here and you said—"

"Not bricks. Rocks. Maisie's rocks."

"You meant diamonds, yes? But by the weight I think maybe rocks."

"She's barmy enough to think that lumps of stone are diamonds. Lumps of stone. . ."

Kijé had drawn his knife and was slashing his way through the crocodile skin. Inside, filling and fitting it exactly, was a steel box. "And didn't you say that her husband Sir Mortimer told her never to let it out of her sight. Sir Mortimer the anthropologist?"

"Lumps of stone."

"You think what I think?"

"I can't believe it. The Equispherians threw it out of the hotel. That mob destroyed everything in here *except* that. How do we get it open? She might have a key."

"I wouldn't want to trouble her," Kijé said. "Stand back." Without any sense of occasion he pulled out his pistol and shot off the lock. They opened the lid and looked in. "Is that what Zayu showed you?"

There was a clatter of running feet. Mrs Fahrenheit, like a Valkyrie, smock flaring, hair streaming, hands outstretched, seemed to fly up the room towards them.

"What was that? You're safe! I thought you'd been killed!"

Kijé caught her in his arms and swung her round so that for a second or two they were waltzing in the rubble. "That was very silly," he said, tenderly, "running about when you hear gunfire. You ought to know better. But yes, we are safe, and we have found the soul stones." He set her down and pointed into the vanity case. She fell on her knees beside it, sifting and caressing the dull little nuggets of space detritus.

"Sorry about the mess," Keith said.

From the Refreshment Room and the Archaeology Gallery the Qantoumis were creeping out, staring about them, stupified at the destruction of their sanctuary, plucking at the tattered relics of their belongings, their voices shocked into tremulous whispers. Through the little noises they made came the heavy tread of purposeful feet over broken glass. From the door to the side passage, by the two-headed sheep, strode an Equispherian Sphinx. Keith, looking at the dead eyes and humourless gin-trap of a mouth realized, shuddering, that they ought to have searched the building before sealing it. This grim interloper had probably been watching them from the window in Prince Andrei's room.

"This is the will of Altaera," he said. Mrs Fahrenheit, still on her knees, gazed up at him, her first sight of an Equispherian in spate. "You are the widow?"

She nodded.

"By your intransigence you have brought this destruction upon yourself and your followers. Now the soul stones will be returned to the Sturyat and they will follow their star as their All-High has promised. Those who oppose the will of Altaera suffer the wrath of Altaera." He turned on Kijé, who was still holding the pistol. "Do you plan to detain me, creature of darkness?"

"By no means," Kijé said. "Take them away, please. Now."

The Sphinx, stooping, brushed Ernie aside, closed the lid of the box and lifted it with alarming ease, the rags of crocodile skin dangling from his hands like swags of Spanish moss. Without sparing the three of them another glance he clove a path through the dazed Qantoumis to the front door, his robes rippling in his own slipstream. The key was still in the lock but with even his considerable strength he could not support the strongbox on one arm, and put it down while he turned the key. He was just pulling the doors open when a peevish squawk rang out.

"Felon! How dare you! Where do you think you are going with that?"

The Sphinx paused as Maisie, Lady Hooke, outraged owner of the crocodile-skin vanity case, careened out of the corridor from the Archaeology Gallery, parasol at the charge, intent on recovering her property.

"Officer! Arrest this person."

"Oh, shit, Maisie, no – " Keith found his voice too late. The Sphinx revolved unhurriedly, raising his hand as if to swat a mosquito, and chopped downwards. Maisie fell where she stood and lay where she fell, neck awry, teeth askew, eyes wide open. Without looking at her the Sphinx picked up the box and stepped out into the portico, stood framed in the doorway and cried, "Altaera lives!" The air was split by a peremptory crack, followed by a crash as the strongbox hit the ground. The Sphinx flung out his arms, a red halo blossomed above his shoulders and he leaped forward, pitching out of sight down the steps. Kijé, creature of darkness, had shot him in the head.

Twenty-two

Maisie, tearfully laid out and shrouded by Ernie and Lizaveta, slept in the cellar, awaiting her last resting-place. The dog and the dog's friend kept the dead watch, one at her foot, one at her head.

They had had another corpse on their hands until Kijé went out to the portico to look at what he had accomplished with his single bullet. He stayed there for three or four minutes, examining the shattered head from several angles, craftsmanly; when he came in again he was smiling, until he met Keith's appalled eyes, seemed to see reflected in them what Keith saw, and gnawed his lip.

"Take that thing off the front steps and lose it," he said. "Drop it down a well, set fire to it, I don't care, but make sure it isn't found." Vlodya and a couple of others wandered out and shuffled uncertainly round the corpse of the Sphinx, after which Vlodya went into the Archaeology Gallery and returned with one of the Bukharas, loosely rolled. He looked resentfully at Kijé as he passed him in the rotunda, saw Kijé's expression and said nothing.

In the Archaeology Gallery Usman wielded a screwdriver with a surgeon's delicacy to recover undamaged panels from the broken cabinets, handling the wood as if he loved it, caressing dovetail and mortise, collecting brass screws and washers in a little blue-glazed shard. Keith, supposing him unhinged by the events of the morning, crouched beside him.

"Is it worth it?" he asked gently.

"To make a coffin," Usman said. He ran his thumb sensuously along a graceful bevel. "I was a carpenter. I am a carpenter."

They had all been struck distracted. Lizaveta, still silently weeping, went to her cleaning cupboard, took out a yard broom and began sweeping the floor in the Zherdin Collection, sightlessly ploughing up and down through the wreckage until Mrs Fahrenheit came out and coaxed her away.

"Liza, darling, go to the kitchen. People must eat; make tea. This can wait." She took the broom and leaned on it as Lizaveta walked unsteadily down the corridor to the Refreshment Room where the refugees were crowded, shocked and hostile in their betrayal.

"Oh, I dunno," Kijé said, loudly. "Send Usman up to clean the windows, why don't you? Use this." He hooked a rag of white cotton, someone's violated shirt, on the barrel of his rifle and waved it about.

"Kijé, for God's sake put it down," Ernie cried, aghast. "Someone *owns* that."

"Flag of truce. Fly it over the door, lure them into range and blow their brains out. They'll be back for their stones any minute now."

"There were no Sturyat in that mob," Keith said.

"So?" Kijé turned and lowered the rifle absent-mindedly. Keith found himself looking down the muzzle which emerged from the shirtsleeve like a skeletal wrist.

"So perhaps we ought to take them back ourselves."

"As a gesture of goodwill?" Kijé said. His left eyelid was twitching, a continuous fluttering tremor like a moth's wing that gave him an air of grisly coquetry.

Mrs Fahrenheit went over to him by a prudently circuitous route and pressed her hand against the rifle until it pointed at the floor and the shirtsleeve down-gyved round it. "Keith's right, we must return the stones. The Sturyat were not party to what happened here. And as far as they know they are no closer to getting their souls back. The only person who knew we'd found them was – is – "

"Out there staining the steps," Kijé said, flirting his eyelashes.

"Come with us."

"No," he said, then: "Us?"

"I'll go with Keith. Be quiet, Keith. I will not be told what I may or may not do in my own house. The stones are my responsibility, they always have been. If the Sturyat see only you or Kijé – "

"Oh, they won't see me. *Don't* worry," Kijé said.

She ignored him with a tangible effort: " – they might

attack you. If *I* go to them they will know why. Keith, can we carry that box between us?"

"No," he said, "but we could use Szusko's cart."

"That's unfortunate," Kijé said. "I advised him to bring it into the rotunda for safekeeping. I suppose it's still somewhere about. Here and there."

"Will you still be smiling when you tell Szusko?" she flashed at him and he jerked his head aside as though she had slapped his face.

"If we made some kind of a sledge we could drag it – the box," Keith said.

They went into the portico, averting their eyes from any sight but that of the strongbox lying where it had impacted into the tiles when the Sphinx let it fall. A little way up the road Vlodya and Makhmud were struggling to convey a long, unwieldy columnar burden towards the corner of Vostok Street. Keith tested the box's weight. "One of those panels Usman's unscrewing . . . perhaps with ropes?"

Kijé bounded down the steps behind them and took a short run, yelling, "Vladimir Nikolaevich!" Vlodya turned in alarm and dropped his end of the carpet as Kijé booted something towards him and shouted, "Give him this! The other one's got a hole in it!" and the head of Setsemhotep III arced skyward.

"We can use another of the Bukharas, a long one, and pull it behind us," Ernie said, taking in Kijé's drop-kick and determinedly looking the other way. "With luck we shall be relieved of our load before we get too far. Bring another to wrap it in."

They were muttering to each other. Keith said, "What about. . . ?"

"It's all right. He's gone inside again. Be quick. I'm going to fetch a shawl."

Far from reassured, expecting Kijé to lurch into his path at every turn or, worse, come up behind him, Keith ran to the Archaeology Gallery where Usman was beginning to assemble his panelling into a sad little box that seemed too cramped to shelter even Maisie's tiny body. The Bukharas hung out of their ransacked cabinet like felted tongues after a rough night. The biggest had been taken by Vlodya to conceal the Equispherian's corpse and he wondered, in passing, where they had taken it. It would surely have been more sensible to conceal it on the premises, and then he recalled that it had been Kijé who ordered its removal, after he had been out to admire it. Keith kept looking over his shoulder as he eased out a lustrous pewter-coloured runner, three metres long. He was just choosing another smaller one to cover the box, when Usman said, "What are you going to do with them?"

"We're taking the soul stones back to the Sturyat. We need something to wrap them in."

"Not that one, please," Usman said. "It's a prayer mat."

"Oh, God. I'm sorry. This one all right?"

"Yes. Thank you. Is the lieutenant going with you?"

"No." He looked sharply at Usman but the man was bent over his joinery again.

"Ah, well, we can always lock ourselves in the cellar," Usman said.

"What do you mean? He'd never harm – never – "

"I knew him before you did," Usman said. "He didn't come here to grow mushrooms."

Mrs Fahrenheit waited in the portico, a thick fringed shawl about her shoulders, another over her head. When Keith came out with the carpets she turned and raised her hand warningly, and he saw Kijé leaning against one of the pillars, arms folded, motionless except for the trilling eyelid and a thin dribble of blood in the corner of his mouth where he had given his lip a particularly ferocious nip.

He watched them as they manoeuvred the strongbox down the steps, end over end, folded the rug around it and laid it on one end of the runner before he said, "Half the weight is in the box. If you took them out you could carry them in baskets."

"Of course. Thank you," Ernie said, as if to a helpful stranger, and went back indoors leaving Keith to contemplate the idiotic arrangement of carpets in the bloodstained snow.

"Not so mad, you see," Kijé remarked. "Perfectly sensible, in fact."

"Why won't you come with us?"

"Because I am not mad. I say leave them out in the street. Someone will be back for them before long."

Ernie came out again with three of the baskets that Lizaveta had carried to market. She paused to speak to Kijé but he turned his back and walked away, deliberately closing the door in her face.

"He hasn't locked us out?" Keith halted, with the lid of the strongbox open. Suddenly the empty streets were filled with threat and the seeming silence was white noise; not no sound, all sound.

"He wouldn't do that." Neither of them went to check if she was right. She began to scoop handfuls of soul stones out of the box and distribute them among the three baskets. They took one each and, holding the third between them, set off down the street, leaving the ambiguous still-life arrangement of an open box and two Bukhara rugs in the middle of the road.

"How can he let you go alone?"

"But I am not alone. I am with you."

"He should be with you."

"Someone has to guard the museum."

"That's not why he stayed. And from what Usman said, nobody wants him to."

"Ach, what do you know?" Ernie said, and they walked on without speaking, a way that Keith had not taken before, through lanes that skirted the Old Town and brought them out in the north-western corner of the Sturyat pasture. As they drew nearer, the sounds of human activity became louder, the customary farmyard bustle, the confused babble of voices they had become used to during recent weeks, overlaid by more organized words of command and instruction, orders given and received.

Keith's first impression as they came to the mouth of the lane, was of a demo in Hyde Park. From one end of the pasture to the other people were swarming in groups, great clusters that bulged and swelled, formed and re-formed, as figures detached themselves, returned, ran from one assembly to another. As he advanced, matching Mrs Fahrenheit step for step with their joint burden, the groups resolved themselves into identifiable entities; the three Sturyat clans with their live-stock, the Sundance Tribe and its minor dependency, the Hobbits; no Equispherians but numerous small clusters, among them the dryads clutching bunches of bare twigs.

Over the heads of the crowd he saw the Sundance benders like a litter of giant piglets, but the tepee had been dismantled and he glanced automatically towards the broken walls of the old fortifications where Theps, Senkh and Khlev had established their compounds. The *kibitkas* were still standing but they had a stripped-down look about them. The Sturyat, confident to the last that their souls would be returned to them, were making ready for their departure at the year's end; and the Sturyat had been right all along.

He searched the throng for a familiar form or face, some-one to whom he could call, and felt, by a tug at the middle basket, that Mrs Fahrenheit had stopped. He looked round to see that she had set down the other basket and was pulling away the shawl that covered her head and partly hid her face. The wintry sunshine of late afternoon lit up her golden hair and she stood, a pale beacon in the dark turmoil of the pasture.

"Wait now," she said. "Someone will recognize me and come to us."

She had not left her museum in years; who would recognize her? His heart skipped as he saw a person move away from a distant group and stump towards them over the grass, in heavy boots, the boots of Tcherk.

"Zayu."

She did not even look at him but went directly to Mrs Fahrenheit. Over her shoulder Keith saw several Sturyat coming towards them, Theps, Gresk, others he did not recognize, and he wondered if this would be the last thing he ever saw.

Zayu stopped in front of Mrs Fahrenheit who took one of the baskets and held it out. Zayu looked in, but without delight. Her features were pinched with displeasure.

"They are naked."

"We brought them as we found them," Ernie said, editing out certain details. "Zayu, we have returned your souls."

Theps and Gresk had arrived. Zayu stood aside as the two men appropriated the baskets and stared at the contents, ignoring Ernie and Keith. They might as well have put down the baskets and walked away, although Keith had a gut feeling that it would not be wise to walk away now. With a circle of unknown Sturyat around them they had no choice but to stand side by side while Gresk sat down and solemnly, unhurriedly, commenced to count the Sturyat souls.

"Oh, dear God," Ernie breathed in Keith's ear. "I never thought they would know the number." He felt the bone-cold fingers of her right hand entwine with those of his left. He suspected that in fact the Sturyat had no idea of the number of lost souls, but they were going to enjoy their pound of flesh.

Gresk was in no hurry. He looked closely at each stone before he set it aside. Theps had produced a tally stick, an ancient rod of black greasy wood, and made laborious calculations with his thumbnail, and all the while the numbers of Sturyat increased, until the circle that enclosed them was ten deep. No one spoke, except for Theps, mumbling over his tally stick, and Gresk intoning a number at intervals. The sun sank behind Qantoum Industrial, the water tower, the barracks; shadows outflanked them and closed in. Flakes of snow fell from a clear sky where the first stars were showing. As Keith had surmised, long ago, the Sturyat were saying, We are the masters now. There was no need to say it aloud.

Why did no one come to find them? By which he meant, he knew, why did Kijé not come to find them? Not them, even; *her*. He could not think of one single reason why Kijé should come looking for him except in vengeance, to exact restitution for every blow that had been inflicted on him since the first encounter, back in April, across the desk in Control Point E.

As silently as they had assembled the Sturyat were withdrawing into the evening shadows and Keith became conscious again of the volatile mass that stirred unseen in the gathering dusk. Theps and Gresk were the last to leave, carrying the souls of their nation in three old wicker shopping baskets, followed by Zayu who began to walk away without another glance. He could not bear to part from her so.

"Zayu. *Zayu*."

She took one more step before turning her head and even then her stride did not falter. It was too dark to see her face. He thought she half raised her hand but he could not be certain.

Mrs Fahrenheit was pulling gently at his arm.

"Keith, come away. We've been gone so long." Supporting each other they stumbled across the uneven ground, unhindered, forgotten. "I thought we would give them their stones and go back. Anything could have happened."

"The Equispherians?" After the numb stasis of their siege in the pasture time engaged its gears again. Anything could have happened and the Equispherians had not been among those preparing to make their exodus with the Sturyat.

"Perhaps the Equispherians. They must know one of their number is missing."

"Go on."

"What do you mean?"

"Aren't you going to say that we needn't worry; Kijé will take care of everything?"

"Oh don't, *don't*," she moaned, and clung to him, trembling.

"What are we going to do?"

"I don't know. It's three weeks to the New Year. Perhaps he'll be better in the morning."

Better in the morning – as if he had had a viral infection. Keith could not bring himself to say, Ernie, he's just blown somebody's face off and remembered how much he enjoys doing it. He saw in his mind's eye the smile, the whirring eyelid, teeth gnawing, gnawing at the lacerated lip, the man who ate his own head, his own heart.

They were back in Museum Street, the snow flurries spitting in their faces. The portico lamp had not been lit but as they set foot on the steps the door opened, an arm shot out and pulled them inside.

"Vlodya?"

"Where the hell have you been?" Vlodya closed and locked the door behind them.

"Taking the soul stones—" Mrs Fahrenheit answered.

"I know, I know. But so long—"

"They wanted to count them. What's been happening here?"

"Usman has finished his coffin. Lizaveta is feeding us. We have all elected to sleep in the cellar tonight; a democratic vote."

"The Equispherians didn't return?"

"No."

"And no one – nothing—?"

"She means, what's Kijé been doing?" Keith interrupted.

Vlodya was lighting a paraffin lamp and as the flame quickened the wastes of the Zherdin Collection were revealed, the fatuous vigil of the two-headed sheep.

"I believe he is on the roof."

"Believe?"

"He is not in the cellar," Vlodya said. "We had a democratic vote on that, too."

"You drove him out!" There were tears in her voice.

"Of course we didn't – with what he's carrying? But we should prefer it if he didn't come in. He frightens people. We are already frightened enough."

"He's had a shock—"

"*We've* had a shock. Kijé knew what an expanding bullet in the back of the head would do."

Throughout the evening, into the night, the Qantoumis sat in the Refreshment Room of their museum behind shuttered windows, and waited for the Equispherians to come looking for their dead. People keeping watch in the rotunda stood shifts and every time the door opened Keith looked up to see Mrs Fahrenheit raise her head and turn in anxious eagerness, look away as Makhmud or Usman or Vlodya entered and left. When people began to go down to the cellar at last, he went over to her.

"Why don't you go up and find him?"

She shook her head.

"Are you afraid of him too?"

"Oh, Keith – how can you – no. Afraid *for* him. What can I do?"

"Don't you think perhaps he's waiting – for one of us to go to him?" Until he said it the thought had not crossed his mind, but now he saw with implacable clarity Kijé alone in the night with only his own frightening self for company. "I'll go up."

She caught his hand in both of hers. "Take him something. Food – I'll make tea."

"I'll see if he's there first." And that had not occurred to him either; Vlodya had only guessed that Kijé might be on the roof. He could be anywhere in the town, alive or dead.

He took a candle lantern and made his way along the darkened corridors to the remains of the door in the remains of the panelling. The catch had jammed and he had to squat and ease himself through sideways. The vertiginous stairs were deathly cold and the lantern, with its guttering candle, made the treads and risers buck and slither under his feet. As he came up under the skylight he saw that the snow had stopped and the sky was clear again. He left the trap open, went down on all fours and headed for the southern turret where he thought he detected movement, a presence; he was afraid to speak, afraid of the shot he might never hear, the bullet he might never see.

"*Put* that light out." The voice was sane and tired. Keith extinguished his candle and crawled towards Kijé's ursine bulk where it sat in the greatcoat at the angle of the turret and the parapet.

"Are you all right?"

"Come here and look at this."

Keith put down the lantern and advanced to Kijé's side, leaning on the parapet. The moon was down and the winter stars seemed close enough to burn the fingers. In the paling eastern sky Comet Colney-Hatch, suspended by its tail, hung like an arrow above the place where the sun would rise.

"Look at what?"

"Wait . . . *there*."

A pale lemon-yellow flash lit the sky along the horizon.

"Lightning?"

"In winter? I don't think so. It's been going on for hours."

"You've been up here all night?" There was no answer. "Ernie says, do you want anything to eat, drink? Tea? She'd probably make coffee for *you*."

"No. I have something to drink." He heard a faint clink of glass on glass, and something cold was pressed into his hand. "Happy New Year."

"As bad as that, is it?" Keith said, tasting the vodka. Another flash, and a shuddering rumble. "It's not the New Year."

"It may be as close to the New Year as we are going to get," Kijé said, discouragingly. "Good health, then, Keith."

"Up yours, Shura."

There came a small surprised laugh in the darkness.

"How did you know that?"

"You let it slip once. Why doesn't Ernie—"

"Erna doesn't know." There was a longer silence, lit by another flash. Then he said, "When I woke up in the cellar after the, uh, incident, the first thing I saw was Erna, watching me. She said, 'How are you feeling? What is your name?'"

"Didn't you have ID – dog tags?"

"I'd already taken care of that. I was not feeling very well, you understand, but I realized that if I had no name I had no past. I didn't exist. So I said, 'Lieutenant Kijé.' She understood. She asked once more, after that, and then never again, even in bed."

"What did she understand?"

"Lieutenant Kijé didn't exist either. That was what he was famous for. If you ever go home Keith, you really must educate yourself; otherwise you will miss all the best jokes."

"It's not exactly a joke, is it?"

Kijé folded his arms on the parapet and rested his chin on them, gazing towards the waning flare of Colney-Hatch. "When I was a child I thought that comets raced across the sky like rockets. I knew Halley's Comet would return in my lifetime – so excited. I thought that people would run through the streets crying, 'The comet is coming!' and we would all rush out of doors just in time to see it roar overhead, leaving a great trail of fiery sparks. But by the time it reappeared I was in Afghanistan. I had other things on my mind."

"Part of that past you don't have?"

"Yes."

"Can you forgive me?" He seemed to have left something out, there, but Kijé picked up on it anyway.

"No – but don't let that worry you."

As the sky brightened in the east the town grew breathlessly quiet. The museum lay hushed below them, and the Old Town, the barracks, the still-smouldering ashes of the gymnasium, Dunkillin. On the silence fell a muffled pattering like the first scatter of rain upon a roof, that swelled to a rushing tattoo, hundreds, thousands of feet. Keith stood up and looked over the parapet. In the Registan and the surrounding streets was urgent movement. The crowds were draining away from the buildings, the bivouacs, filling the narrow echoing lanes with the torrent of their footsteps. Immediately below, the smotered snow of Museum Street was hidden by a surging darkness, a voiceless stream that spoke only with the relentlessly advancing feet. Keith could only think: *Lemmings*. At the edge of the desert a shape thrust out against the snow.

"Moment of truth." Kijé raised his field-glasses. "The Sturyat are moving out."

"*Now?*"

"Why not now? They weren't waiting for the new Millennium. They were waiting for their star and their soul stones. There's the star. They've got the stones."

"No thanks to you."

"I couldn't come with you – think of the *temptation*. I watched you all the way. Every minute. And all the way back. You were always in range."

"It's like the Israelites leaving Egypt," Keith said, as the mass swelled and elongated into a moving column. "Sheep, goats, they're taking everything."

"They're going through the minefield."

"Sturyat don't step on mines." *Oh Zayu, Zayu, may your faith hold you up.*

"Sturyat don't."

The streams of people rolled on, to converge with the Sturyat horde as it left the pasture, pouring out of the lanes and alleys, out of the Registan and through Qantoum Industrial, for as fast as they moved out others were pouring in, the inexorable throng on the railway, coming from the west. In the vanguard, moving with uncanny speed over the snow, white things caught the light of the almost-risen sun, like fat pearls on a necklace of jet, without legs, without eyes, returning by instinct alone like the Sturyat to the place they had come from. As the sun touched the rim of the horizon the first of the land-mines went off, the vindictive crack of its detonation followed by a thunderous boom from farther away. Thick smoke boiled into the sky.

"Shell," Kijé said.

The column did not falter but pressed on into the sunrise, endless, as if all the folly in the world were not enough to feed it, and from the Sturyat at its head rose a deep-throated chanting which was joined by singing farther back in the throng, and buzzing, and ecstatic howling. There came another distant, but not so distant, boom. The black smoke was spreading now, obscuring the sun's disc as it pulled clear of the horizon. Kijé took advantage of the temporary eclipse to make another sweep with the field-glasses.

"Many coming from the east," he said.

"Who are they?"

"I can't tell who. They are coming in tanks."

The sound of the singing and chanting and detonating mines was swamped by a mighty explosion. The whole building shook under them. Three jet aircraft swooped out of the smoke, over the column, and veered away in a steep climb to the south-west.

"Why don't they turn back?" Another mine went off. "They're *dying* out there."

"How can they turn back? They came here to find the end of things, and now they've found it."

From quite close by someone opened up with a sub-machine-gun, bullets smashing into the tiles of the northern turret. In reply a single rifle shot chipped stone splinters from the parapet, a few metres from where they were crouching.

"I wonder if that's anyone we know," Kijé said. "I think you had better go down to the cellar now."

"And you."

"Someone must remain up here."

"Why? I will – both of us – "

"You must go and tell Erna what is happening. They'll be able to feel the explosions down there. Think of their fear."

"And you're going to stay here and get your head shot off? Do you think she wants to be told that?"

"Please get down that staircase. I guess those tanks are advancing upon Iskanderabad. If they intend to take Qantoum then they have been seriously misinformed. Once our own maniacs have finished walking into a war Qantoum will be just as it was before they came here, playing dead. We survived once. We may survive again."

"*You* won't survive if you stay up here. For the last time, come down with me. Let someone else take a turn. Usman—"

"For the last time, no. This is where I belong." A bullet ploughed among the tiles on the turret above them. "This is where I deserve to be."

The shell bursts were now coming so close together that

the thunder was a continuous rolling wave. While they had been talking St Vasili's dome had vanished.

Keith shouted, "What do you mean?"

Kijé turned and the sunshine cruelly spotlit what the night had wrought, his haggard face, the raw lip, the bloodshot eye where he had ground his knuckles in to suppress the maddening tic. "Take this." He thrust the rifle into Keith's hands.

"No. I can't keep it. I don't know how to use it."

"Oh, for God's sake," Kijé said, "you pick it up and fire it. It's a Kalashnikov, they give them to children. Now, get down those stairs." He had the pistol out and, still crouching, advanced on Keith who backed towards the skylight.

"Come with me. Please come with me."

"Go away. I've got nothing else to say."

He pleaded, "Not even to Ernie?"

"Give her my love."

"She wants more than that."

"Love her for me."

"We *need* you." He was at the head of the stairs. Kijé, on hands and knees, lunged forward, reached out an arm and caught him by the back of the head, twisting his fingers in his hair.

"Give her this." He pulled Keith towards him and kissed him on the mouth, then let go, propelling him backwards and rising to his feet in one movement. Keith's last sight of him was a dark pin-wheel of arms, legs, the swinging skirts of his coat as he ran for the parapet and the sniper opened up again, a silhouette nailed for ever against the morning sky.

Another explosion sent Keith slithering down the stairs on hip and shoulder, the rifle clattering ahead of him. He half-somersaulted on to the landing and as he regained his feet a light appeared below, and he looked upon the upturned face of the widow Fahrenheit, lantern held high, scaling the next flight, in search of them. He saw her speak but the barrage drowned the question she must be asking, and he could not make himself heard to answer it, so he leaned down to where she stood on the step below him and passed on Kije's last gift.